THE GOLDEN SECTION

Pernille Rygg

The Golden Section

*Translated from the Norwegian
by Don Bartlett*

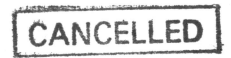

THE HARVILL PRESS
LONDON

First published with the title Det gyldene snitt by Gyldendal Norsk Forlag AS, 2000

2 4 6 8 10 9 7 5 3 1

Maps by Reginald Piggott

The publisher gratefully acknowledges the financial support of
NORLA towards the publication of this book in English

First published in Great Britain in 2003 by
The Harvill Press
Random House, 20 Vauxhall Bridge Road,
London SW1V 2SA

Random House Australia (Pty) Limited
20 Alfred Street, Milsons Point, Sydney,
New South Wales 2061, Australia

Random House New Zealand Limited
18 Poland Road, Glenfield,
Auckland 10, New Zealand

Random House South Africa (Pty) Limited
Endulini, 5A Jubilee Road, Parktown 2193, South Africa

The Random House Group Limited Reg. No. 954009
www.randomhouse.co.uk/harvill

A CIP catalogue record for this book
is available from the British Library

ISBN 1 84343 000 2

Papers used by Random House are natural,
recyclable products made from wood grown in sustainable forests;
the manufacturing processes conform to the environmental
regulations of the country of origin

Typeset by SX Composing DTP, Rayleigh, Essex
Printed and bound in Great Britain by
Mackays of Chatham plc, Chatham, Kent

Dying is an art,
Like everything else

SYLVIA PLATH

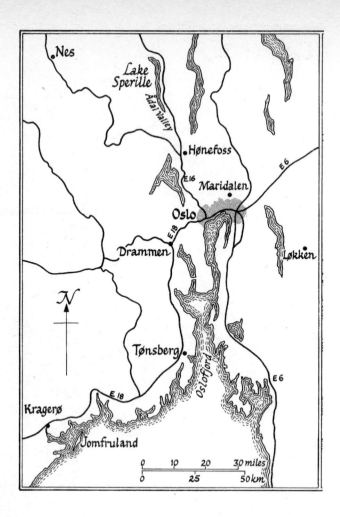

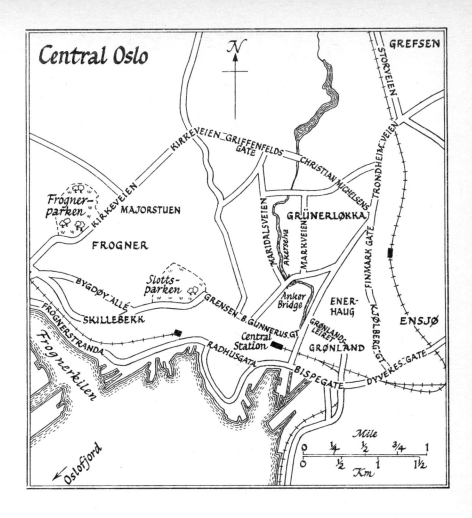

I

IT IS A DECLARATION of love of the most insistent, brutal kind that no-one would want or wish for. *Look at me*, it says, *Love me, however awful I am*. Look, no choice there. Love, I don't know that I can, standing outside the gateway in Markveien. It is an autumn morning, the world is cool and rain-fresh under a transparent, cobalt blue sky. Bad timing for intense, cryptic declarations.

It is all over the house front on the other side of the street, stretches the length of the wall with its soaring, sloping letters. It demands attention. And interpretation. This love says No when it means Yes, it screams when it wants to whisper. And it implores me to understand, implores me to interpret.

My daughter doesn't interpret as I do. She is standing on the pavement with her hand raised to put in mine and she is trembling a little.

"Oh," she says, and stares at the wall opposite our door.

"Someone has written on the wall *again*."

"Yes," I answer.

During the night Someone came here while the streets were empty and tarmac-wet, the house fronts given a thin coating in black and sepia by the meagre street lighting. Someone came here, through the echo of empty streets, listening to the sound of their own footsteps resounding against the buildings in which everyone was asleep, or almost everyone. There were just a few windows forming rectangles of golden homeliness, which have such a glow for those on the outside. Surfaces of gold with bars across, gifts wrapped in golden paper with a black ribbon. Someone brought their gear with them in the night: pot of paint, paint brush, and the urge to express themselves. The urge was insistent, uncontrollable, perhaps irresistible. Intense enough to drive someone out on such a night. Empty streets, windows hiding dreams. Perhaps a little wind between the houses, the sound of a taxi on its way up Thorvald Meyersgate. And then these huge, resolute sweeps of the brush over the wall, metre-long strokes, some of them repeated again and again so that the Message was clearly visible.

"Are they allowed to write on the wall?" Ida asks and frowns sternly and, I know, hypocritically.

"No," I say. For four-year olds this still holds, though it is somewhat dubious everywhere else: law and order with no special nuances, without qualification or mitigating circumstances. *No-one* has the right to write on walls. It is not *nice*. If my daughter trembles, it is because she knows the wicked desire in her heart. Ida, moralist and hypocrite, would like to write on the wall herself.

"*What* did they write on the wall?"

It is not nice to lie either, but for the time being I am the person mediating this form of communication, and, as we know, knowledge is power.

"Mum-my real-ly loves you," I read out staccato with a smile. She knows this code, even if I am communicating on two levels, playing and not playing at the same time. My daughter isn't stupid, she knows that there is no such thing on the wall, but she also knows that I tell the truth. She can gladly interpret me in the best possible light. Later we swing our arms in rhythm as we walk happily along the pavement. We stop at the corner and look first to the left – no cars there – then to the right – no cars there, either – before we cross the street. Law and order of the self-protective variety, a strict code to prevent chaos, social disintegration and sudden death.

The message appears again on the wall behind us – a metre high, slightly slanting letters with splodges of white paint underneath, written in some haste. "HEITMANN THE PSYCHOLOGIST KILLS CHILDREN," it says. It isn't true, of course. It is damned by its own absurdity. It is absurd. That is the kind of love it is. And the hatred. I don't kill children. But some of them don't believe me when I say I like them, even if it is a long, long time since they were small. You need training. And tests, just like Ida is doing, swinging her arm in rhythm with mine.

"Mum-my," she chants, "real-ly loves – ME! ME, ME, ME!" A little ego skipping on the pavement, beginning to learn, as she has to, necessary ways to survive. First left, then right. MUMMY. ME.

You can always hope that she will be spared. You can always take care of her, make sure that cars don't hit her, lie about the writing on the wall. But one day soon she will also learn the alphabet and have to interpret on her own.

Five minutes later, by the nursery, I hope that she can be spared, I hope that she is so busy with her don't-step-on-the-cracks game that she doesn't look up, as I do. Not a bit of it. She stops suddenly, her little foot on a crack.

"Someone has written on the wall here *too*," she says, anger in her voice. Someone has written across the high, crumbling wall that separates the perimeter of the nursery from the road. Also on the end wall of the neighbour's yard. To reach it, Someone must have been standing on the sloping roof of the children's nursery. The paint had dripped on to the roof and the pavement. The arched Jackson Pollock loops reveal the strength of the arm that formed the Message.

Careless, I think, and I feel a sharp knife turning in my stomach. I have been careless, though adults aren't allowed to be. I can't stop anyone looking for my address. I am in the telephone book, like everybody else. Unless they are being stalked or are nervous. But this. Where did Someone stand and watch us? On the corner, by a shop? Did they follow us one morning or one afternoon, meet us on the way to or on the way back from somewhere or bump into us by chance?

Or on purpose. Someone didn't bump into us; Someone searched for and found us. "HEITMANN = CHILD KILLER," Someone wrote.

"You aren't *allowed* to paint on walls," my daughter's superego repeats sternly.

"No," I say.

"But Someone is *still* doing it!" Ida trembles. She puts her hand in mine, her body is shaking. Oh, it is desire and horror and revolt and prohibition and all kinds of conflicting devilry. She is standing right on the crack, tramples on it with her little foot, hops up and down on it, driven by all kinds of conflicting devilry. Pleasure. Hop. Horror. Hop. I don't hop. But I am much more afraid than she is.

That is perhaps why I run away, afterwards. Though it might be just to get to Ullevål hospital on time.

3

*　*　*

In my room the idea that I kill children takes hold. Nothing in the sober atmosphere of the community that my office forms part of can prevent it. Every now and then, between two chairs upholstered in blue woollen material, by the dull birchwood desk, in front of the pale shelves, I turn into an aloof she tyrant, a silent ice maiden, a hardened bloodthirsty child murderer, all achieved without any effort on my part at all. It is a kind of magic. Or simply a method that can be used with variable fortune in this as in any other department of psychiatry.

Community tristesse is a good trick. It is an integral part of the demanding magical illusion, becoming myself again.

My consulting room is in Someone's head. Someone knows my address and the address of the nursery. But it is certain that the anonymous painter knows this room better still. Why else would they draw attention to the fact that I am a psychologist? And my room was also invaded this morning, although no-one painted any generous loops or razor-sharp lines here.

Someone's presence superimposes itself on the cool, azure-coloured, rain-fresh light that floods in with the breaking day, this fury that is love, that is shame, that is hatred, that is despair. It has to be like this. Here I am supposed to turn into someone who destroys the confidence of small children. But, please, let it be just here. Not on street walls.

I believe in the strange, slow magic of words and the interpretation of words. They sound quite different, most of them, when they are spoken aloud, not in your head or on a house wall. That is the method, but it is slow, complicated and delicate. Not many guarantees come with it, even though in this department, in the offices along the endless corridors that we are provided with, in accordance with madhouse requirements, tests are done, statistics are kept, prognoses are worked out that reveal a certain degree of success.

Success: getting up in the morning. Completing a course of study, being able to catch the bus without acute attacks of anxiety, applying for a job. Getting it. Going to work. One day. Two days. A year. Success: sleeping at night. Talking to your father without crying the whole of the following night. Not talking to your father. Washing the floor when it is dirty.

4

It is not so ambitious perhaps, not so exclusive or remarkable. It is stories and the interpretation of them, their meaning then and now. Especially now. It isn't so ambitious, but it is *something*. It is the method. Sometimes it fails totally, as for example when the story isn't complete.

Perhaps Someone is like this. For as long as Someone expresses themselves at night, it isn't a finished story, it is a failure. There are consequences: caretakers have to be rung, also the police. It is a matter of order. It is a matter of law and order. It is a matter of the knife turning in my stomach.

The caretakers promise to paint over the writing, the police promise to include the addresses on their slow car patrols for the next few nights.

And so the day's work has to begin. Success: having a little knife in your stomach and still doing your job.

2

"ORGANIC", BELLA SAYS and blows a cloud of menthol smoke over the table.

"Of course, it's a load of bloody rubbish, but that's what he calls it. *Organic*, fuck me. I mean I *love* the man, but every so often he's so bloody pretentious. An exhibition that is not ready is not ready, never mind whether it's being put on by Mr Bloody Genius, the Angel of Death, Aske, or not."

"My God." She pauses while the waiter comes with the menu.

"We don't want anything to eat, not even a lettuce leaf. Well, Rita could perhaps have a piece of *animal* of some kind."

Rita is Bella's weird, elongated dog lying limp at her feet and salivating profusely.

"Actually," says the waiter, "dogs are not allowed in . . ."

"Come on," says Bella. "Loosen up. Just for once, take a real risk and serve Rita a little meat. We won't say anything to your boss. We only want a drink and the drink is champagne."

"And Farris mineral water," I say. "But in fact I'm also a little hungry and . . ."

"Igi," says Bella, waving the waiter away. "You are not allowed. Over there in the *hellish* chaos that I'm glad to say you've saved me from, there is simply the best cook in this country – he is gorgeous, gorgeous, blue-black, if you know what I mean. We're talking Trinidad or Port-au-Prince here or something like it. In any case, it's impossible to understand a word he says and he's doped up the whole time, but Igi – well, he serves some scallops that you wouldn't believe possible this side of an orgasm."

It is seven o'clock and we are sitting in a nice, boring, all but empty restaurant in Nydalen. We have been swimming. We have been lifting small weights designed for women. We have had a massage.

That is, I have been swimming and lifting weights. Bella splashed around, affecting a curiosity in the pool and staring with much more interest into the mirror in the fitness room. Later, with some relief, she put herself in the expert masculine hands of a masseur. Bella doesn't go in for getting out of breath, unless it is in bed, and she has, as she says herself, the perfect, oddly muscular body some women achieve living on a strict diet of alcohol, black coffee and cigarettes.

The hellish chaos is the opening of the retrospective exhibition for Bella's most important and most controversial client, Aske. It is said he had a Christian name once, but that was a long time ago and it disappeared quite deliberately into the mists of time.

"But what do you mean," I ask, "by organic?"

"Shit," says Bella. "It's some work-in-progress rubbish. You know, painting pictures is a *process*, mounting them in a thoughtful, decorative way one after the other is breaking, *killing* the process, and that's why he refuses to put on a polished exhibition. Of course I can understand it, for Christ's sake. Being given a retrospective is a bit like being declared dead."

"And what does that all mean exactly?"

"That nothing is finished. That there are a whole load of little art students floating around taking things down here and assembling things over there. There is no-one *with any idea* what's going to be in there for certain. I went there last night, and, well, there were just bare leads hanging loose all over the place and people painting the ceiling, drilling holes in the walls and – how shall I put it? – *fiddling* around. And the egomaniac was walking around with that blank expression of his, as happy as a sandboy."

We drink champagne in two seconds of silence. Rita swallows the meat noisily as if it is supposed to be taken in liquid form.

"And Roll coming from London," Bella says.

"I mean, it isn't only Aske's thing, all this."

Of course, that is true. The event referred to earlier, somewhat agitatedly, and the one I am on my way to as Bella's escort and Benny's wife, half of it involves Joakim Roll. Not so strange when you consider that everything which has just a suspicion of involvement with this country's most fervent speculator creates a public outcry.

"The prick," Bella says, and lights a new spike-thin mini cigarette.

"Meaning Aske?" I ask.

"No," she says. "I mean Joakim. What kind of behaviour is it to make yourself totally inaccessible in some bloody glass tower in London and let me stew here with a load of fucking demonstrators and *trade and industry journalists*. You have no idea the things they ask you. Igi, they ring me in the middle of the night and ask me if I know about *share regulations*. My God, I don't even know the highway code. Try saying something like that to one of these journalists, Igi, and just watch what they do."

"Print it," I suggest.

"Right," Bella says. "The dickheads."

Bella has a broad, select repertoire of foul language and she uses it with enthusiasm. I am not for one moment taken in by what she says about share regulations. Bella has been running her own very lucrative gallery for at least ten years, and she has presided over the most sensational combination of culture and capital this country has seen since the purchase of *The Four Greats*, according to various hysterical commentators.

But of course it is difficult. The country's richest and most controversial financier working together with the country's most scandalous painter and then, hey presto! – fantastic, hundred-year-old factory premises converted into a permanent exhibition room for Aske and for touring exhibitions of his slightly less successful contemporaries and younger colleagues. All the result of mysterious and much discussed large-scale purchasing of shares in the company owned by Bella's father, Otto Troels-Jacobsen, a renowned figure in cultural and industrial circles, who until very recently owned the factory.

I have never heard Bella speak of him. In fact I thought, as I'm sure others did, that he was dead. But from the series of articles about the purchase of the shares and the closing down of the factory it was clear that he was, after all, still alive, more than eighty and living a somewhat secluded life.

"The slimy bugger," Bella says. "I don't want to talk about him. He thinks that in principle art stopped some time in the Fifties when everything was clean and abstract and – *scientific*. Kiss my ass. And that is about the most interesting thing you can say about him. What do you think? Are we ready for the *show* or not?"

She gets up from the table and waves her gold card hither and thither. Rita gets to her feet with great difficulty and stands at her mistress' side, a soggy piece of meat dangling from the corner of her mouth. Rita is old and not very comely. The bi-product, Bella maintains, of a great Dane raping a dachshund. Or the other way round. One way or another, it is not an image I want to dwell upon, but Rita makes it difficult for you to ignore. It is, in fact, exactly what she looks like.

"Tell me, Igi," Bella says as the waiter approaches with the bill. "Have you got a lover?"

"No," I answer.

"It's just that's there's a guy over there staring and I thought for a moment it was at you."

The guy in question, tall, thick-set, wearing dark clothes, leaves the restaurant. I only catch the back of him and I don't recognise him. But then, how many people's backs would I recognise? *Heitmann the psychologist kills children*, whispers my little knife and twists again.

Anti-pornography protesters stand in the cold autumnal air. Red noses and blue chins, numbed fingers around a ragged banner on the banks of the Akerselva river, shoulders hunched in flimsy clothing. The crackle of the megaphone sounds forlorn, in the same way that the hollow sound of applause from begloved hands does. Between them and me there are waves of people on their way to the exhibition; there are a great many more of us than of them and we know it. And we don't feel the cold so much. And we are wearing broader smiles. Heitmann the hypocrite doesn't begrudge the demonstrators the TV camera crew they have surprisingly attracted. Generous of her, as those with the temperature and broad support on their side tend to be.

"There are also some *workers* among them," Bella says, rolling her eyes to the heavens. "From the factory, can you imagine?"

And then my knife twists again. Makes me crane my neck and stare. There, on the other side of the wave of smiling faces, among the demonstrators, there is for half a second in the confusion of movement, a face. The thick hair falling over the forehead, the rounding of the cheeks, the red blotches over chin and neck –

"Anlaug," the little knife in me says and turns in my stomach.

9

"Can you see someone we know?" Bella breathes into my ear the warmth of menthol cigarettes and champagne. Someone we should know the name of, she means, be attentive to, wave to, invite to join us *inside*.

"No," I say. "I made a mistake."

Anyway, Anlaug isn't anyone Bella knows or would like to be associated with. Bella believes that all my patients, past and present, lie screaming in small padded cells, bound by straps, and it is too wearing to explain to her that this is not true.

I can't see her among the demonstrators anymore. Where I thought I saw her there is now a shoulder, in green, perhaps Anlaug's and perhaps not, beside it another face, a little like a squirrel's, pointed, with big, furious eyes.

We are standing on a narrow advertising agency-style bridge, painted white and prettied up, stretching from the east bank of the Akerselva to the west, and at this moment it forms an exaggerated, caricatured, dividing line, perhaps a bit like a small class boundary, between those inside and those outside elbowing their way further and further up, like Bella and me, and those who, sad or angry, are left behind, alas, on the *east* bank.

It is not intentional, of course. No advertising agency would consider building a bridge over this country's most symbol-laden river to mark anything to do with *inside* and *outside*. This bridge, which doesn't lead to an advertising agency, but just looks as though it does, is definitely intended to be a fetching tribute to unity rather than division and it is so undesirable, so old-fashioned, this *inside* and *outside* that we are part of.

But it has entertainment value, no doubt about it.

"No-one," wheezes Bella, "and I mean no-one, Igi, has demonstrated against an art exhibition since the Kjartan Slettemark exhibition in the year dot, the Seventies, wasn't it?"

Perhaps they have been hired, I wonder, from a dynamic little company called Rent-a-Demo, or something? Perhaps the TV camera crew has been hired too? When it comes down to it, TV camera crews are just as rare at the openings of exhibitions as demonstrators, although Aske is probably the only artist in the country capable of attracting both.

The jostling behind us is increasing. Bella has to get through more than anyone else and doesn't miss a chance to let everyone know. They're bloody waiting for her inside and she hasn't got time for any of this, and she makes good use of elbows, nails as well as her dazzling smiles. Elbows for the women, smiles for the men, Bella operates with her own class distinctions.

And she has an *animal* as a *guide*, she asserts, although Rita doesn't appear to notice the crush at all, she is just as sluggish and overweight as always. Rita was exposed to a great deal of hash smoking in her, and Bella's, younger days, and since then her state of mind has been peculiar.

"You should've brought your little one with you, then we would've been at the front of the queue straightaway, just like on planes."

I think that is the first time I have heard Bella suggest that there was anything positive to be said about children.

"What have you *done* with her?" she asks, as if I have mislaid her somewhere.

"Benny organised some child care," I say. I get a raised eyebrow from Bella before she shoots off and tackles the couple in front of us. She always behaves as if Ida is something I had produced on my own and so I shouldn't burden her beloved Benny with her. Benny is the reason that I know Bella, – he regularly takes pictures for her catalogues.

Bella is now quite frenetic in her endeavours, rougher in the way she takes her fingernails to the tight packs of anorexic girls, more open and generous with her leopardskin bosom to the men. It is difficult not to be impressed by her tactics, especially when someone like me is *inside* and on my way, if not up, then at least through, albeit strictly as her appendage.

Now there is shouting coming from the west bank, from the crowd gathered there in a semi-circle around the cobbled square. Here too there are cameras, belonging to the TV crews with greater foresight. They are resting on the photographers' shoulders like bulky little bazookas pointing in the air. Well-trained young men in black T-shirts and baseball caps, the latter worn back to front according to convention, shove the crowd into the wall, keeping the square free with outstretched arms.

It is overwhelming. It is a vertical landing, sudden and with a jolt and staggeringly beautiful like a second coming. Whoosh! Thousand watt cones of light on the right side of the river, the west bank, on the reverently prepared, pseudo-antique cobbled square kept free for this purpose. Whoosh! The light floods down from above, and Bella becomes a little less choosy about genders: a really nice looking young man gets a leopardskin elbow in his stomach, I just catch hold of Rita's collar before Bella storms into the circle of light. She belongs there, the leopard woman, the Fifties babe with the nerve to have bleached hair, a whisky-soaked voice and her own gallery. The light from the helicopter streams over her, a second Anita Ekberg, the sex-bomb in her fountain, and the two men who jump nimbly from the helicopter crouch in the downdraught of the rotor blades and let her bathe in it, bathe in the light, in the applause that belongs to her or to them or quite simply to the special effects.

I stand on the edge of the dazzling white circle and watch, overwhelmed, like everyone else, by the helicopter's descent. Joakim Roll has come to earth, bringing if not his prophet then at least Aske.

In the white light from the helicopter: a ballet. Bella is embraced first by one very self-assured male celebrity and then by another, and although she is too toasted brown, leopardskin-clad and bleached, no-one doubts that she can keep up with them. With a man on each arm she struts in her high heels towards the entrance. The worlds meeting by Bella's side, as by the banks of the river earlier, are not exactly east and west, nor are they up or down, or inside and outside, but Art and Money and it is by no means the first time they have gone hand in hand.

On the way towards the five-metre high open doors in the brick wall in front of us I am squashed against an art critic and her decorative husband. Behind her black rectangular glasses the critic has a sharp art critic's look, behind the fiery red lipstick a sharp art critic's tongue. With it, she gives the demonstrators a going-over to energetic nods from the decorative husband. The anti-pornography group, factory workers, whoever, they are all basically a mob, I am given to understand. Aske's use of pornography, the art critic's tongue makes it clear, is subversive, deconstructive and – but here perhaps I mishear – anthropomorphic, something the demonstrators, if they could have been bothered to read the art critic's articles, would have understood.

The decorative husband is standing close to the art critic, so it is not for his sake that she is shouting. It is possible that she would like to assist me with my potential lack of clarity concerning Aske's subversive anthropomorphism, but it is of course also possible the TV camera crew stuck to my other shoulder has something to do with it. She has a Message, as well as a strong commitment to her obligations as an educator of the people. And I know that she has a biography of Aske coming out soon because Benny has taken some photos for it.

Furthermore, she is very nicely made up. Alas, the TV crew miss the opportunity and thereby display their lack of interest in educating the people, and despite vigorous attempts they still fail to push their way through the doors before the art critic and her decorative husband. I make an unsuccessful bid to say hello to her, but the art critic seems not to like women any more than she likes demonstrators.

On the other hand she gives a fleeting hello to a man in his fifties wearing a Norwegian cardigan who looks anything but deconstructive. He seems a little nervous and earns my sympathy, as does anyone who appears the slightest bit insecure in large crowds or at exhibitions.

He and Rita and I sail in through the doors like gatecrashing surfers on the art critic's deconstructive wave.

3

ONCE THROUGH THE high sliding doors we find ourselves in a long-abandoned industrial landscape. Heavy, dusty, cast iron machinery, the function of which we can only guess at, surrounds us, glistening conveyor belts stand significantly still among it. Two rows of bare light bulbs cast a dark, greenish light, rusting pipes with an impressive circumference rise to the roof. The once-whitewashed walls are covered with yellowing stains and something that looks like soot. Buckets of paint and grease-smeared tools lie in the corners, apparently forgotten.

Between the machines, people carrying slender glasses mingle with each other; their faces are impassive, signifying their familiarity with dead machinery as backdrop. Because that is what it is. This isn't how the factory looked when it was closed down a short time before. This is how it has been recreated for the occasion, with care and not a little irony. We don't need to believe in the illusion, we can just look at it. Enjoy it, if it suits us, or leave it.

The man in the Norwegian cardigan latches on to me.

"I know him, I do," he says. "Aske, I mean."

He is in his fifties and very grey, both his clothes and his hair. He is sweating in the Norwegian cardigan.

"From when we were young," he adds.

I am not surprised. Like me he is obviously an appendage here, and I realise that I am in danger of ending up on the margin of the action. Rita sniffs at his shoes.

"We went to sea together," he says. "Well, he wasn't much of a seaman, and that's the truth."

Now he wants to introduce himself. Rune Skjalgson. Igi Heitmann. Rita.

"Did you see the demonstrators outside?"

"Of course," I say.

"One of them is his *brother.*" He says it in a whisper.

"You don't say," I say.

"That's quite something, demonstrating against your own brother."

He is dead right about that. My goodness, it is. "Why is he doing that?" I ask.

"I heard him talking to the *media,*" he says. "Said it was because they closed down the factory, but I don't know, I don't."

Nor me. And I am not that interested, either. "See you," I say, not meaning it, and escape into the centre of the floor.

A particularly squat, weird-looking machine is doing service as a bar. A young woman and a young man, both with bare midriffs and navels pierced with silver rings, are serving drinks from the dusty surfaces of the machine. One of the conveyor belts is covered with narrow glass serving plates; the multi-coloured open sandwiches that fill them make a delicious counterpoint to the industrial mono-chrome of the rest of the room. Bright orange: caviar or salmon marinated in cognac. Yellow: capelin roe? Green: pesto, I presume.

Over and through everything reverberates heavy industrial rock music, extinct for decades, but that too has been revived with mock seriousness, as much a sideshow as the ancient machinery. The rock music is delivered from a stage set between two high-arched windows; a band is playing iron plates and drills with such vacant expressions that they provoke the desired laughter from the guests on their way to the sandwiches. The flames from the welding torch are especially well received; even a shower of golden sparks from an angle grinder gets a burst of applause, their industrial fireworks fizzing towards the tiled roof for a few brief moments.

Aske's art student assistants in their black T-shirts whizz round with drills and sledgehammers pretending to be busy taking to pieces the machines that they must have assembled during the night.

"Excuse me."

A man in a diving suit appears in front of me. At least that is what it looks as though he is wearing: a tight, black diving suit, head to toe. On top of the helmet is a small box, also black, inside which is the reflection of a lens, glistening like an eye. The face behind the helmet is compressed and seems squeezed by the thick rubber, but of course I recognise him. Javed Prasad is not happy to see me.

Which is not so nice. Most of them find it unpleasant to meet their therapist in the real world, in much the same way as I felt about running into my teachers away from school. If it really was Anlaug I had seen outside, that made two patients I had encountered inside half an hour, though to be precise one was an ex-patient. And the other in a diving suit. *Child murderer*, the knife turned.

"I didn't realise it was you," Javed mumbles, making even more wrinkles in his contorted face. "I just saw *it*. You are not . . ."

"Allowed to bring dogs into the gallery? This is Rita, she's working here, so to speak."

On one of the big video screens mounted in the ceiling my mouth forms a void of about half a metre. Javed emits a brief, nervous laugh.

"It's a camera," he says, fiddling with the little box on top of his head. "Live, you know."

On the screen above us my head is tilted to one side and looking away from him, a sickly green colour in hostile lighting. The camera, black and glistening, stares at me. Below this third eye are his own eyes. Dark and uneasy.

"And the diving suit?" I ask.

"I'm not quite sure," Javed says. "I think it's supposed to seem virtual, somehow."

And it does, somehow. When Javed, with some relief, has found other people to record *live*, I follow the flickering pictures on the screen in the ceiling. There are several diving-suited cameramen in the building, and their catches are recorded directly on to the screen, alternating with some of Aske's own famous videos and scenes the news team are filming outside.

One of the demonstrators mouths silently on a screen. In fact it seems to be Aske's brother, at least it says *Sjur Aske, elected trade union spokesperson* right down at the bottom of the screen under his lean, angry face. He has dark, curly hair and does not look much like his brother as he opens and closes his mouth before the clip is interrupted by Aske's gloomy, staring eyes.

On another screen a bird dies, its wings twitching. The bird is part of "InNoSense", an early Aske in black and white with carefully fumbled camera work and a complaint from the RSPCA to its credit. It is very difficult to distinguish between what is in real time and what was pre-recorded.

Above me the art critic nods graciously, caught at last by a camera. Aske reappears, talking now to the man in the Norwegian cardigan. He looks as bored as I was.

I follow my husband's erect back on one of the screens until I have an idea where he is in the room and make for him, threading my way cautiously between rusty iron surfaces and glasses of champagne.

His ponytail rests on one of his shoulders; his brows are slightly knitted and there are bits of pale pink nail varnish on his beautiful middle finger.

"Whoops," I say and lift his finger up to his face. "Careless, Daddy."

Since Ida's birth, Benny has got into the habit of borrowing my make-up or, on rare occasions and usually because I force him, of buying his own – I do *not* use pale pink nail varnish. Not because I think it especially suits him, though he knows how to put on his make-up better than I do, but because he gets so depressed if too much time goes by without him being able to leap into one of the somewhat boring dresses for which he seems to have a penchant.

It has only been in the last year that he has realised, Daddy or not, that he is a much easier person to be with in the house, if now and then and preferably without any brooding he can have as much make-up, granny-ish women's clothing and flirting with the boys as he needs. A depressed Benny, a Benny abstaining from push-up bras and eyeshadow, does neither Ida nor me any good, but so far, I am the only one to have met *Bente*.

She is fine, and Ida will get to like her, but Benny is still in a somewhat protracted coming-out process with regard to his daughter, and although I consider it rather boring there is nothing else I can do but defer to his timing. I can't exactly *out* him for our four-year-old. I think he is doing his best in that direction himself with his and Ida's wild enthusiasm for blondes, glitter and something tacky called My Little Pony.

That is why make a point of showing him the finger with the bits of nail varnish on.

"Hmm," Benny says. "Okay. So not enough time this morning. The caretaker over the street was pissed off. I don't know, perhaps we'll have to pay him. Must be something like the seventh time now he's had to paint it over and . . ."

Paid back in kind. His nail varnish, my misdeeds. But I don't want it, I don't want us to play this kind of marital ping-pong, and since it was obviously me who started it I take his other hand and kiss it. In it he is holding a pink plastic thing, a familiar object, one we haven't used for a long time. A baby monitor. Ida isn't a baby any more.

"Couldn't get hold of a childminder," says Benny, and this is why he looks down in the mouth.

"What do you mean?" I ask in my role as mother, wife, suspicious-but-calm chief child expert.

"Childminder went down the pan," he says. "Her team got through to the next round of some football competition or other and . . ."

"But Mother and Karsten," I ask, "couldn't they . . .?"

"The opera," Benny says. And then he didn't have too many others to ask, at least not at a moment's notice. Benny's family is pretty distant, and my father died a few months before Ida was born. She looks like him, sometimes. When she's thoughtful or lonely, that is. But I much prefer her looking like him, than all the other types who did, shortly after his death. Drunken men. Troubled men. Thin, unshaved men in sad raincoats, looking like failed cops and private eyes. Like my father. Lost men, that is.

Lost.

"But, my God, Benny, where *is* she?"

"Here," he says, seeing the hysterical look in my eyes. "Relax. She ran amok with the industrial rock group while they were practising, stuffed herself with sandwiches and then flaked out in someone or other's lap. She's in a room above us, perfectly comfortable.

"Benny, I could . . ." I begin, "I don't have to be here. There's no reason for her to . . ."

But then I shut up. I don't need mournful Benny eyes to remind me that it was I who institutionalised this mid-week, child-free day, I who consecrated it with stingy crypto-feminism. I know all too well that Benny could never have interrupted my time in the swimming pool and the sauna, the mother's well-deserved massage and a couple of glasses with Bella before coming here. He had tried once before and it hadn't been a very good idea.

"You know," he says.

"Yes," I say. "But you're working here in a way, and I'm not."

"I don't think it would be wise to wake her now," he says. "You know how cross she gets."

"It'll be fine," I say. He looks relieved as he escapes the ear-bashing he had been dreading. Benny is a very good Daddy and a well-behaved husband, too well-behaved. He has so much going for him, but from time to time it is hard to convince him of that. I blame the damned make-up, and I remind myself to talk to Bente about it some time. Benny doesn't owe me anything just because he uses make-up, and nor does Bente.

I tie Rita to the bar and then we go.

Ida is up a flight of stairs, behind a door, and she is sleeping in the way we dream about sleeping, soundly and quietly behind feather-light curtains that sway gently. This room is going to be one of the offices in the Cultural Centre, and it is furnished with an elegant sofa covered with linen upholstery, big enough to hold three Idas under an eiderdown. There is a comforting smell of milk and the warmth of a child's body here. An open window looks out on to the shadow of the ruins of a half-demolished factory; the deep blue twilight with a single early star, sparkling in cartoon style, settles over the rounded black silhouette.

Which is it, the evening star or Venus, or are they one and the same? We don't know that kind of thing, Benny and I, and we always feel a bit guilty, a bit serious and at the same time giggly for that reason. It is there, the cartoon-style star, and it is beautiful. Perhaps it really does feature in our daughter's dreams, which are strange, inaccessible, sweet and fragrant.

The chief child expert casts a surreptitious, but critical, eye over the surroundings and approves them: the window is too high for her to reach, Ida's meticulously groomed mouse is by the tip of her nose, and the sofa is so low that she could not hurt herself if she fell off.

The baby monitor is pink, stupid and silent in Benny's hand as we close the door behind us. I ignore my little knife. Women should show their faith in men. Anyway, the door is locked.

Bella is whining, or perhaps it is the angle grinder.

"My God," she says, "I've been looking for you everywhere. You simply *must* meet Joakim."

And then, for a second or two, my fingers brush the country's most expensive hand, rest in the dry, golden brown fist of Joakim Roll and receive in return the light pressure of a *handshake* more used to sealing contracts worth billions. Hands belonging to the country's Prime Ministers and ministers responsible for oil have rested, like mine, in this hand. These well-manicured fingers have closed around the outstretched hands of trade union leaders, captains of industry, shipowners and media moguls; rumour has it that Bella has *sucked* them on occasion.

"Joakim," she says, "this is Igi. Igi is married to Benny and she is also a psychologist."

"Psychologist," Roll repeats. His famous glasses glisten cheerfully, but the look which meets mine for a tenth of a second is quite dead. "Is there any money in it?"

"It depends what you mean by money," I say.

"Joakim, you're such an evil bastard," Bella says in her Marianne Faithfull voice. But the small retinue surrounding Roll finds him amusing. They have shining faces, broader stomachs than his and also brighter ties. The court likes fun. Fun is buying shares for breakfast, selling them for lunch, eating a company for dinner and spitting it out again in small pieces for supper. The court often has fun.

On Bella's other side there is Aske, whom I *have* to meet, but who doesn't stretch out his hand. No surprise there. He is well known for not wanting to touch. All the better then, I think, as the greenish light that reflects so cheerfully from Joakim Roll's glasses also causes Aske's silver-coloured little finger to sparkle. The artificial finger is almost as famous as the glasses.

It is difficult to keep your eyes off it. If anyone out there had come to the exhibition because of Aske it would have been his little finger that clinched it. Like most little fingers it is in private ownership, but in this case the private ownership is not Aske's, but Roll's.

The amputation of Aske's little finger is his most scandalous manifestation to date, and furthermore the only one that really deserves the name as the prefix *mani* comes from the word *manus*, meaning hand, which no-one at the amputation could help but notice. The amputation is documented on videos in a series of exclusive collections; clips of these videos have also been shown – copyrighted and raking in the cash – on TV stations all over the world but no-one – *no-one*, Bella emphasises – has seen the little finger *live*.

20

It has been embalmed, presumably in a highly skilled way since this is one of Aske's particular abilities, cast in glass or put in formaldehyde, or for that matter the brand of vodka used in Aske's previous conservation projects for some shameless sum of money. No-one knows because the little finger has only ever been viewed *live* through Roll's cheerfully reflecting glasses. Until this evening.

Bella and Roll's court are immersed in what I presume is the story about the blue-black cook's scallops. For that matter, large sections of the public have moved to the furthermost end of the room where the organically growing exhibition has been for a long time. I follow the scattered stream of spectators past an enormous soot-blackened iron oven with a tiled chimney pipe right up to the ceiling. Everything around it is white. The floor, the walls, the ceiling high above us, everything has been painted in the same chalk-white.

Cobweb-thin strings of microscopic, intense, shining bulbs are hung in intricate geometrical patterns at several levels above and beside us; not a corner, not a cubic centimetre of space is given over to the darkness of the factory building.

It reminds me of a laboratory, or a surgical department; at the very least that we have entered a new illuminated world, a world for clear thoughts and for clean, perhaps intellectual, creation. It is here that some of Aske's works are to be found, some mounted and finished, others work in progress. These are the *Impossible Bodies*, Aske's most famous and most controversial works apart from the little finger and pornography, the still unfinished collection of objects that arouses disgust, hilarity and serious critical attention.

The *Impossible Bodies* consist of bones, all of them, of skeletons, parts of skeletons, scrupulously cleaned, polished and reshaped fragments of various animals' bodies, taken from various bodies and reassembled with the precision of a watchmaker into animals that *aren't*. Aren't able to move, to reproduce, to nourish themselves, animals which have not existed, could not exist, except in an unbounded, somewhat grotesque imagination. Although they *look* as if they could have done, could have lived strange painful lives with these misshapen bodies, and that is why it is so difficult to keep your eyes off them.

Impossible Body V rests its colossal, much too heavy, ox's head on its fragile, splayed front paws, the slender spine behind the head curves over long multi-jointed legs as thin as spikes. In the middle of the back a number of tiny birds' skulls with pointed beaks burst out of the vertebrae; or that's what it looks like.

Impossible Body III raises itself as if in protest on two powerful hind legs with its long headless neck thrust wildly over one shoulder; the skull for this animal has enormous curved horns and it protrudes from the abdominal cavity where the stomach should have been.

Impossible Body IX–X is, as the title suggests, two quite similar, monstrous, oversized fronts of bodies grown together that taper into a pitiful, fungus-like, weak pelvis without rear legs. Number XII has all its eight-metre-long legs growing out of two bodies. One body lies twisted under the other with its beautiful polished sheep's skull barely raised off the floor. It points towards the snake's head and the rest of the body, which is tensed, as if about to break free.

Number VI has its tooth-crammed mouth open, not as if to attack, rather to cry out in terror; it is a tangled, intricate pile of bones. Everything is there: skulls, claws, hip sockets and wings; nothing is in the right place but it is all connected. It takes a great effort of will to study it.

The pussy cat in the exhibition room is Number II. I have seen it before and it is a comfort. The small pile of bones may be too compressed but somehow it gives the impression of sleeping, or at least that it is unaware of its deformity, in contrast with the others that without doubt *experience* their deformity in all its horror. Experienced it.

This is the laboratory we find on the other side of the soot-blackened oven. Scrubbed, with aspects of great craftsmanship, white, open to inspection and judgement from all sides. And I think to myself that not one of these constructions could be a stranger, less appealing or more fragile body than the one which stands erect on two curving legs, the one that is me.

Under my skin I can feel where bones meet, where the bones press together or move away from each other, where vertebrae settle evenly and noiselessly above one another as I move. I don't think I am alone in this. But we take it well. We have been exposed to art before and we study it without a hint of emotion appearing on our faces, none of us lets the disgust, the wonder or the horror these objects arouse in us to be reflected in any way at all with the muscles and the gestures that *we* in fact have at our disposal.

Our bodies, which are nothing like the rudimentary experiments we observe, are a lot less expressive than they are. All the power of expression in this whitened laboratory is contained in these *things*, these objects for our deliberation. We ourselves are quite incapable of expressing anything at all. Only a child or an animal would have behaved otherwise here, would have been awkward, would have made a spectacle of itself or cried out. But there is no doubt whatsoever that many have screamed here, though soundlessly.

A path opens up through the crowd of people and allows a small group to pass by the heaps of bones towards the wall at the end where the altarpiece in the room, Aske's little finger, is on display. Until this moment it hasn't been possible to get through as the crush over there has been much as before the Mona Lisa in peak season. So I slip into the accompanying group and scurry along like a fame fly after the royals: Aske, Roll, the camera crew and the famous *liberal* presenter of high culture who is going to interview them.

Aske's lean, wolfish face flickers above us, tense in anticipation of the amputation. Through the loudspeakers we can follow the unnamed doctor's assurances and dry explanations, all given in broken French; doubtless no-one in the room is taking it in, and most of us have probably seen this video before.

The end wall is bathed in neon light, and a stressed production assistant gives the cameraman the thumbs up. Between him and Aske there is a five-centimetre-wide, one-metre-high, grey pole standing in a glass showcase. A groove has been cut into the top of the pole and covered with glass, beneath which there is something pale, greenish and worm-like. The little finger.

There is a countdown. We are *on*.

"Hello," Ms Liberal says calmly to the camera. "I am here, as you heard, at today's top cultural event in the capital and I would like you to look very carefully at the work of art beside me. Aske, you created this work of art, surrounded as it has been by so much secrecy. Tell us what we are looking at."

"It's called *The Relic*," Aske says in a voice as deadpan as his face.

"As in *corpse*?" Ms Liberal asks.

"No," Aske drawls, "as in . . ."

"But what we can see," Ms Liberal interrupts, tossing back her head of curly hair, "what we can see is your amputated little finger. It must have been painful, mustn't it?

"All artistic activity," Aske says, his pale face pasty in the fierce lighting, "inevitably involves a certain degree of pain. Not one of my works has . . ."

"With us here in Nydalen, in Oslo," Ms Liberal interrupts, "we have not only the controversial artist behind the little finger, but also the *owner* of the work. Welcome, Joakim Roll. Why haven't you exhibited this work before now?"

"There's a time for everything, as someone once wrote," Roll smiles. "And that moment is right now. The TroJa factories have at last come into our ownership and we will carry on the cultural commitments that are bound up with such a prestigious name as Otto Troels-Jacobsen in the cultural life of Norway, and we have found a solution for *these* rooms that are so rich in tradition. Here, in one of Oslo's richest and oldest industrial areas we in RollOn will open a progressive, innovative Cultural Centre, dedicated in part to our most important contemporary artist, Aske, and in part to his younger contemporary colleagues."

"But the little finger," Ms Liberal asks. "The little finger?"

"What about it?" Roll asks, bored.

"Let me put the question another way," Ms Liberal says. "Why do you invest your money in art and not in something like football, for example?"

"There's not much fun in owning a football team," Roll replies lightly. "Everyone owns a football team."

"So, that's why you would prefer to own Aske?"

"There's owning and owning," Roll says, his famous glasses glinting. "At least I've got his little finger."

Laughter. The laughter spreads. Even Ms Liberal has to allow it the nano-seconds she can afford on the screen before she remembers that she is in fact a confrontational journalist.

"But it hasn't been entirely without protest," she says, turning to Roll. "Some of the last industrial jobs are disappearing here, and that must have an effect on a man who is so dependent on his relationship with the trade unions as you are?"

"You can't have *innovation* without protests," Roll says quietly. "There will be about thirty jobs lost here and, if I may say so, the

Cultural Centre alone will make up for many of those lost jobs. We are opening a restaurant here, with service and public entertainment functions. In addition to all the other things that RollOn's takeover of TroJa will mean."

"But what about all the demonstrators we've seen outside earlier this evening?" Ms Liberal says, turning to Aske. "One of them is your brother. Doesn't it make any difference to you that your own brother is making a violent protest against the new owners and the exhibition of your works?

"My brother," Aske says, and his face on the screens above us concentrates, stiffens. We are just seconds away now from the bombshell. "I'll tell you something about my brother. He has worked in this factory his whole life."

"Yes, that's what I mean," Ms Liberal says.

"Just as my father did," Aske drones on. "I worked here too, a long long time ago in the summer. And right here where we're standing now, right back in what was then the storeroom, my brother stood and watched one of his workmates rape me without lifting a finger to prevent it. I think he enjoyed it. That's what I've got to say about my brother."

Ms Liberal's eyes turn to bullets.

"Cut," she whispers. "Cut, for fuck's sake."

Above her Aske's face distorts as his mouth opens to scream. Beads of sweat break out on his forehead. Then it's cut.

But only on the video screen. Either the producers don't hear Ms Liberal's entreaty or they misunderstand, whatever, the little red light on the side of the camera continues to flash. In a panic-stricken attempt to avoid a scandal Ms Liberal points up to one of the two screens above us.

"You're also famous for your video work," she gasps. "The most famous one of them is being shown above us now. Can you tell us a little about what happens?"

But the amputation is over. On the screen we can see the yellowing picture of a naked young man stretched out on a bed. The camera gently and lovingly follows the body, the sweaty thighs, the erect penis, the rippling muscles of the stomach. A hand strokes his chest. The Norwegian TV cameraman is sensitive this time to his broadcasting time and to the limits of public decency. He pans quickly away

25

from the screen in the ceiling to the liberal presenter. Above us, however, the pictures of the man in the bed still keep rolling.

"My God," Ms Liberal whispers.

"It's *live*," someone else shouts.

"It's *porno*."

Laughter. Close-up of the young man's face, he's lying on his back, with closed eyes, his lips parted. There is a black belt tightly bound around his neck. Close-up of the hand caressing his stomach. It's an attractive masculine hand with a small tattoo in the soft part where the thumb meets the palm of the hand.

"Aske," Ms Liberal whimpers, "can you comment on . . ."

The belt around the recumbent boy's neck now seems frighteningly tight; red blotches appear on his face and his body starts twitching. The hand again: the tattoo is very clear now; it is a delicate little orchid, elegant, accomplished. And I have seen it before. In the close-up the boy's face has turned purple and his eyes are protruding from their sockets.

"No," Aske says quietly, "I didn't make this one. This is not one of my works. But the make-up is very good, don't you think?"

By then I had turned and caught sight of a black silhouette by the oven at the other end of the room. As it disappears I begin to make my way in pursuit.

4

THE AREA IN front of the factory lies empty in the gathering dusk. The TV camera crews are indoors, the occasional demonstrator is still shivering at the other end of the bridge. Two sounds reach me. Somewhere a car is starting up. And somewhere, round the corner towards the river, someone is running.

I shout his name as I round the corner, I shout even though I can't see him on the narrow pathway that runs the length of the factory building, I shout even though I can hear nothing except the sound of my own footsteps now. In my haste I don't question anything, I just run. Between the river and the wall, past the arched windows that reflect a dirty brown, dark colour, in between two low brick buildings where all the sounds are magnified and explode between the house fronts. There is no-one in the tunnel that is formed by the two long red-brown walls. I don't see any black shadows disappearing round the corner at the end of the tunnel. Nevertheless, I put on a spurt and run strongly and with silent determination.

I stop and draw breath by the corner of the warehouse. In front of me, about 200 metres away, is the narrow end of the ruins of the old factory, a black, open abyss where there was once a wall, now a gaping wound torn into the brick wall after the demolition was begun but never completed.

I move with care towards the pitch-black, serrated giant jaws of the hole. I listen as I move forward, tense, controlled. No sound of a car engine, just the rushing noise from Ringveien, the distant running of the river and, somewhere in the dark before me, something else. Not thundering feet, not even cautious steps like mine. But something.

A shuffling sound?

I am momentarily blinded as I step over the threshold that the shadows from the inside of the building have formed, but, blind as I am, I can feel the huge scale of this empty space. My dainty, girlish steps resound inside these walls that I still can't see and the roof somewhere high above me. It smells of damp and decay. Deeper into the darkness there is something dripping, the clear, regular dripping of water on metal.

I call the name as my eyes begin to get used to the dark. The inside of the building reveals itself to me in the same way as a photograph is developed: a wall there; to my right a number of oil barrels, a metal cupboard mounted on the wall; a torn wet cardboard box disintegrating in a pool of water on the floor. In my controlled voice his name resounds around the walls and up towards the roof and I stand still in the great silence as the echo fades away, so that my footsteps don't drown his answer. There is no answer.

The bricks form intricate patterns up in the dark near the vault of the roof. The pipes covered in thick layers of dust disappear into an even deeper darkness. I still can't see the end of the room. Moving forwards into the room I can feel the muscles in my back stiffening as if in readiness for an attack from behind, if it should come.

Halfway into the room I stop calling him. Halfway into the room I stand still so that my eyes can get used to the dark again. The dim light from the huge opening behind me doesn't penetrate this far.

He's not here, I think, I say to myself. Look elsewhere. My foot encounters a stone. I bend down, pick it up and throw it into the dark.

The stone hits something, makes a dull, ludicrously small sound, drops and stays put. Even the echo sounds foolish, futile and trivial. It must have hit the end wall, I think. And so what now? He isn't here.

But there is something here. Something other than me and the echo. Somewhere in front of me I hear a small shrill sound, like glass cracking perhaps, or metal rubbing against metal. It is not the water dripping because that is now on the left of me, in by the wall somewhere. I stand still and listen. The shrill sound has gone. Was it there at all?

Above me I can feel there is a change in the dark, as if I were close to shadow and the sound of my steps has changed. I am standing under a mezzanine, an old division between floors, and the fact that there is perhaps a floor over me, a separate unit, a different world of dark above the one I am moving in, makes me conscious for the first time of my own terror. I put my arms out in front of me and mumble something incoherent.

"Are you there?" I say. "Are you there?"

My hands close around thin metal rods. A staircase. A spiral staircase. Above me at the end of the staircase there is a grey circular surface. Some light from somewhere seeps in there. Where would I have hidden if I had been him? In a corner somewhere? Perhaps up there, perhaps not. And I am not sure I would have answered a call, even if I had wanted to be found. So I will have to find him. I move awkwardly on the stairs, trip and make a noise.

A corner somewhere. I know him. But I don't know him that well. I know what kinds of hiding places he prefers. In any case this dark landing is not a corner. There is a wall and a closed door. But through a metre-long opening at the side of the door it is possible to peer into the denser darkness inside. I can't see anyone in there, or hear anyone either.

But I manage to open the door. My fingers, suddenly nimble, busy, grope along the side of the door opening and find a switch, and I am blinded for a moment by the powerful light; he, on the other hand, is caught and paralysed by it.

He is lying on his side and he is naked. It is not a bed he is resting on, but a mattress laid straight on the floor with a crumpled sheet on top. Even though the back of his right hand is covered I know that I won't find the small orchid at the base of his thumb. This isn't the young man I had called out to and followed. I wasn't expecting to find a victim. I have seen him recently but I haven't a name I could give him, or a mantra that could turn him into something other than body and flesh.

The narrow black belt is still tied around his neck, his face is still swollen, a deep reddish-blue colour in the piercing, cold light from the naked bulb above him. He is not on film, despite the camera tripod at the foot of the mattress. And though everything in my senses tells me it is meaningless, that he is not some meticulously made-up piece of fiction, I have to touch him.

It feels contrary to nature, like frozen sun or warm ice; skin isn't like that, shouldn't be like that, not so cold, not as hard. All I want to do is leave him, but I can't. The strap holds me back. It shouldn't be like that, around his neck. I fumble around. I press my fingers between his neck and the strap, but I can't loosen the knot. As I take my hands away, one of them brushes his Adam's apple. It moves. It reacts under his skin, allows this part of his body to move although he is dead. That is when I begin to cry.

And although my hands are stupid and clumsy in my pocket, I find the bunch of keys and cut the strap with one of the keys.

Somewhere, far behind me, by the serrated jaws that break up the building in the dusk, there is that same dry scrunching noise, like teeth crushing bones or feet crunching on gravel. It only lasts a second and there is no echo. It is the strangely muted sound of Out There, of departure. And it tears me away.

Out of the dazzling light, into the cramped stairwell, my feet slipping on the steps, stepping into thin air, remorselessly kicking the steel rods and sharp edges of the spiral staircase. I meet the damp floor on all fours and stagger towards the jaws and the dusk.

I can feel my hands burning all the time, where that part of my body touched his, like a branding, a trembling frozen patch. My hands try to understand what they have touched; I stretch them out in front of me, as if they were damaged or as if they had witnessed something important, something I mustn't forget.

Back in the exhibition rooms I still have them in front of me, show them to others, as if they could explain anything. Then I say what they have touched.

5

THE STAIRS ARE half-lit. I round the corner on the landing and find the light switch with my right hand. In my left hand I hold the baby monitor. The lamp above my head has a meagre 25-watt bulb in it and spreads a golden but inadequate light over the steps in front of me. Nevertheless, it suits my purposes, which are simply to go up and check that Ida is sleeping as deeply as the silent handset suggests. Behind me I have left the exhibition rooms, the people, the unrest and the activity that I set in motion when I arrived there, running over the cobblestones from the half-shattered jaws in the side of the storehouse.

Behind me they are talking on mobile phones. There are calls for order and authorities and organisation, groups split up, half understood rumours are exchanged and ill-tempered commands are given.

I shake them off on my way into the corridor, up the stairs. The sounds behind me flow into one and become a mumbling, a regular, unbroken drone of noise and disappear in the same way that the shadows of movements disappear in the dour, warm yellow monotony of the corridor and then the stairwell.

The handset is silent. The little red eye that flashes when she makes a sound is dead. It means that she is sleeping, that she is breathing evenly, undisturbed. When she sleeps she doesn't need me. But right now I need her. I need her breathing, the light breeze from the window and my child's tranquillity.

"Igi," comes a whisper from my hand. It is flashing furiously, the little eye on the baby monitor is bright red. In the corridor I turn to ice. I can see the door in front of me, she is behind it. From outside, from downstairs, the distant sound of police sirens reaches me. They are getting closer.

"Is it you?" my hand asks, the stupid pink thing in my hand asks. "Igi, is it you?"

"Yes," I say.

Silence. And the sirens getting closer.

"Can you hear them?" he asks.

"Yes," I whisper.

"Can you hear them? Speak up!"

He can only hear me through the door. The pink plastic thing in my hand is only one-way. From her to me, it should be. From him to me.

"Yes," I say. "I can hear them, Javed. Open the door now, will you. Be a good boy and let me in. It's just me. I'm alone. I only want to check Ida. That she's sleeping. That she's okay."

I can hear his breathing now. He must be holding the baby monitor close to his mouth, it is flashing wildly at my end, it looks like an inflamed scar, like an open wound in my hand. The sirens rise to a scream outside the building, howling on the other side of the wall, forcing their way in, filling the corridor, filling my conscious-ness as I know they must be filling his. Just don't wake her up, I think, I pray, foolishly, in vain, as if I had telepathic powers. Sleep! screams my conscious will. Sleep! But whether or not my mouth opens, no sound comes out.

And then the sirens die away, dropping to a protracted, deepening whine down the scale to zero; the sound becomes dull, sluggish and yearning, a pathetic lament, a desperate surrender before it fades away and becomes nothing, no sobbing, no crying, just one final, sudden incomplete groan as if from a large dying animal.

"Shhh," Javed urges. "Shhh." And it is not me he is talking to. I have already frozen. I can't open my mouth because I might wake her up. I can't move because . . .

"Igi," Javed whispers.

"Yes. I'm here. Please tell me if she's asleep."

"She's asleep. They almost woke her up, Igi. All that racket. You don't want them to wake her up either, do you?"

"No," I say.

"What did you say?"

"I said no, Javed. I don't want them to wake her up either."

But I would like to see her. To join her. To join them.

Behind me the light penetrates the corridor. I am a black mass as this knife of light hits me in the back. Someone calls. Someone behind me calls, not with any vigour, not in panic, like with the light. But somebody calls my name. The sound of feet on concrete carries up the small stairwell.

"Igi," Javed breathes into my ear. "Igi, don't! Get them out!"

And behind him I can hear muffled, indistinct sounds that I know come from her. I turn and run towards the light.

We are under siege, Javed and Ida and I. Those inside the door, me between them and the others, this great unknown outside. I am bound to them by the umbilical cord of the handset and I am isolated from them by this locked door. On the semi-circular drive outside the blue light flickers between the house fronts and cuts up any movements into small separate fragments without any apparent connection, as if we were part of a jumbled silent film. There is a wide swathe of no-man's-land in the drive now, where there is no more activity, a vacuum between the crowds that have been pushed back and the police cars in front of the building.

"Is the door locked?" someone asks me.

I answer that I don't know.

"Is he armed?"

I don't know.

What does he want?

Don't know.

"Has he done anything to her?"

I don't know. Don't know. Don't know.

He won't let me in. He wants them to go. He just wants to be left alone. He says she is sleeping. That he wants to have a think. It flashes red, the handset flashes red, in a different, more urgent rhythm than the light cutting up the drive outside into blue fragments.

She's sleeping, he whispers again. But there are other sounds behind him. And then the handset stops flashing. The little rectangular eye is dead, black for ten seconds, twenty, thirty and behind me on the stairs there is whispering, rapid breathless activity, and the creaking, rustling noises you hear when all noise is forbidden.

I can't hear her through the door. So she isn't calling. But there is nothing reassuring about this certainty. Doesn't she dare? Is she not in a position to? Is there something over her mouth preventing her from screaming? The hand with an elegant orchid at the base of the thumb?

I can hear rustling behind me. Creaking. Somebody puts a hand on my shoulder. It is one of the policemen.

"Igi," he whispers. "We have to . . ."

And then it flashes. It flashes in my hand, red, black, red.

"Igi," my hand whispers.

"Yes," I say.

"Can you get them to go?"

"Yes," I say. "If you let me in."

"I'm holding her," he says.

"It's only me coming."

No rustling. No creaking. I don't know how many people there are, standing behind me. But I can't even hear them breathe.

"Can I open the door now?"

Silence.

"Wait," he says. Seconds pass: the click as the lock is slipped from the inside. I don't shoot forward to get my daughter. It is as if there is an adhesive sticking my feet to the floor until he gives me permission to move. Fear is stronger than fury, wiser and more disciplined, too.

She is standing erect on the sofa and looks at me with wide open eyes. He is not holding her. He is sitting on the floor, huddled up against one corner of the sofa with his back to her. He looks at me, him too.

"Hi," I say. "Hi, Ida. Hi, Javed."

Ida says nothing. Her small hands show the white of her knuckles as she holds on tight to the sofa. I have to loosen them for her. With one arm round her body, which is still rigid in my embrace, I release her grip. I don't look at him while I do it, though I can feel his gaze through all the nerve cells in my back. Her body is like a metal pipe against mine, a tensed mass, unyielding in my arms, against my chest and stomach. Then she moves her head back a tiny bit and rests her forehead against my neck. Her eyelids tremble against my skin, then she presses her nose into the hollow of my throat. There is an artery there, in my throat. It beats against her face. And then I can feel her body softening a little.

34

"Can Ida go?" I ask. She stiffens again. I stroke her hair. "I'll stay here for a little while, together with Javed. Daddy is outside, you know."

"You can't go," Javed says.

"No," I say. "I'm not going. Just Ida."

"Don't go with her to the door," he says. "You can't. You have to sit here."

"Okay," I say. "But Ida can go to the door herself, can't she. Is that okay?"

Javed doesn't answer. Ida moves her head backwards and forwards against my neck, and now she is no longer a dead weight in my arms. Now she holds me the way she held the back of the sofa, she holds me with all her body.

"She can go," Javed says.

"We'll sit here for a while first," I say.

"She can go!"

Ida presses herself tighter against me, more frightened. But not a sound passes her lips.

"Can I sit down?" I ask. He looks anxious, but nods. I take two cautious paces towards the door and watch his eyes grow and his fists clench. He has something in his left hand, but I can't see what it is. I lower myself slowly into a sitting position while I whisper into Ida's hair.

"What's that?" he asks. "Speak up so that I can hear you!"

"Ida, you can go to the door," I repeat. "You can put your feet on the floor, like that. Let go of Mummy and just walk over to the door and open it. Daddy is there."

But I have to release her fingers again. I keep talking to her the whole time. One foot on the floor. Then another. And always hoping that some of this is being picked up on the baby monitor, or the mobile phone I fastened to my belt. That they can hear me outside.

She is on the floor now, between my legs. She stares at me. I put my hands on her hips to turn her round. She shakes her head.

"Do you want to find out if Daddy is out there?" I ask. She doesn't answer.

With some reluctance Javed passes the baby monitor over to me, and I ask for Benny.

He answers through the door, perfectly calm. He is waiting for her, he says. She shakes her head. I begin to press my hands against her hips. And then she goes, her body half-turned towards me, half towards the door, backwards, sideways towards the door. Then she turns her face away from me, rushes over the last few metres, lunges for the door, gives it a shove and shouts. Javed grabs my arm and pulls me into him; I can hear Benny calling to Ida who is hammering with her small fists on the door and shouting for her father.

"The door handle," I say in a voice that is not mine.

"Hold the door handle, Ida, and pull the door towards you. It opens inwards, sweetheart. The door opens inwards!"

She hits out. Javed raises his left hand, the one holding whatever it is I can't see. I throw myself on top of him.

"Get hold of the door handle, Ida," this strange voice that must be mine calls out. And then she does it. She pulls the door towards her and disappears into the chink of golden light that opens itself up to her and she is gone.

We are panting. I am lying half over him in the soft new darkness and I can hear him breathing, and myself, too. As well as Ida's sobbing outside, which soon dies down, and Benny's voice that fades into a mumble as he carries her downstairs. Javed and I disentangle ourselves.

"I'm sorry," he says. "I didn't mean to . . ."

He means my hair. He had grabbed hold of it at some point and bent my head backwards. I didn't realise. I can't take it in now either, as he relaxes his grip and lets me go.

Our breathing is hard, irregular, unsynchronised and feverish in this dark room that is now ours. Somewhere deep inside me something asks if I am afraid. Too late, I think, as if it were someone else asking. Why do you ask now? When it no longer has any meaning. The sweet fragrance of Ida's sleep still hangs in the air, hazily, giving way to the smell of Javed's fear and my own. I don't know what her fear smells like.

He asks me if I have a light. A lily-shaped flame illuminates his face for a second. He looks young.

"What do we do now?" he asks.

"What do you want us to do?" I ask.

"Nothing," he says. "Die, perhaps."

36

And that is understandable. It makes sense although he won't be able to do both. I still can't see what it is that he has in his hand, but all the same he will want to use it more than anything if it is a weapon. Dying is not something you do *perhaps*. I suppose. I have to suppose.

"There is no other way out here," he says and half gets up. "Just out of the window. But that wouldn't do much good now. They're there as well. I've checked."

"Is that how you came in?" I ask.

He nods, pensive, not interested.

"I shouldn't have let her go," he says. "That was a stupid thing to do. Just as stupid as coming here. I don't want to be here."

"But we are here," I say. "Right now."

A low, deep growl emerges from his throat. One of his feet begins to twitch. "I don't want to be here," he mumbles. "I shouldn't have come here. But I couldn't go anywhere else in *all this*."

He means the diving suit. It is still stuck tight to his body and looks more conspicuous than ever. He has taken the helmet off and his hair is soaked with sweat, shiny and black with spikes like horns or thorns.

"There were some people by the bridge," he says. "I couldn't run over there. I couldn't go anywhere, you know."

A corner somewhere, I think. A window. The reassuring smell of a sleeping child.

"That wasn't supposed to happen," he mumbles and I assume he is not talking about Ida. "I don't want to talk about it. I don't want to think about it, either. *I don't want to talk about it!*"

He is with his therapist now. She is the one who puts pressure on him to speak.

"You don't have to talk about it," I say, "if you don't want to."

"It was his idea," he says. "All that about . . ."

The window facing the backyard lets in a soft breeze, it circles us, lingers, then disappears, returns around our cheeks, knees, arms and then goes away.

"Is he?" Javed asks. "Do you think he . . ."

Is dead, he means.

"I don't know," I say, as someone used to lying.

But I know that he is lost now, it is all just a big white expanse. Fog, perhaps. Thick white fog devouring him and enveloping his thoughts, his feelings, burying them, lying on top of them, deaf and mute.

I guess we have been sitting for quite a long time. We talk a little. His hands are restless, fidget and make small jerky movements now and then, like his feet. It was a camera he had in his hand, black and compact like his diving suit. It must be the one he had on his head when he was filming me and when he . . . I don't want to think about it. I don't want to think about any of it.

"Shall we go," I say at last. And then we go. I hold the door open for him. In the golden light from the corridor his face makes him look like a three-year-old. A three-year-old wolf. But he doesn't bite as they take hold of his arms. Only once does he open his mouth, show his teeth and call out. Then he disappears round the corner of the landing in front of me, down in front of me, his gaze locked into mine.

6

THE DAY IS like blotting paper. It sucks the darkness into itself like water before letting it dry out and disappear. I am sitting by the kitchen window and watching, watching the sky being drained of colour, watching it turn pale and fade until it is nothing more than a grey, unbroken surface again. Fog. In the fog the shapes of the town assume a heaviness, become de-energised surfaces and indistinct striving diagonal shapes.

And I am not making sense. I haven't slept for a second but I don't want morning to come, I want this night to remain, though it has gone on all too long. Ida and Benny are sleeping in our bedroom. They don't need me to keep watch. Last night she clung to him on the way to the car and didn't let go during the drive, up the steps or when they got home.

Not that I would have been capable of carrying her, not with my limp, muscle-less legs on the way home, I was like a kind of jellyfish, a strange, twitching jellyfish. Later she stared at me from the bed with her grey mouse by her cheek and one of Benny's arms to ruffle her hair.

Once, hours after she succumbed, with some reluctance, to sleep, she called out, a brief, shrill cry, and then they both slipped back again. Neither stirred as I sat down at the kitchen table.

As the town takes shape outside the window I perform the morning rituals – slices of bread, milk, picking up the newspaper from the mat outside the door – and I turn into a normal citizen, no longer the jellyfish, the jelly of the previous night. Things do that for me, things and the rituals they belong to. It doesn't spring from me.

Our names aren't mentioned in the morning papers, neither Javed's nor mine. We are protected by the photographs of the drama taken through a telephoto lens; the indistinct, mysterious surroundings that frame us are no more than diffuse shadows. In the bottom corner of one of the pictures there is a black, fuzzy-looking diagonal shape – is it a pipe, a ceiling, an open car door?

It is the Peeping Tom's perspective raised to an art form: indistinct, dark, rushed, the further away, the more exciting. Once upon a time most pornography looked like this. All the woolliness of the foreground highlights the intense focus on the background. The jacket covering Javed's face is grainy, every fold is chiselled out with the care and strength of Michelangelo, the contour of Benny's arm around Ida's shoulders is reproduced with ice-cold precision, every hair on her head can be counted. But her face is turned away, as mine is in a sloppy, coarse photographic study that could be entitled "In Flight".

Our names are not mentioned and we are protected by a well-established aesthetic; we are given large, well-defined roles that can be recognised immediately, so who would recognise *us*?

They are asleep when I leave them and will wake up to a packed lunch, coffee and a big note from Mummy on the table, covered in felt-tip cartoon hearts. A recognisable aesthetic. Necessary rituals.

There is no massive reception committee dressed in black waiting for me in the clinic, there are no whispering councils of war in the meeting rooms, the flag isn't hanging at half-mast. Nevertheless this neglected Victorian building could have been marked with a large cross with dripping black paint. Every voice here, every metre of lino, every exploratory smile and every familiar movement gives the same unambiguous signal: the effort to maintain the necessary calm. Underneath it the crisis pounds away. We know things like that, we are used to reading faces other than our own.

Doctor Welle is careful not to draw hasty conclusions. He sets great store by being objective, well-mannered and professional. Of course there is also room for emotion, though unorthodox, after all we are in the feelings business, but it is for the most part limited to running your hand through your hair, needlessly scratching around in your papers on the table or taking particular interest in the coffee machine, which is more sluggish than usual this morning.

If the doctor is boiling with suppressed fury there is not a hint of a reproach in the brown eyes under the heavy eyelids. We are in this together, the look is supposed to tell me. That I don't believe him can be put down to the fact that he and I have what is called bad chemistry, which we both politely and in accordance with our well-mannered professionalism have acknowledged.

There are strategies. Systems. A framework for well-mannered, objective and professional treatment. That is after all what we do, we deal with crises. Though not usually of this dimension. They don't often come here, the ones who have committed real acts of violence. Not until now.

"Nothing?" he asks, his fingertips playing under his chin in the coquettish way that so irritates patients. I remember Javed parodying him in this way. "No previous acts of violence at all?"

"No," I say. "At least, not in our records."

"And the tests? They don't show any such tendencies, either?"

"I don't think so," I say. "I would have remembered. That would, of course, have been very pertinent. But we will go through them again."

"Please be so kind as to run over his case again. Just the bare bones. I have to confess that I don't remember him very well. It's senile dementia, you know."

He is past pensionable age and in the last of what he calls his years of grace. According to rumours in the department, plans are being made for his seventieth birthday, a Festschrift is on the way and he is just as coquettish about his age as he is with his fingertips, the cord trousers and the Hemingway beard.

"Twenty-three years old," I say. "Unipolar personality disorder with extremely withdrawn behaviour patterns, scores consistently high on feelings of shame, no alcohol problems. He is the younger of two brothers, strong attachment to his mother. Sexual identity is unclear, limited circle of acquaintances."

"Unclear sexual identity?"

"Yes. He's had some homosexual experiences over the last months. It was his sexual debut, so to speak. The others in the group sort of applauded that. He was very proud and very quick to point to the problems."

"What problems did he point to?"

"It wasn't love, he said. And on top of that, of course, it is quite impossible to talk about at home."

"I see. Mother and father?"

"Mother's a housewife, hardly any Norwegian. Father – strict, traditional, active in a rather conservative Pakistani union. Independent businessman. Occasional violence during Javed's childhood, the older son on the receiving end most of the time. Apart from his mother no-one in the family knows that he is a patient here."

"I will want to see the records and the results of the tests," he says, looking at me with his self-assured brown eyes.

No-one needs to tell me that this is being reported upwards and, what is more, of necessity, outwards too, if only to a limited degree: to colleagues, to the media and right to the very top, I suppose, to the politicians of the town. Since it is not necessary, no-one bothers to tell me that either. I am not deaf. I can hear the telephone ringing in his secretary's office.

It is when there is a message from the police that I realise. It is what I didn't want: the humiliation. The indignity. I sit there with the telephone in my hand and I know it is there, I know that it has been there since the morning. I hate it and I despise it and I am not enough of a psychologist to excuse it. Not when a young man is dead and this when it was *my* Javed who confessed to killing him some time early this morning. Then I don't excuse the pride that makes me feel humiliated. I don't excuse the possessive pronoun either. My Javed. My patient. Shouldn't do that sort of thing.

And this time it is I who perform the magic, who makes myself his mummy with my little pronoun.

It is ten past twelve when the police phone us, and by that time the official machinery is up and running in preparation. Reports confirming the confession go to the top of the system, to the professional and administrative heads, who have been forewarned. The checking of records and tests intensifies, clarification about immediate measures is given and the right to make public pronouncements is restricted.

There is a system and an order. Action is a wonderful remedy for heightened sensitivity. It is not the aim of the system; that is not why we become so zealously industrious. It is a side effect. But side effects are effects nonetheless. Even long-term schizophrenics can hold off a psychotic attack by keeping themselves busy. It is not so surprising then that I start to forget my self-contempt over the course of the day. However, it is okay to have a loathing – well, in retrospect.

Ida *does* want to go to the nursery, Benny says. Necessary rituals. Action.

7

"POLICE STATE," BELLA snarls into my ear. It is one o'clock in the afternoon and she is pulling on what I guess is a morning cigarette.

"Igi, they've *arrested* him."

"Charged is the word," I say. "Yes, I know."

"But it'll be one hell of a *scandal*! It's persecution. We're talking about Gestapo methods here, Igi."

"Well," I say. "It's shaken me too, of course, but they didn't have that much choice, did they? When he confessed, I mean."

"Confessed? What the fuck are you talking about? He hasn't confessed a bloody thing, has he? He's not altogether doolally, is he?"

I thought we were talking about Javed, I say, with the incredible composure I sometimes have with Bella.

"About Javed? Which Javed? I don't know any Javed. Igi, listen, Aske rang me. At *this very moment* he's at the police station! Do you realise?"

"But Bella, you dear old thing. Being questioned is just a routine matter. I'll have to be questioned, Benny will, you as well. Bella, it's got nothing to do with persecution."

"Piss off," Bella hisses. "Give me a cigarette first and then piss off. Go and have a shower or something."

"What?" I ask.

"I wasn't talking to you, darling," she answers. "There's some prick lying in my bed, I can't imagine why. The point is, Igi, that the police are holding Aske."

"Bella . . .," I begin.

"But I know what I'm going to do," she says. "We shouldn't put up with all this harassment, should we? I'm going to report them to the Human Rights Commission in Cherbourg. Pure and simple. Go right to the top."

"It's Strasbourg," I say.

"I beg your pardon?"

Bella has this wonderful, cutting West End tone of voice that she sometimes uses. I rarely get the chance to enjoy it.

"The Human Rights Commission is in Strasbourg," I say, "and I don't think it's the sort of thing they really deal with."

Bella has had a very active past as an anarchist, and so she is a little bit paranoid, but after a while she calms down. After lighting her fourth ultra-thin cigarette she can also remember Javed.

"Not my responsibility, Igi," she says. "I've *no idea* who roped all those art students in or whatever they were. I want *nothing* to do with that organic mounting crap. I told them, but of course it's me who'll have to pay the *bill*. Isn't that typical? I mean, they managed to find the *sex killer*, Igi, sorry to put it like that."

"So it was Aske, then, who hired them," I ask.

"I've no idea, Igi. No idea. Everything was just chaotic. My impression is that people just dropped in, as it were, and picked up a drill or something. And now they've closed the whole place. Igi, down in the gallery they're saying that people are crazy about coming. Everyone wants to see the exhibition, just *everyone*. We're talking busloads, Igi, busloads of *pensioners* from Askim. And then the police closed the whole caboodle down."

"It won't be forever though," I say. "Since Javed has confessed."

"Who's defending him, do you think? An idiot? I mean, confessing. But that may help us. Whatever, I'll still have to order guides right up to Christmas, just to get the pensioners through. It'll cost a fortune. Have you heard if they've identified him?"

"No," I say.

"The one who died," Bella says. "Well, it was one of those trade and industry reporters, one of those bloody limpdicks."

"Who was killed?" I ask.

"No, who rang me. They always know everything that's going on. And it's scandalous, Igi, I have to say. Of course I should have recognised him, but then I had never seen him – how shall I put it? – *dead* before."

"Did you know him?"

"My God, who do we ever know? Igi, I don't think I know *anyone*. Well, he was one of those young superguys, you know, twenty-something with a Master's in something great, worked for *Daddy*, can you imagine? And then one day – wham – he's in management, in TroJa, and was really helpful, I've got to say that, with all that shares stuff and so on."

"Bella, cut it out," I say. "He's dead."

"Well, that's what I'm telling you, darling," Bella says. "Isn't it shocking? One day he's sitting there smartly dressed, very proper, putting forward plans and asking me to sign bonds, and the next day he's stretched out on a bed, purple and stone *dead*. It's crazy, Igi, and that's what I'm trying to tell you, it's crazy this life we're living."

"What's his . . ., what's his name?" I ask in an effort to get Bella's feet more or less back on the ground.

"Something quite run-of-the-mill. Martin Olsen or something like that. Maybe Andersen. You know what I'm like with names."

Someone is screaming wildly somewhere in a room behind Bella.

"He was good-looking as well," Bella continues without remorse. "I think he was in training. For rugby or something. Do people do that?"

"Bella," I say, "There's someone screaming over there."

"Oh that," Bella says. "That's just Rita."

"Does Rita scream?"

"No," Bella says. "No, that's not Rita screaming of course. That's the guy who was in my bed. Rita's *snapping* at his toes. She is very jealous, you know."

"Rita isn't jealous," I say. "Rita's a *headcase*."

"Yes," Bella says, deep in thought. "It must be all the hash she ate when she was young, do you think?"

I am smiling when I put down the phone. I can feel my lips curling and I instantly despise myself for it.

That is how easy it is to despise, but it takes about half an hour before Javed drifts away and becomes a vague memory. I am sitting on a school-style chair next to Dr Welle. He has insisted that he should be the one to inform Javed's group, which is meeting this Thursday, as every Thursday, in this rundown room where the windows don't close properly and where the once white door is scored and has dark patches where the paint is peeling off.

It is an essential part of a well-thought-out system for the Head of

46

the Department to be present; that I lose a little dignity in the process is a side effect. However, the balance is thereby upset: there is one therapist more and one patient less. There is no free chair where Javed should have been sitting.

And after a mere thirty minutes Javed's absence has created associations that are strong enough to become personal, his action has entered their lives, pieces of his history have been changed into theirs. Javed is a switch, a point of departure for convoluted or very direct references to their own lives. It is because the same has happened to me that it hits me so hard, that it is so tough and so dirty. My pride. Their lives. The scientific validity of our tests.

Gerd opens the window. She is forever opening the window. Ottar uses the occasion to state that I am the worst therapist he has ever experienced, and he has experienced a few. Ada's neck is a botanical display of red, inflamed smudges. Torstein's tics have rendered him inarticulate; he looks up to the ceiling and slaps his hand against his knee before he begins to stammer. He feels obliged to retell a sexual fantasy.

"There should be two free chairs here," Gerd says at last. "There was also someone who died, wasn't there?"

And then the session is over. Jackets rustle as they are lifted up and thrown over their shoulders, bags are opened and packs of cigarettes are taken out. The curtains flap even more as the door to the corridor is opened, feet stamp or shuffle on the lino floor. The chairs are free again after our departure and form no pattern of any kind.

Perhaps something in me expected this, even wished it. In the drive in front of the brick-built Victorian hospital that reminds me of the TroJa factory I smoke an unmotherly cigarette, as far away as possible from the acrid smoking room and its yellowing walls. Departments of psychiatry have the most effective smoking rooms you will find anywhere; you can stand outside their windows and still have a good chance of contracting lung cancer.

Five minutes for the distaste, for the pointless self-contempt, more often than not accompanied by a woolly, unclear, vacant feeling. Maybe I am thinking about something while I am standing there, but despite my best efforts it remains inaccessible.

And then: pandemonium. A chink in the veneer of good manners

47

that were there, even in the group, where we seldom insist on them. However, it all begins well enough.

"I'm looking for someone called Heitmann," he says. He is large and muscular, wearing soft, heavy cotton trousers and soft heavy shoes; his T-shirt is stretched to regulation bursting point around his upper arms and chest.

"That's me," I say, and drop my cigarette on to the ground. Not to free my hands so that I can protect myself, because I don't work in the high security unit. There isn't even a locked door on the way into our long corridors. He could have gone right in and found my name on the door and I would have been just as defenceless there.

"I thought it was a man," he says, and his brown eyes meet mine for a second. The car he just got out of is parked at an angle, and illegally, on the pavement. Three of the doors are open, and the younger, thinner man is getting out on the driver's side, behind him a woman in a green sari is holding on tight to the car roof with both her small hands. Her face beneath the shawl is thin and the strange, sooty greyness that comes out when skin which is naturally golden brown is streaked with sleeplessness or distress or terror. I have never seen her before, but in any language it is clear that she is a mother.

The bodybuilder kicks out the front headlights of the nearest car with his soft heavy shoes. It is not mine, but he is not to know that. His ham-like fists thud once, twice, ten times on the car roof before he turns towards me. Now I can place him. Javed's brother, and beside him in the flapping, cheap brown jacket a cousin, a cousin or a second cousin, because there are no Javed brothers other than this one, who until today did not know that Javed came here, did not know that Javed was not doing some nonspecific four-month course, but was here every day, did not know that one day some months ago – how many was it? – Javed told us, eyes big with embarrassment that he had had a *trick* and it was with a man.

The bodybuilding brother kicks off the side mirror on Dr Welle's Volvo as he approaches me. The one called mother in any language of the world has covered her eyes with her hands. And I don't remember what the bodybuilder is called. As if that meant anything now, as if calling out his name would have any effect, lists of names run through my mind – khalidalimohammednadimosmanfikretsalim! – as he drives his fist down into one of the soft pockets of his tracksuit

48

bottoms and raises it towards me, shaking it and scattering a shower of small white saccharine-like pills over the pavement between us.

"Do you know," he roars, "where he got this from? From her house, in the bathroom cupboard, eh? It's *shit*! It's shit like this he got from you and he was turned into shit like this *here*. Wasn't he? Wasn't he? Perhaps you were there when they rang her, were you?"

I don't remember his name. I wasn't there.

"*I* was there," he screams, his large swollen face close to mine now. "I was there when they told her that he was a murderer and a *dicksucker*. My brother!"

This last came in such a shrill, piercing falsetto that it could have been a woman screaming, and though this is no high security unit, it is nevertheless a department of psychiatry and not all that far away from departments where people working are forever on the alert and physical, and where there are, yes indeed, both straps and padded security rooms. And now there are two men on the footpath coming over towards us, who at least together can measure up to his constructed butcher's body of brawn. He senses them behind him, but still he holds my gaze.

"My brother," he says, now calm and without any need to draw breath after the roars and kicks and blows with his fist. "Not any more he isn't."

He reaches his sleek, carelessly parked Mercedes before the two interns and before I wave them back he has the engine started so that the hollow-cheeked cousin and the one called mother in any language can hurl themselves into the car. Of course he revs up the marvellous German engine, and of course he slings the car sideways so that the two male nurses racing after him have to leap to the side. He backs up. Tears the wheel round with his enormous golden brown fists. He roars off, the engine whining again, but as the car purrs past me seconds later he opens the window on the driver's side.

"I've got a SOLICITOR, you know," he yells. "Norwegian as FUCK!"

"It's all right," I say to the two male nurses and I wonder from which film I have stolen such a stupid line as that.

I have another smoke and I am back in my office when the message comes in, flashing on my screen. At first it seems in poor taste, then it is tempting. An e-mail headlined "murder" is something I hope not even Bella would send me on this day of all days and I feel like deleting it without reading it. But the temptation lies in the content.

Temptation: the little deviation from the main thoroughfares, the leap into a more fantasy-filled, obligation-free universe. The opportunity to succumb can be drawn on a multi-dimensional system of coordinates: time, occasion and degree of vulnerability. At the end of this working day the coordinates meet neatly on my little screen and I know very well that I am vulnerable.

The message comes from someone called i–c.dahl. I have never heard of any i–c.dahl, except for the painter years ago, but this current version hits me right in the vulnerable place where my pride and humiliation meet, in the middle of my desire not to have any responsibility for Javed's actions. Suppose, i–c.dahl suggests, it *wasn't* him who took the life of the young man whose name i–c.dahl, unlike me, does not know?

In fact i–c.dahl is quite sure that it was not Javed and furthermore i–c.dahl believes that since I am an intelligent woman I will also be convinced that this is the case, if I am willing to receive further information via a more suitable medium. A meeting, for example. In i–c.dahl's flat in Grønlandsleiret, for example.

That place where my pride and my humiliation meet smarts just a little and I would like i–c.dahl to be right, I would love something to loosen the moorings to my obligations – hey presto, just like that. Most of us can tolerate twinges of pain; it is the persistent pain that we want to get rid of.

But I do what once in a while one should do and what one has to do in a psychiatric department: I refer him or her to the police. I–c.dahl should talk to the police, I write, if he or she knows something about Javed or about the murder, not to me. I won't allow myself, I muse, to be taken on a tour round the narrow, winding pathways of my imagination. Not for a second will I succumb to the temptation to wish that i–c.dahl was right, and so I won't ask myself how on earth i–c.dahl, he or she, found me, either.

Nonetheless it is irritating and I feel it beginning to nag at me as I walk to the car that will take me home and to Ida. Where did i–c.dahl get my e-mail address? It is not important, I know, it is just the temptation that sneaks up on me, that wants me to deal with i-c.dahl in order to avoid other more painful thoughts.

In the car park I see again the trail left by Javed's brother, the smashed glass and the reminder of my own fear. I am not a masochist, there is nothing cleansing about having humiliation written in capital letters, no catharsis in his brutal outburst.

I mustn't believe that by following small winding passages of thought I can get away from Javed. Ida will achieve that for me. She will take me away from him and from myself.

8

SHE LOOKS AT me with her father's eyes, big and dark and deeply serious. We spoke a little on the phone during the day and she consents to come into my arms. She stands with her erect little body between my knees as I squat down in the cramped locker room and make small talk with her metre-high peers. But she doesn't want to wear her sweater, she won't take out her socks from the little locker labelled with an apple, Ida's mark, to distinguish her from her friends' blueberry or carrot. Ida's section of the locker room is strictly vegetarian on the symbol front.

Her little head moves heavily from side to side, for a long time. Afterwards she looks at me with her serious expression. The owner of the blueberry, whose name is Thomas, is hopping around us in manic fashion, his arms seized by a kind of spasm. He seems to be fawning for attention. Ida gives him a big smile and looks across at me with those thoughtful eyes. People are different. Just now I doubt that Thomas is as silly as me.

Afterwards we talk a little about Plasticine and about a variety of events in the sandpit where Thomas has celebrated important triumphs in the course of the day. Ida puts her hand on my arm, her hips rest against my thigh which, if nothing else, I suppose is warm. I blow into the back of her neck.

"Silly," she says and shivers, and it is okay to take out her socks, it is even okay to put on a sweater. Ida also has a few sandpit stories of her own to share with me while I tidy up zips and shoelaces as best I can and I am such an appreciative listener. I know that there is a very serious ban on silly people here among the blueberries and carrots, but I am not so silly that I take any notice of it while Ida's body nestles around mine and her eyes glint.

"Mummy . . .," Ida says.

"Yes," I say.

"Mummy? Mummy . . ."

"Yes, what is it?"

"Nothing."

We have a good laugh at that and then she repeats the success all the way home. Like all children she has a terrible sense of humour, but it is so infectious.

A yellow plastic car is on the receiving end of the horrendous story about being alone. In reality the plastic car is on the top of the kitchen table, but metaphorically it is out in the BLACK OF NIGHT and it meets LIONS. It has been a while since THE LIONS appeared in various places in the flat and the general neighbourhood, but they make their comeback while Benny is preparing lunch.

What helps against LIONS is mainly stories about them, and Ida has the plastic car meet a lot of them as she pushes it up and down along the edge of the kitchen table. Food also helps, even if it turns out to be a feeble and rather un-Benny-like affair.

"It's called spaghetti carbonara," he says. "And obviously it's not nutritious or even that good, but it's *something*."

"It's okay," I say.

"That's what I said," he says.

When Benny makes food like this he is depressed, but with the whole kitchen full of LIONS I can't be bothered, I just cannot be bothered, to show any interest. He is not the only person who didn't sleep well last night. It wasn't his patient who . . . And after that I am distracted by a LION. It turns out that it likes carbonara; at least one of us does.

Down over the wide green slopes towards the Akerselva she is a Daddy's girl, holding on to his trousers, drawing his attention to important observations about the landscape, riding on his shoulders. Sometimes the best thing you can do with an unruly emotional life is to take note of it. It is not important that I am jealous of my daughter's father as she stands behind him on the slope doing something very absorbing with his hair. I have been closer to the LIONS than he has of late and perhaps there is still the smell of NIGHT in me.

While we are drinking coffee from a thermos she shadows three interesting girls all about the age of six, and she is willing, it seems, to do anything to be allowed into the circle. She succeeds with one of the six-year-olds, the chubbiest, who just at that moment has been excluded from the secretive whispering going on between her poker-slim friends. Ida and the chubby girl start a kind of business activity involving lilac leaves and small black stones.

"I've got to go to the police station this afternoon," I say.

"I suppose we all have to at one point or another," Benny says, emptying the coffee dregs on the grass. His fine profile facing the water, his ponytail coiled over his shoulder. He isn't normally as remote as this.

"Hello," I say. "What's up?"

There may have been a touch of irritation in my voice, there could also have been a hint of gooey female patronising, it might have been been the LIONS for all I know.

"What's up?"

"Nothing," he answers. And among the unwritten agreements in our marriage there is, of course, this one: sometimes nothing is nothing. Ida and the chubby girl are involved in a discussion about the exchange rate between small black stones and lilac leaves, and Ida seems to be sticking to her principles. It won't be worth her while in the long run, I think to myself; the chubby one is starting to look longingly at her graceful, ice-cold whispering girlfriends.

"There is no such thing as nothing," I say.

"I know," says Benny and looks at me with his daughter's eyes. But that is all. And I am not my husband's psychologist.

"I have to meet them this afternoon," I say.

"Mmm, that's quick." And this is marital ping-pong and, what is more, calculated in some way or other, although not premeditated. His "nothing" against my absence.

The chubby one has been reintegrated into the trio of six-year-olds and Ida is thus abandoned to her own four-year-old's fate. Standing in front of us she has strong opinions about the shockingly low exchange rate for lilac leaves and in compensation receives biscuits from us. She doesn't care much whether a Mummy, who smells of LION, doesn't follow her home and into bed. Nevertheless Mummy still gets a kiss and biscuit crumbs on her mouth and on top of that a handful of sticky lilac leaves. Perhaps she thinks I should buy myself some friends with them.

"Men don't come from Mars," I say to Benny.

"And women don't come from Venus," he adds. "I'm just a little tired."

When I leave them they are absorbed in an entranced study of the saris worn by the mothers of the trio of six-year-olds. Benny goes for the turquoise one, Ida for the copper green. Hardly surprising. That is the one with the most golden embroidery.

"Copper green," she sighs. "Copper, copper, copper."

Over the tops of the trees towards Telthus Hill and Gamle Aker church the sky is uniform, a consistent, undifferentiated white, high, sluggish and blank. It's nothing, I say to myself, he's just a little tired.

I am a little frightened of women like that, I know, frightened of them and frightened of being like them. Chief Inspector Kielland has a delicate, thin, elastic smile that is quick to disappear, and a delicate, slim, elastic body that seems comfortable behind a desk as sad as mine. She is new, I think, which is why she still likes her office so much. She must be new because she is so young.

I have seen her before, of course, well-dressed in grey in several hundred cafés and in several hundred shop windows. I know that she can distinguish between *caffè latte* and *café au lait*, and the wheat from the chaff in every sack, in any office where she and her experienced, rather uniform fellow women officers work.

"I would like to say first of all," she says, "that I have the greatest respect for the *professional competence* of your specialist branch."

Oh dear, I think. The lady doesn't like psychologists.

"But it is not a precise science you represent," she continues.

"No," I reply. "It's fallible, the same as criminal law. But we try our level best."

She thinks that is amusing. Her laughter is thin and a little angular like the rest of her. Maybe she thinks that psychologists are people who look right through you. Yes, baby. At least we try our level best, most of all when we are nervous or tired. I also prefer to find myself on the right side of the desk. Kielland, Eva, chief inspector and young&pretty, busies herself with her papers for a moment and then throws me a look that is clear, clean and without question professionally competent.

She is very interested in his medical history and in his bilingual upbringing. In the brother with the sleek Mercedes and the silent mother, and of course in the events that took place in a little room with Ida, as well as in a hand with an orchid tattoo. I must be close to the best thing she has experienced all day. I imagine this is how a model interrogation is supposed to be. Small, subtle pieces of circumstantial evidence flow out of me like confessions from a jaded alcoholic.

There is an almost audible click as Javed is slotted nicely into a compartment that Eva Kielland is familiar with from her previous experience. That is what they fear, the ones who come to me, that I will be able to look through them immediately in this way.

"Javed Prasad has been a patient at your department for almost two years," she says. "Isn't that rather a long time?"

"Yes, it is," I say. "But he was only in daily therapy for four months, and at no point was he brought in for round-the-clock observation. To simplify things, you could say that instead of being transferred to a psychiatric polyclinic – which is what tends to happen after admission to hospital – he continued his weekly treatment with us. This is something of an exclusive offer we make only to a specific group of patients."

"The particularly dangerous ones perhaps?"

"No," I say. "We don't treat anyone at all with violent behaviour. No active psychoses. No serious drug or alcohol abuse. No acute suicide cases and no dangerous cases whatsoever. To follow this treatment you have to be capable of withstanding a long-term committed process of group therapy. It is quite demanding and not for people with a low threshold for displays of aggression or losses of contact with reality."

Professional competence, my girl, is quite boring, not least when it is used to boost your self-respect, as I am doing.

"I would like to see him," I say rather meekly.

That can't be done. Ban on mail and visits pursuant with Magistrates' Court order and indictment and some paragraph or other belonging to Eva Kielland's area of competence.

"But why not, now that he's confessed?"

"The confession has been withdrawn," she says. "After taking counsel from his solicitor. In addition he refuses to explain himself further to us. The indictment is upheld however."

So Javed has met another competent person. Who, like Bella, doesn't like confessions. Eva Kielland really does need me. And I don't know, have no way of knowing, if Javed does. But I give her a pathetic little lecture on the accuracy of our tests.

"And so it's your opinion that there is nothing in this material that points to Prasad being violent?"

"Yes," I say. "Not up to this point in his life. But that doesn't mean that something didn't happen that could have triggered it off. Something acute or something violent."

"Anything that points to that?" she asks. "A change in his behaviour, irritations, anger?"

"Nothing," I say. "He didn't seem to be under pressure of any kind."

"Nevertheless it still happened," Kielland says with a look of scorn in her eyes. "You'll probably have to review these *tests* of yours, won't you? Unless it's a case of human error."

"It's likely to be that, whatever happens," I say. "A case of human error."

"Did Javed talk about Martin Andersen?" she asks.

"No."

"Can you really remember all the names of the people he talked about?"

"There aren't so many," I reply, remembering the brother whose name I couldn't recall. "His family mostly. Some friends, no-one called Martin among them. We have conversations, not interrogations."

"What you're saying is you don't know any more about him than what he told you?"

"I thought I'd explained that. I know his somatic and psychiatric history – through the tests as well as through conversations and the way he functioned in the group – and his personality. Pretty well."

Eva Kielland flicks through her papers and takes some notes, though the cassette is still running, and what looks like the hint of a smile passes over her face again. Cut it out, Igi, I say to myself, you are stressed and worn out, you haven't been brought in to stand trial here and no-one is trying to make you feel that you have been accused. But I don't believe the nice girl's voice in me for a second. Even while she is whispering I know that she is lying.

"These casual sexual liaisons, they were with men?"

"Yes."

"And where did he meet them?"

"It varied, I think. Cruising mostly. Parks, saunas, nightclubs."

"Uhuh. And how did he feel about them?"

"The men?"

"I was thinking more of the meetings, the casual sexual encounters, how did he feel about them?"

"Ambivalent, as most people do about their first sexual experience."

"It was his first sexual experience?"

"Yes."

"Behind a tree, as it were?"

"Well," I say, "very few of us are lucky enough to lose our virginity in particularly dignified circumstances. Isn't that your experience too?"

"But isn't it rather late? How old is he – twenty-three?"

"It's much later than the average starting age, of course, but it's not so unusual for homosexuals."

"No?"

"No."

"I sort of had the impression that they were pretty much, how shall I put it, on the ball as far as sex is concerned. That they come out early, that is."

"Your impressions are not that pertinent here, are they?"

"But yours are?"

"I'm not giving you *impressions*. I'm talking to you here on the back of clinical experience and quite extensive training."

"And I'm grateful for that." She smiles coldly. "But your long period of training and your clinical experience didn't prepare you, then, for Javed Prasad murdering someone?"

"No," I say. "In no way."

"Am I to understand, then, that you don't *believe* that he did it?"

"If it weren't for his confession and . . ."

"And?"

"And for the video, I probably wouldn't have believed it, no."

She has been to a psychologist she loathed, I think. She's got a surly mother. She thinks what men do with each other is disgusting. There must be some reason for this lady being so damned hostile. Unless, the cool young girl's voice inside me says, it is you feeling guilty and acting out *transference*. Oh shut up, I think.

Eva Kielland places her nice hands on the desk and gives me a winning smile.

"But then he had confessed," she says. "Originally."

"Yes. And there's also a video."

"Not for the time being," she says. "A pity. But we'll find it. It is pretty chaotic up there."

"What do you mean?" I ask.

"We haven't found it yet," she says. "The statement given by the man operating the filming equipment is, what shall I say, not exactly crystal clear, but it'll turn up. In fact it's a shame that NRK didn't broadcast it. At least we would have had a sort of copy."

"Has it disappeared?" I ask.

"With all the cameras around, for all we know what you saw on the screen could have been *live*," she says.

"It bloody well couldn't," I say. "I *saw* Javed, I was following him."

"Are you sure it was him you were following?"

"No," I say. "I can't say for certain. But anyway the autopsy must show . . . he was cold when I touched him. He must have been dead for a while."

"Okay," Kielland says. "All this will become clearer when we have the autopsy report in front of us. Until then I don't think we have much more to talk about. But I will be calling on your competence again."

All the way along the unending gallery in the police station, the architectural expression of the state's openness and social accessibility, I am embroiled in a bitter discussion with my inner angel. I have got over the age when I refused to listen to her, but for the moment I walk quickly and let my body make it clear that I think she is stupid.

"The lifts are that way," a great bear of a man says to me. "That is, if you want to go down."

He has a powerful jaw and gives me a friendly smile, then points towards Eva Kielland's office. "There's not much down there apart from a smokers' room."

"Thank you," I say, and turn away before we feel obliged to exchange some smokers' room jokes, as we always do when we are standing around in corridors. Walking around the enormous police department's *glasnost*, the four-storey high atrium in the inner part of the building, I am not big enough to deny the pleasure I feel that Eva Kielland has closed her office door and does not see my pitiful retreat.

In the lift I am hostile to such architectural hypocrisy: the open areas for milling around, the market thoroughfares, the glass-covered openness designed to be a contrast to the awful local community and state monoliths that through their uncoordinated appearance guarantee that they cannot produce anything but mistakes and tyranny and idiocy. *Glasnost* interpreted literally, expressed as glass. What crap, I think. There isn't an architectural style in the world that actually reveals a building's contents.

You seem extremely aggressive, my angel whispers. Oh shut it, I reply.

After passing through two heavy, lead-coloured and anything but open doors, I am met by the autumn air and the small golden lights in the park in front of the old penitentiary, where there is a multi-ethnic exhibition. As I walk slowly down the slope towards Grønlandsleiret reason begins to replace rage. As a result my internal angel doesn't need to open her mouth. It all hangs on the confession, I think. Which has been withdrawn. And on the video. Which has disappeared.

9

T HE POLICE ARE not the only ones who reside in Grønlandsleiret. There is also, at least virtually, someone called i-c.dahl. It is foolish and childish and I'm quite sure just because I have been humiliated by a competent policewoman, but I am tempted anyway. My angel tells me to go home like a good girl. The angel can go back to Eva Kielland, where she belongs. But to be on the safe side I do a little negotiating with myself: four entrances, five at the most, and if there is no i-c.dahl in any of them it is straight back home to bed.

It is the second button from the top in the fourth entrance. At least it could be. *Dahl* it says in the little window beside the button, no initials in front of it, but there would not have been room for them on the little strip. Because there is another word there too. Loaf. *Dahl Loaf* it says.

Not Dahl the painter, but the baker? A little home bakery that sends e-mails marked "murder"? Doubtful. On the other hand, temptation's spokesperson inside me asks how often it is you get the chance to ask a question like this.

"Am I talking to I.C. Dahl?" I ask into the mouthpiece of the intercom. I feel as if I am thirteen years old and I am making a hoax call with some name and number I found in the telephone directory.

"Pardon?"

I'll be taking a shower in a quarter of an hour, I think.

"I.C. Dahl," I repeat. "Perhaps I've got the wrong house?"

"Yes, indeed," crackles the thin voice in the intercom. Masculine, I think. "She is in, actually. It's just me who . . . I always call her Ingeborg, actually."

"I received an e-mail," I say.

And it is true that technology opens doors, because that is all I needed. An e-mail and more mumbling, this time from behind the lock on the door.

Loaf, I think, as I push the door open. Perhaps it is nothing to do with baking, but a name? Could be living with someone from a different culture altogether?

Maybe Asia, I think, on my way up the stairs. Or the Czech Republic? Zdenek Loaf? Loaf Ho Cheng? Africa? Mbeke Loaf?

I don't know which floor it is on, but it is impossible to make a mistake. There is a piece of white A4 paper stuck on the door to the right on the fourth floor. LOAF it says in what I presume are the biggest letters you can print from a normal PC. Once upon a time you had to order that sort of thing at the printer's. Now anyone can make a more or less professional-looking poster for themselves. Though normal A4 paper doesn't look that professional after a while.

Under the A4 sheet there is a thin brass sign screwed into the door. Just Dahl. No initials.

"That was quick," he says, opening the door.

I shake his hand and introduce myself.

"Dahl," he says. "Søren Dahl, actually."

As if it were an unusual name. He is small, a good 10 centimetres shorter than me, and thin with it. But he is not hunchbacked or sunken as men of his age often are. He is quite simply a little squirt of a man at full stretch, and he looks very spry, although he must have been at least seventy-five. He is wearing jeans and a short blue nylon zip jacket, the kind that carpenters and plumbers often wear. And a typical plaid flannel shirt underneath, with trainers. He has thin hair and thick-rimmed glasses.

He smiles, cautious at first. Apologetic. As if he would like to help me, but he doesn't know quite how.

"Yes, Ingeborg Caroline is busy," he says. "Actually. But in a couple of ticks . . ."

"Loaf," I say, and point to the piece of paper. "Is that an association?"

"An association for victims of crime. I thought you knew," he says. "I thought . . . yes, well, that's why most people come here. It's a short form actually," Søren Dahl adds, blinking behind the enormous glasses. "It stands for *Landsorganisasjonen for Ofre og Foresatte*. In other words, LOAF."

I have a feeling that I should drop it, but I can't help asking.

"But where's the second F? I mean *Landsorganisasjonen*, I get that, but how does it go on? Where does the A come from?"

"Well," says Søren Dahl, looking somewhat desperate. It *is* a problem, actually. You'd better talk to Ingeborg about that. Actually, I don't know. It should have been LOAOFFOF maybe. Or just LOFF."

"LOAFFFF," I suggest. "LOOFOFO?"

Søren Dahl blinks frantically. Someone calls out from inside the flat.

"Who are you t-t-talking to, Søren?"

"There's a lady who wants to talk to Ingeborg," says Søren Dahl. "Actually."

"Well, a-a-sk her in then!"

Søren Dahl looks at me with these desperate eyes, which are magnified by his glasses.

"Of course," he says. "Here we are standing on the stairs. Actually, come in," he adds, waving his thin arms. And then he smiles tentatively. I like him. Actually.

The narrow hallway is dark. There is a coat stand to the right of me, piled high with outdoor clothing for most seasons it seems; canvas jackets and waterproofs hang pressed up against heavy coats and sweaters tossed over the hooks. In the wall diagonally opposite the entrance there is another closed door, decorated with a little dough figure of a troll child on a potty. As if anyone could miss the bathroom in local community flats like these.

The kitchen I assume, even if there is no sign up, is inside the opening to my right, beyond the coat stand. The bedroom is to my left; this too, like the bathroom, is behind a closed door. The opening on the other side leads into the sitting room. That is where the person is calling from.

"Torstein," I say, my face appearing through the opening where once there was a door.

"Do you know each other?" Søren Dahl asks. Torstein is silent. He is staring open-mouthed and I know, having the advantage of surprise and knowing the sound of his voice and his personality so well, that it will take a little time before he is able to overcome his stammer now. At least I don't need to speculate where I.C. Dahl got my e-mail address from. Tidying things up is always satisfying. Reassurances are, too.

"I didn't know you were here," I say. "I came to meet Ingeborg Dahl."

"Would you like a cup of coffee?" Søren Dahl asks. "While you're waiting. It's ready actually."

"Yes please," I answer.

"Sh- sh- she s-s-says . . ."

With whistles and a few wild, uncontrolled slaps with his hand it takes him almost a minute to tell me what I already know, that Ingeborg is in a meeting. It gets better. Søren Dahl comes in with the coffee; my mug is white with the word "LOAF" printed on it in black letters. Søren and Torstein each have a burgundy red mug. Perhaps, I think, taking a sip, I am drinking my coffee from the only one in existence, the official LOAF mug, so to speak.

That doesn't seem so outlandish. The sitting room has been turned into a kind of office with two big public service-type desks at 90° to each other in the middle of the room. It still gives the impression of its being a provisional arrangement. What was perhaps once the sofa and coffee table are downgraded to a kind of seating area. The coffee table is decorated with a line of brochures across the surface, the sofa is complemented with two sorry armchairs of the beige institutional variety. Posters on the walls. Reference literature, judging by all the yellow pieces of paper sticking out of the books, periodicals perhaps, all in a line in red and blue files. There are telephones on both desks. And PCs. An ancient photocopier in one corner.

It is a kind of headquarters. There is only one thing that sticks out here – the large portrait on the wall above the sofa. It is a massively blown up photograph, at least 90 × 50, plus a wide, deep green mount. Plus the gold frame. Søren Dahl follows my gaze.

"Yes," he says. "That's her. Actually."

And of course I recognise her.

She looks like twelve-year-olds tend to when they are being photographed by a professional studio photographer. Her smile is stiff, her eyes are almost lifeless, her hair is neatly brushed. But she is holding a football in her small hands, which are resting on her lap. In the newspaper version of the portrait I saw the football had been removed. It does look strangely out of place between the girl's hands on her burgundy red velvet skirt, which is held in round her waist with a narrow black belt. It was her face they printed the picture of. With these eyes that already seem so lifeless, perhaps because she is bored or maybe just a little nervous.

She played football, I tell myself. As if it makes it easier to comprehend that she was alive.

"A junior," Søren Dahl says. "She was good, actually. But it was just a game of course. When they're so small."

"I didn't know that," I say, sounding stupid. "That she played football. Are you, I mean, were you . . .?"

"Her grandfather, actually," he says and looks at me strangely as if he is beginning to wonder why I am there. And I can remember catching her surname. Helena Dahl. But it is only the Christian name I remember and I would have been able to connect it with her face any time. Helena, as in "the Helena Dahl case". Søren Dahl had a grandchild who became known as "the Helena Dahl case". How long ago was it, I ask myself. Sixteen years? Eighteen? It is a long, long time since she disappeared. And a long time since the only possible assumption was that she was dead.

"My only grandchild, actually," he says and narrows his magnified eyes. "Margrete and I only had Ingeborg, we did. She was born here in the apartment actually. In 1959. Yes, Ingeborg didn't play football. Girls didn't do that then. But Helena did. Played for the juniors. We played together a little, we did. Just playing of course. For fun."

He seems to have the impression that I think there is something wrong in that. My face doesn't show the right emotions as he reminisces. When he talks about Helena she is alive, she hasn't disappeared and she isn't dead. And that is why I hasten to give him a smile, a forced one.

"She was devilishly good at dribbling," he says. "For a junior. Actually."

I don't know when I last heard the word. Devilishly. And then I think what a gift it is, with squinting apologetic eyes, to be able to create a living image in outline and in a single second. I don't know where he played football with his granddaughter, I don't know how often he played, but I can see it.

"I was actually on my way down to the cellar," says Søren Dahl and writhes in his nylon jacket. "Actually. For the tables. You know."

He looks at Torstein for help.

"Ingeborg is sure to finish the meeting soon," he adds.

"J–j–just go," Torstein says.

Søren Dahl lifts his hand up to reach for an imagined cap, then runs his fingers a little awkwardly over his forehead instead. He glances at the closed door leading to what must be the dining room. I can't hear the sound of any voices coming from inside, but then the flat laminated door closes tightly into the door frame.

"H–he lives here," Torstein says when Søren Dahl has disappeared down the stairs. "It's a–a–actually hi–his f–f–lat."

"But you don't live here, do you?" I ask.

He looks deeply offended and slaps his thigh with one hand. I wonder what complications these gestures cause him in the central administration at the university, but no doubt he will have other, more appropriate forms of expression there. Most of us, psychologists included, find the form of expression our workplaces demand of us. Torstein has worked at the student office at the university for almost twenty years.

"Of c–c–course not," he says. "You kn–n–now that, d–d–on't you?"

There is a terrible frown on his forehead. It is not so many hours ago that he told me about a sexual fantasy in great detail. It involved a great many oils. And then me. I assume that it is this, among other things, that is causing his brow to furrow and to increase his stammering.

His hand shoots down to his side three or four times and I have no desire to have him endure the torment of his Tourette's syndrome.

"Are you a friend of Ingeborg's then?" I ask. "Or of Søren's?"

And then it hits me how stupid I have been. This is no normal flat. It is a headquarters.

"You're here because of Loaf," I say. "Isn't that right?"

"Of c–c–course," he says, and since he is still waving his arms about I ask him about very concrete things. What Loaf is. What they do, and if there is anybody else beside him and Ingeborg?

As expected, the whistling and stammering disappear when he is on secure neutral ground. Loaf has existed for nearly five years and it is a support group of people who – as the Norwegian name says – are victims or kin.

"Used to be victims of crimes, but the target group," Torstein says without a hint of a stammer, "turned out to be somewhat narrow."

"Today," he continues, giving me the opportunity to see the student office at the university in action, "we have members who are victims of a failure to provide care, local authority incompetence and tyranny, as well as purely economic victims. There's still a core of victims of violent crime, of course, but we also have many cases of psychiatrists infringing citizens' rights and authorising compulsory treatment."

He gives me a stern look during this last comment, as if expecting me to protest. I don't.

"A future area for activity," Torstein says with a rather superior air, "will be *media victims*. It has been adopted into our work programme."

I ask him if there are not already other organisations working in similar areas. He fixes me with a cool stare.

"Isn't there something called . . .?"

"The *Losers' Association*," he interrupts. And snorts. I don't know if I have really seen anyone literally snort before, but Torstein does this. He doesn't want, he says, to say one word about them. I have a suspicion that the competition for members is not such a small matter.

"The *Losers' Association*," Torstein says, not wishing to say a word about them, "has never lifted a finger for media victims. That's just one example. Of *many*."

"And Ingeborg Dahl?" I ask.

"Is the head of Loaf. Of course," Torstein says. "Ingeborg started Loaf, she built up the organisation from nothing, she has the whole network of contacts. And the *competence*."

Ida has always had an introspective, deeply serious expression in her eyes when she eats ice cream. It is a grave sort of happiness. When Torstein uses the word "competence" he has something of the same expression.

"Not only the personal competence," he adds, "though of course everyone can understand what a background like hers really means. There is no-one, no-one who would consider suggesting that anyone else could head Loaf. No Ingeborg, no Loaf."

Sounds reach us from inside the other room. Perhaps chairs being pushed backwards as someone gets up. It is hard to discern through the closed door. But they have a dramatic and sudden effect on Torstein. One arm shoots into the air as if he wanted to say something at a meeting, then it falls back on to his thigh and sweeps out to the side. He clicks his tongue loudly against the roof of his mouth several times, and whether he wanted to say something or not, now it is no longer in his power as his face puckers up into agitated wordless stammering.

There is silence in the other room again, and I realise now that it is late. I should have been home a long time ago. Torstein's leisure activities are none of my business. As soon as Torstein recovers from his acute attack of Tourette's syndrome, I'll go.

The sounds he is trying to produce are at first quite inarticulate and nasal; then they become easier to comprehend. He is stuck on an "h".

"H-h-here she is, she's *finished*," he howls. "She h-h-has finished!"

"Ingeborg Dahl?" I ask, suspecting some shocking internal Loaf tragedy.

"N-no! Not Ingeborg, *Anlaug!*"

More scraping sounds emerge from the adjacent room, and Torstein looks at the door in unholy terror. I am slow. Very often, and especially in the evening.

"Anlaug?" I ask, as if I have no idea who he is talking about, though of course I do. Anlaug, who was a day patient along with Torstein for some months before she discharged herself from me and all my therapist's devilry. And who perhaps was standing by a bridge not so long ago.

I follow his gaze.

"Is she in there?"

He looks at me in utter desperation.

"She's finished," he repeats. The poor man had been sitting here and talking away, almost stammer-free, about his association, all the while feeling he has been caught in the act. Not just in new surroundings together with me, but caught red-handed, nabbed by Miss. We recommend that our patients do not associate outside the department during the time they are receiving therapy. When the treatment is over, of course, it is different.

This is not because we are authoritarian or killjoys. It is solely to avoid clients, patients, consumers or whatever the bloody politically correct term is at any one time forming alliances or loyalties which may prevent them from receiving the full benefit of the treatment.

"She's finished," Torstein repeats with all the suppressed fury of someone who has been obliged to get involved with the complicated system of public authorities a serious psychiatric case or a sufferer will inevitably meet in this country. There is an infinite number of well meaning but very complex rules everywhere.

"Of course," I say. "Torstein, of course you can make friends with whoever you wish."

"I'm not f-f-friends with her," Torstein says and then fixes his eyes on a point a little to the side of my head.

She is about 1.90 and must have passed the 100 kilogram mark since the last time I saw her. As then, she looks as if she is from a different decade, wearing as she does large, loose drapes of a rather indeterminate African and batik-influenced origin. Her long, loose oat-coloured hair tumbles over her shoulders. Over the squat nose sit her strange glasses, which can perhaps best be described as tragic. The look behind them is, essentially, deadly.

"What is SHE doing here?" she says in her deep Wagnerian voice, pointing at me. "GET her out!"

There is not one organisation, not even Loaf, that receives potential members in this way. Torstein starts his wild, uninhibited whistling again, slapping his thigh and making arm movements that seem nigh on impossible, as if his arms were missing a joint or had three too many. I know him well. If I had had just a touch of Tourette's syndrome I would have straightaway gone into spasms under Anlaug's cold, jellyfish-like look.

"OUT with her," booms the ponderous, toneless voice.

Shame, I think, that Torstein's Tourette's syndrome does not include bad language. Some imaginative variations on *fuck* would have been appropriate right now.

"I'm meeting Ingeborg," I say.

"You're meeting Ingeborg," repeats this massive slab of woman who still has not budged a millimetre from the door opening. "You. From the PSYCHIATRIC clinic."

"Yes," I say. "Hello, Anlaug."

"Perhaps you would like to recommend her some CHEMICAL preparations," Anlaug drones, "so that you can prevent her from

69

expressing ABSOLUTELY NATURAL SORROW and a HEALTHY RAGE."

The capital letters are audible all right.

"No," I say. "That's not why. I don't want to prevent her doing anything."

"You," she continues undaunted, "are the kind of person who wants people to willingly subject themselves to a CHEMICAL LOBOTOMY and you come here? Hah! But we're not IN FAVOUR OF such things here, are we? Are we, Torstein?"

Torstein is now a kind of vibrating heap of jerking limbs.

"TORSTEIN," she roars.

It is an elephant trumpeting. And still there isn't the slightest movement, not so much as a quiver in this body borne by its pillars of legs. And under those pillars, stuck on her surprisingly small feet are . . . court shoes. Those immediately become my friends. I remember them. It isn't possible to be IRRITATED by a whale in pumps.

"As I said, I'm here to meet Ingeborg Dahl," I say in my most unpleasant therapist's voice, as gentle as a happy pill, "not to torment either you or Torstein."

"I'm the SECOND-IN-COMMAND here," Anlaug says, "and I decide who gets to talk to Ingeborg."

Torstein whistles. Anlaug doesn't move a millimetre when the other woman sticks her head out of the doorway beside her.

There is something familiar about her pointed little squirrel face. I must have seen it in the newspapers or something, and away from Anlaug's rounded, heavy ham-like shoulders I would have thought it was there that I had seen her. But I have seen her in the last few days. Beside the little designer bridge over the Akerselva, with Anlaug. Then her face was distorted with rage, but it is still easy to recognise her. Ingeborg Dahl. Helena's mother.

"Anlaug," she says in a delicate, silky soft voice. "Torstein, it's late. I don't think I need you any more this evening."

Torstein somehow gathers his mutinous limbs together; Anlaug stands immovable and stares at me.

"See you next week," I say to Torstein.

Torstein forces out some indistinct sounds. Anlaug turns round and stares at the slender woman beside her. She could have broken her like a twig. But she lowers her head and lumbers towards the front door. Torstein is by now on his way down the stairs.

"Would you care for a cup of coffee?" Ingeborg Dahl asks me.

"No thank you," I say. "I've just had one."

"TORSTEIN," Anlaug roars. "WAIT!"

10

I T IS A SECULAR altar. A whole wall of what must once have been her grandparents' dining room is covered in photographs of Helena. In contrast to the enormous portrait in the other room, these pictures are small, just the normal photograph size. But there are a lot of them. And they have been stuck with great precision; not one of the pictures has curled up or bulged in the sunlight; not even a corner has come unstuck, although none of the photographs has been framed and many have been cut to size.

The sideboard beneath them still contains what is probably Søren and Margrete Dahl's Sunday dinner service – a heavy, chalk-white dish, a pile of plates of the same colour, a row of green engraved glasses with rattan stems – and above its curved front this enormous collage stretches up to the cornice moulding. Twelve small candles have been lit on the sideboard. One for every year she lived perhaps.

Someone has run a scalpel around Helena's leg, or an arm, round a multi-coloured beachball or a Christmas pixie and placed this cut-out of a day in her life, like hundreds of others, next to each other. Placed them together, with the normal rectangular photo-graphs beside or under these neatly made cut-outs without a single joint coming unstuck from the base. There is nothing here that doesn't fit together, that doesn't reside in perfect harmony with its surroundings.

"Contact glue," Ingeborg Dahl says in a low voice. "You spread it on both surfaces, the surface you want to stick and the base, and then you wait until they take. It's strange that they don't stick until both surfaces are dry. After that is quite impossible to unstick them. You have to be precise, of course. It's important to spread the glue right out into the edges."

In the glow from the candles the wall looks as if it it is made of nuances of black and gold. It is only close up that all the green and blue stand out. Trees, sky, water. All the things that surround a child. Standing beside all the adult bodies. They are here, too. Søren Dahl wearing swimming trunks and an older woman, perhaps Margrete. Ingeborg. But mostly it is Helena. In a Christmas dress. In football kit with the ball under her arm. On a rock, sitting on a wet bathing towel, thin and perhaps freezing.

"I had a lot of time," Ingeborg Dahl says from behind me. "There were some years when the only thing I had was time. And it's no good trying to take them down. It would be impossible, from a purely practical point of view if nothing else."

There are very few things that it is impossible to tear apart, but you would at least be forced to use strength to destroy this finished puzzle.

"If you would like to sit down, this chair is all right, I think." She points to an armchair by the desk, behind which she herself takes a seat, her face turned towards the sideboard and the thousands of photographs. Her smile is stiff, stuck to her face like the photographs to the wall.

"I didn't know who you were," I say. "When I got your message. I didn't know that you were Helena's mother."

"That's what you become," she says. "More than anything that you can imagine you were or would be. Your child's mother. You have a daughter?"

"Yes. Her name's Ida. Four years old."

"That's a nice age."

"She makes things up. You know, she sees things."

"Helena saw bears," Ingeborg Dahl says with her calm squirrel face and her hands placed on top of each other on the table top.

"It's mostly lions with Ida," I say.

She nods, perhaps there is the shadow of a smile over her thin lips.

"Anlaug," I say. "I didn't know that she . . . was working here. It seems I don't know very much."

"To be accurate, she doesn't work here," says Ingeborg Dahl, sitting upright in her office chair. "But she is here a great deal. Did Torstein tell you anything about Loaf?"

"Yes," I say.

"I didn't contact you as the head of Loaf, even though . . . when you live as close to a mission as I do it isn't so easy to change *rôles*, as they're probably called. But this is not primarily a Loaf matter.

"You don't believe that Javed killed the young man," I say.

"No. I don't. Exactly twelve years ago, that is, twelve years ago yesterday, my daughter Helena disappeared. She was twelve years old. I saw on the net that the young man, as you call him, has been identified. His name is Martin Andersen. He was twenty-four. The same as Helena would have been, that is, if she had continued living."

Her pinhead eyes stare at me; it is a shiny and black and very intense look. No, I think. This is not a Loaf matter, it is a Helena matter. As perhaps everything is for her.

"Twelve plus twelve is twenty-four. He was killed exactly twelve years to the day after she disappeared. At the opening of the exhibition dedicated to the man who did *this*."

Without lowering her gaze she pushes the piece of paper her hands had been resting on over the table top to me. The paper is glossy and A3; it is a colour reproduction of a famous work by Aske from the time when he still painted. I recognise it immediately although the original must be about ten times bigger. And I would have remembered the title as well, even if it hadn't been written down at the bottom of the sheet. *Hommage à Helene* created a furore the first time it was shown and it confirmed Aske's reputation as a *provocateur*.

The main figures in the picture are a man with a doll on his lap, and there is still a powerful threatening atmosphere reminiscent of Goya's gruesome *The Satyr Eating His Child*, although the figure in the man's hands is not missing its head, as in Goya's picture, but its hands and feet. The colours are Goya's, a piercing ochre and terracotta. The red in Aske's picture does not have anything to do with the missing parts of the body; the doll's limbs don't terminate in bloody wounds, but in neat black stitches. The blood red is part of the background, made up entirely of newspaper and magazine cuttings of the child's body and face, all placed together and covered with a rough varnish or a scarlet glaze.

Helena's face doesn't appear in the picture, but when the picture was shown for the first time the name was immediately associated with her alone. "The Helena Dahl case" had dominated the newspapers for months. In addition, child pornography was being discussed openly for the first time, and some of the pictures in the collage were without question approaching that category. Although it is not possible to pick it up in the little reproduction there is something I remember from the controversy that followed the picture and I may be wrong. As I may be wrong about him not using Helena's face.

I ask her about it, cautiously, almost as if I am blaspheming. Behind me there is another collage and here in this room I push the impression of a similarity in technique as far back into my consciousness as I can.

"No," she says. "Not in this picture. But in some other less well-known ones. I've got reproductions of those as well, if you would like to see them."

"Like" is a strange word to use, just as I think it is strange – or impressive – that she can rest her hands so calmly on this picture. But then I haven't had twelve years, night and day, of dealing with pictures a lot more shocking than this one, pictures produced by her own horror-filled imagination.

"There's a second picture I would like you to see," she says. "This one."

A shiny new reproduction is pushed over the table top towards me. I may have seen it before but it didn't make any impression on me. The subject has been spread across the canvas roughly; jagged black spruces point angrily at the golden sky and in front of them there is a powerful reddish figure, a bold diagonal line, who appears to be dragging the naked body of a boy behind him into the trees. Under the picture is written the word "PAN" in capital letters.

"That's a few years older," Ingeborg Dahl says, "and not as well known."

The last remark comes out with almost imperceptible bitterness from her thin, stiff, smiling lips.

"He was seventeen when he disappeared and he's never been found. Not much effort was made to find him anyway. Seventeen-year-olds are almost adults, aren't they. People assume that they just take off on their own. Especially if they're boys. Per Anders Nilsen his name was."

P.A.N. I am sitting in the golden glow from the small candles behind me and from the few lamps switched on in what was Søren

75

and Margrete Dahl's dining room, between the secular altar to their granddaughter and her mother's motionless body.

"Would you like me to take these with me to the police?" I ask, nodding in the direction of the two reproductions.

"Oh, I can do that myself," she says, and I can hear the lameness of my suggestion reflected in her voice. "I've had rather a lot to do with them. I don't mind the police. I just don't have much confidence in them."

"You know, Pan," I continue, blushing as I speak, "is a very familiar mythological figure. Aske isn't exactly the only person to have used him."

I hear myself saying the word "used" and it sounds cold and cynical here.

"That was his name," she says. "His initials were sewn into the jacket he was wearing when he disappeared. PAN. Like the god of the woods indeed. There was also a very distinguished art critic who got a lot of column space explaining that *Hommage à Helene* was a reference to Homer. Perhaps you can remember the other title of the picture?"

"No," I say.

"It was *The Rape*. As of Troy."

And I can see her small enraged face in front of me pressing against Anlaug's rounded shoulders on the banks of the river as Bella and I fight our way over the designer bridge. Over the river to what is no longer called the TroJa factories.

"I thought," she says, "that since the matter concerns one of your patients you would feel a certain responsibility."

"I do," I answer. "But then Javed confessed."

"After how many hours of interrogation?"

"I don't know. And – on top of that we almost saw him do it."

"On the screen?"

"Yes."

"Really," she says. "Well, I wasn't inside, so I didn't have that . . . advantage."

The awkward pauses, defining or testing. There must have been several of them in this room.

"What do you want me to do?" I ask.

"What you think you should."

76

And then she follows me to the door. She is still smiling, the most horrible of all smiles, the fixed smile on the face of someone carrying a sorrow that will never end. And a fury without vent.

The lights are still on in some of the windows in the police station, small patches of gold behind the neat black foliage of the trees in the park on the other side of the road. Grønlandsleiret is a broad sweeping road, empty, damp on this dark autumn night. High above me on the rocks the Enerhaug blocks of flats tower up. No cars making the soft swishing sounds on the wet asphalt. The traffic lights beneath the mass of rock flash their lonely red and green signals.

On the empty pavement fragments of sentences, glimpses of unclear golden pictures come back to me. I recognise them. It is me in some shabby dive something like ten years ago, enthusiastically defending the inalienable revolutionary right of art to break with norms and bourgeois sensitivities. And no doubt flinging around expressions like freedom of speech and fighting censorship.

The occasion was Aske's *Hommage*. Hazy golden glimpses of forgotten, meaningless nights. Rows of cheap amber pints on tablecloths that were either white and soon became stained with the ash from our cigarettes or large orange and brown flower patterns so that when we missed the ashtray the stains wouldn't show up.

The right to be outrageous, obnoxious, uninhibited and *dangerous*, vigorously defended around tables until we went home or up to someone's flat to drink more or slip between clammy, sweaty sheets with some other body.

Beneath the vast jagged cement-laden mass of rock of Enerhaug I am absorbed by the yellowing glimpses of a past. That is why I am so startled. The man is thin, dressed in dark clothes, with his shoulders hunched. I only catch sight of his face in the brief moment when I turn round towards him. He doesn't look at me, but I recognise him. I have seen his snarling face on an enormous screen up in the TroJa factories, expressing his anger about the closure and Joakim Roll. And his own brother. *Sjur Aske*, it said on the screen, and though he isn't snarling as he walks there is no doubt that it is the same man. Aske's brother, walking in the direction that I have just come from, going into the big bend on Grønlandsleiret.

II

THE LIGHT FROM the entrance forms a perfect rectangle in the darkness of the narrow room, and it smells of leather here and also of wool and of Ida's small red rubber boots. It is joined by other, subtle scents: caramel, rose petals, white freshly pressed sheets. I close the door behind me again and lean my back against it for a second as I get used to this touch of fragrance and the deep golden colours of the hallway. They don't come from the light from the entrance but from the living room, and it is also from there that the muted sounds reach me.

She went there from the bath and left this cool trace of a fragrance behind her. She didn't do it for my sake, but I am still grateful to her for it. I know who is child-minding in there, almost certainly with her knees pressed together, and it gives me a little time to adapt. She doesn't often appear unannounced, as it were; she has her fixed routines.

With my head leaning against the back of the door I think that I might ask her right now to get the hell out of the rooms I live in, but in the hallway I have a chance to draw breath and here there is a comforting homely darkness. I haven't slept that much in the last twenty-four hours and she is certainly one of my best friends. In formal terms, of course, I am married to her.

In the sitting room the strongest smell is of herbal tea. She has lit a number of candles and she has also tidied up, as she always does. There is a pile of magazines kept in meticulous order beside the teapot on the coffee table, and the plaid rug we got from Mother and Karsten is placed diagonally and elegantly over the back of the sofa. Bente is more thorough than both Benny and myself as far as putting Ida's things away in her small boxes with wheels on is concerned; the boxes stand side by side in the corner.

The only thing she has missed is the answerphone, which is

flashing. I count at least five. Now the biggest difference between Bente and Benny is not in the voice, so I wonder if she doesn't feel like talking to anyone. I don't give a shit. Tea with Bente is about all I can manage.

"How well you've done it," I say. She is squatting elegantly in front of the wood fire and has her arms round her knees. I think her blouse is new, at least I can't remember having seen it before. At the opening there is a slender woven gold chain resting against the modest cleft between her breasts. She got it from me and she is very pleased with it.

"I think we should do something about the bookshelves," she says. "It's tedious of course, but don't you think we should create some kind of system? It isn't healthy to have books in your bedroom."

This is not, despite her domesticity, a Bente theme. She is gaining time, just as she did, perhaps, by not answering the phone.

The golden reflections from the flames of the fire flicker over her face and body, and colour the delicate waves in her hair almost the same colour as Benny's. But Bente is a brunette and, no thank you, she has never been interested in using Benny's ponytail.

She pours out the tea for us and strokes my cheek before she goes out to the kitchen to boil some more water. Then she takes her place again in front of the fire, her hands resting in her lap, the tea cup in the saucer-shaped hollow of her hands.

"I know him," she says to the fire. "No, that's not correct. I've *met* him. I didn't know he was one of your patients."

"You mean Javed," I say. Bureaucratic, professional, I am punctilious in the golden glow of my own fire, as if I were thinking of writing a memo in my own flame-lit living room.

"Yes," Bente says, "although I didn't know his name. I didn't know what he was called. He just appeared from time to time and came *along*. You know, one of those who just strings *along*. I met him at some parties round about."

She looks strangely decorative in the sensitively matched nuances of beige and olive green for which she has such a predilection. I have long thought there was something grandmotherly about Bente, and therefore I find it so difficult to see her having anything to do with more exotic kinds of sex.

"I didn't talk to him that much in fact," she continues, pensively, and I lose my cool and become unsympathetically primitive for a moment.

"What did you do then?" I ask very pointedly, brutal and direct in contrast to the welcoming warmth of the fire's glow. "Did you sleep with him?"

I have seen it before, Bente's rather bourgeois, wounded look.

Rules of the marriage, and I also had a hand in making these. It isn't Benny who refuses to tell me what Bente does, it is me who doesn't want to know. At least not the details.

"What do you mean then?" I ask, quieter now, and later, but not, not right now, I will have to react to my husband having sex with one of my patients.

"I mean that I didn't protect him."

"You are not talking about condoms, I presume."

And I think I'm trying not to sound sarcastic.

"I'm not messing you around, you know," says Benny or Bente or both or someone.

"No," I say, biting my lip. "I know."

And it was an off-the-record Javed, of course. A Javed outside the group, inaccessible to the long conversations and the series of inflammatory provocations and tentative interdependence you find in groups. Also psychiatric patients have their private lives. Bente wasn't picked up by the records, the tests or me.

"He was really – on the lookout," Bente says, talking about him as if he were dead. "Friendly, curious and so keen to *experience* something. The urge to have experiences can make you very vulnerable."

"You can drop all that stuff about being in touch with your emotions and not having to do anything you don't want to," I say. "I'm exhausted. Can we talk about this tomorrow?"

"He was a beginner, wasn't he?" She continues as if she hadn't heard me.

"Bente, I mean it. Not now."

"I should have protected him."

But it is Ida who screams, not me. And whatever she might think about LIONS and mothers who remind her of them it is me, for primped-up reasons, who has to go in to see her. Protection, I think, and I am an old biddy too.

And perhaps that is why it is my body that she curls up to and winds herself around towards morning, when THE LIONS have made it impossible for her to sleep in her own bed. It shows trust and I value that, but it doesn't make me sleep any better. Benny, the ever popular mascara-stained Daddy, is fast asleep on the sofa in the living room. The mouse smacks me in the mouth before seven o'clock.

"Silly," I whisper.

The mouse doesn't answer.

The men are not at all threatening; on the contrary, they greet us and they are friendly to Ida, but she still grabs my leg and won't let go. It is the flashes that do it. She remembers them from the previous night. There are three of them and they are very busy with their cameras trying to *catch* something very banal, mother and daughter on their way out of the house one morning. Of course we know we are caught. Trivialised perhaps. I remember the busy answerphone and wonder if it was people like these ringing.

"Where's your Daddy?" one of them calls out to Ida. She is a polite child and almost always answers when adults ask something, but this time she clings to my leg instead.

"Clear off," I say, taking Ida up in my arms. One of the photographers laughs, with a note of scorn. None of them makes a move to clear off; on the contrary, they move backwards along the pavement in front of us. No mother and daughter stroll today then, not even the couple of hundred metres to the nursery. Whether they want to clear off or not, I want them to. The car to the nursery, the car to work, the car a shell to hide in, from what I'm not sure, except that it is creepy, like the Message the other morning.

What is more, it is also there in the department. Welle's attractive secretary looks embarrassed and one of my more-saddened colleagues gives me a cautious pat on the shoulder. We can *talk* about it later, he whispers.

"Talk about what?" I ask, leaving him looking quite desperate.

There is an explanation. Someone published a Message during the night. It is on Dr Welle's desk, and it is in red, white and black and it is tough. Unlike the painter in Markveien, the writers of the Message reach not only me and a few neighbours, but about a hundred thousand newspaper readers as well.

It is the same out-of-focus picture. Benny with Ida on his arm and me in profile, almost blurred, behind them. But the headline is different and the soft-focus golden tones of his close-up too. It is a nice one of him. Though, of course, it is Bente. "Taught sex games by the psychologist's husband", and under the picture of Bente the tasty little follow-up: "Or is it the wife?" No caretaker can paint over this.

Not surprisingly, less care is taken over Javed's picture. Very dark-skinned, he is staring with wild desperation into the camera. It is a passport photo, always unbeatable as a representation of the accused party.

We are civilised in those long, quiet corridors and in the offices giving on to them. We treat pain with caution. Doctor Welle has no intention, he says, of engaging in any kind of interrogation of his employees. There is trust here. Cooperation. Understanding.

"But you know, of course, that there is some concern," he says. "Senior management must be briefed. Kept informed. Know how to deal with . . . this. And that is why I have to ask you some questions."

Then he rests his chin on his long attractive fingers. Grey hair swept back from his temples, a roll-neck sweater, sharp green eyes beneath these impressive bushy eyebrows looking into mine.

"Is it true?" he asks. "Not in any tabloid sense, but true in any form?"

"No," I say. "Benny met him and talked to him, but I don't think he taught him any *sex games*, either tabloid ones or otherwise."

"Think?" he asks, without lifting so much as a bushy eyebrow.

"Yes," I say. "I don't think Benny knows that many sex games."

"But he did . . . meet Javed?"

"Unaware that he was a patient here, yes."

"Did they have sex?"

And I know that he sees it, I know that this man with whom I share bad chemistry sees life as shrivelled and pitiful, and as dry as a small raisin when he asks. But he asks nonetheless. That is his job, I think, his job and his report and his superiors who have to be *briefed*.

"Not as far as I know," I reply, "and that is no business of the department anyway."

There is a strange, ominous conversation after this and I am outside the door to his room before I realise that I have accepted the decision that I am not one of those who should be involved in going through Javed's tests and records.

And it has a name, I think, on my way down the quiet corridors. It has a name, I think, and stop by one of the arched windows. It is ineptitude. Incompetence. In-something, like the 'in' in indisposed, incapable, in when you mean to say *out*.

I don't even have to pretend to have a cough. I can go in to see the doctor's lovely secretary or to see the man himself at any time and then leave the department with unspecified, indefinite sick leave, and it would be a relief for them if I were to do so.

"You'll have to speak up," he says, his eyebrows meeting in the middle. "Say whether you need any changes in your work programme or a few days at home. In the country. In your mountain cabin. Where is it? Jomfruland?"

"My stepfather has a cabin there," I say. "We go there sometimes."

"Right," he says. "Just so that we can get hold of you. The surf up on the smooth, sloping rocks in autumn is just fantastic, isn't it?"

That's a fact. There are some fantastic breakers up by the smooth, sloping rocks in autumn.

An hour spent tapping my pen on the desk. Smoking furiously by the window – what the hell, with sick leave and sex games looming I really live it up. Making ten phone calls to a Benny who still isn't listening to the answerphone. I don't give in until a saddened colleague comes in to *talk about it*.

Welle's secretary is helpfulness itself and cancels the day's appointments. That is kind of her.

Now, rather fearfully, I make my way towards the car park. Not in fear of Javed's brother. But in fear of *them*. Of course there are no photographers waiting for me behind the car bonnet or in the bare bushes. But they are still there anyway. I can feel them in my nervous, girlish steps. Fantastic breakers in the autumn.

The car is a shell, and the shell gives strength and strength doesn't create fear but fury. If Benny had been a passing motorist I would have given him the finger, right there and right up and turned it. Bente on foot I would have knocked down without a moment's hesitation. I don't drive well down Kirkeveien, but isolation in a shell has its positive sides. Igi, I think, while waiting for green at the Majorstuen crossing, you are a *media victim*.

Yes. Oh yes. It is pathetic, but it gives my life a direction, a purpose. First to Bella's Frogner Gallery to beat Benny up, if he is there. Then wherever the need takes me. *Media victims* strike back.

12

I AM BEING observed, in the white rooms in Bella's Frogner
Gallery. From shadows, as black as a gorge, his eyes stare at me, he
fixes his gaze on me, and he doesn't let go, no matter where I move
to.

It is the old trick, used just as imperiously by Renaissance princes
as by rock stars. The full-on portrait with the eyes staring ahead has
this persecuting effect; the power of the gaze is the result of a single
effective technique. Eyes like these seem to want something from
you and they don't let go until they have achieved what they want.
However, what they want you to do is a mystery. Do they want your
secrets or do they want to impose theirs on you? It is said that animals
cannot stand a fixed gaze; they either have to flee or to attack.

In this case the intensity of the look is increased by the fact that I,
the onlooker, know the circumstances in which the picture was
taken. The many versions of Aske's concentrated, hushed presence
surrounding me are all stills from a video tape of the moments before
the amputation. What is awaiting him is pain.

I heard it catch up with him, heard the scream that came from him
seconds after the picture was taken. But before that, while he is
waiting, he doesn't lower his eyes, there is no faltering of the gaze as
with those whose thoughts are elsewhere. This man is alert before the
pain reaches him, and his open eyes challenge the onlooker to
accompany him, to stay. How does it *actually* feel, they seem to say,
wouldn't you like to know that too?

"Ow," a voice behind me whispers, and when I turn round, all too
quickly, showing my nervousness, I meet the same eyes sitting in
their dark sockets. Of course he can see that he frightened me, from
where he was standing leaning against the door, and now he winces
a little and jiggles one hand up and down in the way that you do

when you have hit yourself. His steel finger glistens as he lifts it and blows on it, rather theatrically. The edges of his mouth hidden in the stubble of his beard turn up into a little smile.

"I'm looking for Benny," I say stupidly. "I thought he was here. The lady at reception was on the phone, so I just came up."

"There's no Benny here," Aske says. He is wearing a crumpled linen suit with a black T-shirt underneath. His face has the pale, pasty look some people get when they haven't slept enough. "Just me. And you. And these pictures. What do you think – does your husband capture my likeness better with his camera than I have done? Funny expression, isn't it. *Catch*."

Then he puts his head back and howls, a wild piercing parody of his own cry of pain. A brief blast of laughter puts an end to the howling. Afterwards the silence in the building becomes a dull pressure on my eardrums, on my skin. He crosses the floor towards me with dance-like steps, his arms stretched out, almost coquettishly, and his feet describing semi-circles over the parquet floor.

"Oh," he says, "this body of mine is worn out. This body needs sleep."

"Have you been in for more questioning?" I ask. "Bella rang me yesterday . . ."

"And was ready to send Amnesty in, I assume," he says laughing. "You have to give her that, Bella is committed. It's a terrible and impressive commitment. No, I haven't come from there. By God, I've had longer and more unpleasant interviews with the police than yesterday's. They were so polite, *so* polite."

"There's no reason why they shouldn't have been, is there?"

"No," he says. "There wasn't, thanks to your garrulous patient. Is that what you teach them, that it is better to tell the truth straightaway?"

"I'm not a teacher," I say.

"No, but you work in the truth business, too," he says and stops dead in the middle of the floor, his bony hand placed in an affected manner under his chin. "What is your theory, as a professional I mean? Was it a sudden urge that overtook him or was it something deep inside him that wanted it?"

He stands there now, quite still in front of me, like a schoolboy, squeezing his hands in front of his crotch. But he is not in the slightest bit interested in my answer. Not yet, anyway.

86

"Provided, of course," he continues, "there is such a place deep inside us. Something inside what is outwardly visible. A second person inside that person. Like a Russian doll, small dolls inside the big doll. At least that is an interesting construct. What is it inside I wonder, a *Homo nuculus* perhaps? A little Mephistopheles in the Faust?"

"I suppose there is a Mephistopheles in every Faust," I say. "The crucial thing is what we do with him."

"So well put. Do you feel any *guilt*?" he asks with childish curiosity.

"Yes," I say.

"Even though you didn't strangle anyone. That's noble of you."

That is very annoying. *Media victims*, I remind myself, strike back.

"Do you know anyone called Ingeborg Dahl?" I ask.

He gives me a tired look. I have interrupted him and I am not a liberal cultural commentator.

"I don't think so," he says. "Is she the one who does, what's it called – *tapestry*?"

"No," I say. "She's the mother of Helena Dahl. You remember, 'the Helena Dahl case'."

"Oh," he says. "Child pornography. In one form or another I suppose we can say. My picture, the pornography lady's *case*. Is she one of your patients or what?"

"No," I say. "I have spoken to her, that's all. But your brother knows her, doesn't he?"

"No idea. Do you think I talk to him? Do you think it makes sense? That I, well, have coffee with him on Tuesday and then on Wednesday I accuse him of enjoying watching me being raped? No, it doesn't, does it?"

"You can't have any idea what I hear in my job," I say, boldly, the *media victim*.

He likes that. In fact he likes that very much. He is in raptures and his childish reaction makes me want to give him more. Torstein's variation of Tourette's syndrome perhaps or Anlaug's Wagner voice. Something stupid and kinky and *fun*.

"What's it like being a psychologist?" he asks, not smiling. "Do you have lots of friends?"

"I wouldn't say that," I reply. If psychologists don't have any friends, they do, however, have a party trick. Answering a question with a question. "Much like artists?"

"Bella maintains that I've only got friends who have *done time*. But I had a friend once. A real blood brother. It consumed a huge amount of energy I have to say. Now it's customers in the main, I guess. And young people of course; they're a type of customer as well. Friendship is so, so wearing, don't you think? Like relationships, in a way. You can't get any work done. Although it gets easier with the years. You don't have to worry about people's motives any longer. They are so obvious. But I assume you have to worry about them."

"About people's motives?"

"About what is inside them. About the *Homo nuculus*. The doll inside the doll. Leonardo, of course, wanted to see it, all the insides: the intestines and the sinews and all these *lumps*. They are such strange colours, the lumps. Is there anything attractive about them or are they merely revolting? And so you wonder whether he was just *good* at looking at it or whether it means anything, all this knowledge about *insides* when he was painting what was on the outside."

He talks about Leonardo if he were a neighbour and there is, perhaps, something *sweet* about it, too.

"Why did he do that, do you think?" he asks. "Was he really looking for the *soul* or was it just morbid curiosity?"

"Is that important?" I ask.

"Those demonstrators outside the factory think so, think that motives make a difference, I assume. Think that they can look at child pornography because they have noble motives for doing so, while I can't. Maybe there were noble motives for Leonardo's doctors, when they peered into bodies, while other people were not allowed to."

"But he was given permission," I say.

"Yes, he was. Within limits and in secret. He was considered noble enough. In the same way that I wasn't convicted of being a porno-grapher. I wasn't even charged."

"Ultimately because of your noble motive. Art."

"That's right, isn't it? It's touching, in a way."

And perhaps a little irritating, I think. What wouldn't a conviction for pornography do for a rebellious artist? More or less than for Joakim Roll?

"Did you know the man who died?" I ask.

"Bella claims that I've met him. I don't know. It's possible.

Anyway, I don't remember meeting him. But I'll never forget the video. The picture of him. It's so remorseless, isn't it?"

"Completely."

"Nobody likes that sort of thing," he says. "It's a horrible, horrible thought. But thinkable. Will *Hommage* outlive Helena?"

"Of that there is no doubt whatsoever," I say.

"The memory of her, I mean. You know what I'm getting at. Will she live longer as a memory with or without *Hommage*?"

"That depends on the quality of the picture, I imagine. And how long her mother lives, among other things."

"When I am knocking my piles of bones into shape," he says, "which don't even have any *lumps* to drive them, people like to think they have something to say, that they make some kind of statement."

"Don't you see it like that?"

"I go my own way most of the time," he says, "wondering how I can put them together. A bit here, a bit there. A bit for me, a bit for you, maybe. A sheep. A bird. Do they fit or don't they? I speculate. That's a funny word. Speculate. On the Stock Exchange or with bones. Do you think when you get closer to Javed and go over him with a fine-tooth comb, so to speak, that you will be able to put him together? Make a complete person out of him?"

"Understand him, you mean? Understand why he did it, if he did it?"

"There's no doubt about it, is there?"

"He's retracted his confession," I say.

Aske is leaning against the large table now, with his back to it, his hands holding the edge of the table close to his body. It is the kind of pose that lecturers often like to adopt. He is drawing breath. The deep cavities under his cheekbones are vibrating just a little.

"He's got himself a solicitor," he says with a suggestion of a smile playing on his lips. "That's very sensible, of course. My point was really the one about *truth*. The feverish search for it. *How could this nice boy have done something like this?*"

"I don't know," I say, now weary. "I don't know how nice he is."

"I thought you *knew* him," Aske says.

"Did you?"

"No," he says. "I'm only speculating."

"And I'm not so keen on speculation."

"No," he says. "And now you want to go. Can I drive you anywhere? Home, for example?"

"I've got my car outside," I say.

"Of course," he says smiling. It's a strangely attractive smile in this lean harrowed face. "Bente's *wife* is her own master. That shouldn't surprise anyone."

Aske reads newspapers too. He goes through the door in front of me and down the broad stairs. The sunshine from the window into the open stairwell hits us right in the eyes, makes dazzling rectangles on the white walls and causes the steel railings to glisten.

"When you talked about your brother," I ask, "what was it? The truth?"

He bounds down the last steps, turns at the foot of the stairs and raises the hand with the prosthesis towards me. And the look he gives me is the same sunken look that all the endless variations in the room above us have. Must have been a reflected light, I suppose. The steel prosthesis that should have been his little finger flashes.

"Aaahh," he says. "So you can ask awful questions, too. It was the truth, of course, or a variation of it. Probably not Sjur's, but if you put the two together you will have it, won't you?"

A sheep. A bird. A little here and a little there. Fantastic breakers in the autumn.

13

Just morbid curiosity.

Igi, in her car shell, where she is Bente's wife and her own master, driving through the elegant, looped tram lane in Lapsetorget, a small piece of the urban design that is also intended to be attractive, because it is real. It has an undeniable function, doesn't lie about it, and it is neither unsophisticated nor rough for that reason. It doesn't hide anything other than, in its rather splendid way, the skill with which it was created. It is beautiful, no doubt about it. And so unostentatious.

One of the trams Oslo Tramways inherited from Göteborg is pulling its way through the semi-circle and is the antithesis of elegance. It is in bad shape, in every sense, and thus reminds me of myself. The voyeur, morbidly curious – about a brother and a friend and about pictures and their *motives*. Who will live longer, the artist or the artist's subject? The victim, one could say, or the perpetrator? If someone like Aske likes playing with words. As if they didn't mean anything.

Some words mean something, I remember, as the lights turn green above Karl Johan. "TAUGHT SEX GAMES." Morbidly curious. You can put things together like that, a bit here and a bit there. Schizophrenics do that all the time. I don't even treat schizophrenics; I'm not competent enough for that. Put together, from here and there: Aske's pictures and his life. But Helena's life? Her death? Ingeborg Dahl is in deepest mourning, and she is crazy, as many of those who grieve are. Like someone perhaps who doesn't talk to their brother, but talks *about* him. Why the hell would Aske *exhibit* a murder if he hadn't committed it?

I have to go through a tunnel to meet my husband. It's extremely physical and not at all metaphorical. Once inside it I remember that

I have to beat him up. It feels neither important nor tempting. This does though: Ingeborg Dahl. A homage. A brother, of course, since families cause all psychologists to prick up their ears. I'm morbidly curious all right.

And I know, gliding down Torggata in my shell, that I have dreadful motives like all curious people. Defeat and fury. On top of that, escape. Morbid.

There is not much fury left as I enter the studio Benny rents in Maridalsveien. Whatever is remaining dies quietly and quickly when I meet Benny's girls. However, you can accept defeat in an unequal battle with them.

These girls are supple, their movement between chairs and tables almost imperceptible, as if they were not there at all, like mere shadows, as insubstantial as dreams crossing the large surface of the floor beneath the high steel beams of the roof. One of them leans over my shoulder to take a piece of chicken from a dish next to where I am sitting at the long table. I don't notice her until she has the chicken in her mouth and gives me a sweet, apple-cheeked smile.

"Hi," she mumbles into her chicken and holds out her hand to me. "I'm Majsan from Sweden. Sorry to keep you waiting."

There is a Lene and an Ane here too, talking in low voices to each other as they walk to and from the table, to and from the half open door into the studio, with light, gentle movements and elegant fingertips that stroke their own or others' facial features with sudden concentration. A strand of hair out of place, the lipstick not quite even. Ten seconds of deep, rigid, total attention, then their bodies collapse into the same cheerful lethargy as before. The large window surfaces along the west wall of the room reflect their poses in whatever they are doing: an averted face – controlled desire; the refined lines of a hand on a raised hip – poised expectation.

"Would you like anything? Majsan speaks Swedish. "Coffee or tea? We've got just about everything here. I like the herbal tea they use here. Astral tea, I think it's called. It's great."

"I've got my own coffee," I say.

"Fine. Do you use your own foundation or what?

"I beg your pardon?"

"Well, some of the girls use their own and that's okay, they're almost pros, but . . ." At this point she looks at me with regret and goes quiet. It is something to do with my foundation, I assume, something almost scary, if I can believe her wide-open eyes.

"I'm not going in there," I say. "I don't want my photograph taken."

"Nooo," she says thoughtfully. "Fine."

Then she leans over and stares at my eyes. Without eyeliner, I imagine they lack the personal touch. I can feel my mascara start to coagulate under her gaze.

"Are you Benny's wife?"

"Yes, I am."

"Cool. Very *original*. Girls, this is Benny's wife! What? They're married, for Christ's sake. Is that something or what?"

They smile, preoccupied. Majsan's shadow-like, submissive colleagues have read the newspapers, if nothing else. Benny and me, we are just pretty *cool* right now to the natives.

Majsan finds what she is looking for – a bad-tempered, very short-haired urban poetess, who appears on the stairs with her own immaculate foundation and with very little time, but who, as Majsan is asking, says she would like astral tea.

Majsan puts a hand on my shoulder as she passes. There is a summery and, I suppose, astral scent from the cup in her other hand.

"How long have you been married?" she asks.

"Eleven years," I say. "Soon it'll be twelve."

"Bloody hell," she says. "I mean, *shit*."

The urban poet gives us a furious look. Majsan glides over the black and white squares of the floor, tea cup and pack of ten Marlboro Light in hand.

"How do you manage it?" she mumbles. "I mean, fifteen years, almost. I can only take it for *a couple of months*."

Majsan and the poet disappear into the studio and are engulfed by its heavy-duty sound system. The poet will find help or hindrance there, or whatever it is that they call the unremitting, deafening beat that makes up a *foundation* for their personal expression. Unless they are here for the photographer, the man with the sex games.

Ane and Lene glide, lithe and almost imperceptible around the room. I take in the staggering view of the rooftops of the town away below us. The treetops beyond the roofs circle round the Akerselva. Above them the sky is hazy, almost as white as the walls inside.

Benny has his hand on the bad-tempered urban poet's shoulder when they come out of the studio. Her face is heavily made up with deep violet stripes under her eyes.

"That was good," Benny says in that calm voice that I want to wake up to all my life. "You looked very friendly."

The urban poet kisses him and disappears down the steps before Majsan, with her wads of cotton wool with face cream on, reaches her.

"Is it lunchtime?" Benny asks. There are big blue lipstick marks on his cheek.

"I thought you might finish early," I say, suggestions of marriage and pram and newspaper cuttings clear in my voice.

"Yes," he says. "Yes, of course."

"There are no *photographers* out there," I say. And then of course he looks quite miserable.

"Shall I go?" I ask.

"No, you stay. I would like you to stay."

And then it's lunch. Lunch with the perverts and the maidens. So what.

Pretty soon there aren't any maidens. Those supple, insubstantial women disappear one after one in a very supple and insubstantial way. All of a sudden they are no longer there; perhaps one of them was waving a hand by the stairs, another playing with her hair. For all I know we give off trace elements, a vague odour of defeat and tristesse, of impending marital showdown, pervasive enough to penetrate the layers of fragrance of peaceful tea and delicate cosmetics. No-one can avoid picking them up, the trace elements, the smell, the famous body language, whatever that is. Even those who like to stay close to such excretions notice them, it just attracts them, it doesn't repel them.

Perhaps the ratio between those who are attracted and those who are repelled is a constant, unaffected by time and space. No-one knows, and thus there are still mathematical puzzles to ponder. Benny's supple women, however, belong to the majority and therefore have what is called healthy instincts under the thin layers of cream, the silicone implants and the masochistic diets.

There was no big showdown after all, no elegant exchange of *why didn't you say* and *you didn't give me a chance*, no heated or quiet replay

94

of the recent past and the persistent established patterns of our lives. It can't have been the trace elements that called him, at least not the ones we are giving off at the moment, although it is the connection, the link, the relationship between us that brings him here.

Edevart Riel looms large, even in the great masses of empty airy space surrounding us. There is an interesting contradiction between his body and the clothes he is wearing. Boxer's body, broker's gear. Bespoke tailoring and foppish attention to detail devoted to the knot of his tie, his shirt collar and his breast-pocket handkerchief. His muscles threaten to burst the neat seams of his jacket; from his shirt collar a shiny shaven head rests on a tree trunk of a neck. He could be a common shark, the type that beaches around the Aker Brygge, if it hadn't been sorrow that drove him here. Sorrow and drugs.

"Two days," he says, "and I haven't slept a wink." It happens, that. It's a question of chemistry and also fear.

Edevart Riel hasn't dared to find out if he's capable of sleep since his lover was found murdered in the ruins of a factory in Nydalen. Brokers in bespoke suits don't have to have family in Oslo's West Side, sorrow doesn't have to be expressed with humble charm. Edevart Riel's north Norwegian dialect is polished but obvious. And there is nothing helpless about the way he smashes his enormous, sunbed-tanned fist down on the table. Under his fist is the newspaper.

"Is this true?" he asks Benny.

"No."

"And this?"

Under his fist the newspaper, under the newspaper a photograph. He pushes it across the table.

It is a copy of a bad amateur photo, blown up to A4, an out-of-focus, fairly run-of-the-mill picture of a party, with two meticulously groomed décolleté trannies in the foreground, each with a champagne glass tilted towards their red-painted, pouting lips. One of them is well built, a very tasty, chocolate brown mulatto. The other is, of course, Bente. There is nothing at all interesting about the picture, apart from the young man in the smiling group behind them. Javed is wearing a sort of sailor's outfit, he is strikingly attractive and there is no question that it is his hand resting on Bente's shoulder.

Depraved enough for any tabloid newspaper, of course, for any kindergarten assistant, for most of the parents in Ida's kindergarten.

"That's the kind of thing they're after now," he says. "I don't need to tell you that, do I?"

He does anyway, holds forth and with his wide open, Ecstasy-affected eyes he sees swarms of journalists and police in front of him, buzzing round Oslo's modest repertoire of saunas and leather bars.

"They must all have been there," I say, interrupting the journalistic harangue that is as boring as ever. "It wasn't me who let on about the sex games, if you must know. And it wasn't Benny either."

"And it wasn't me either," Riel says. "Yet."

Benny's eyes are glued to the photocopy in front of him, which is why his head is bent over.

"Of course, no-one can stop you giving the picture away," he says in a gritty, tired and persecuted voice. "Or stop you selling it."

"Thank you, I don't need the money," Riel says. "No-one needs money. The only thing we occasionally need is information. Isn't that true? And there is never enough of that. Never. Rumours, dirt, small, exquisitely polished reports. You have to swim through it like a baleen whale with your jaws open. You never know when you're going to pick up something good."

Sorrow, I remind myself, my hands resting on the table top with the photograph. It is all about sorrow and, whether chemically produced or silenced, that is what brought him to us, reeking as we do of it or having it vaguely hovering around us like a delicate exotic perfume. "Shame" by Hugo Boss. "Despair" by Calvin Klein. "Sorrow" by Edevart Riel.

He turns to me.

"Do you know anything about dealing?" he asks.

"Not much," I say. "I don't know a lot about dope."

Then he smiles. It is stiff, distorted. It is chemistry which makes this possible, his own and the legal or illegal medical industry. The knowledge. The causes and the strange effects.

"I don't mean that type of dealing," he says. "I mean the straight-forward exchange of goods that we all carry out. I get something from you, you get something from me, love or security or sexual release or knowledge. You know."

"Yes," I say.

"I run a business," he says. "I know that it's a good thing to have a little prior knowledge about the opposition. As Javed's therapist you take a vow of professional secrecy, for example."

"Yes."

"And I have this." Sunbed-tanned hand on the photograph.

"I'll make it a little easier for you," he says. "I want two things. Two stories. About Javed. And about Martin. About how you found him."

Soap was once manufactured in these rooms. A small, semi-essential product. Benny manufactures pictures here now, perhaps truths, versions of the truth, moments torn out of time, processed and made accessible in a language of which we recognise at least fragments. This grieving boxer wants to buy stories and gets them. There are costs involved. For the most part I detest the notion that love is about giving and taking, but I may have turned Benny into a veritable victim of this debt.

He sits silently beside me. And I hope he isn't counting. Even as I hope, but don't know, that I will stop keeping mean-spirited little accounts.

Riel's smooth amphibian face remains impassive as I tell him about Martin's death. And there is no doubt he is aware that no story is ever completely satisfying. He is an adult after all. He went through a great deal *afterwards*, the crumpled sheets, the continual restlessness, the clearing up after a purchase, a party, a night. But he nods when I have finished, when I have delivered the goods, I suppose.

"We didn't bother much with rubbish like fidelity," he says. "Martin went his way and I went mine. I can run on about a whole load of ideology any time you want, but perhaps I don't need to?"

"Not really," I say.

"More life," Riel says in a voice that, if not dead, is more than a little weary. "Extra. Added value. A superabundance, we could call it."

And maybe that is the businessman in him still talking. Maybe there is a little calculator punching out his ticket and recording a deficit. It's a good habit to pay your debts on time.

"This Javed," Riel says, "he wasn't very *experienced*, was he?"

This question is to Benny, who shakes his head.

"I barely knew him," he murmurs.

"Know," Riel answers brutally. "He isn't the one who died."

"No. He was . . . er . . . like most people at first. A little leather, a little make-up, a piercing or two. Some effects maybe. He was trying things out. Sniffing around, wasn't he? Thought everything was exciting or frightening or perhaps both."

Riel nods.

"That's how they come unstuck," he says. "The ones who don't know what they're doing. That's not like Martin. I suppose I've been waiting for it to happen to *someone*. It does happen. It has to happen, the statistics say so. I mean, the stuff's there. All you have to do is click on to the net and you've got all the titillation you could wish for. Anyone can get it. I try to tell all the young ones that. There are rules, though, aren't there? You have to take care."

It is called oxygen deprivation and it has a terrible reputation. This more than eccentric form of sexual pleasure leads a shadowy life on the margins of what is already a margin, as I understand it. It is talked of only in whispers, picked up as a rumour and passed on nervously from one place to another. It can be found on the net, Riel said, like so many other frightening things. As if there was anything virtual there. As if it didn't belong to this world.

"Because this is different," Benny whispers. "That's what they don't understand. It requires almost . . ."

"Medical knowledge," Riel interrupts. Then he turns towards me, the inbred representative of the big outside world. "Experimenting with oxygen deprivation," he says, "requires great precision, attention and expertise."

I gaze into Riel's eyes. There is nothing sentimental about it. We are talking about strangulation. Of his partner, what's more. But then he is also equipped with *chemistry*.

"You mean," I say, "that this type of sexual pleasure requires the partner to be precise, alert and utterly responsible. At the same time as he – or she – is being sexually aroused?"

"Yes," Riel says. "That's required, of course. But that's true of anything you do. Even normal sexual intercourse requires you to be sensitive to what is happening to your partner, doesn't it?"

"But aren't we talking about small margins of error here?"

"Yes indeed. Dangerously small margins. We are talking here about *le petit mort* in a quite literal sense. That's why I've never tried it myself."

This is said with emphasis, his eyes resting on mine.

"Martin did?" I ask. And this is where we find the traces, or at least a hint, of the sorrow awaiting him when the chemistry wears off.

"Not that I know of. And it's not like him," he says. "I would have thought that Martin, if he did . . . that he would have taken care that it didn't . . ."

Didn't go wrong. That is what they say, that is what it is called. Like accidents that happen on slippery, sheer mountain sides or in rapids that turn out to be wilder than you thought. It is all to do with knowledge and experience, trusting your partner and control of your equipment, challenging nature's forces. Karabiners, ropes and lines. Or thin black straps. Degrees of incline, the structure of the rocks, the rotation of the whirling eddy and the strength of a hand. Saying yes when you mean no. Saying no when you mean yes. Free flight, resting on the airstreams, diving down and down and down, then coming up and breaking the surface of the water the second before your lungs burst.

"Shame," Riel says, thumping the newspaper, "that it wasn't true."

"I could never teach anyone that," Benny says.

The chemical treatment that has kept Riel awake for two full days is probably the same thing that enables him to talk about Martin with such remote objectivity. And also deliver an important piece of information. *He* hasn't tried to achieve *le petit mort* by strangulation.

I can't follow his calculations and I don't know what determines his pluses and minuses. So I don't know if he is paying off a private debt with his little piece of information or if it is more than chemistry he is dabbling with. It must be because I don't have what he called prior information that I think it is so odd.

It changes nothing. Perhaps it is just a part of the unseen, wakeful grieving.

Anyway, now there are supposed to be more frightening or compulsive things on the famous Internet. Riel has heard that the video is somewhere in the ether. That there is evidence of its existence, like the rumours about the sexual potential of strangulation, a long, long way out into the other dream-like world, one secured to our own only by thin threads.

If he still wants to stay awake it may be difficult for him to close his eyes to that knowledge. It is not easy to keep away from the one thing you desire when you first discover that it is accessible.

"Is that what you were supposed to be protecting Javed against?" I ask Benny as we walk silently, hand in hand, along the path by the river.

"The knowledge?"

"I don't know," he says. "Perhaps that too."

He should have been protecting him with his presence, his greater experience, although he had no experience of this. He only knows this through interpretation and comparison, the same as I do with my patients' suffering. What protection is there in interpretation?

This is how to gain knowledge: the empiricist Francis Bacon said that we should put nature on the rack and force her to reveal her secrets. But nature is no longer a witch with esoteric knowledge, nor is she a mere slip of a girl from whom confessions pour in swift-flowing streams of statistics, in the way that admissions from my clients do.

And knowledge from others. Do I want Ingeborg Dahl's visions or Edevart Riel's information? I know what I dream about on the banks of the river. It is filters, stupid and boring child protection, buffers against unwanted intrusion. I am an adult and so I am not exposed to it. Javed may have stood under one of the many outflows where bits of undigested information flowed and he was submerged. Or Martin Andersen, who was supposed to have been so well versed on safety procedures.

And if it was not like him for something *to go wrong*, who was it like? If I wasn't following Javed into the factory ruins, who was I following into the dark? And who would play a video like that or display a murder, an accident in the rapids, as if it were just a picture? Or a calculation. Twelve plus twelve.

Two ducks make long, razor-sharp slices in the surface of the water as they land. Behind them the water sprays up, white and green and agitated, leaving two V-shaped trails, and afterwards there is the wild flailing of wings and the hoarse guttural cries. Under the thin, leafless branches of a weeping birch there are more ducks, busy in their own ways. Before the ripples reach them they have become vague, just a small almost imperceptible nuance of the surface, black and shiny like the rest of the stream. The ripples hardly touch them, they have no further significance.

We'll be there much too early to pick her up.

Ida holds her parents' hands, one each in her own. She has an idea that she might be able to get something from this unexpected meeting at the nursery, perhaps a currant bun. As this doesn't turn out to be the case, she makes do with our double presence, lifts her legs off the ground and uses us as a swing along the pavement. It isn't a currant bun, but it is *something*. Modest ambitions.

Under the line of windows in the yard, diagonally opposite us, the wall is shiny, newly painted and clean. As always with running repairs or work of this kind, though, it is not quite right. The paint covering the underlying message is a slightly different shade from that of the rest of the wall. It shines, it stands out. Like a scar. It is easy to see that something had been written there, but not what. There is *something there*. Modest ambitions.

We are Peeping Toms in our own street. We stand in an unholy trinity on the corner and peer in. It has been cleaned up. The danger seems to have gone, unless it is hiding between the parked cars. But we don't know for how long it will be like this.

"It's still too early," Benny the photocynic whispers to me. "They're waiting until people have finished work."

We don't mind. Ida certainly doesn't. She does not feel like going home at all when Charlotte Andersensveien is an option. Modest ambitions. Mother and Karsten are in fact among the most exciting people she knows.

14

KARSTEN IS STANDING on the covered patio in front of Mother's and his house in Charlotte Andersensveien. He is wearing a bright, checked short-sleeved shirt with well-pressed khaki trousers and light moccasins, each with its own festive tassle. He doesn't feel the autumn cold in the slightest; there are heating elements in the ceiling – long red-hot pipes which give the patio a summer warmth. He is putting sausages on the grill while his closest friends stand around him, men of his age wearing similar colourful shirts. One of them has put on a sober blazer, though it has an interesting lemon-yellow pocket handkerchief in the breast pocket.

Some of the children have come round, attracted by the smell of smouldering coals and the drops of fat already spitting on the fire beneath the grill, but they realise that they are a bit early. The sausages are being prepared by an experienced, a patient specialist in the art of grilling, and a job of this sort takes time. There will be no sausages or hamburgers blistered black or red and raw on the inside here, that's for sure. And the children run down across the smooth deep-green lawn, chasing each other or the neighbour's spaniel or a balloon or a croquet ball.

It is not one of the children but Karsten who is celebrating a birthday with grilled sausages, friends and their grandchildren. Benny finds it touching, and of course he is right. It is just me, the offbeat stepdaughter, who thinks it is also a bit *weird*. Me who brought something *weird* along with me. They read tabloids in Charlotte Andersensveien.

But you'd never have guessed. At the grill Karsten is surrounded by me and a few close friends whose deep intimacy he and Mother, as far as I can see, cultivate mostly on the golf course, over the long, undulating, manicured stretches between the tees. They don't talk about sex games or shares. They talk about *the grandfather figure*.

"Life has taken on a whole new meaning," my stepfather says, turning a shiny greasy sausage, "now that I've become a grandfather. A new dimension. I can't put it any other way."

There is the clink of glasses as his friends toast him and there are well-defined laughter lines in the tanned, robust faces turned towards me. General agreement, it seems, among the golfing fraternity about the new *dimension*. I know Karsten's library. It is full of curious literature about the tyranny of genes, about the male's exclusive interest in spreading his genetic material, and I know that Karsten, as his friends do, nods in gentle agreement with the cultural significance of this on long flights over the Atlantic or in the golden glare of a civilised hearthside fire. Karsten the gene slave does not, however, share one chromosome, not one hint of a DNA molecule with Ida, and he still hasn't killed her or eaten her, as alpha males are supposed to do. Instead he has discovered the role of grandfather and the pleasure of balloons.

Weird, I think. Or perhaps alpha males imagine that despite everything, they should be able to save Ida & co. from their crazy parents?

I leave the little male society to share its newly acquired experiences of the grandfather role as they generously hand around perfect grilled sausages. Benny is embroiled in a discussion about financial allowances with their wives on the patio. The shadows under the blackcurrant bushes are beginning to turn dark and chilly. Some of the children begin to feel tiredness creeping in and they are whinging. I help Mother with the coffee.

"Ida wants to stay over," she says.

I am Mother's only child. I hadn't planned to change her life, but of course I did when I was born. It was even more of a surprise when Ida did the same – not only to me but to Mother, too – when she arrived, but nevertheless it is a fact. I have, if nothing else, never been served grilled sausages in this house before. If it had been up to Mother we would have eaten her strange experimental child-friendly versions of pizza every single Sunday.

Ketchup in a plastic bottle. Mustard for the sausages. Placed neatly between the Dijon and the balsamic vinegar, the oyster sauce and the small bottles of Henckel Trocken in the fridge door, side by side with Mother's battery of vitamins and minerals. On the shelf Litago yoghurt beside Karsten's strong Gorgonzola.

"I think she should sleep at home tonight," I say. Push and Pull. We are like polar magnets in the kitchen, gliding past each other as we put together cups and plates, find silver cake forks, fill the porcelain coffee pots and lay thin slices of kiwi fruit on the cheesecake.

"It's no problem," Mother says.

I don't know if she still has anything other than vitamin tablets in the house, and I don't want to know either. This is one of those ruthless adult choices: to decide what you don't want to know, and then to be able to put up with not knowing. To stop looking in the bathroom cupboards.

One of the golfing friends stands beside me as I put the cake dish on the patio table.

"She seems to have recovered quite well," he says. He is talking about Ida – Ida and the BLACK of the NIGHT. She is standing by the steps below us, absorbed in a complicated balloon and water project, the sort of thing that adults must not, must NOT, interfere in.

"Yes," I say. "She talks about it a lot, and she's unsettled at night. It'll take its course."

But this man is not preoccupied by the grandfather role. This is fine by me.

I suppose it is the ridiculous, rebellious daughter in me that makes me think Mother's and Karsten's new friends look so much like each other. But Håkon Middelthon is good looking in a casual, tanned sort of way: his grey hair is soft and recently cut, he has strong, broad hands and the lines on his face come from squinting into the sun while leaning on a walking stick in the mountains over Easter or taking the helm of a sailing boat. This man certainly paid his dues to the tourist association for more than thirty years before spending 200,000 kroner on membership of the Oustøen golf club.

"So, you're interested in art," he says, "as you were at Aske's exhibition?"

"Not really," I answer. "I was there primarily as Benny's wife. He's taking pictures for a book about Aske."

He blinks at the sound of Benny's name, but nothing more.

"What do you think, then, of the works of art?"

"They're . . . quite shocking," I say hesitantly, as we amateurs always do, when faced with this sort of question. This area more than any other can reveal our prejudices, our ignorance and our uncertain taste. "And sad perhaps. They seem lonely, his bodies, even though they have grown into each other. Or perhaps that's why."

"Yes," he says a little absent-mindedly, as if he has asked a question to which he doesn't want to hear the answer. "Of course, you can't really call what we've got a collection, it's much too modest for that. But we have made some small investments, my wife and I, and I must say it's an incredibly interesting market. In fact, we do have some small works of art by Aske."

"Really?"

"Older ones, that is." I'd say it's five or six years since we bought them and in the meantime they must have increased in value by several hundred per cent. There's a picture of his childhood home. And a portrait."

"Not one of the expensive ones then?"

"They're very valuable and on top of that there's some doubt surrounding them. He's got a very good gallery director . . ."

"I know her," I say.

"Really?" He doesn't like me interrupting him, I notice. He is not used to that. "She's controversial, just like her father was in his day. Very few people remember him, but, you know, he has not always been seen as – shall we say – *sound*. There was a time when it was not thought to be safe to buy from him."

"Why's that?"

He hesitates.

"You have to be able to rely on the gallery director's judgement," he says. "On the value of the goods. Anyway it's a long time ago. But his daughter – of course, she has promoted Aske skilfully, and, my goodness, she's not the only one. He's had incredible publicity, and that affects the prices, of course."

"But?"

"But. There is always this *but*. It's all tied up, of course, with the boom in the Eighties when there were a number of sensational artists hyped out of all proportion and prices exploded. This is especially true in the USA, of course, New York, but to a more modest extent here too."

He looks at me with that air of paternal gravity which is never that far away when this type of older man talks to younger women.

"It burst," I say, largely because I can't resist the temptation to break his self-conscious pause for effect.

"It burst," he says, breathing noisily through his nose. "It burst because the underlying values and the prices were out of kilter."

This is crucial, I understand. Perhaps he didn't come to this conclusion all by himself, he may have read it somewhere – in the *Dagens Næringsliv* or *The Economist*. He must have forgotten that.

"Is it what they call a bubble?" I venture. "A speculation economy? Like the one we have now?"

"Quite right." He doesn't exactly pat me on the back, but I can almost feel the touch of his hand.

"So the underlying values in this case are artistic?"

"Right. That's just what they are."

"And such values are, I imagine, rather more variable and problematic to determine than others?"

Now he is where he wants to be; it may be a while since he held guest lectures at the Norwegian School of Management, and I can see it makes him feel good to have a younger female listener's interest. Even if she is quite a bit older than the usual management student.

"Artistic values," my mentor says, "are ultimately subject to the same laws as other values. They're affected by expert opinion *and* by demand. When this particular market burst it was because the market took account of changes in the experts' opinions. It was certainly devastating enough."

"And the experts' opinions are in turn influenced by . . ."

"An exaggerated demand. Which forced a re-evaluation. In principle, it's a healthy sign that bubbles like this burst."

"Even if investment in a market like this is based on the assumption that this won't happen?"

"Wise investors keep tabs on expert opinion."

"And as far as Aske is concerned this means . . .?"

"It's very exciting right now, isn't it," Håkon Middelthon says, very pleased for the time being with his student's interjections. "Now that Joakim Roll has invested heavily not only economically but also, shall we say, prestige-wise, it is bound to lead to an immediate jump in prices. There's no doubt about that."

"But?" I am flirting with him now, I know, but I am also interested. Supply and demand. Dealing.

"We're talking dangerous money here," Håkon Middelthon answers. "And Roll is controversial, too. Will he get anything other than publicity out of TroJa? Because a lot of publicity is not necessarily a good thing. If there is anything in the takeover that wasn't done according to the book the publicity can overshadow the underlying values in the company. It certainly doesn't look that way now. But this is what the market has to consider with respect to Roll . . ."

"And with respect to Aske?" I ask, ever the bright student. "There will have to be expert evaluation of them both?"

"Precisely."

"And the murder, will that affect the evaluation?"

"Not seriously. Not now that the man has confessed," Middelthon says. "Something like this just causes fluctuations."

"It doesn't affect the underlying values?"

"No. For the time being there are no investors who would dare to take a chance on Roll making a mistake or, for that matter, having made a mistake, but there again no-one is willing to risk putting everything on him. This is true for Aske in a way. The uncertainty is greater than the value he has at the moment."

"They suit each other very well then," I say.

"Perfectly," Håkon Middelthon says.

"And if you were to give me some some advice," I ask. "About Aske, for example. What would you recommend I do?"

"Buy," Håkon Middelthon says. "And then keep yourself posted as well as you can."

Trust, then. Belief. And a little professional judgement.

15

B ENNY RUNS WITH long strides down the hill towards Vindern, with long strides and gentle but vigorous swings of the hand holding mine. I run awkwardly, in a wifely way, with my skirt hitched up like a girl's to keep up.

"Hey, macho man," I say. "Take it easy!"

"Child-free macho men," Benny growls, shaking his ponytail, "don't take it easy. Child-free macho men just go for it, without mercy, and don't listen to the whimpering of women."

Ida, Mother and Karsten, together, won out in the discussion about Ida's overnight stay, and this gives her parents time to slow down.

"We can always swap, of course," I say. "It's you who *likes* skirts."

"Here? Do you want to swap here?"

The pavement in front of the Chinese ambassador's residence would be the right place for really depraved, Western-style striptease, but I am not the exhibitionist in the family, so he gets to keep his trousers on. Anyway, we behave like young idiots all the way down to the tramway, frolicking like lambs, as leggy as calves, groping and grappling, not in the least bit funny to anyone else but ourselves.

Three teenage girls, staggering along on their thick rubber-soled shoes, look at us through narrow, lifeless eyes as we reach the tram stop. They chew world-wearily on their gum bought from the kiosk; they carry this sophisticated needle-sharp knowledge of the world in the limp, anorexic sort of way that is peculiar to those who don't have a clue.

They yawn and roll their eyes knowingly, belying the clumsiness of their make-up.

"That's how Ida will look at us in about three years' time," I whisper to the back of Benny's head.

"Let's bum it," he says.

"Let's take a taxi," I say.

The wallet is, of course, our remorseless, ultimate weapon against the eternally hard-up sprog. They can't imagine this, any more than they can imagine that we have the sex that they lie about. We wave to them merrily from the back seat of the taxi, not expecting a response.

Then we pretend that it is very elegant – and how – that we are going to a hotel. Benny insists that this is an incredibly extravagant child-free idea, and if it were not for his colleagues in the photography business I might have believed him. He is such a bad actor, but on the other hand that is one of the many things I love about him.

We get out at Benny's studio and take the car since I haven't been drinking and Ida still has to be picked up next morning. Benny chooses the hotel. Flight from the photographers has to be carried out in style. On top of that he *likes* the Oslo Plaza, whatever he might mean by that. I haven't stayed there before.

"Dearest," he says. "Neither have I."

It is pleasant and anonymous and looks just like any other hotel room. And that is pretty much it. But it *does* have a wonderful view.

He thinks, as usual, that I could have taken more care shaving my legs. But, I can't complain about his because they are always freshly waxed, like his chest. I'm a bit stubbly but he forgives me. His face isn't exactly a baby's bottom, either.

"It's a bit stupid," Benny mumbles. I have one stubbly leg resting against the inside of his and the back of my head in his armpit. If I could be bothered, I would find out exactly where his other limbs end and mine begin, but one of the privileges that comes with rumpled hotel bed linen is that you don't have to bother.

"We're not even smoking," he says.

"Are you trying to tell me something?" I ask. "Are you complaining?"

"Not at all. I just mean . . ."

"You mean, what shall we do now?"

"Something like that," he says.

"Evening off, sort of."

"Mmm."

"We could get up and go and collect her? She might not even have gone to sleep yet."

"Cut it out."

"There's something called more of the same," I say.

"Of course," Benny says.

"Then there's the minibar."

"That's not a bad idea. More?"

"Pay channels? They're supposed to be interesting."

"Absolutely not."

"Nice conjugal conversations in a restaurant?"

"But we have them all the time, don't we?"

"That's true," I say.

"Not that you can get too much of them," he says.

"But?"

He doesn't need to strain himself to find some adult entertainment. The mobile phone rings. And it *could* be our daughter.

It isn't. It is Søren Dahl. Actually.

"I hope I'm not disturbing you," the reedy voice on the phone says.

Yes, you are. I think. Actually.

"It's just," he says and then breaks off. "You haven't seen Ingeborg, have you? She hasn't been here all day, actually, and there was supposed to be a board meeting and all. She's not answering the phone either."

"Does she usually?" I ask, still sleepy, still tired, the knife turning in my stomach.

"Oh yes," Søren says. "Especially if it has anything to do with Loaf, actually. It's as if . . . But for the board meeting I doubt I'd have thought it so strange. Though she rings me on the days when she isn't working here too. After Margrete died it was as if we only had each other. Actually."

"So she doesn't live in your flat, then?"

"No, no. I rang the doorbell, but there is, well, but . . . She doesn't seem to be at home, actually."

"But why are you ringing *me*? Not that it matters, but I hardly know her."

"I thought that you left here together last night, didn't you?"

"No," I say.

"That's strange. She wasn't here when I came up from the cellar, actually, and that's why I thought that you . . ."

"She didn't leave with me," I say.

"I was wrong, then. Yes, well, I won't bother you any further. I'm sorry to have disturbed you."

And of course I should go back to duvets and the adult entertainment but I can see him in front of me in the strange flat. The headquarters of the The *Losers' Association*'s little competitor and the altar for the missing Helena. I hope he uses one of the telephones in the outer room and not by Ingeborg's desk facing the black and gold colours of his daughter's collage. Although he does live there. That's what they are like, the rooms in which he lives his life.

"Just a minute," I say. "What are you thinking of doing now?"

"I don't quite know," he says, "actually."

"Will you report her missing?" I ask.

He hesitates. "I've got a key," he says. "To her flat. I should do that. Even if it feels odd. Going into hers like that. Actually. But I ought to do that first."

"Where does she live?" I ask.

"In Tveita," Søren Dahl says. "You can get there in no time by tram."

"I've got a car," I say. "I'll be around at your place in ten minutes."

Ida's Daddy has gone to sleep and is snoring lightly in the hotel bed. Søren Dahl is also a Daddy, though to a more grown-up girl than Ida. And he has had such awful experiences with girls who don't come home when they are expected. Even though I am leaving him, Benny is a great deal less lonely in a strange, wifeless bed than Søren Dahl is in his own flat.

It is not such a bad deal I am offering him; it is a while since Benny had declarations of love written in lipstick on a hotel mirror. At least from me.

He is waiting by the front door, and I can see that it is not something he is used to doing. Søren Dahl sorts out his own transport, as he does most things. He belongs to a generation and the personality type that regards a taxi as an unimaginable luxury and seldom asks for help.

He is small in the seat beside me, and he has to say "Thank you" and "Sorry" and "It's very good of you" several times before he can settle. But when I glance at him his profile is clear though anxious in the orange light from the halogen lamps on the main street up towards Helsfyr.

Benny has his own tribal name for people like Søren Dahl. Salt of the Earth he calls them. Salt of the Earth people pick up pieces of paper from the pavement even if it is not their job. Water plants even if they are not theirs. Talk nicely and probably stupidly to children no matter how drunk or dirty their parents are. Sweep up in front of the front door when the caretaker can't be bothered. Pay much too much tax, though perhaps not that willingly.

They are modest, conscientious and dedicated, and they treat their neighbours and nature and the law – it doesn't matter which – with the same great respect. They may well have appalling political opinions but they don't flash them around. They have almost always some kind of tool in their pockets. There is always something that has to be repaired. Or maintained.

Salt of the Earth people are without doubt a dying race, but they can still be found in most small communities in this country. In a block of flats, for example.

"You love them, you know you do," Benny usually says.

"Of course I do," I answer, because I'm nothing like them.

"Most of them didn't exactly invent the wheel, either," Benny usually says.

"No, but they look after it," I say. "Someone's got to do it."

Now Salt of the Earth is sitting beside me and he is afraid. There are no words for this in the language of his tribe. Instead he gives me directions with exaggerated thoroughness, right down to the exact visitor's parking spot by the blocks of flats in Tveita.

It is sad and inelegant, but you would have to go up to Holmenkollåsen to find this twelve-storey block's equal in terms of a view over the town, and as is widely known that costs a great deal more. Or to the Oslo Plaza.

The blocks tower like bleached bones into the indigo sky and only take on human proportions when seen from inside, from the golden rectangles of light that mean *home* wherever you see them. Outside the golden rectangles you feel restless and long to go inside, whether what surrounds the light is elegant or not.

Søren Dahl must be freezing in his nylon jacket. If he had been here on his own, I think to myself, he would have wandered up and down in front of the middle block several times before making a decision. With me there is nothing else he can do but go straight to the door. He looks up and counts, there is still no light in her windows.

But that is obvious. He rings first of all. Once. Twice. Three times. Then he pulls out the bunch of keys. Ingeborg lives on the sixth floor and there are neither initials nor the word "Loaf" by the doorbell or on her door. The fact that only her surname is on the nameplate on the door must be a sure sign that the person living in the flat is a woman. A single woman. Exposed. Clumsy anonymity.

The little hall is immaculate. A brown varnished writing desk with a narrow cloth runner on top, a niche where jackets and coats hang neatly side by side, a slim mirror immediately in front of us by the door and next to the mirror an attractive framed picture of Helena and Ingeborg. To the right of us a bathroom door with a sign on, a porcelain sign this time, but in essence it is the same child sitting on the potty as at her father's house. These are the family's rooms where the missing child's presence is everywhere.

Søren calls her name and knocks on the glass door of the sitting room. He fumbles around until he finds the switch. Here, too, there is a consistent sense of quiet order. But there is no-one here. The bedspread covers the single bed neatly, and in the alcove two chairs are tucked under the table with an embroidered cloth. On the sofa there are cushions that seem to be there rather for decoration than for comfort.

Beneath us lies the town. And the Oslo Plaza. Ingeborg Dahl also has a writing desk in this room, next to the three adjoining windows looking into the night. Outside there are the thin coils of light along thoroughfares, the infinity of vibrating points of light that make up a town surrounded by darkness, the thousands of signals identifying movement and arrival and loneliness in red and green and gold contrasted against the overwhelming black of night. Søren Dahl's face is reflected in the glass, thin and white.

Then he turns away and opens the door beside the alcove where Ingeborg Dahl sleeps. This is Helena's room. Her bed, resplendent in IKEA colours, her bedside table, the red table where she must have done her homework in the few months before she disappeared. A teddy bear on the bed. A clothes cupboard covered with stickers. Before he closes the door again I can see the biggest one is Smiley, that simple smiling face, yellow and shiny and dated, until it was reinvented. But Helena was dead long before Smiley became an advert for fancy dope.

In the sitting room our faces are reflected in the black window panes, white and in duplicate and indistinct. I don't like them there and turn on the desk lamp to get rid of them. The only place in the room where Ingeborg Dahl allows herself not to be industrious and methodical is here. Her desk is covered with newspaper cuttings, reproductions of pictures on glossy paper, magazines and photographs. Most of them, it seems, are about Aske.

There is a telephone in the hall, on the writing desk, probably the least convenient place to have a conversation in the whole apartment. But she has an answerphone and it is flashing red, wordlessly.

No-one has rung apart from him. However, he left a series of messages. In his reedy voice he asks again and again if she is there, if she can hear him. It is almost unbearable, and we have nothing to say to each other when the machine finally stops. Only one of the messages is different from the others and that is the first one. When rather apologetically he wishes her good night. After coming up from the cellar and finding his flat empty.

I look at him questioningly. "Yes," he says. "The first one is from yesterday." And behind his thick glasses there is enough loneliness to fill a whole universe.

"Do you know if she knows someone called Sjur Aske?" I ask.

Søren Dahl blinks. "Is that the artist?"

"No," I say. "His brother."

"Ingeborg doesn't know either of them," Søren Dahl says. "As far as I know."

But I find his number in her telephone book.

"This is probably just nonsense," I say, "but I saw him in the street outside your flat as I was leaving. And he may . . ."

"May what, Igi? May know her even if her father knows nothing about it? Or may have seen her leaving? Or something."

However, no-one answers the phone at Sjur Aske's and he doesn't have an answerphone capable of receiving a message and flashing red, wordlessly. I make a note of the number on a slip of paper and put it into Søren Dahl's hand. It is not much to go on. Almost nothing.

16

IN FACT, IT is really Benny I am looking for in this dreadful place, half multi-storey car park and half warehouse with large depressing posters announcing the sale of some cheap, tacky product. It is Benny I am looking for, but at the back of my mind I am also worried about this woman. As I glide round the corner into the garage I see her and know at once that I don't want to know about the nature of her pain.

But I also know that it is terrible, that her suffering must be unendurable, just as the man's is, even if it was him she was so afraid of. But one thing is clear: she has come here of her own free will. And the look she gives me expresses predominantly grief. Then shame. He, too, looks as if he is about to cry. He gropes around for her but can't find her, because, separate and yet together, they are locked inside this thing, the precise function of which I want to know nothing, the physical results of which I want to know nothing, but which I know is called a Pain Machine.

I also know that what it does to their bodies, whatever it is – I catch a glimpse of something purple and decomposed, perhaps a nipple – is monstrous. That I couldn't bear to know exactly what it is. That is why I wake up, so that I can get away from it. I have no objection whatever to my consciousness protecting me in this way. As I lie there paralysed, terrified out of my skin, I am grateful for it.

I don't need to wake up Benny because it's obvious I have already done that. Whisperings in the night. Little movements in the bed. There is something reassuring about this dream dying away in the retelling as others do and Benny not being stricken with fear of the Pain Machine, as I was. Anyway, he offers to raid what is left of the minibar for me.

It is only three hours since I came back from Grønlandsleiret.

Søren Dahl got out of the car close to the police station and didn't want to be accompanied *there*. Benny took me in his arms and listened to me, and now even he can't get any sleep. Well, that is not such an unreasonable deal. A call on the baby monitor here, a nightmare there.

A couple in an immaculate hotel room, sitting huddled up in a strange bed. The dense night suspended in silence beyond the windows. The sounds of the town that are not ours. Benny puts on a light. A night light, a sparse, limited range.

I am awake because I am frightened of sleeping, like Edevart Riel.

"This is stupid," I say.

"Yes," Benny says, "no more nights in the hotel. How long do you think *sex games* can stay interesting?"

We have a wry, nervous laugh at that.

Then I find myself talking about Javed even though it wasn't him I dreamt about. How I would very much like to believe that he didn't do it, but can't let myself since it is so obviously in my own interest if it is true.

"And in mine," Benny says.

"And in yours."

"But really that's not a particularly *good* reason," he says.

"Just a complicated one."

"Complicated by women," he adds. Well, he should know.

"If he did it, you are the world's worst psychologist, is that it?" he asks.

"Something like that."

"And I'm the world's worst husband."

"You didn't teach him any sex games, did you?" I say.

"Nor did you," Benny answers. "Anyway, Javed has withdrawn his confession, hasn't he?"

"Yes," I say. "And no-one believes he did that for any other reason than for his own advantage."

"Lot of advantages here then, aren't there?" Benny says. "It's to his advantage to withdraw his confession and on the other hand it's to yours to believe he withdrew it because in fact he had nothing to confess. The equation doesn't quite work, does it? Is that why you don't believe it? Because it's to your advantage?"

"That's what I don't know," I say.

"What do you think then? If you had to bet on it?"

Long pause, as if with a patient. It's a good thing to wear two hats at the same time; I search for my own answer in all seriousness and see Benny parodying me while I ask other people similar questions.

"No," I say. "Not only that. That too. But not only that."

It tends to be me who extols the virtues of talking within the family, but Benny's the one proud of his score in *practice*. It is a great deal higher than mine.

"There's only one thing to do, then," he says. And I know the rest. "Check the sources. Find out. And then you can tackle the wretched feeling of shame afterwards. When you know that you have good reason to do it."

"But that's so silly," I say. "These ideas of Ingeborg Dahl's are so absurd, so hysterical, wherever she may now be. I mean *Loaf*, Benny. I feel sorry for her, but it's absurd."

"But she's gone missing."

"Maybe. And maybe there's a friend her father doesn't know about and she's staying there for a few days. Things like that happen. She isn't any less crazy for running away for a couple of days."

"But being crazy, if she is, doesn't automatically mean that she's not *right*?"

"Being active," he whispers into my neck later, "isn't so silly."

No. It is a temptation. And a very respectable way of surviving. I can recommend it.

"Comfort," Benny says half-asleep. "Being active is a comfort."

And it is his body against mine that allows me to sleep although I am so afraid of dreaming about the people trapped in the Pain Machine.

The next morning I have a disembodied Ida with me in bed and an excited monologue on the mobile phone. She wants me to pick her up, but *later* after she's done lots of thrilling things like visiting Karsten's cellar and Saturday shopping in Vindern. She sniffs her way round the world as a small animal does and in return it heals her. It is an excellent deal.

We take a late breakfast in the pretentious Sonja Henie room and dare to read newspapers. Bente has been moved to page eight with quite a small photo. Welle defends the department's honour – and mine — as best as he can. Edevart Riel has kept his side of the bargain and hasn't done a new deal with any of the newspapers.

No more nights at the hotel. No more self-centred wallowing in defeat.

"How well does Bella know Aske?" I ask.

Benny smiles mechanically. Check the sources.

"Extremely well, I should think. She has organised most things for him for years. From paying fines for minor drug convictions to doing his tax returns."

"Have they known each other since childhood?" I ask. "I think he worked at her father's factory."

"No idea," Benny says. "It's possible. Ask her."

"That's what I'll do," I say. "But it's a bit early yet, don't you think?"

Benny has to drop in on Håkon Middelthon to see whether his Aske paintings are any good for the biography. Being active is no bad thing.

Streams of sour sunlight chase between the rows of houses as I drive the few minutes it takes over to Grønlandsleiret. It is still dark, however, in Søren Dahl's hallway.

His hands are stained black and he waves them around in confusion in front of his thin body.

"I can't see you today," he says. "Actually. I'm sorry."

Behind the thick lenses his eyes blink a couple of times, as if it is this that makes him so desperate that he can't shake hands.

"I understand," I say. "Are you working on something?"

A trumpeting sound reaches us from inside the flat.

"WHO IS THAT?"

Søren Dahl blinks a couple more times. "Yes," he says. "Or rather no. I'm not really working. I'm just trying to, actually. The photocopier has overheated. At any rate it has stopped working. Actually."

I raise my eyebrows and nod towards the hall. My cautious smile may be like that of a social worker in its warmth, but Søren Dahl needs as much as he can get of that kind of thing, whether he has heard any news of his daughter or not.

"Have you . . .?" I ask him in the dark hallway.

"No," he says. He seems very small standing there in front of me. "I rang the police at seven this morning, actually, but they had nothing new to tell me."

"SØREN," comes a howl from inside the sitting room. Søren scampers off like a squirrel through the doorway in front of me.

Anlaug is standing with her legs apart in a sea of crumpled paper. One panel of the photocopier is open, and a mangled piece of paper is sticking out between the rollers. The rest of it is dangling between two of Anlaug's outstretched fingers at the end of a raised, beefy arm. It looks as if she is holding a rat by the tail, one she has found in her voluminous batik clothing and now she is ready to *sue* someone over it.

"But I told you," Søren stammers. "Actually. I told you not to turn it on again."

"WHAT IS SHE DOING HERE?"

"This is . . .," Søren begins.

"I know who she is," Anlaug thunders. "The question is: what is she doing HERE?"

"I came to talk to Søren," I say. "To find out if he had heard any more news about Ingeborg."

"He HASN'T. Now you can GO."

"I don't know," Søren says, blinking behind his glasses. "Perhaps you would like a cup of coffee?"

"Yes please," I say.

"I'll have to wash my hands first," he says. "It won't take a moment actually. It's ready and I've got a tube of Kjemrens in the kitchen."

I couldn't actually get a clearer invitation to stay. Anlaug stands motionless with the scrap of paper in her hand.

"So it's broken down, then," I say, to make conversation. "The machine?"

"YES," she says emphatically. "It's overHEATED."

"What are you copying?"

"That's got nothing to do with YOU."

"No," I say. "It hasn't."

Outside the clean shiny windows the sun falls low over the roofs of the houses, striking the church tower and the treetops in front of the prison.

"It's the ARCHIVE," Anlaug says.

"You're copying the archive?"

119

"EVERYTHING," Anlaug says.

"But why?"

"In case they close it DOWN."

"In case someone closes down the archive? But who would?"

"The POLICE, of course," Anlaug says and looks at me as if I were an idiot. "You NEVER know what they'll think up next."

The idea is a little grotesque. But then everything around Anlaug is a bit grotesque. "You think . . .," I begin.

"If they don't FIND her they'll SEAL the office. Any FOOL can understand that."

"I don't know," I say, looking across at her from the office chair I am sitting on. "It's possible that they'll do that. Maybe. If they suspect that she may have come to some criminal harm."

"PAH," Anlaug snorts. "They won't STOP us. When Ingeborg comes back she'll FIX everything. In the meantime, I MAKE THE DECISIONS here."

Søren comes in with with three mugs on a tray. Once more I get the Loaf mug.

"Anlaug thinks it best that we take copies of all the material," he says. "So that Loaf is . . ."

"OPERATIONAL," she continues.

"Actually," Søren adds.

"Of all the material?" I ask.

"ALL," Anlaug answers.

"But that's a lot, isn't it?"

"YES."

"That's why the machine overheated," Søren says. "Actually."

And I reflect that she might be doing him a favour without realising it. It may do Søren Dahl good to keep busy doing something, getting his hands dirty and having to wash them with Kjemrens. Although I don't believe for a moment that Anlaug is here to help Søren.

"Do you know where Ingeborg is?" I ask Anlaug. She glares at me through her tragic glasses.

"Are you STUPID?" she asks.

There is no answer to that, not in the nursery nor anywhere else. But I can see that the prospect of a quarrel flaring up makes Søren nervous. His gaze wanders between the two women in the room, intruders in what must once have been his private territory.

"I'll ring you later," I say. "If that's okay."

Later is better. Later is easier than his being hemmed in as he is now.

Now there is a photocopier that needs looking at. Søren Dahl puts his mug down on the edge of the desk and bends over the well-ordered system of rollers, plates and cogwheels inside the photocopier. He is an elderly man whose fingers may tremble, however little, or may be clumsy, at least to begin with. The situation improves after the options for repair have been examined.

At some point the machine will work again, of course. At some point both Anlaug and I will leave in peace.

There might be a few bits of wood he can salvage in the cellar to work on. On the way to Vindern I wonder what significance the copying has, whether Anlaug believes that Ingeborg has gone for good or, on the contrary, that she knows where she is. What do I know? Maybe Anlaug just needs to be active too. As Ida does, as I do.

So it doesn't hurt to make the DECISIONS for a while.

17

MOTHER SPECULATES ABOUT what Benny and I got up to while she was child-minding, but whether it was excruciating rows or a flamboyant sex life she imagines I prefer not to know.

"Not quite enough sleep." I leave it at that.

"I can tell," she answers.

Ida can't see it. Ida can only see her new accessories for the rather nasty little pony. They keep her busy and distracted while we say our goodbyes. She would like to put her grandparents in her little rucksack and take them home with her. As that doesn't work she has to fiddle around with little bits of pink plastic as best she can.

But I can tempt her with Bella, for whom Ida nurtures a deep, albeit unreciprocated, affection. Bella allows herself to be roused, and yes, she would like to see me.

"I've got Ida with me," I say cautiously.

"Oh God," Bella says. "Okay, then the *poor man* will get a few hours off."

The poor man is Benny; Ida and/or I are his burdens.

"I'm dreading it," Bella says.

"Meeting us?"

"No, no. We're going on a trip," she says.

"Where to?" I ask.

"Into the Past," Bella says. "With a capital P."

Bella lives in what she calls *a hole* in St. Hanshaugen. I have never been there; no women apart from Bella and Rita are allowed access. She keeps us waiting for ten minutes by the kerb in Schwensensgate before she stalks briskly over the tarmac.

"Very robust," she says peering at the back seat of the car with gratification. "A kind of straitjacket. Look, she can barely move her arms."

With Bella you never know. You would think it was the first time she had ever seen a child's seat, at least one with a child in.

"I didn't realise that you were so smart," she says as she twists her pencil stroke of a body on to the passenger seat beside me, flips her sunglasses into place and fidgets with her oversized, elegant handbag.

"What's the deal? Can one smoke with her on board?" Bella asks.

"I'd rather you didn't. And in the car smoke might make her feel so sick that she would vomit all over you."

Bella is not keen on that. I roll the window down a little way – for all I know the clouds of perfume Bella sprays all over her may also affect my daughter's stomach. On top of which, I don't think Rita smells that good.

"Go," Bella says.

Rita licks Ida noisily.

The Past with a capital P is in the embassy area of Skillebekk and is called Villa Troels. Ida doesn't like it. That doesn't surprise me. I don't know how My Little Pony *lives*, of course, but I imagine that a pink plastic stable is more Ida's sort of architecture than this. We park a few hundred metres down from the National Library and Ida goes into raptures over the several gaily-turned towers and parapets with false embrasures in the street.

"Look, Mummy," she says pointing towards the neighbour's house where narrow Gothic lattice windows encircle what must have been the brick version of a Muslim seraglio, in the guise of a long balcony embellished with caps, tassles and bunches of grapes in heavy stucco work.

"A castle! And there's another!"

Ida has distinct hopes as Bella unlocks the smooth white metal gate to the house. Once inside, she stands motionless. The drive in front of the house is paved with flagstones, a modest grey in the autumn sun; here and there they are cracked and have thick tufts of grass growing between them. Under the rows of neglected bushes there are deep shadows of cobalt blue.

"Brideshead revisited or what!" Bella says, striding away towards the broad concrete steps. "Roll is busy patching up after the blunder at TroJa, so he wants to show it off to lots of *cultural correspondents* this very morning. *Containment*, he calls it in English, the snob. Give them something else to think about, you know? Roll, the saviour of neglected Modernist architecture. That sounds good, doesn't it? I just thought I would have to look at it to make sure it hadn't gone *rotten* before the hordes turn up."

There is a thin, once white, metal balustrade beside the steps leading up to the door which has a round brass-framed window at head height. On either side of the door glass stretches the length of the central section of the door; there are small ceramic glass panes in this part of the façade and they continue around the door and two floors up, set in a broad rectangular concrete frame.

The sections that break up the centre consist, on the left-hand side, of a compact white concrete block almost windowless and, on the right-hand side, a tight curved structure in which the high windows follow the form of the façade. This section is half a floor higher than the other and is vaguely reminiscent of a ship's bridge, complete with towers and windows with cracked teak frames.

It is famous. Clear, cool thinking converted into space, volume and axes, imperious, secure, confident. As if mathematical proof were clad in glass and concrete and now invited us to follow its series of calculations, to draw valid conclusions and to verify its logic.

Inside the hall Ida starts to rouse herself, advances hesitantly over the many square metres of parquet flooring and whirls energetically on her own axis, secure in a child's awareness that the important thing is to keep yourself busy. Rita stands and *gapes* at her.

It is cold inside and there is no furniture. The open staircase continues to the full height of the house, but is surrounded by galleries on both the higher floors. Ida discovers the echo and experiments with the different options.

"It's . . . overwhelming," I say to Bella who has put down her handbag in the middle of the dark parquet floor.

"You're telling me," she says, looking at me askance. "I was born here, baby," she says in English.

"You grew up *here*?" I ask because, although in some vague way I must have known that Villa Troels belonged to her family, I never really imagined that anyone lived here.

"God no," she says, lighting up one of her ultra-thin menthol cigarettes, "thank heavens I didn't grow up here. He tried, sort of, in the Fifties when I was a baby, almost, but – you know we absolutely *froze*, Mummy and me. Can you imagine that?"

Now she laughs, her gruff whisky-and-Bella laugh.

"We froze in this hell here, his two ladies, so he had no option but to wrap us up in Persian carpets, velvet curtains and stuff up west. I'm not sure that he ever forgave us."

Her heels go clack-clack-clack sounding like dry machine-gun fire as she walks round in front of the curved teak staircase, her elbow resting on her hip and her hand with the cigarette forming a stiletto in front of her. Ida, collapsed in a heap on the floor, follows her with big eyes, a first-time spectator at the catwalk.

"This was his very own work," Bella says, "and it was supposed to prove something, apart from covering over all his ill-gotten gains. And then we *froze*! No-one has lived here since then. To begin with he probably hoped that his little family would warm up and return, but then Mummy went and died – on top of everything else."

It smells of damp concrete here and the dust billows up around her legs, which she can't keep still.

"But now at last it'll be of some use, one way or another," Bella says. "Who would have thought that a global billion-dollar business would need no more room than this? Although it isn't exactly *small*, let's face it. There is enough space to romp around in here, isn't there?"

She casts her eyes over Ida who is doing anything but romping.

"Shall we have a look at the other rooms?" she asks. Clack-clack-clack across the floor. Flat white sliding doors open under protest and we enter a wing where the light of the high autumn sky is filtered through the foliage and forms pale intricate patterns on the floor and along the white walls.

"I think this is called the music room," Bella says. "Imagine a grand piano in front of you by the windows there, if you can. Mummy was supposed to play it. But, you know, I don't really think her piano skills stretched much beyond *Für Elise*, or thereabouts. Eric Satie or Shostakovich would have been way beyond her."

Bella's voice tends to be rough, rasping and a touch aggressive, but I have never heard anything resembling hatred in it before.

The rooms we make our way quietly through may be bare, everything sober, serious and clean, but the light filtering through the high windows colours the wooden floor in dark rich nuances, forming long tongues of red in the woodwork and creating golden vibrating circles and deep henna hues where the shadows fall. This is not a dead house, not at all.

But one thing is clear. For Bella it is dead, and as she opens the door with the paint peeling off to go to the kitchen I can feel it too, the death this house was left to die.

"Kitchen," Bella says, "right next to the dining room, of course, no ridiculous cramped corridor separating the *domestic staff* from the rest of us, as in the awkward Frogner flats. It's very light and practical here, isn't it."

It is big and white, of course, and without the table that must once have been in the middle of the room it looks more like factory space. There are long narrow benches along all the walls, an infinite number of drawers, shelves and yellowing cupboard doors. Three zinc basins in a line look as if they could absorb anything, the carcass of an ox or a human body.

Bella sits side-saddle on one of the benches furthest from the zinc basins and lights another cigarette.

"They'll have to use this as a kind of canteen," she says. "There are laws protecting it and that makes things complicated, but Roll doesn't give a shit. However much he has to spend on plumbing, central heating and antiquities he will never get anything like this anywhere else in the country. Unique, isn't it. None of the yes-men have anything like it. They still go in for *chesterfields* and illuminated globes with built-in bar cabinets."

Bella goes over to the zinc basins and stubs out her cigarette. She lights up a new one. I have never seen her like this before. But how have I seen Bella? Vulgar, cursing Oslo's West End, and cheerful, devil-may-care, always secure even if she's drunk and balancing on that particular knife edge that exists for Bohemians who have no regard for personal safety and the economic safety net of the family.

"Did you know Aske when you were small?" I ask.

"God no. Do you think he let us have anything to do with *workers*?" she says. "I never once went to the factory. Aske maintains that Daddy hung around their house, though God knows what he would want to do there. Escape from his frozen women possibly."

She looks ravaged, ravaged and bitter, and gets through her joint-thin Superlights in two or three deep drags. Ida tries to play with Rita. She fails completely.

"Do you think that Aske could have killed someone?" I ask.

"Three or four art critics perhaps," Bella says. "Or me from time to time."

"Bella . . ."

"Are you serious? Crazy. Is it your little patient you're worried about?" she asks. "Well. I presume he could have. He *is* crazy after all, in a way. His *screaming* is terrible when he gets into a temper, and he never apologises afterwards, the prick."

"The deal," I say. "With Roll."

"Yes?"

Provocatively.

"How did it come about?"

"That was the Frogner Fannies," Bella says baldly.

"Who?"

"Some old ladies who have a load of shares and decide for once to listen to common sense," Bella says. "Just imagine, they supported me and Roll instead of Daddy. That was really very sweet of them."

Then she looks at me and narrows her eyes.

"How exciting," she says. "If he had killed someone. Oh God, the *prices* we could have charged."

Then she hops down from the bench.

"I could do with a Bloody Mary. This place is just as run down, depressing and bloody cold as I thought. Though I doubt they have anything like that at McDonald's or wherever it is *she* usually eats."

Maybe Bella is not entirely unaffected by Ida's devotion at her feet after all. She doesn't touch her, but she looks at her, follows Ida with her eyes as my daughter walks shyly across the floor towards the deep zinc basins.

"What's that?" she asks, pointing.

Above the zinc basins there is an old-fashioned board with small white enamel squares with numbers. The numbers represent each room in the house and under the board there is a chain with a handle, just like the ones hanging from the lavatory cisterns of my childhood. At the end of the handle is a little button for the *maids* to acknowledge that they had heard the call from one of the big empty rooms in the house.

This building is an attractive equation, but it belongs, if only in part and perhaps with some reluctance, to a time when a household of this size had more staff than labour-saving machinery. The number three on the little board quivers faintly. That must be Ida's footsteps on the floor causing the wall to vibrate, or perhaps it's Bella walking quickly now towards the door.

"It's just a stupid game," she says, shrugging. "Come on, let's go."

And perhaps I'm just imagining it, but I think for a second that she looks frightened as she turns her back on the board and the room. Clack-clack-clack she goes, as she crosses the floor on her way out.

The sound is like that of an old-fashioned fire alarm or of an especially loud alarm clock, the kind of panic-stricken ringing produced by mechanical devices, not by electronic ones. Somewhere inside the board there is a little hammer continually striking a ringing metal bell at lightning speed, and the little enamel square with its painted figure three falls through the slit at the bottom of the board. It sticks out like a prominent tooth, vibrates a little, then settles. It looks as if it is staring at us. Although, of course, it is we who are staring at it.

Houses like this don't have ghosts or shouldn't have at least; they are built to a certain extent so as to dispel the whole idea of ghosts.

"Someone's ringing," I say cheerfully and hypocritically to Ida. "Can you see? The little number falls down when someone pulls on the wire in another room."

Ida looks at me as if I were an idiot. I studiously avoid looking at Bella and walk over to my daughter.

"But there *isn't* anyone pulling on the wire," she says. "Is there."

"It's a very old piece of equipment," I say lifting her up in my arms. "Perhaps it's broken."

Clack-clack-clack, Bella's small hard heels are followed by mine through the dining room and across the music room where there is no grand piano standing sedately by the arch of the window, where the shadows of the treetops outside cast silhouettes of intricate patterns over the floor.

Bella holds the door with the porthole open for us. She stares at her feet, then shrugs and tosses her head back, her Monroe hair a swift, sharp protest across her forehead.

He is standing in a long horizontal shadow in the gallery on the first floor with one hand resting on the banister. It is turned golden brown by a shaft of sunlight while he is bathed in dark dense light and I can't distinguish his features. But it is an old hand on the banister, heavy and wrinkled, like a captain's hand resting on the bridge. Bella stares at him for a few seconds, then she waves us out.

She lets the door close behind us, but she doesn't lock it. She walks down the paved drive with her arms folded against her chest.

"Was that your *father*?" I ask.

"Yes. Yes, of course it was," Bella answers, pulling out another spike-thin cigarette. "And that house has got shit to do with him. *The prick.*"

Bella has a talent for making the most sexually laden language sound almost everyday, but this time her talent deserts her. *Prick* sounds as if it means exactly what it is as we walk out into the tranquillity of the gardens of Skillebekk. *Prick* sounds raw, dark and old beside the historical pastiches surrounding us with their towers and their overblown stucco fantasies.

"Do you think you could . . . ?" Bella asks haltingly by the car. "Do you think you could let me borrow her for an hour and just stick your head in there to find out what he's up to? I mean I damn well don't want him standing up there and staring *tomorrow*."

"What do you say," Bella smiles persuasively at Ida, "to a Big Mac with a double portion of fries and a mega-Coke and Mummy will come back a little later?"

Ida doesn't want a Big Mac. She wants a Happy Meal with Disney games. This is something she has studied in some depth with Karsten and she is bought of course, bought and sold. Maybe I could have imposed myself on them, but when the goddess at last smiles on you for once, you don't ask your Mummy to come along with you as a chaperone. Ida manages to tear herself away from her rising sun for a few seconds to give me a half-apologetic look.

"It's absolutely fine," I say. "Off you go."

She smiles with relief, just as she will in ten years' time, when she wants to go off and enjoy ecstatic living with some pimply youth. They are lost in intimate conversation about the subtle differences in the world of hamburgers when Bella starts the car. No different, I think, from the conversations she will be having about music and clothes not so long from now.

I am not even sure how up-to-date I am on minced beef, although I think, as I close the metal gate behind me, that there have still to be opportunities for me to catch up. There is something called *nuggets*, I remember, but I am not quite sure whether or not they are served in breadcrumbs.

Ida will surely be able to tell me. Many, many years from now she will be able to tell me something without despairing of my ignorance. It is a long time before she will consider me hopeless.

He is still in the gallery with a hand resting on the banister, as if waiting for one of us to return. But it would have been odd if it were me he was waiting for. He too has a daughter. I don't know how I should address him. I can't remember his first name and perhaps that is because I thought he had died a long time ago; nevertheless I flick through my built-in cultural lexicon searching for his first name. Not that I would have dared use it in the presence of someone elevated to the status of royalty.

"*The Adults' Party*," he says. "Do you know it?"

"André Bjerke," I answer, still playing Trivial Pursuit.

"Now it's not good manners to peek between the railings of this balustrade, though it is nice. Peeping in on your children's party."

"It wasn't exactly a party," I say, disappointed for a moment that he chose such a simple book. Somehow I had imagined that this was more of a complicated Modernist milieu. Though why should I demand something more obscure when I am struggling to find the name of the country's biggest art collector, even when I am standing face to face with him?

"But they're coming," he says. "There will be parties here. I am quite sure they're coming. As far as I know there will be something like a party here tomorrow. Would you like to come up or shall we stay here, like Romeo and Juliet?"

"If I may," I say and hear the curtsey in my voice, as if I were in the presence of genuine royalty.

"Otto Troels-Jacobsen," he says amiably, his captain's hand outstretched, and he frees me from my futile race through the *Who's Who* of Norwegian cultural life.

"Igi Heitmann," I say. "I am a sort of a friend of Bella's."

"Really," he says. "Sort of. I have the impression she has lots of those. Sorts of friends."

"I don't know," I say. "I haven't known her that long."

"And I don't know her any *longer*, Bella's father says. "Perhaps you would follow me into the, what shall I say, office?" he asks without shifting vocal register.

He is a head shorter than me, compact and firm-fleshed, though rotund. He has the kind of curved stomach called *embonpoint* that caricaturists before the war loved so much and reproduced so affectionately with a single masterly brushstroke.

He just managed to avoid them, I think, although I have a feeling that I have seen a drawing done of him by Hammarlund, with his whisky hand clearly defined and his heavy jowls dark like meat. Perhaps it is hanging in the Theatercafé, deep in a corner where he and other heroes from the Fifties are yellowing behind their thin frames.

"The office" is as empty as the other rooms here. There is a fragile writing desk with curved steel legs, a chair and a couple of cardboard boxes under the window. And nothing else.

"Spartan," he says. "Not that I mind that. There is a certain logic to it. There is another chair in the other room, if you don't mind following me. I don't much like *carrying* anything any more, not even for a lady."

The other room is likewise deserted. The bed, a narrow white rectangle, protrudes into the room from the shorter wall. There is also an open suitcase. And a chair by the window.

It is a *camp*. An eighty-year-old man's bivouac, in the middle of a dead house. His cheeks are flushed as he sits back behind his matchstick desk and offers me a cognac. He has two glasses – for situations such as these, he says – and a bottle of dependable VSOP Napoleon brandy. His hand shakes just a little as he pours, possibly because the bottle is full and heavy.

"Nothing works here," Troels-Jacobsen says with delight. "There's no electricity, no water, no heating. I have to go outside to go to pee. The only thing that works is the bell I rang, and that was only meant as an experiment. But there was life in it all right.

"You startled us," I say and I can see that that cheers him up. "How long have you been living here?"

"Three days," he says. "I've been living here for three days. There is a man who comes with hot water in the morning and also a thermos of coffee. He didn't need to bring the coffee, but it's a fine gesture, don't you think?"

"But why?" I ask.

"They're behaving as if I were already dead," he says. "And I have decided to show them that I'm not. You can tell her that. I may not have any authority in my own company any longer, but I can still manage my own life. They weren't quick enough, you see, they didn't think about taking the key to this house away from me when they took everything else."

"Who's they?" I ask.

"Bella and that upstart. It's true that Bella and I have not seen eye-to-eye, but you don't expect such treachery. You don't. And the time I transferred the house to the company it was simply, as is well known, with a view to keeping it."

This is said in a way which suggests that some tiny little tax motive may also have been involved. He is an observant man and he sees my doubt, although that is not necessarily the reason why he continues so hastily.

"Keeping the house up has been a chore for a long time, as you can see. There are antiquated laws and regulations on all sides and letting the company take over the house was supposed to have been the best solution. There were countless plans, drawings, exciting portfolios and declarations of intent by the community that are worth about as much as lavatory paper. Everything would be okay so long as I transferred the house to the company. Hah!"

He leans towards me, across his fragile writing desk, and lowers his voice.

"Reception rooms for a status-obsessed upstart! That's what they want to turn this into. And there is no-one apart from me who is willing to lift a finger to prevent them. As you can see, I have to do it. It's a question of decency."

"Was it Bella who recommended you transfer the house to the company?" I ask. For a moment he squeezes shut his glistening old man's eyes.

"I don't remember that exactly," he says, tapping his forehead lightly. Old people flirting with a worn memory have a fine range of evasions at their disposal. "It may have been her. For all that she seldom talks to me. About anything. On the other hand, on the rare occasions when she does turn to me it's always, without exception, about money."

He raises his glass to his mouth and moistens his lips.

"It was her block of shares, you see, that tipped the scales. Secured the majority for this vulgar person."

"I know," I say. The shameless deal: Roll got the company and Bella got her mausoleum for Aske. And Otto became a one-man demonstration.

"You must be very angry with her."

"I could be perhaps. On the other hand you can also see it as — a little frightening. Have you any children?

"Yes," I say. "She . . ."

"Yes, of course, I saw her, didn't I," he interrupts. "Wouldn't you think it was creepy too if you knew, were convinced, that she would rather you were dead?"

The house is still. There is a draught from the big windows. The teak frames are old and cracked and don't close flush any longer.

"Do you think that Bella does?" I ask. "Wishes you dead?"

He doesn't answer that.

"It's also going to be a kind of cultural centre," I say hesitantly. "The Aske collection and the exhibition rooms up in Nydalen."

"Cultural centre?" The old man spits the words out. "For what? It'll be a rubbish dump, a rubbish dump for inertia, for muddled, cloudy thinking. You may not be aware, young lady, that I've collected art almost all my life. But I draw the line at other people's *fingers*."

"Indeed," I say. "I don't suppose they are indispensible."

"And now I've got nothing. I have this, a table and a bed, otherwise nothing. They took my entire collection away from me and now they're selling it piece by piece to get the money for a *museum* for junk. That's why I'm here. To make things less easy for them."

"What have you been doing?" I ask. "I mean what have you been doing these last three days?"

There isn't a single book here, there are two newspapers folded nicely on the desk, otherwise there is, as he says, absolutely nothing.

"Waiting," he answers. "For someone to come. You came. Tomorrow there will be more. Skål!"

This time he has to hold the glass with both hands before wetting his lips, and it is obviously embarrassing for him, so I look away briefly.

133

"All you have to do is change the lock on the door, you know," I say. "That's all you need to do, if it's no longer your property."

He smiles.

"But that's why I keep a look out," he says. "I'm on the inside. So they have to choose whether to lock me in here or to get the police to carry me out. That would be something, don't you think? That this multi-millionaire and my daughter send the police in to carry me out? There are still a few cultural commentators left in this country. I may have a word or two with some of them tomorrow."

He places his plump fists on the table to help himself up. It's not a rapid process, and it asks a lot of his eighty-year-old lungs, but I just stand next to him with my arm proffered in the traditional way, should he need support. As I thought, he doesn't. The audience is over, apparently.

He escorts me as far as the gallery.

"I've got an Arnold Haukeland down in the garden, which you ought to have a look at before you go," he says. "I have great respect for Arnold Haukeland even if, sadly, he has the most wretched of successors. You'll find the door out to the terrace in the conservatory," he continues. "Behind the stairs. I don't think you went in there before, but it's very easy. The double doors behind the stairs."

So he watched our every movement from the moment we arrived, I think. Stood in the shadows up here in the gallery and watched us go into the music room and the kitchen. Watched us and waited. And then looked for the right moment to ring the little bell. That must have amused him. Now he, too, is smiling wryly while I shake his hand and say goodbye.

"I assume that you will talk to Bella," he says.

"Of course," I say. "That's what you want, isn't it?"

He smiles again his sardonic smile, and his face is at once ancient and evil. He waits.

I look up as I am about to go in under the gallery and open the sliding door to the conservatory. He is still there peering down at me with a plump hand on the banister. The captain on his bridge. Waiting.

The conservatory is as empty as the other rooms. It is in the shade now and it is grey and a little bluish by the deep rectangular bay windows, glass on all sides. In the middle of the centre section of the bay window there is a French window, double glass door, which opens easily out on to the concrete terrace. The air is fresher out here and it is only now that I realise how much dust I have been surrounded by, how much bare, damp-stained concrete.

Beneath the terrace's moulded concrete steps there is an area of shingle sloping down to what were once elegant, wide flower beds. They are overgrown now and contain a strange assortment of wilting nettles, dry grass and the odd surviving perennial.

The pathway to the pool is almost entirely overgrown and beyond it is a towering Arnold Haukeland sculpture in polished steel in a jungle of shrubs. There is a gate among the shrubs, a pale metal shape standing half-open.

The pool is empty. It is cast in grey, furrowed concrete with a bottom that is covered in withered leaves and, where the shade is thickest, slimy black layers of leaves on their way to becoming compost.

On the other side of the statue lies Ingeborg Dahl, curled up like a child under the strong penetrative will of the sculpture.

18

THE CANDY-STRIPED plastic tape that the police have put up flutters feebly above all the dark green overgrown moss that has taken over this abandoned garden. Haukeland's matt silver sculpture reaches up into the cool afternoon sky. Silence no longer surrounds this transfixed will. There are no longer any hiding places between the overgrown trees. The police, wearing baseball caps like adolescents, wander around the overgrown paths setting up floodlights on branches for the approaching dark. The sweeping blue lights penetrate the garden from the street, filtered through the foliage. Soon there will be no secrets left here.

It is Ingeborg Dahl they are taking photos of, not the Haukeland. The body under the will, this soaking wet, abandoned, prostrate body that is now being packed in green plastic and is ready to be removed. I am neither victim, nor kin, but I watch what they do with her all the same. I have seen the marks on her neck and felt the lifeless body. If I am not moved away I would like to make sure that they, mmm, treat her well.

So I stand on the shingle outside the conservatory smoking. I won't be in the way there. I soon realise what a sod it is to find technical clues in shingle. I have made my own arrangements, my preliminary reports. Benny is picking up Ida, something Bella was more than keen to help with since she didn't want to come out here *under any circumstances*.

I spelled out Ingeborg Caroline Dahl's name for one of the men in baseball caps. The head of Loaf. *Landsorganisasjonen for Ofre og Foresatte*.

"Has it got anything to do with the *Losers' Association*?" baseball cap asks.

"No," I say, bumming a cigarette.

The cool Chief Inspector Kielland registered the moment she arrived that I was the same Igi Heitmann *who* . . . before. And she immediately gets a grip and a perspective on this and the comments the baseball branch make, and afterwards she *doesn't* confuse Loaf with the *Losers' Association*. She has no cigarettes I can bum off her, but she listens keenly and handles me competently as I talk about Ingeborg Caroline Dahl's singular theories. Pictures and the person who painted them. Lives and the person who took them.

The inspector nods and puts her hand on my arm. She has clearly taken a course in *empathy*, I think irritably, and I know that I am unreasonable, post-traumatic or perhaps pre-menstrual.

"Of course I know Helena's mother," she says. "Not personally, but her case. As all the police chiefs do. An unexplained disappearance of this kind is never forgotten, neither by the police nor the bereaved relatives. And it is absolutely right of you to tell me about – this theory of hers. We'll take it into account along with everything else."

But I hear before she says it. *But something*, in the same way that I have said *but* hundreds of times to some unreasonable proposal or desperate demand.

"But I think I should mention to you," continues Eva Cool Kielland, "that this is not the first of Dahl's theories, if I can put it this way. She has flagged up several supposed killers for us. Including the officer leading the inquiry at that time."

We are professionals, each in our own not quite scientific field. We know a *nutcase* when we meet one.

"You don't know if she had a *man friend*?" she asks.

"No," I say. "No idea."

But it is a truism that most murders take place within the family, and I can see that Eva Kielland is mentally exploring the range of Ingeborg Dahl's family. *Nutcases*. Loaf is full of them. For all I know some psychologist may now have taken his place on the social map that Eva Kielland obviously finds so useful, following my own not quite exact science.

"Can we leave it at that?" Kielland asks empathetically before disappearing on her many duties.

"Sure," I say.

All the same I bum another cigarette off one of the baseball boys.

It is the last of my little jobs and I squat against one of the steps smoking.

Otto Troels-Jacobsen's occupation is over even before it started, and there are enough police here to escort him home, though they won't have to carry him out now. I thought I would spare him the irony and loneliness of such an escort, but Eva Kielland, cool and competent, has already talked to him. It is okay with her.

Old men who have to be accompanied home by the police state have loneliness reverberating around them, whether they are demonstrators or not. I was careful how I put it to him since I knew that I couldn't offer him his daughter as company.

And now I am waiting for the only person he could come up with. The kind person who brought the warm water in the morning and the coffee, I suppose. Sjur Aske.

In time old men's eyes go yellow, they tear easily, become shiny and red-rimmed. Perhaps it is the fury that turns them yellow. With his bent back and not resembling a sea captain at all he is like putty in Sjur Aske's hands as the trade union official from the defunct TroJa factories takes him out to his old Golf.

Three abreast, we shuffle up towards Troels-Jacobsen's oak door leading to a sumptuous stairway in Oscarsgate. Either Sjur Aske is not enthusiastic about my coming along, or his eyebrows are permanently knitted under that curly black hair of his. As they were on the news clip at the opening of the exhibition two evenings ago in Grønlandsleiret. Pressure perhaps of a different kind.

The door is a heavy Renaissance copy, covered with small delicate squares in a pure mathematical design without any ostentatious hierarchy. Otto Troels-Jacobsen, who had a kind of empire taken from him, passes the key with trembling hand to Sjur Aske to unlock the door.

Sjur Aske knows his way around in the dark corridor; he helps the old man out of his thick coat, takes his hat and scarf and puts them in their place. Very much at home for an ex-employee, trade union official or not.

In the same way that children's body language can at times be heart-rendingly direct, so can older people's. Otto Troel-Jacobsen's hands hang heavily by his side, his bull neck is bent over his chest and his round tummy, which is no longer that exuberant brushstroke. We could take him anywhere now, so long as it isn't too far.

Sjur Aske puts him to bed. Teeth have to be cleaned first, and all that sort of thing. While Sjur holds open the bathroom door he stares at me challengingly. The way out is *that* way, I interpret without difficulty.

"The lady must have a cognac first," Otto wheezes. "We aren't barbarians, are we."

"The switch is on the right," Sjur Aske says curtly, nodding in the direction of the dark doorway. "You'll find the bottles in the cupboard by the desk."

If you don't count the electric light, which has limited powers anyway, this room is as close to a five-hundred-year-old north European Renaissance style as you will get in Frogner. The dark oak floor has been laid in strict geometrical patterns. Along the wall there is a line of heavy rectangular cupboards, plain save for the intricate square inlays. The high-backed chairs in golden leather or *petit point* embroidery look too comfortable and too valuable to sit on. The Gobelin tapestry in subdued green tones and faded red is a copy, I hope, but a meticulous one for all that. If it is genuine the insurance policy for this room alone would be frightening.

Maybe there is some logic to it. He wasn't able to perform modern number magic with the house, but he was able to adapt his flat to the requirements of another stern, rational and more mathematics-friendly age. As collectable items the objects here are not to be sneezed at either, not *nothing at all*, whatever he says. I stand there like an alien interloper and I would rather go my own way.

Sjur Aske rushes through the room in his high rubber boots, lights a small golden candle by the desk, finds the crystal decanter, pours a glass and heads for the doors.

"To take to bed with him," he says. "Like a teddy bear for adults."

I hear him whisper "Sleep well" and look at the clock. It is half past six. A bit early for the ever so slightly excitable of any age. Ida, for example, will be watching children's TV now.

Sjur Aske offers me a glass from the crystal decanter when he returns; he pours it by the desk standing with his legs apart in his mud-stained boots and his worn jeans. Then he turns to me and his face is at once as lean as a wolf's in the golden light thrown from above, just like his brother's.

"Will you let mè drive you home with this inside me?" he asks.

"All right," I say, thinking that I have seen enough of the police for one day. "Or I can always take a taxi."

He raises the small round glass in front of me and shows me how much alcohol he is legally allowed to take. Apart from the lean face, there is not so much likeness to his brother, but perhaps that is because his head is not shaven.

"Troels-Jacobsen asked me to ring you," I say. "Just you."

He sits down by the desk, a few yards from where I have perched myself on an attractive, uncomfortable Renaissance chair.

"I knew that you were working in Nydalen," I say. "But not that you were so . . . close."

"No?" He moistens his bottom lip with cognac, in much in the same way that Troels-Jacobsen does.

"We are, I suppose. Close. He's old and lonely. And I didn't just work in Nydalen. For Christ's sake, I ran the place for the last few years."

This rolling of his shoulders and his way of sticking his chin in the air. The ambitious trade union boss all of a sudden.

"We can't live by sending e-mails to each other in this town, can we. We have to do something else as well. Apart from what calls itself art, I mean."

This is not a discussion I need to get embroiled in. These proclamations are not directed at me in particular; they just roll out as if they are on a conveyor belt.

"How long have you known him?" I ask. "Otto."

A little laugh. Not a smile in sight.

"All my life, I suppose. He didn't really want to run this lousy business, you know, he just wanted to drop in and be a kind of friendly prince, but in those days he was quite dependent on Father. Of course there were always lots of employees and managers and so on, but Otto liked the idea of the family business, the extended family, building up a paternalistic organisation."

"It sounds as though you saw through that."

"Of course. Because it was so strange that this celebrated figure should hang around at our place and eat stuffed cabbage leaves as if it was something he offered his guests at the Etoile. Don't you think?"

"Emotional deprivation somewhere?"

"An emotional hunger. Perhaps. He certainly needed it."

"Needed what?" I probe. "A normal home life?"

This time the laughter is accompanied by a broad smile.

"A normal frost. They weren't very affectionate, those two."

And then he becomes cautious. "Have you talked to my brother?"

"Yes," I say.

"Were you at the exhibition? When he . . ."

"Yes."

"It was lies, like everything else that spills out of his gob. I know nothing about art, so I have no idea whether what he does is good, and I don't care about it either. But talent is innate in some way. So the talent for lying could be too. He's hardly said a truthful word for as long as he has lived. And he managed to get into trouble all by himself."

With the light over his face and the hollows under his cheekbones, he looks again like the brother he loathes.

"I don't know why he does it," he says. "Where does he get it all from, all the lies? I haven't exchanged a single word with him for . . . my God, it must be at least fifteen years. Since Father died. But he's not interested in that, if it is not public, can't be hung and exhibited so that other people can see it. I shouldn't be surprised, should I? He did exactly the same with Mother and Father. But he could have just left it at painting them."

"Did he talk about them in public?"

"Oh yes. About the terrible poverty, as if we were something special, as if we weren't all pretty poor – yes, most of us – in the Fifties. And then it wasn't even true. Father had work, we had a house to live in. He describes his childhood as if he grew up in rags. As if Father was a block of ice and Mother was, I don't know, a *mad woman*, because she had a job doing washing or perhaps she was a little depressed at times. It is such crap."

I sit a few paces from him, but the air around him is thick with the bitterness. He gives it off like rays; it settles on the darkness surrounding him and creeps inside me. Is this what he *is*? his brother might have asked. Is this the core of the man in the feeble light behind the desk that doesn't belong to him? If so, what combination of bones would be able to characterise him?

"He's made a good living off the poverty, over the years."

Is this what it is? Is this the root of it? Money?

Then he yawns, the best way in the world to show you want to change the subject. Whatever it is that makes you short of oxygen when you're talking about something unpleasant has probably got something to do with what his brother calls *lumps*. That is true of my experience.

"I expect he's asleep by now," Sjur Aske says, looking past me to the open door. Beautifully stage-managed. Conjurers do that, too, look away and divert your attention from the little trick.

"How was it," I ask, "that you ran the factory, as you say?"

"I knew it inside out, didn't I? That's why."

"But, as I heard it, it went badly at the end?"

I meet this almost daily, this cautious expression that moves across his face, this twofold wish: to speak and to keep your mouth shut. Ambivalence.

"The people who do the paperwork," he says sullenly, "can make everything look the way they want. It didn't go that badly, but it's true that with more investment the surplus would have been greater. Somehow that's what the little prince should have fixed. Investment."

"The little prince?"

"Martin Andersen. Mr Dangerous Sports."

"Did you know him?"

"I met him. In Nydalen. The few times that he was there."

"What types of dangerous sport did he go in for?"

"Anything that could give him a kick and show how macho he was, I think. Paragliding, rafting. Just nothing *normal*."

"It sounds as if you didn't particularly like him."

"I don't think I had any grounds for it. But I was proved right. All the same I didn't think . . ."

"You didn't think what?"

"We shouldn't talk badly of the dead. But if he was supposed to take care of Otto's interests he didn't get very far. You could say."

Then he laughs.

"I've never seen Otto so furious as after the last board meeting. I thought he was going to have a heart attack. But, by God, he survived."

"What happened at the board meeting?"

"Er, nothing except that Roll found he had the majority. That came . . . as a surprise."

More brief laughter.

"Weren't you furious too? I mean with the demonstrations and . . ."

"Of course I was furious. But I didn't take it *personally*. She isn't my daughter. Or sister, more like."

The little glass is lifted to his lips, the rest of the cognac goes down in one gulp and a shiver runs through him. He puts his hands on the desk. They are thin, with prominent bluish veins like tiny slithering snakes.

He half gets up.

"How did you know Ingeborg Dahl?" I ask.

"Who's that?"

"The woman who was found dead in Otto's garden," I say.

"Aha. I'm sorry, I have no idea who she is. Wasn't it an overdose?"

"She was strangled," I tell him.

His hands are stretched across the leatherbound writing surface, his body bent forward as if ready to jump over it.

"And she was at the demonstration, wasn't she?"

"Possibly. There were so many people there, different kinds of people."

Different kinds perhaps, I think, but not that many.

"Shall we go?"

It isn't a question. It is a command.

"You should come forward as a witness," I say.

"As a witness?"

"You passed me on Grønlandsleiret, don't you remember?"

"No," he says. "When was that?"

"The evening before Ingeborg Dahl was reported missing," I say. "The evening she disappeared. Or died. She lived there. Weren't you on your way to see her?"

"On my way to see her? Why on earth should I have been? You must be mistaken."

He turns off the lamp. The wall light by the door is on, but the light doesn't reach us and the only illumination we have is the fading light from the windows and the limited reflected light from the unchanging dignified silence of Oscarsgate.

On the little table under the mirror in the hall there is a glass of cognac with dregs in the bottom. Otto's? Did the old man put it there and then shuffle back to bed, or did he stand by the sitting room door listening? His bedroom door is closed; behind it he is either asleep or lying awake. Sjur Aske pointedly ignores the glass and holds the outside door open for me.

If the old man didn't want us to see that he had been listening, I think, wasn't it stupid of him to leave the glass there. On the other hand, Otto Troels-Jacobsen doesn't seem to be stupid.

Sjur Aske's old Golf is parked between two deformed-looking family cars which, they say in certain parts of town to the west of here, can carry five children.

"Where are you going?" I ask after getting in beside him. "Is Grünerløkka out of your way?"

"I'm going home."

To my left his profile is sharply defined and dark, the curls over his forehead black and pointed like thorns.

"To Maridalen. It's not far out of my way."

He scarcely says a word during the drive and I don't know if it was me he was talking to up in Otto Troels-Jacobsen's Renaissance room either.

"What are you going to do now?" I ask while we wait for green in Alexander Kiellands plass. "Now that the factory has been closed down."

"Adapt," Sjur Aske says with a rough little laugh. "Isn't that what we're supposed to do?"

19

THE STORY IS long and complicated although it's mainly about hamburgers and the freebies that come with them. I am not in the slightest bit interested, but I listen, absorbed. Because I get it anyway; I get the long, halting story about hamburgers and the freebies, and the torrent of experiences an intense four-year-old's passion can give rise to.

Because I need it, because I need the reassurance of listening to her chirpy voice, because I need to know that I'm still an integral part of her life and experiences, I let her chatter for a bit longer than she should. She is still babbling away even while she's cleaning her teeth.

But it may also mean that she will dream about them. I don't begrudge her hamburger dreams. The freebies come in lurid colours and take pride of place on her bedside table. The happiness *objects* bring is rich and varied: here a Renaissance cupboard, there a plastic freebie.

Benny is standing in the sitting room, holding the phone at arm's length, nodding mutely at it and looking for someone to relieve him.

"The asshole," Bella is saying as I take over. "He's buggered off."

"Aske?" I ask.

"No, damn it. Roll, of course. Gone to his tower in London or a private island for all I know. Who do you think will have to sort out the *mad* hordes? *Mother,*" she snarls. "Bella, alone as always, against the cultural and the crime correspondents. Igi darling, could the pervert have *arranged* this?"

"Roll?"

"*Father,* darling. I mean, a dead little drug addict in the garden. That'll look *great* tomorrow, won't it?"

"Bella, first of all she wasn't a drug addict. And she isn't simply dead, she was murdered. Do you seriously believe that your father would have arranged something like this to destroy your little event?"

"Is that a bit over the top?" Bella seems to consider this for a moment or else she just pauses to strike up a Superlight. In any case I hear the click of her little gold lighter.

"You never know with him," she continues. "Father holds grudges for such a long time. And Igi, they're *occupying* the whole of the pavement outside, and I mean usually you can sort things out with cultural correspondents with a bit of real *alcohol*, but it's a complete waste of time with this lot. Perhaps I should set Rita on them?"

"Do that," I say.

Bella continues her tirade with increasing injections of invective, but there are reassuring signs in it as it is familiar territory. Yet there is one disturbing feature in her torrent and for that reason I cut her off.

"Everything went well with your father," I say. "Well, under the circumstances."

"The man is *immortal*, as you know," she mumbles, but then seems to have no further need to talk. That may have been why she rang in the first place.

"She has a point," Benny says afterwards. "it does look like an attempt to sabotage Roll."

"Dire sabotage," I say – to quote Bella. "One or two murders for . . . for *what purpose?*"

Benny is feeding the houseplants with what I believe is dried fish bone and he is quietly humming one of David Bowie's songs to them. It seems weird to me somehow, but it is better than songs about troll mothers, on which there is a total ban, unless it is to Ida, though he insists that the plants like them too.

"To punish Roll for the attack on TroJa, as it were?" I continue. "Wouldn't it be natural to bump off the man himself in that case?"

"Natural," Benny mumbles. "Please, you're beginning to sound like Bella." Anyway it's difficult to get at Roll, I would think. Glass towers, helicopters, private islands."

"And an eighty-year-old man would do that?"

"Maybe, or someone who wasn't fond of Roll. Sjur Aske, for example. As a theory," Benny continues, "it's no more unlikely than the idea that Aske did it. Have you noticed, by the way, that those sweet little photographers have gone?"

146

"They weren't sweet and they're at Bella's," I say. They can't be everywhere.

"There we are," Benny says, taking the dead leaves off the coffee plant. "Action, you know. Who would have believed you would ever succeed in appealing to some editor's *morality*?"

As he stands by the window I notice how very attractive his back is and whether I believe in his morality theory or not is of no importance. I am tired; I lie down on the sofa and I am very happy to have him. Either it is Benny's appeal or more pressing issues mean that Bente ceases to figure in the pages of the newspaper. I am happy for him and for her. And Ida as well. But I have a feeling that it will be difficult for certain people to keep their hands off the picture of Bente for the morning editions.

"Tea?" he asks.

"Yes please."

The pile of manuscripts sitting on the low table in front of the sofa would have been cleared away if Bente had been around. Benny is not as untidy as I am, nor as pernickety or as obsessed with the symmetry of things as Bente.

"Strictly confidential" the top sheet reads. "Under no circumstances to be shown to unauthorised personnel." Women, I think to myself, can never really be considered to be lacking the necessary authority.

Aske's forthcoming biography amounts to about a hundred pages of manuscript. Here and there the author has stuck yellow Post-its with notes about which pictures she wants to illustrate the text. Benny has put a cross by some of them or added "ok"; in a couple of places he has written big question marks and in one place "halfwit".

It is not a biography in the traditional sense – real biographies aren't written until the subject is dead – and Aske is not that retrospective yet. The text comprises overblown and complex tracts about everything that Aske has so much as touched, and apparently unedited interviews with Aske himself.

Since there aren't any illustrations yet the manuscript is the perfect soporific. Aske acclaims his own status as an autodidact and holds forth on the damaging effect of all formal training. On page twenty-nine he calls Otto Troels-Jacobsen "phoney", and he hasn't anything very nice to say about his colleagues either, not that that is surprising.

"Anything interesting in it?" Benny asks, returning with the tea, made from something a bit like grass that one of his homeopathic friends recommended him. "I've only read bits."

"He has to concede," it says, "that Francis Bacon was 'good at painting'," I say.

"Oh dear," Benny says.

"And that Giacometti 'was essentially on to something'."

"Oh no," Benny says. "So embarrassing."

And it is.

"Did you know he had been to sea?" I ask after a while.

"Well, yes," Benny says. "For three months or thereabouts. He went to Amsterdam and did a load of dope."

"That is obvious," I say. "Are you sure boiled grass is that healthy? A small espresso might be nice."

I ignore his disapproving look and flick through several years of Aske the street artist and notable pickpocket in Paris.

"Have you got to the bit about the dwarf?" Benny asks, returning with the coffee.

"Yes."

"Isn't it fantastic?"

"The bit about the dwarf? Yes, it is."

But it is not until I am well into the text that I wake up. Perhaps it is the coffee, perhaps my professional training, but I suspect it's more than that. Aske's *childhood* stands out as being a great deal more sensational than anything in his adult life, fame and dwarves notwithstanding.

This is one of the things that is difficult to get some of my clients to believe: my unstinting admiration for the fact that they are standing at all. Clearly there are some people who are stuffed full with such admiration for themselves, and their superficial self-love camouflages a deep contempt for others. But as a rule it is the other way round: the laboriously repeated stories about endless humiliation and deprivation tell you more than anything about the will to live which the survivors neither recognise nor show any respect for.

"Doesn't it get boring in the long term?" Benny sometimes asks when I come home from work. "All the *complaining*?"

It does. But the unusual, innovative methods for surviving that my clients teach me more than outweigh the daily tedium. An apple tree for refuge here, the sweet delights of a giant chocolate bar there –

they are flashes of gold to help keep a life and a world going. The apple tree generally represents escape and the chocolate consolation and both are objects of boundless contempt. As if it were an aim to be able to live without escaping and ever being consoled.

It comes as no surprise, therefore, that there are no flashes of gold in Aske's description of his childhood. Flashes of gold are the true secret, and good sense tells us to hide them well, for they really must not be stolen. They exist somewhere in this terrible deprivation and there is some connection with all the bones, with the jagged spruce trees he surrounds himself with, but the tips of trees and the bones are more visible.

Methods of punishment. Silence. The father's blank face. The monstrous mother's sudden, uncontrollable changes of mood: the clammy, fumbling hands that could be so kind, and then the brutality in the cellar, in the barn where the dead *cat* was found. This refined, possibly premeditated terror, nurtured over many years, that exploded all over him. On and on until the moment – mercifully, blessedly – she saw fit to stop.

He looked for the key, for the ever elusive *something* that could bring it to an end, prevent it from happening. A word, a gesture or a thought. But he didn't find anything, for he was a child and very vulnerable. Victims of torture are also tormented by this: the mind's intense search for something that can stop the savagery, the pain. Torture sets our survival instincts against us, demands that we should be able to prevent what we are powerless to confront.

It is the ultimate cruelty, the belief of our consciousness in its own superiority. If I could only find the *explanation*, then I won't be hurt again. The world goes to pieces every time this fails to happen. But of course there is not one religion, not one ideology, not one amazing technological advance that is not based on this demand and this notion: the dream of the end of pain.

But the pain doesn't end on even one of the eight neatly typed pages describing Aske's years in his childhood home. It is razor-sharp, monstrous and exacting: Look at me, it says. Do you think you can hide from me? That I won't *find you*?

Next to the silence of my soul, which always comes on when I encounter reports such as this, I have another pressing cause for unrest as I put the manuscript away. It has nothing to do with this sharp collision of worlds: an atrocious childhood on A4 and a Benny in the sitting room fiddling around cheerfully and rather arbitrarily. He turns off a light here, folds a newspaper there, takes a teapot and cups into the kitchen, tidying up as if it's the end of the evening. He maintains order as needs must, and whether or not he does it to keep from falling into the abyss makes his modest rituals no less important. The tightened strings of unrest within me are not due to dizziness after such a clash between universes.

The reason is this: Aske has exactly the background I imagine that a deeply tormented, dangerous human predator would have.

Even if his brother maintains that it is all lies.

"Take me in your arms," I say later, once it is dark. "Comfort me."

That is how the relationship between sexuality and brutality has been interpreted for almost a hundred years: as the latent urge to die and to kill, since we are so contemptuous of comfort, of the body and the soul.

20

THERE IS A snake around my legs. It slithers along my knees, rests heavily and sweatily against my skin and I want it off me, off the tangled bedclothes it is hiding in, away from my body. The snake noses the back of my knee and *tickles* me, and somewhere in my drowsiness my brain registers with increasing panic that it is *scratching* my thigh with what must be snake claws.

I am about to rid myself of it with a panic-stricken blow when I realise that snakes don't have claws and that my daughter is happily riding something that is not a snake or as far as she is concerned probably not my legs either, but a pony exactly matching in size, that has happened to find its way under my duvet.

She is ecstatic, of course, and has red blotches on her cheeks, probably an early sexual experience while galloping over the prairie astride my knee. Sensible parents shouldn't interfere in any of this, and I am far too tired to do so. Anyway I should be grateful, I suppose, that I haven't encouraged some ghastly trauma by dragging her into all this.

"Yaa," she whinnies. "Yaa!"

"Was it good for *you*," I mumble into the pillow.

"What did you say?" Ida asks, interested.

"Nothing," I answer. As is well known, that is the one answer in the world that makes a child's ears prick up, one that no-one, whatever their age, will accept. Nor does Ida. She hits me instead. Small fists rain down on the duvet without much power and do no damage.

"Silly," she wheezes. "Silly, silly, silly." Then she doesn't want to be held, but wriggles out of Silly's grip and rushes out of the bedroom, to never quite as silly Daddy. Silly goes to the shower. Embarrassing confession: even soft blows hurt when the skin or the soul is already sore.

While I dry myself off I can hear her laughter from the living room, breathless, wild, thin outbursts into the ceiling. It isn't Daddy who is making her laugh. Aske is crouching on the sitting-room floor and Ida is standing between his legs, thrusting her head against his chin and laughing her little girl laugh.

He looks terrible, pale and emaciated, and it seems as if he is baring his teeth rather than smiling.

Death and the Maiden prettily laid out on our Sunday morning living room floor, and I have no reason to be frightened. My daughter is standing between the legs of a sort of acquaintance and I am waving too, participating in the general grimacing competition, twisting my lips into the awful ape-like grin I am known to have mastered, and the knife turning in my stomach is a mother's hysteria. They must look like both *The Satyr Eating His Child* and *Hommage à Helena*, but the world doesn't consist of images and associations, it consists of Sunday mornings, and where's bloody Benny?

"I used the opportunity," Aske says, "to get away last night. No photographer fancies standing on the pavement all night, we know that, so I went up to the workshop at five. I never invite anyone there, so they don't know where it is. You have to fix yourself up with a bolt-hole in life, don't you?"

His parchment-white hands rest against Ida's hips, her small fat fists settle with child-like intimacy on his thighs. We laugh. Benny appears from the kitchen, having made breakfast. I find some domestic excuse to drag him back in there.

"What's he doing here?" I whisper.

"I don't quite know," Benny whispers. "He came to the door while you were having a shower and I couldn't not invite him in. Perhaps he's hungry?"

Ida was given a kind of killing machine by Karsten, an Action Man with bulging muscles and an authentic laser weapon which she is whirling round the kitchen. The doll inside the doll; Ida with a dangerous little man in her hands. They are both firing away.

"Bang," Aske says, following her into the kitchen. What is it that makes young children like weapons so much? Makes them want to pretend to kill people?

"They're very small," Benny says. "I might carry weapons if I were 70 centimetres shorter than everyone else around me."

Ida kills without mercy, it seems.

Aske looks starved, but he doesn't want anything except coffee. He sits on the edge of the kitchen stool and smokes restlessly while we eat, running his bony hand through his hair. He worked all night, he says, without achieving very much with all the disturbances going on.

"All this *unpleasantness*," he says, his gaze resting on Ida's head, which is bent over her bowl of cornflakes. Benny nods. He is wearing a sloppy T-shirt and he is unshaven. He doesn't look as if he has ever learnt a sex game, never mind *taught* one. As for me, I suppose I look frightened, frightened or stressed, or both.

"We look like a month of wet Sundays," I say. "The only person with a bit of life in her is Ida."

"And she only wants to shoot people," Benny says.

Aske laughs then. Loud and dry. The laughter turns into a cough, not a particularly bad one when I consider my psychiatric experience, but bad enough.

"Shouldn't you get some sleep?" Benny asks. "If you've been working all night, I mean."

"I can't," Aske says. "Not yet. It's got something to do with rhythm. With sleep you have to wait for the right moment. As with many other important things."

He lights another cigarette and accepts another cup of coffee.

"Bella phoned me last night," he says. "She told me about . . ."

"Not now," I interrupt, nodding towards Ida. It takes a few seconds before he gets the hint.

"Of course," he says. "Of course. So, what do you do on Sundays? What does *Ida* do on Sundays?"

"Walk," Ida says. "Me and Daddy go for a walk."

And Aske and I are allowed to go along with them.

He is a wading bird, out of place among the preening, promenading, sportswear-clad families in Bygdøy. Long and ungainly in an over-sized coat that flutters behind him. That is interesting, he says, as if to convince himself that it really is interesting that there are so many people out walking. In flocks, almost. The flocks aren't over-whelming yet – it is still too early – but in an hour's time people will be queuing up.

153

Some people recognise him, others look away as he passes and then turn round to take a look. It is not easy to say whether he notices it; in any case, he gesticulates a lot at the beginning, speaks at the top of his voice and describes enormous circles in the air with his hands as we walk through the sparse, leafless forest behind Kongsgården.

If he wants to avoid *photographers*, I think, this is not the ideal hiding place. I presume there are enough mobile phones in the pockets of all those nice padded jackets everyone's wearing. I imagine the caption would read "Murder Therapist, Sex Games Bente and Bones Aske out for a walk with delightful small *child*."

"Is this really so clever?" I mutter to Benny as a woman in regulation green velvet cord three-quarter-length trousers with the standard dog for the West Side, a drooling setter, stares at us as she passes.

"Clever," he says, "it's Sunday. Do you think it would have been a good idea to take him to the *gallery*?"

The sky is like glass, a dazzling blue. Ida kicks at leaves and squeals, scurrying about like a puppy between the trees a secure metre or so off the path; Benny, who knows the rules of this game, takes up pursuit.

"I'm coming now and I'm going to catch you," he shouts. In among the trees. Over the treacherous forest floor with the roots and dry branches to trip over and the strange, frightening distorted shadows that come out of nowhere. The little girl and the big man and her rapturous, panic-stricken shrieks. Of course they are preparing for something, escape and pleasure and embraces and knowledge of the dangers between the tall black trees.

"No, no," she gasps, meaning he should carry on frightening her. No when you mean yes. And when in-between you mean no. Benny doesn't make a mistake, so there are breaks and unrestrained laughter before the pursuit starts anew. Perhaps there is a rhythm there. Aske watches them.

"Bella sa— . . .," he begins. "She told me about this woman. In the garden. It must have been awful?"

"Frightening more than anything," I say. "No. Not that either. It was sad. Shocking. As if she had been humiliated. As if I humiliated her by looking at her."

"Or as if *she* humiliated you by letting you see her? Weren't you just a tiny bit angry?"

"She was dead," I say.

"And still caused you a lot of trouble. Do you think it's always like that, that death is humiliating?"

She had talked about him. Thought about him quite a lot. Hated him. I don't want her to be treated in an abstract way on a Sunday morning in this civilised forest.

"Her name was Ingeborg Dahl," I say. "We talked about her recently. 'The Helena Dahl case' and *Hommage*. Why did you paint that picture anyway?"

"It was about innocence, you know," he says. "There is something so provocative about innocence. No-one likes to admit it, but there is. There was a lot of fuss about that picture. People make a fuss about so many strange things. As if it is *tasteless* to depict the simplest connections. Some people think it is beautiful. The picture, that is."

He is right about that. There is an insistent, painful beauty about it. It landed right smack bang in the middle of the intense publicity around the case and on top of that made him famous overnight.

"Ingeborg Dahl thought you killed her daughter," I say.

He laughs at that. A brief, harsh and bitter laugh.

"That's original, if nothing else," he says, still smiling. "I don't mean to be indelicate or maybe that's what I am, but that is a pretty *stupid* connection to make. You know, the connection between life and art. If I had done anything as repulsive as that I wouldn't have *painted* it."

That is a very facile response, but I don't get another chance to ask him if he could have resisted the temptation to paint or film it, if he had done it.

"Bella said that she was strangled," Aske says. "Is that correct?"

Could be *morbid curiosity* and if it isn't, what is it? Life and work? The need for a story, for information, just like Edevart Riel?

"As far as I know it is," I say. "She was strangled either there in the garden or somewhere else. The latter is probably the more logical, although Troels-Jacobsen doesn't potter around much down there I imagine."

But he did ask me to have a look at his Haukeland sculpture, I remember.

"You've known him since you were a child, haven't you," I say. "How angry do you think Troels-Jacobsen is about losing control of TroJa?"

The short laugh again. Louder this time, so that it attracts the attention of people in the queue in front of the waffle stand in Paradisbukta.

"You'll have to ask my brother about that," he says. "Though Otto can get very angry, as I remember, when he wants to. I've heard him yell. He doesn't have much finesse, even if he gives that impression. Do you know that he has never bought anything from me? Stupid perhaps, or spiteful. But one can manage without him. If one wants."

"When he did he yell at you?"

"A long time ago. It's of no importance."

He strolls in front of me down to the water's edge. Ida stumbles over the rock on her way towards us holding a shell she wants to show us.

"Something lived in there once," Aske, the bone specialist, says. "A strange kind of creature. All soft and lumpy."

"Where is it now?" Ida asks.

"It's moved," he answers with the same seriousness as her.

"Then it hasn't got a shell any more."

"No."

"What will it do?" she asks, her fat little fist still resting in his.

"Well. Maybe move around in the sea, with nothing on. Could be worse, couldn't it?"

Benny has brought a woollen blanket and tea in a thermos. We sit on the uneven rock with our faces turned towards the Fornebu landscape and a chilly sun. We look like all the other small groups here, just another couple with a child and a family friend who didn't get enough sleep on Saturday night. On the other side of the bay someone is lighting a barbecue.

Ida tentatively throws stones at a duck and is told to stop, after which she resumes more legitimate activities with the kind of knowing look that says that she hasn't forgotten what stones can be used for.

"I found some older works of yours," Benny says. "That is, Igi met the owner, a golfer called Middlethon. The pictures are hanging on a posh sitting room wall and look a little strange, but they were thoughtfully hung and the photos came out well. One is called *Home* and could certainly be used and the other was a portrait. But we're not interested in that, are we?"

This infuriates Aske. He rocks his upper body and folds his long arms over his stomach.

"That's why I came to see you," he says. "There's not going to be a biography. You can forget the whole business. That idiot of a writer woman is making some quite ridiculous demands and is impossible to talk to. I've had enough. I'm not going to waste my time messing around with *amateurs*."

Benny has also got a little pebble. Now it is going from one hand to the other in an even rhythm before a fist tightens around it.

"You don't mean that," he says. "We're much too far down the line for that."

"If it is money you're worried about you'll have to talk to the publishers," Aske says coldly. "It's not my problem. They'll have some standard clause or other to take care of that. But there won't be a book, pure and simple."

"But why not? If it is the text that is the problem . . ."

"Yes, exactly, it's not the pictures," Aske hisses. "It's that talentless, self-centred bitch. There's nothing to discuss, it's over. Finished."

"Is it the content that bothers you?" I ask.

"What's it's got to do with you?" His eyebrows have locked into a tight V over the top of his nose, and he is sweating around the hairline. "Your husband will manage okay on his own, I imagine. Or have you got a little mortgage you're worried about? There are plenty more nutters to cure, aren't there?"

The atmosphere has changed suddenly. Ida looks up from whatever she's doing in the sand. She is clutching a wet stick she is using as a drill.

"I am aware that it wasn't correct of me," I say, "and it wasn't Benny's fault, but I have in fact read the manuscript. I think it was interesting. What is it that you don't like?"

Maybe he always laughs in this rough, convulsive way. It sounds solitary, in the way that angry weeping does.

"It is difficult to keep agreements, I know," he says, getting up. "It may amuse you to know that you are among the few who will ever read it. A privilege of sorts."

"But I'm sure changes can be made to the text if you're not happy," Benny says.

"It's not the text we're squabbling over," Aske says as he stands above us, wrapping his coat around him.

"What is it then?"

"What do people normally squabble about? Percentages. Status. Money. The hack wants to use me as a ladder. The dwarf on the giant's shoulders, you know. Well, she won't get it. Can I get a taxi anywhere around here?"

He waves vaguely to Ida with his bony hand but gets no response.

"It's really *nice* here," he says before leaving us. "Sorry to ruin the Sunday idyll. I am so gauche with things like this."

Benny trudges after him up to the road with his hands deep in his jacket pockets. When they stop by the waffle stand they find they have a few spectators. Aske silences them with a long look, then he pats Benny on the shoulder and fights his way through the oncoming stream of prams and leisurewear-clad middle classes leaving the car park in Huk. At the top of the hill he disappears behind the trees. He doesn't look like the man in my dream, the man in the grip of the Pain Machine, apart from the fact that they are both so thin and have such grimy, pain-racked faces. There may be enough similarity to explain why, as he disappears, the dream about the Pain Machine returns to me as a flashback.

"What do you think is he frightened of?" I ask when Benny comes back. "Stories about his childhood?"

"Maybe. Or that bit about Bacon being good at painting – all things considered."

Benny gives Ida the big fatherly smile. She falls for it and resumes her excavating.

"I think he wants something bigger," he says. "He regrets choosing a not-established writer. Perhaps he wants a monument, as it were. All this retrospective stuff has gone to his head."

"You don't think it's about money?"

"You never know. Well, it'll pass. It's only nerves."

Nerves don't always pass. It is not only exhibitions that are retrospective. And life and art are seldom altogether disconnected from each other.

"Bollocks to him, anyway," Benny says.

"What did you say?" Ida asks.

"Nothing," Benny says, suddenly hurling his pebble at a gull. His daughter chortles merrily.

21

BENNY REGISTERS WITH sadness that his moral appeal for fairness has not been effective. He is sitting at the kitchen table flicking through the Sunday papers and, though Bente is not given any prominence, she is still there. There is something called a follow-up and that has outweighed Benny's appeal. Fortunately not prominent enough to create a new siege of Markveien, but Bella is probably still under the cosh. Roll's glass tower too, if it is sensitive to flash. Nor does Villa Troels stand out as cool logic in physical form, either.

Ida has joined the health sector and equipped herself with her little stethoscope to take care of the cuddly animals she has just slaughtered. But, since surgery is her preferred branch within medicine, it is not certain that they will fare any better for that. She is not the only one playing games; while preparing Sunday lunch I am rehearsing a number of strategies for getting away. Not far away. Not for long. Just long enough to find out something about money.

What do people squabble about? Percentages. Status. Money. Aske said that. He should know.

Bella's money and her father's. Joakim Roll's money and Martin Andersen, who must have known quite a lot about it but who is now dead. While frying the chantarelle mushrooms in the pan, I think about him and his pumped-up lover who also knows a bit about money and grieves in such a strange way. Edevart Riel. The one who was wide-awake because he didn't dare to sleep.

Benny is peacefully drinking wine at the kitchen table and when I refuse a glass I am playing games too. I may need the car, I say to myself.

Ida, for her part, needs kitchen towels.

"Bandages," she says with a charming smile.

"I talked to Gran this morning," Benny says and gets a stern, old biddy's look from the direction of the stove.

"You talked to who?"

"To your mother."

"Gran" is not one of my favourite expressions. "Gran" has stuck with Ida, but like songs about troll mothers it has also been affected by the ban on the childish behaviour by adults. It is a sensible ban, but there are also other motives at play. I am hypersensitive to Mother's and Benny's post-Ida friendship, despite it having lasted all her life and the fact that I know I ought to appreciate it.

"What would you say to a few days on Jomfruland?" my childish husband asks.

Mother and Benny have quiet morning chats about me. Before Ida they only communicated stiffly and needed me as a go-between. Nowadays they meet at a café. Two ladies stuffing themselves with cream cakes work out what they want to buy for Ida, then go straight out and get it. Of course I am jealous and I know it, but that hasn't been a great help to me so far.

"You sound like Dr Welle," Benny's old dear says, neatly avoiding any mention of Mother. "Do you want to send me somewhere to convalesce?"

A few days in a holiday cabin, a voice says inside me. To recover, to think about something else, to get things in *perspective*. Nice crashing waves, a little sea air will do you good, I hear. It isn't Benny saying that, it is just the old dear inside me.

"I don't want to send you anywhere," Benny says. "She and Karsten are travelling down early tomorrow morning and were wondering if we wanted to join them. And if Aske is serious about withdrawing the book I've got the whole week free. I was going to use these days to concentrate on him and his bones."

Staying in town is not that enticing, understandably enough, either for Bente's male counterpart or for his daughter. Escape is no bad thing.

"And you," he adds.

"Yes?"

"Could use a walk to . . . or something."

Ida's teddy bear protests noisily about an unavoidable operation.

"Do you think she would be very unhappy if I didn't come?" I ask, nodding towards the surgeon.

"Nooo," he answers. "It'll be fine. But there are others to think about."

"You'll have Mother," I say. Escape is not to be sneezed at, but then again it is not action. Sound advice for nagging thoughts of all kinds: check the sources.

"Yes, of course," Benny says. "I will, that's true."

"Edevart Riel should know something about Martin Andersen's position in TroJa," I say, frying, turning, fiddling with the mushrooms in the pan Benny is so proud of because it has something known as cooking quality.

"Check the sources?" my husband suggests.

"Yes indeed," I say.

"Don't do anything silly then," he says. He gets a kiss for that, the man who, on occasion, likes to strut about in his push-up bras and his ridiculous high-heeled shoes.

"So, that's very well done," the surgeon says in the sitting room. "Just try to think about something else for a moment."

"What do you think she's doing with it?" I ask.

"Something gruesome no doubt," Benny says.

It is a deal. A simple calculation while the chantarelles get their dollop of cream. He gets his trip to the sea, I get my little evening out if I put the surgeon to bed first.

"Now, naughty teddy bear. Lie still," Ida says. "That's the way, yes. Oops! There was no need to cry, was there?"

"Did we teach her that?" I ask.

"I hope not," Benny says.

"The teddy bear has lost its leg," Ida wails. "Naughty teddy bear!"

The surgeon has gone to sleep and Benny is slowly getting the necessary gear together for Jomfruland as I try Edevart Riel's phone number.

The high-pitched voice that answers is welcoming and over-excited and, no, the girl can't find Ed *right now*, but just come anyway.

The flat has taken over the stairwell, judging by the sounds coming from it. The whole of the top landing under the glass roof has been converted into a provisional hall with a good-sized palm tree on the right of the door and an overburdened coat stand on the left. By the side of the palm tree, as if to increase the flora, hangs an elegantly framed Robert Mapplethorpe photo of that rare kind, *sans* penis, though the light grey *Anthurium scherzerianum* is erect enough.

Six floors below I can follow the vibrations of the bass line through the concrete, two floors below the digital treble whipping beat. If a wake is being held in this penthouse no-one's keeping quiet about it. The door is wide open and it is the only one on this floor, so I assume I haven't come to the wrong place.

But if I'm in any doubt there is a name on the door; Martin it says. And Edevart. Inside, a large grinning frogface, copper green and childish, and I assume, deliberately vulgar in contrast to the cool black and white elegance of the photograph. Inside no doubt there are some of those expensive Alessi utensils in the kitchen as well.

There is little point in knocking, so I go straight into the hallway.

"Hi," says a sun-tanned young girl leaning against the grey wall, clinging to an equally youthful sun-tanned boy. More precisely, she's the one being clung to. He is enthusiastically drooling down her neck, and she is only half paying attention. Opposite on the wall facing them is a full-length mirror and she is more interested in what is going on there.

"I'm looking for Edevart," I say.

"Who isn't," she says, running a lazy finger through her gently cascading hair. "Everyone is *checking on* Ed. He is being looked after like a big baby. Like an *enormous* baby."

She laughs a little at that. Her stomach curves in and 20 centimetres of it are exposed between her trousers, which rest on her hips, and her tight top, which ends above a navel with a little ring in it. The boy's sun-tanned hand is fumbling around her chest, as if he is searching for her breasts. Perhaps it was her I spoke to on the phone, but I doubt that she remembers.

"Will I find him in there?" I ask, nodding in the direction of the wide doorway from where the music is emanating.

She nods amiably, about as uninterested in whether I find Edevart as in the success the blond-haired boy has in his explorations.

The room is enormous; the broad arches stretch 20 metres across and on the longer sides meet something rare in attic flats – windows at head height, two parallel rows of them beneath the raised dormer sections of the roof that rest on the lintel over the uprights. The whole of the short side is made of glass, from the pitch roof down to the floor; in the middle it opens out into two glass doors that at this moment are releasing whirling torrents of sound over the terrace and roofs, out into the deep blue evening sky.

Black leather Le Corbusier-style sofas, low, varnished cherrywood tables, scattered elegant, slim furniture for sitting and contemplating, or for more independent enjoyment of the impressive sound system than is possible at this moment. Pure style. The fun element is the zebra-striped cushions on the sofa – they are *flaws* of just the right kind. In here it is chilly, airy and right now very dope-laden, which is to say, urban.

This is what happens at some point after the age of thirty: anyone ten years younger, not even that, becomes incredibly attractive. The beauty of young bodies such as those surrounding me now increases year by year, as does my sympathy for old goats.

People smile at me from the sofas and the armchairs and I get a hug from an ecstatically happy young man in combat kit. It is not warm in this jungle of his, but his scanty outfit reveals his tanned, smooth muscles: biceps, triceps, pectorals and what they will surely here call the abdominal muscles.

The weapons he carries I am led to believe are exclusively peace-loving, uppers and inners and downers and outers of varied and impressively coordinated kinds, a whole arsenal, but tablets don't take up much room, so he might have the whole lot in his baggy pockets. I thank him for his offer and my stupidity is pardoned with good grace. Each to his *own stuff*, each to his own *fix*, even temperance is regarded with surprised tolerance by the urban guerilla. They are *love machines*, they and their youthful beauty will last for ever, or at least until Monday.

Edevart is, when I ask for him, in some unspecified place close by, and in the meantime I tear myself away from the young bodies – it is not seemly to stare at objects like that, even though that is partly their purpose – and I devote myself to the study of another, more mysterious beauty.

In the middle of the room, a short distance away from the end wall, facing the hallway and the kitchen, there is a dark, green world covered with glass. It is more than a metre long and a third of it is an aquarium; it is less than half-filled with water and there is room for luxuriant, humid foliage too. There are no fish here, but amphibians, soft white midway creatures that need access to water to swim in and plants to climb up.

In the big terrarium there are salamanders with slim green bodies standing motionless on a stem or staring hypnotically from a leaf, under a rock, as speckled as the shadows beneath it. There are many different kinds of frogs here: some heavy, some lethargic, others surprisingly big and some tiny scarlet ones.

It is the complete stillness that fascinates, the immense patience that is only broken a split second before the body in response to a mental impulse disappears or reappears somewhere else, on a different leaf. It is a world of extremes: absolute calm and absolute activity. Between them there is nothing, not even so much as a blink of a moist eyelid.

I see a reflection of his face before I realise that he is standing behind me, because of the music, I suppose, or the hypnotic effect of this world of stillness or sudden movement.

"They eat flies," he says. "Usually. And they don't need to be fed more than once a week. We had a snake for a while and it survived for a month on a single mouse. Incredibly long period of digestion. It didn't move at all for something like ten days after eating. It's a form of sleep or coma, but for the most part a time of risk; it is never more vulnerable to being attacked than at this time, when it has killed and eaten. Satiation is a dangerous state to be in."

Then he laughs, his strong face bursting open into a broad, rather jaded smile.

"And no," he adds. "I've still had hardly any sleep. I daren't find out that I can't sleep. Although I did get a few hours yesterday when I was *out of it*."

"All this," I say, spreading my hands and pointing to the room, the music and the mass of youth.

"The result of not sleeping," Edevart says. "It's what comes in the wake of sleeplessness. It sneaks up on you. Do you think it undignified?"

"Grief does not have much to do with dignity, does it?" I say. Where is grief attractive? Ritualised and strict and slow in a monastery perhaps, but then that is only in the chapels. What happens in the cells afterwards no-one knows. Edevart Riel has his *chemicals*, which may also be a kind of ritual.

"Come with me," he says, "and I'll show you what you can do with grief."

He leads me by the hand over to a corner of the room where a young woman, gone to fat and with a shaved head, is sitting in front of a computer screen. She is wearing an Icelandic sweater and blue jeans and her way of dressing marks her out from the surroundings, as our ages do for Edevart Riel and me.

"This is Lill," he says. "The most experienced *dominatrix* in the town, though at the moment she is in civilian order."

"Cut it out, will you?" this version of the female dominant figure in homosexual and heterosexual SM mumbles. She even blushes as she stares fixedly at the screen. How interesting, I think, a shy *dominatrix*.

"Have you found anything?" Edevart asks.

"No. Just chat," she grumbles. "There are enough people who maintain that they've seen it, but either they don't remember addresses or they're quite unapproachable. It's mostly boasting, anyway." "It" is the video from TroJa. This shy girl Lill surfs the oceans of chat in cyberspace, skims the waves of gossip, dives into arbitrary small talk, bathes in pornography, searching for a few minutes of hardcore reality: a death. It must be possible to find it, she says. At any rate there is no shortage of claims that it exists.

Edevart's smooth, shaven amphibian face is chiselled and heavy next to mine; he carries his lack of dignity borne of grief with his head held high.

"If it can be found somewhere out there who has more right to watch it than me? *Le petit mort.* And then the big one."

He turns round and drops his great weight into a safari chair beside the desk.

"I want her to search at least. If she finds it, I don't have to watch it."

It will be difficult to avoid it, I suspect. It is a long, long time since the three wise monkeys, hear no evil, see no evil, and speak no evil, were anything but an object of contempt in our jungles.

Enormous fists on each knee tremble.

"Is this what you came for," he asks, "to see how undignified my grieving is?"

"Not really. I came to find out more about TroJa."

"TroJa."

"Where Martin worked."

"Well, did he? I'm not so sure," Edevart says, lifting a one and a half litre bottle of Farris water – as light as a feather in his giant fist. "TroJa has been slowly but surely run down over the last fifteen years or so. Partly as a result of a poor business sense – the factory in Nydalen has not been especially economical, and the others weren't much better. But it was in Nydalen that there were real losses."

"To the tune of how much?" I ask, choosing an appropriate register.

"A very worrying tune for any management team, catastrophic for an ambitious one. But TroJa has never had anything approaching an ambitious management team in recent times."

It is the professional in him talking now, the shark from Aker Brygge working smoothly.

"On top of that the industrial sector was subsidising the company's other activities, wasn't it?" he adds.

"And what we're talking about there is . . ."

"The collection. Until very recently TroJa was closer to being a machine for pumping out revenues that Otto Troels-Jacobsen could use to buy art with. It worked fine in the Fifties. The factories could churn out roof tiles and lavatory bowls and rather inelegant bathroom furniture, and he could merrily buy art with the surplus."

"Then it was a private company, wasn't it?"

"Originally, yes. But he turned it into a limited company some time in the Seventies. Anyway, it was at a time when the company was still going well and the fine ladies buying the shares got a little more than exclusive access to the gallery's private viewings in return for their investments. In recent years it must have been the private viewings of exhibitions, the champagne and the exciting artists that persuaded them to keep their shares, because they didn't get much more than that."

"Why?" I ask. "Why did it go so badly?"

"Idiosyncrasy," Edevart says. "Troels-Jacobsen's hobbyhorses. He was squeezing the company for more than it could stand and he consistently failed to invest in a serious way. He spent more or less the entire Eighties dealing with the national and local governments to get a Troels-Jacobsen Museum."

"And after that?"

"After that he left the company alone to plough its own furrow.

After that the Frogner ladies who owned the shares became old and apathetic, and so did he. And after that he refused to let his daughter take over the gallery, so she started her own from scratch in competition with his.''

Edevart falls silent, musing. He drinks his Farris water. Around us the jungle is alive, not a sound inside the terrarium, very noisy outside. It is the quiet ones you have to watch.

"Now you have the background," he says.

"Before Martin appeared?" I ask.

"The backdrop for Roll as the *deus ex machina*," he says. "He saw that the inherent values of the company were greater than its value on the stock market and he saw that here was a chance to invest in prestige. Roll is so terrified of being any Tom, Dick or Harry, you know."

"Everyone owns football teams," I quote.

"Quite. But before TroJa could become anywhere near interesting he would have to get rid of the dead wood."

"That's the industrial bit, I take it?"

"Of course. Everyone knew that Otto did not want to close the business down. Whatever happened. So Roll had to acquire a majority on the board, and he knew that Otto would be against him. Sjur Aske, the trade union representative, for another. That left Bella and the three dozy Frogner women, who all loved Otto. An open bid from Roll would send the prices sky high and also make it possible for Otto and Sjur Aske to lobby for their point of view. Not the ideal position for Roll."

"But?"

"He managed it anyway. At a decisive meeting of the shareholders there was the majority nobody had expected. The industry is run down, the properties outside Oslo and part of the collection are sold. A Cultural Centre is set up in Nydalen. Hey presto. As far as Bella's vote is concerned, it is significant that she was appointed the director of the Cultural Centre immediately afterwards."

"A deal then?"

"It must have been."

"But Bella's vote can't have done it on its own, can it?" I ask.

"No. The interesting part is the Frogner shares. The old ladies started to demand proper business management. And sent in proxies at the casting of the votes."

Still no more than a fleeting wry smile on that mahogany face.

"Martin was the proxy," he says with great calm. "And he also managed to get hold of a devastating report on the business management of Nydalen. And so Otto loses a kind of son."

Strange, I think, the use of that word. Loses. If anyone lost Martin Andersen it was Edevart Riel himself, though much later.

"But wasn't Martin employed by Otto?" I ask.

"Employed? Bloody hell, no. If you could imagine Martin being an employee anywhere it would have been with Roll. He was obsessed by him and it is important to understand that. He's a golden guy in so many ways."

"Not just money?"

"Not just money, not money at all in point of fact, although he's rolling in it too. It's life, he just glistens with it. More life. He sparkles with it, real throbbing *life*."

"As they have," I say, indicating the room behind me with a sweep of my hand.

"It's similar. And I could see it in Martin, you know. When he'd been near him it just radiated from him. I could recognise it, of course, because I admire it too. I desire it."

Yes. For all those who remember that they will have to die it is difficult to avoid it, the desire. It shines off all the bodies around us too, though I don't think that Edevart Riel sees it, even if he doesn't even dare to close his eyes at night.

"And he wasn't so demanding," Riel goes on. "I don't mean that Martin was cheap, more that he was saving himself. Waiting with his demands for as long as he had the glow. You know, these sumptuous lunches, a late jacuzzi in a boat out in the fjord, a private jet out to an island with tennis courts. Tax deductible, all that kind of thing, but it can shine light into the dark all the same."

"Was this going on all the time that Martin was supposedly working for Troels-Jacobsen?" I ask. "When he was actually working for Roll?"

"Yes. And that was part of the glamour, I assume. The secrecy, Martin being involved in plans, being active and making himself indispensable to an old guy and loads of old dears, it was part of a plan, it had a purpose. Martin trudged round, charming the Frogner biddies as only a gay can and he did it all for the glow."

169

Dangerous sport, I think. Gets your pulse racing. More life.

"There wasn't a . . .," I begin, and he quickly interrupts. He knows this kind of allusion.

". . . sexual relationship between them? God forbid. And not with Roll either. He was a son to Troels-Jacobsen and as far . . . a kid brother or useful simpleton to Roll."

"And the only thing Martin got out of it," I say, "apart from quite a lot of money – was the glow? Being close to Roll?"

"Closeness to Joakim Roll means more than *quite a lot* of money. And Martin probably imagined that it would mean more to him, too."

"You said that he was saving himself," I venture.

"Yes. He was pretty out of it with excitement when the vote was finally home, after the big meeting. I suppose it was naïve, but he did have some ideas about moving up and into the treasury. Into the stratosphere. A job at RollOn, managing director, administrator and yes man, something anyway. He was trained to be demanding, you know they are now. And he had something to apply pressure with."

It is sad. As are his heavy body in the canvas chair, his massive fists and these dreams of the glow he is part of. I don't need to tell a muscular survivor of AIDS how dangerous it can be. Before he died Martin Andersen managed to betray Otto Troels-Jacobsen and Sjur Aske, his competitor for the rôle of son, and in addition, to deliver a threatening demand to Joakim Roll.

At least Edevart has suggested the possibility to me that this is how it was, from his knowledge, and now he doesn't want me here any longer. Around him the results of his own sleeplessness are full of life: exultant and chemically love-filled lives. It is just in the terrarium that there is the menacing silence waiting for the one right moment.

The shy dominatrix Lill joins me going down the stairs.

"What will he do with the video?" I ask. "If you find it for him."

"Don't know," she mumbles, her mouth part-lost in the neck of the Icelandic sweater.

"You know the police would also like to see it."

She snorts.

"At any rate Edevart won't give it to *them*."

"You will?" I ask.

Heavy steps on the stairs, a hand out to hold the outside door open for me. Lill is a *gentlewoman*.

It is no surprise she takes out her lighter to light my cigarette on the pavement outside. I let her light it and offer her the cigarette afterwards. Little deals in the empty streets of Vika on a Sunday. You can't see the evening star for the rows of houses and the over-powering quantity of light in the town. It is out there somewhere in space anyway. In a different scenario from our own you would see the light trail it leaves, just as Lill will probably be able to run the video to earth in oceans of cyber noise.

Sunday evenings. Trepidation about the following day or a sleepy nursing of the last hours of true freedom that can only make sense in the context of a measure of obligation. In the windows across the street the yellow glow alternates with the blue light of TV screens. Lill and I shiver in the autumn night, though not from any sense of danger, as the faint strains of bass and treble reach us from Edevart Riel's attic balcony.

"Do you think it will do him any good to watch it?" I ask.

"Dunno," she whispers.

"Would you give it to the police, if you found it?"

Soft laughter.

"Phone me," I say, "if you find it. *I* can take it to the police, you know."

She looks at me for a long time from under her furrowed brow and shorn head.

Nods and takes my card. Little deals. "I'll have to think about it," she says.

"Of course," I say.

She doesn't want to sit with me in the car, but she gives me her latest Internet trail. It is: down.boys. And it is as open to interpre-tation as everything else is under the sky.

22

I AM NO DOMINATRIX, but this is how all women of my generation drive at night: we steer, make decisions, accelerate or slow down as necessary and harness much more powerful beasts than the poor horses we thought we had tamed in our teenage years. We are in control but we don't feel it. Somewhere within my complete confidence as a driver there is the knowledge that if the engine seizes I will not know what to do. However, it exerts no influence on my undiminished sense of power. None at all. The engine purrs into life.

The halogen street lamps are yellow and high above me; the town beneath them glitters, flashes red, blue and green, and reveals occasional black ravines, the dead gateways between rows of houses.

They don't frighten me. I glide. I glide powerfully along as I know the loneliest, the wildest and the sickest people in the town do, powerfully because it is possible to move without being hurt and without being seen in the night. I glide along with the same arrogance, concentrating on my own egoistic thoughts. Or wild, sick fantasies.

Edevart Riel and a preference for the dangerous sports he may have shared with his partner. In finance, sport and sex. Otto Troels-Jacobsen with the yellow eyes of an old man and a desperate need for a son and whom Martin Andersen savagely betrayed. Joakim Roll who may have faced – who knows? – the *unfeasible* demand for more life or more money. Enough tangled thoughts to occupy a simple journey through the town, enough perhaps to satisfy a tormented therapist searching for explanations for the catastrophe, other than her own failure.

The only time molluscs are vulnerable, we know, is when they leave their shells or are sated.

And that is when the predators go for them.

Bunches of keys are recommended as weapons for women. They are solid, sharp and accessible. Carrying knives or pepper guns is not so sensible, we have been told; it is stupid to give the assailant a weapon. The same is true for tear gas. Wailing alarms are supposed to be good. You believe in alarms and even think about buying one; but you have lived in the city centre for a year and you know how long it takes for anyone to ring the police when a car alarm goes off.

So the bunch of keys, as dependable as ever, with one key sticking out between my fingers. If nothing else it can mean a nasty wound or a lucky poke in the bastard's eye. Knowledge on my way home at night.

But you need to have an opportunity to use the keys. They must not be left in the car door, for example. As mine are. The door into the backyard should not be left open. As this one is. And the backyard should not be situated below the open window of my daughter's bedroom.

But it is. I bellow, I swear and I resist, and I am furious and tenaciously halfway through the passage way into the street despite the blows, but it is while I am crawling backwards over the tarmac into the middle of the yard that I look up and know.

A mountain of flesh casts a shadow over me, black and heavy and driven by a fury that I have never experienced, but which humiliates me kick by kick over the tarmac but which nevertheless ignites every resistance I have in me. I want to scream, I want to roar at him. Four floors up I catch sight of something that silences every sob, every scream of rage or pain within me.

The half-open window of Ida's room. Inside she is asleep. I could wake her now with my breathless screams of rage.

I can still hear the sounds we are making in the courtyard. His metal-framed toecap driven into my stomach, the cry I can't hold back. My clumsy attempts to turn away, his foot crashing into my ribs, my spine, my shoulders.

I am sitting half-upright against the pretty rundown outhouse in the centre of the yard taking blow after blow. The kicks. I have the open window inside me and he could kill me now and I wouldn't want her to hear what it sounds like. There are supposed to be women who have bitten their tongues off in such circumstances. I know what drove them.

There is a ringing. Inside me, I suppose, in my head. I have my arms around my head as a shield, and that irritates him. He spits at me. He kicks me again, in my side where I never dreamt I had something that could create such violent pain. The kidneys, some people say it hurts like hell in the kidneys, and it's true. So much so that I bite my lips until they bleed. The warmth of a blow across my chin. This is what I am reduced to, to recognising random physical sensations without a centre to relate to. There is no me left, just kidneys and chin and arms that instinctively protect this precious entity that is the brain somewhere behind my face.

And the open window.

And now nothing exists except our frenzied breathing, unsynchronised, disunited in every way. Silence almost, long enough for me to think that I should go over there, to the door and the doorbells. I reach out in that direction before he stamps my arm.

And then I hear before I see what he is going to do.

The smooth zigzag swish of the zip. The warmth, sharp and emphatic. Above us is the white rectangle of Ida's window, half-open to the night. He soon finishes pissing on me. It doesn't hurt. I know, more than he realises, what he could have done to me, wordlessly in this yard, and I may use that knowledge to put myself together again after his streams of piss cut me into pieces, like a jigsaw puzzle, before he leaves.

His friend stands leaning against the arch to the gateway and his eyes under the balaclava follow me with interest as I crawl across the tarmac. Don't look up, I think, don't show him your face. Don't look up, look at the ground, be like vermin for him.

He lifts his head towards the night sky for a second and whistles softly as he follows his bulky leader out through the gateway passage. I don't know if it is my daughter's open window or the distant stars that makes him whistle so. The stars didn't fall. They didn't change one iota, and if we extrapolate from the backyards and beatings of our world, then we can say that nothing ever changes, nothing ever leaves an impression.

Life is lived, even if it is a kind of perverted amoeba's life. Life is heaving and seething with them, even in dead bodies. Even this courtyard, dark and damp and given up on by its owners, is teeming with life. Worms and beetles and fungus and minutiae of different kinds. Perhaps I am not so different from them as I wriggle towards the door. At any rate they smell better than I do at the moment.

Above me the open window. Above me the unchanging sky. But it does not mean, as I get to my feet, that he is right. That I am a clod of earth he can piss on. That my life can be equated with that of a larva. That all things that heave and seethe are in some way equal.

If I were a worm, I think, if I were the same as the level of life he wanted to bring me down to, I would not have so much as looked at the open window. Although he could have made me forget it. And I take it as a blessing, a gift of mercy, that he didn't do that. His gift to me. The torture victim's final humiliation – the overwhelming gratitude to his oppressor for stopping.

Along my back: stretches and weals of blood, hidden under the skin and thus multi-coloured. Yellow, brownish, darkening to purple here and there, one thigh has a broad band of inflamed redness where the skin is punctured with a series of tiny superficial dots.

I have peculiar painful swellings on my body, subterranean explosions that are only slowly bringing the evidence of the shock to the surface. My body is being developed as if through a slow photographic printing process: shortly the purple will turn black and the yellow will turn blue.

I study this with care in the shower. I don't show my husband during the night for reasons that I still don't understand. I can understand the intense discomfort of getting undressed. The desire to gather myself into a neat little heap under the blanket on the sofa too. But not why I still won't show him, still won't tell him about the open window and the backyard.

It is while I am forcing myself to stand in front of the mirror and see that my face is untouched that I realise. Benny won't go anywhere if he sees my body. And I want him to go. Because he is taking Ida with him.

There are various levels in the tidying up process. Benny will need the assurance of regular telephone calls, for example. Sleeplessness is an acceptable explanation for spending the night in the sitting room and looking terrible, but sleeplessness itself can give cause for concern, too.

Then there are the remains of breakfast and discarded toys, your own terror and the simple task of calling in to work to report sick. I walk very gingerly through the flat in my comfort clothes, Benny's big thick dressing-gown. Naturally there are child-free freedoms too, peaceful and not too melancholy music on the CD player mid-morning and the knowledge that, mile by mile, she is distancing herself from my contagious presence.

They might have been after my purse. They could have been anyone, a gang of drunken psychotic rapists. But I don't believe that. They were so purposeful and so quiet, as if they were carrying out a specific mission and withdrew when it was finished. Beat the bitch up. Piss on her. I loathe them whatever the purpose, even the glimpse of the dark-skinned face that forced me to think so *typically*.

I drink coffee in the safe corner of the sofa with the blanket over my legs and I know that the balaclava could have been concealing Javed's brother. Or any other gorilla that does that kind of paid work. Who would have paid them? Aske with his acquaintances from the *clink*? His brother who lied so unconvincingly about his visit to Grønlandsleiret? The furious old man in his empty flat in Frogner, who Bella insists nurtures grudges?

Or just Edevart Riel, who can't lack for well-built, pill-popping acquaintances? I am not certain that I should stay in Markveien, either. But then I said that I would water the plants in Charlotte Andersensveien.

There is a lot that can be said about a beating, but dwelling on it isn't to be recommended. The part of me that only wants to stay like a bundle under the blanket forever doesn't manage to come up with anything better than a single interesting question about kicks and punches and backyards. Small bundles don't go in for interesting things, they just want to enjoy long-term self-care without inter-ference from an obtrusive outside world.

Seen in this light the question is not so bad: was the beating a punishment or a warning? If it were a punishment, I think, as I reluctantly interrupt my bundle-life and get dressed, if it were a punishment, it must have come from Javed's brother who thinks that I turned his brother into a contemptible homo or from the part of Loaf that collapsed and died in front of the Haukeland sculpture, so to speak, directly after I entered their little headquarters. *Nutcases.*

Anlaug and Torstein. And their unwitting fellow victims or kin.

As I prepare to escape and gather my things together – toiletries, clothes, the biography and Benny's portfolio – I gently go over in my bundle-brain the warnings kicks and punches can deliver. Lay off – that is what kicks and punches tell you.

Lay off the exaggerated interest in Martin Andersen's enjoyment of dangerous sports. Lay off Joakim Roll's skilled transactions, which if they turn out to be murky can affect the conversion rate of his hallowed shares. Bitch, don't stick your nose into what Sjur Aske was doing in Grønlandsleiret. And don't pry into the *silly* connection between Aske's life and his works of art or the body of his biography that could tell you something about it.

It doesn't smell of Bente's perfume in the hall as I roughly pull my jacket over my heavily bruised biceps or triceps, it just smells of leather and a child's woolly clothing, and then I have to ring them before I leave. They are in a place called By the Way which involves if not hamburgers then fizzy drinks at any rate. Ida makes bubbling noises into the receiver and she says she has seen a horse. It is almost as great as seeing a pony.

I lock my getaway stuff in the car – it is daylight now and modern-day trolls in balaclavas don't like that. And if you don't want to be a little bundle, you had better move, even if it hurts. I'm going to do what skivers and malingerers invariably do, go into *town*. This has the advantage that there is less need to be a bundle. In my workplace we deal with anxiety-induced bundle-life in the following way: first, walk to the corner, then scuttle home. Next day or the week after, walk to the bus stop. And then, in stages, try the places that buses and streets can take you.

It is like training programmes for beginners. Run a hundred metres, then walk three hundred. Run two hundred. Walk five. Modest ambitions. *Something*. Sniff at the world, as small animals and children do, and let it heal you.

I am limping and my movements are ungainly on the pavement going down Markveien, but that is one of the advantages of this part of town: there is always someone limping and looking ungainly and strange on the pavements here. Today it is my turn. I owe my neighbours this much, that they can enjoy my quirks, as I enjoy theirs.

The feverishly smoking mothers with their prams in Olav Ryes plass. The brisk minimalist with his rectangular glasses on his way to some long awaited and, it seems, vital *project*. The proud Pakistani gentleman in freshly pressed, dazzling white pyjamas and quilted jacket. Mother and daughter, like two peas in a pod and pissed, probably on their way down to get the deposit back on the bottles for more cheap beer.

And the alarming woman who flits by, the one with the voluminous flowing veil which covers everything except the slit for her eyes. She is *strange* all right. She won't get much joy from seeing me.

Grünerløkka's proud isolation is down to the fact that this part of town has a bridge, like an old-fashioned gateway to the town. Anker Bridge with its odd rustic folktale statues – a bull and a reindeer – is the only viable road to the centre if you are walking. Before the bridge you are at home, beyond it you are visiting. Some inhabitants of Løkka would like *us* to receive as few visits from the outside world as possible. Newcomers like me dare not presume such community feeling.

Walking through the part of Torggata which is a relocated *Paris du nord* – confused, filthy, with kebab shops and slow-moving traffic because of the continual deliveries to vegetable shops from Turkey and Vietnam – my bundle-mentality begins to whirl from more than the beating I received. There is busy trading here of all kinds, but the really big money is not changing hands in some Asian jeweller's or in a scruffy Greek restaurant.

The world heals; it has an effect. I am a long way from Joakim Roll's glass towers and shrewd share dealings. On the other hand, I am not so far from Loaf's headquarters in Grønlandsleiret. Life and art. Pictures and the person who painted them. Life and the person who took it. If Ingeborg Dahl ran some strange theories past me and the police inspectors, did she do the same with others as well?

A picture called PAN and a boy called Per Anders Nilsen. He too must have *close kin* a Loaf activist or a battered old cow can look up. As Ingeborg Dahl herself has. The Salt of the Earth is still worth a visit.

Something has changed in the little hallway. The chest of drawers with the cloth with the big flowers on is the same, the little souvenirs hanging in a line the length of the frame of the door into the kitchen, too – a porcelain donkey, a miniature straw hat with a dried flower stuck in it, a plate portraying Greek gods in a respectable scene. The troll child made of dough is still sitting on its potty on the lavatory door.

But all the outdoor clothing has gone. Perhaps most of it belonged to Ingeborg, and the visiting Loafers. And there is an overpowering smell of detergents: ammonia, chloride and soap.

Grieving doesn't come easily to the Salt of the Earth. The decorative plates on the wall in Søren Dahl's kitchen have an advertisement's sparkle and shine, and the curtains are still damp where they border the newly cleaned windows. He has hung them up before they are dry, just as Mother used to do when we lived in Grefsen. Maybe it's a generational thing, something that will die with them. There is a small square cloth runner lying across the kitchen table and two porcelain cats – one for salt, one for pepper – on the part of the cloth closest to the window.

Søren Dahl has brushed the cloth down and put the cats there. And now there is nothing else to do. He will manage to find something, I know, something trivial perhaps, a nail that has to be hammered in or a plant to be repotted, tomorrow perhaps, in the cellar, in the backyard, and these things will help to make the minutes pass, the hours, the days, and it will save his life. But right now everything has been done. Perhaps it was harder than he thought, perhaps time was going too fast.

They are taking good care of him, he says, the people in the flats and from Loaf. Lots of people have phoned. More than he thought, actually. Newspapers too, but he would prefer not to talk to them. Apart from a nice man from the TV and gossip magazine *Se&Hør*. He knows him from before – he took pictures of Søren and Ingeborg in here, actually, in the kitchen. That is some years ago now.

He has received letters and cards, too. Would I like to see them? I go with him into the sitting room, which is still dominated by the two Loaf desks. He has put the letters and cards in a nice little pile on the coffee table by the chairs beneath the enormous portrait of Helena. Some of the cards are folded and he has placed them upright, as you do with Christmas and birthday cards.

It is as if the lenses of his glasses have expanded and become even bigger. His lean squirrel face disappears behind them and his eyes, a long way back, blink rapidly. Where he sits, shrunken on the sofa under the photograph of his granddaughter, he seems smaller than her and he has less colour. Everything in here is light. The high autumn sky outside sets the room in a crystal clear, chilly day, which seems as if it might last for ever: that is how the sky should be – high, blank and serene. Nothing else can happen here, other than that in one distant moment of truth he too will die.

And for the moment he is not even complaining.

He doesn't know what to do with it, he says, indicating with his thin hand the office landscape he inhibits. But he doesn't feel like thinking about it yet, actually. It's up to Loaf, as well, isn't it.

The police have been here and they too were friendly. He doesn't know when the funeral can take place, but it is important to him. The rituals, the order.

We talk in low voices and while we drink the obligatory cup of coffee I mention PAN. It is awkward.

"Ingeborg may have had some contact with his relatives," I say.

Yes, indeed. The boy's mother. The police have got Ingeborg's address book of course, but he leaps up and fetches his phone book. Something to do, action.

It is one of the old-fashioned kind that opens at the right place when you run a little lever down the side and stop at the right letter. N for Nilsen.

"Here it is," he says, pushing the little book over to me. *Fru Nilsen*, he has jotted it down in pencil so that the name and number can be rubbed out at the appropriate time. I put the name and number in my own little book. There are no *Fru Anyones* there from the past and nor do I have the characteristic handwriting of those who have learnt calligraphy, but don't write that much in their lives. Nor do my hands tremble yet.

There is a ring at the door and the sound of it makes us both start as if it could only be ghosts wanting to come in.

"That's probably Anlaug," he says. "She has a couple of boxes in the cellar she has to pick up, actually. Could you help me to carry them?"

Before we have closed the door behind us Anlaug has rung the doorbell twice more, one short and one LONG. He scoots down the stairs in front of me, past the door out to the backyard and down the steep cellar stairs. His part of the cellar is orderly with a carpenter's bench and an old piece of kitchen furniture serving as a worktable. Two long neon tubes light up his tools, which are neatly hung up, set against their contours painted on to perforated board. The cardboard boxes are in the middle of the floor, five of them, and we take one each. They are heavy and stuffed with papers, Anlaug's paranoid copies.

Perhaps getting stuck with this job right now is as awful as I imagine, or perhaps every single job he gets is a blessing. At any rate, I shouldn't get so worked up about people who give old men work. I can't even get my cardboard box as far as the cellar steps before my bruised shoulders force me to put it down.

"Don't worry," Søren Dahl says. At least I can hold the doors open for him.

Anlaug is waiting on the pavement in front of the gateway in her dirt-coloured batik smock. She pulls a face when she sees me. Maybe I am wrong. Perhaps it was already distorted. Behind her, on the other side of the road, there is an enormous van; it's called the *Dream Machine* but it's probably more likely to give nightmares about gang bangs than dreams.

"WHAT IS SHE DOING HERE?" Anlaug says as usual when she sees me.

"What's happened?" I ask.

"That's got shit to do with YOU," Anlaug says, a little apprehensive.

"Well," Søren says, blinking, "Igi dropped in and so I thought . . . She's helping me to hold the door open, actually. But my dear," he adds, "have you hurt yourself?"

Anlaug grunts. "Accident," she mumbles. "I fell."

Fell a long way then. Fell right down the stairs, hit the door frame, tripped over the threshhold, fell against the chest of drawers and hit the edge of the stove, whoops. Anlaug didn't hit *herself*. Someone hit *her*. And unlike my backyard man he didn't spare her face.

I have seen her face like this before, about two years ago just before she left the department. She had also had a bad fall then. That was one of the reasons we wanted her to stay. But Anlaug is a grown up and we didn't detain her against her will.

"Accident," I say dryly. "I see. Let's get this box in your car, shall we?"

"I can take it MYSELF," Anlaug says.

"Fine," I say. "Then Søren can go down and get another one." I am halfway across the street before she waddles after me with this extra weight attached to her heavy body. I have swung open the back doors of the *Dream Machine* before she catches up with me.

She is, her numerous falls and her sympathy-sapping, verbal trumpeting-style defence and her body fat notwithstanding, also a *wally*. She has left the bucket in the car, standing in a small cardboard box with the brushes wrapped in plastic next to it.

"Have you gone back to him?" I ask amiably.

"I have NOT," Anlaug pouts. "He" is the guy who made Anlaug "fall" so badly that time. "He" is also the father of the child she didn't have, almost certainly because I recommended she have an abortion. "HEITMANN THE PSYCHOLOGIST KILLS CHILDREN", I am reminded.

"Is that his car?" I ask.

"NO," Anlaug says.

"Whose is it then?" I ask.

"That's got shit to do with YOU."

She may have met someone new, someone with a long staircase and the *Dream Machine*. It can take time, but most of us discover that all the people we *fall* headlong for tend to resemble each other. On the other hand "he" whose name I can't remember was Anlaug's first, and there wasn't a single person in the department who took much notice of her when she swore that she had finished it.

Things suggested that she was slowly beginning to fall again.

"Do you have any regrets about the abortion?" I ask.

Søren arrives with a cardboard box and scampers off like a squirrel to fetch another.

"YOU have got a child, haven't you?" she says. "Do YOU regret having HER?"

"No," I say. "I'm very happy about it. You know I didn't mean that *you* shouldn't have a child, but that it wasn't such a clever idea for you to have one *then*."

"My Mum had ME," Anlaug says, "and there's no saying that that was so CLEVER."

Anlaug fell a lot in her childhood as well.

Søren is back already with yet another box. He puts it down in front of us on the tarmac and scurries away again.

"I know it hurt you," I say, "and I'm sorry about that. If you feel that I pushed you into doing something you didn't want, I'm terribly sorry."

"That's BLOODY easy to say."

And it is. It is banal and stupid. But it is also necessary. The most desperate regrets, if they are genuine, have a far greater effect on the person hearing them than the person expressing them. It is just to begin with that it appears to be the other way round.

"This painting . . .," I begin.

"YOU just SHUT UP," Anlaug interrupts. "You have NO IDEA what you're talking about ANYWAY, so you can just shut your BLOODY MOUTH."

She snatches the cardboard box from the ground and shoves it sideways into the car where it falls over and a stream of A4 sheets spills over the floor and on to the road.

"WHAT THE FUCK DO YOU KNOW!" Anlaug roars, bending down awkwardly to pick up the paper. "You come here and INTER-FERE! NOBODY wants you here. Ingeborg was ALIVE until YOU came knocking at her door."

"Heitmann=death," I think.

"Anlaug," I say.

"But LOAF won't stop, YOU KNOW, even if INGEBORG has gone. Now I MAKE THE DECISIONS."

She flings a handful of paper into the back of the vehicle and slams the heavy doors to. Then she shoves me hard in the chest and marches up to the driver's seat, settles herself and starts the engine with a ROAR.

I stand by the side window gesticulating. It is dark, the colour of smoke; squinting, I can just make out the outline of the heavy shape that is her through the glass. The *Dream Machine* speeds off, leaving behind a minor blizzard of A4 sheets.

Søren stands in the shadows on the opposite side of the road with the last cardboard box in his hands. I pick up the remaining sheets. So many things might be going on. "Regrets" might be starting to kick in.

Søren retires without waiting for me to finish picking up the paper.

As I flick through the photocopies to see that the page numbers tally, the occasional word filters into my consciousness. Not because I look at the papers that carefully. It is because some of the sentences are underlined.

I recognise the cat. The one she kept for so long after it had died, the one she frightened him with so much so that he stopped sleeping at night. The shrivelled cat, stiff and shrunken, its exposed gums grinning into his face. The smell of it. This cat from hell, there can't be more than one of them in the world, and as I read on I find the brush too and the strap she used to tie him up with in what used to be the sheep pen.

There is a reference number at the bottom of the pages together with the page number, but it is meaningless as the first page is missing. There is 574/2 on one sheet and 574/3 on the following one.

So strange, I think. If Ingeborg Dahl hadn't read the biography – and how would she ever have had the opportunity to do that? – she can't have got this information from anyone but Aske himself. Or from an unusually talkative Sjur. Who passed me here in Grønlandsleiret on the night she disappeared. On his way to her? To talk about the closing down of a factory or a brother?

Søren Dahl is helpful by nature, but I am not allowed to go up and see the rest of the archive. It is HOLY, I assume. And anyway it's not his DECISION.

As I have NO IDEA whatsoever I'll find out from *fru Nilsen*.

23

FOR ANYONE WHO has taken a beating of any kind the world becomes something of a challenge as you sniff at it with suspicion. After bouts of training: rest. Run a hundred metres, walk three hundred. Anlaug is a hundred metres any day, and I take note of any big men around the backstreets of Grønland and on the way home to Markveien. I see them not only because I am vulnerable to them, but also because I am exhausted.

Outside the gateway with my car key in hand I can feel something smarting more than my bruised muscles. *The pissing*. He pissed on me because he could.

It is the middle of a crystal clear, sky blue autumn day and I know today's trolls don't like it like this, but walking on the pavement I am still afraid of them. Of course, I am escaping. Of course I, like Aske, have found myself a bolt hole in life. I haven't had a reason to use it, however, for more than fifteen years.

I park the car in front of Karsten's showy garage door in Charlotte Andersens vei. There are just as many clever inlays in it as in Otto Troels-Jacobsen's Renaissance cupboard, but it is shinier and sparkles more. Something else they have in common, one can assume, is that they are marking the value of whatever lies behind the doors.

Mother's kitchen is clean and empty; the new kitchen range with the Provençal tiles reigns supreme in the corner under its copper hood. I put my bag down on the kitchen table, which is thick and *faux*-antique, made by an *absolutely fantastic* carpenter in Lom.

It is a long time since the telephone was kept in the hall, in this house as in others. When I lived here I sat at a flimsy table in the hall, hunched up on what we called the telephone chair, putting my finger in the holes and dialling the appropriate numbers. Sniffing at the world. Letting it heal me, I presume.

Now the telephone is in Karsten's library where he reads strange books about the dominance of the alpha males and about golf. I don't need to sit down on one of his chesterfield-style chairs, however, as the phone is cordless and works just as well by an imitation country table in the kitchen. Beside the bag I have my little calendar and the pile of manuscripts containing Aske's biography.

When Ingeborg Dahl gained access to Aske's childhood history it needn't necessarily have been through him or his brother. It could also have been the person who wrote the biography. A sharp art critic who has just had her assignment cancelled.

However, first of all I ring *fru Nilsen*. Family of the boy known as PAN.

She isn't at home, she doesn't live there any more. But someone called Edel Amundsen does.

"Did she move a long time ago?" I ask.

"She didn't move," Edel Amundsen says. "She took her own life."

Quick and tough and with a metallic ring of defiance.

"I'm sorry," I say. "I didn't know."

"Not in the house," she adds. "She hanged herself from a tree in the forest here. It's two years ago now."

"You don't know," I ask, where I can find any other relatives of Per Anders Nilsen?"

She considers this for a few seconds. "You're not ringing from that – not the *Losers' Association*, but . . ."

"Loaf?"

"That's it, yes."

"Not exactly," I say.

"Okay. It's not that difficult to find any of PAN's relatives. For example, I'm his sister. Are you a journalist?"

"No," I say, "a psychologist."

"I see. And you're *not exactly* ringing from Loaf. I'm sorry, I don't think I've got anything to talk to you about."

Bang.

As well as being angry, Edel Amundsen is also quick. She has either left the house or pulled out the plug when I ring again. But she is not difficult to trace; thanks to directory enquiries her name and a telephone number soon give me her address too. If I am standing on her steps tomorrow, I think, I could put my foot in the door, if necessary, before she shuts it.

Before I continue ringing round I raid Mother and Karsten's fridge. I have a choice between Litago yoghurt and Karsten's Gorgonzola. I take the Gorgonzola.

Which certainly would have been the art critic's choice. Aske's biographer might also be angry. After all she has just lost a prestigious commission, but mostly her tone on the phone is scornful.

No, she hasn't spoken to anybody called *Ingeborg Dahl*, not about Aske's childhood, nor about anything else.

"Who are your sources then?" I ask.

"You can ask your husband about that," she says. "You can find them in the manuscript."

She goes into a longish harangue about *breach of contract* and the law about intellectual property, and while I listen to this I leaf through the first pages of the manuscript. There is a contents list; after the chapter entitled "Home", which I have read, there is one with the rather pompous title "Momentous Experiences in Amsterdam".

"What I meant was," I interrupt, "who was the source for his childhood stories?"

"Aske, of course. Who else?"

"And you're sure," I say, "that you never talked to anyone about the contents of this chapter?"

"*I* don't break contracts," she says pointedly, "unlike . . ."

She is off again on the laws relating to intellectual property.

I flick through to "Momentous Experiences in Amsterdam". They are not there. That is, the chapter is not there. The page numbers continue unbroken, so neither Benny nor I has removed it.

"Was there anything else?" the art critic asks abruptly. "I'm quite busy here."

"Just one little thing," I say. "I've got the manuscript in front of me here, and it seems as if there is a chapter missing."

"That's not very important now, is it," she says. "In fact there are several chapters missing. We were going to do a series of interviews, but the amateurish guy . . ."

"Do you know what they were about, the chapters? The one called 'Momentous Experiences', for example?"

"No idea," she says. "But I can tell you one thing, that it is of little importance for me or for Norwegian art. Aske is a completely *insignificant* figure."

BANG. If she doesn't actually slam the receiver down, she does so metaphorically. That's how it is in her line of work.

Don't do anything silly, Benny said before leaving. He hasn't seen my body, so he doesn't know that I have already done it. Today I may not have done anything silly, but I haven't done anything important either. No *momentous experiences*, to be precise. I move my bag from the steps to the second floor and amble through the big rooms downstairs. And I miss Father, I know, despite never having lived here with him.

And that is why. This house was the structure around a year-long teenage yearning for him long before he died, something that Karsten, picked up on. I have been a poor stepdaughter, and I suppose I still am, cynical as I am about his garage door and chesterfield-style chairs.

Momentous experiences. I'd have thought Aske would have had them in his childhood home, but we move on from there, in various ways. There is a picture of Aske's *Home* in Benny's portfolio, the last pointless assignment of his at Håkon Middelthon's. *Home* is blazing red and gloomy; the little house in the middle of the picture is surrounded by a turbulent sky and a heavy ridge of hills. On the left of the picture there is a single angry brushstroke, the line that is called the golden section, the one that is supposed to give optical and metaphorical balance to what is there.

Middlethon's other picture by Aske explains at least why he had to concede that Francis Bacon was "good at painting". The deformed face is almost a Bacon pastiche, if it weren't for the much coarser brushwork. "Portrait of Rune Skjalgson" Benny has noted down in his neat handwriting on the little yellow Post-it stuck on the photo. "50 × 83 cm, oils on canvas, 1969."

I knew him, I did, a voice says inside me. The art critic is making a path through TroJa's exhibition rooms in front of me and briefly greets a man wearing a Norwegian cardigan. *We were at sea together.* Now it is not certain that this means they went ashore in Amsterdam together, but it is not inconceivable. And he was certainly called Rune Skjalgson. His name does not appear in the ostentatious list of "sources" in the typescript biography, but on the other hand he is in the telephone directory.

Momentous experiences, it sounds promising, but I am not in the mood for another bad-tempered phone call. You can also check sources face to face.

As I imagined, the man peering at me through the crack of the door didn't look quite like Aske's portrait of him. His nose is in the right place, as noses are, and his skin is neither cyclamen red nor toxic green, as one would expect. In addition, though I didn't have the picture handy to prove it, he is much older than when the picture was painted.

Rune Skjalgson is wearing the same attractive knitted Norwegian cardigan, grey Terylene trousers and a greyish T-shirt under the cardigan. His hair is grey, combed back and damp. He looks at me with calm, narrowed eyes through the crack, but he lets me in, falling for my rather feeble excuse.

"My husband and I," I say, in the way that I think people of Skjalgson's age will like, "my husband and I are looking to buy a picture, a portrait by Aske. Or, to be more accurate, in fact, of you, depending on how you look at it." Was it true, I ask, adopting the friendly tones of the art buyer, was he *the* Rune Skjalgson?

Skjalgson nods.

"Well, we would very much like to know something about the picture. When it was painted and where and . . ."

It is easier than I thought. Although of all people I should have known, working as I do in the confessions business, when I'm not lying, and there being no shortage of people who like to talk either. Noncommittally and perhaps in confidence. The one assumes the other, here as in my consulting rooms.

His rooms are cramped. Little boxes with low ceilings, decorated with large-patterned wallpaper that steals space from him; perhaps he keeps the windows open in an attempt to gain more space. The room is soberly furnished in an old-fashioned but well-maintained Sixties style, more reminiscent of a museum's reconstruction than a home. None of the furniture would have made even the most ardent Sixties enthusiast gasp; it is much too solemn for that.

He shows me to one of the two small armchairs upholstered in green, with heavily tilted, narrow backs made of wavy-grained birch. He himself remains standing, as if undecided.

"I think we met once, briefly, at Aske's exhibition," I say, looking up at him.

"Really?" he says. "I don't remember that."

"That's not surprising," I say. "We weren't on our own there. I had a dog with me."

He remembers the dog. Rita is not easy to forget.

Skjalgson likes to have the neutral, office-like variation of the Sixties around him. A small, pale coffee table with a brown ashtray. True to type, the anonymous landscape on the wall matches the potted plant in the window. It could have been a nice but dull hotel room, the kind that doesn't have a TV but does have a Bible in the drawer of the bedside table. If you can still find anything like that. If this room isn't the last surviving example of it.

Rune Skjalgson brings a thermos coffee pot and two small porcelain cups and carefully pulls his trousers up at the knees before he sits down. I wonder if people still do that any more and try to picture Karsten or Troels-Jacobsen in front of me. Karsten does it when he crouches down to play with Ida, but not otherwise. Troels-Jacobsen probably does it routinely. Skjalgson is no more than twenty years older than me, about the same age as Aske. Perhaps his gesture is a habit that is dying out, at least for people like him who don't have great fortunes they need to underpin with old-fashioned manners.

"It was in Amsterdam," he says. "In our wild youth. He painted it in a little room there, down by the port."

As an artist's myth that is perfect, of course. It is exactly what *my husband and I* would go for, I think to myself.

"I have the impression," I say, "that Aske regards the time he spent in Amsterdam as momentous for him in some way. That he had important experiences there."

"Uhuh."

"What do you think it can have been?"

"Well, it must have been getting drunk or the prostitutes. Or he found out that it was okay to paint *ugly pictures*. It can't have been the sea because he didn't exactly have any success with that."

Very matter-of-fact and to the point and it sounds altogether out of place against the background of this insipid, meticulously clean room. Rune Skjalgson sips his coffee and dries his lips after each sip.

"You were at sea together?" I ask.

"We were sort of left behind. Aske had behaved appallingly on the crossing; when we got there we hung around and waited for another trip. Drank and ran wild, as one does."

"What did he do that was so appalling?" I ask.

"He was so contemptuous and he got everyone's back up. And when we came ashore he drank a tremendous amount. The others did, too, of course, but . . . Well, he was young and couldn't take his booze."

"You can't have been very much older," I say smiling; it is the wildness of youth we are talking about, at our ease now, years afterwards.

"I was two years older, maybe, and I had been around before him. But I didn't drink like that. Not in that way. And that makes a difference."

"So how did Aske drink?"

His big fist holds a thin, delicate porcelain cup in the air. His hair is combed over his bald head in stripes, letting gravity do the rest. But his gaze is clear and calm.

"Aske's drinking was so out of control, you know. Even though he was very young. And it made him very quick-tempered. He talked and fantasised a lot. He regretted it, or so I imagine."

He looks out of the window for a few seconds, his gaze wanders and becomes remote. If he does see anything, it is not the roof of the Esso garage over the road.

"Anyway, we took a room there. My goodness, I think she was a sort of prostitute who got it for us. And that's where he painted the picture. We laughed like idiots about it. He painted the prostitutes too, he was very keen on that, but then he didn't like any of the pictures."

"Why did you stay?" I ask. "I mean, if he had behaved badly you didn't need to . . ."

"I suppose I was sorry for him. It was his first trip and then he was booted off at the first opportunity, in Amsterdam."

I laugh and Skjalgson doesn't appreciate it.

"It was no joke that. What's more I felt a kind of responsibility for him. As if I had persuaded him to go to sea."

"Oh. Did you know him before then?" I ask.

"There's knowing and there's knowing. We worked together the summer before I left for the first time. Up at TroJa. He wandered around drawing then too, not on shifts of course, any way he could. Hanging around there drawing the factory chimneys. You didn't exactly make any friends doing that."

I also worked for one summer at TroJa a long, long time ago, Aske had said at his exhibition. Was that the summer?

"Did you also know his brother?" I ask.

"Well. I knew who he was. The type to suck up. The sort who wants to become the foreman, you know. He was a brute, he was. Bad."

"The foreman?"

"No, Sjur, the brother. He *paid* guys to beat up boys who were smaller than him because he was too cowardly to do it himself. They lay in wait in the forest, on the road above the river. We used to go swimming there, in the Frysja. And those guys would be waiting there and attack people."

"Did he pay anyone to beat his brother up?"

"Course. Especially him."

"Did he do anything else?" I ask.

"He worked, as we all did."

A small dry laugh escapes his lips. It sounds more like a cough. If this is anything to go by, Rune Skjalgson doesn't laugh much.

"When his exhibition opened recently," I say, "Aske made a very strong allegation. I don't know if you remember it."

"Not that well," Skjalgson says.

"No? He said his brother had stood and watched him being raped by some workmates."

"I never heard anything about that," he says. "But it wouldn't surprise me. There were some very rough people working there and that Sjur was a bastard."

He rubbed the palms of his hands against his knees a few times, as if to dry them.

"Aske talks a load of rubbish when he's drunk. It wasn't something you would want to listen to, so I soon forgot it."

Skjalgson pauses and allows his gaze to rest on my coffee cup.

"He was furious with his brother, you know. Hated him almost. I used to think it was a case of *when the manger's bare the horses begin to bite.* But there could have been other reasons."

"What do mean by the manger?" I ask.

"Their mother was utterly mad," he says, looking at me calmly.

"Did you know her too?" I ask.

"Nooo. But he talked about her, just when he was drunk. And I thought it was her he was getting away from. But it could have been the brother as well."

"Did he tell you much about his childhood?" I ask.

"Not that much and not that often. But enough. When he was standing in the tiny little room by the port in Amsterdam painting prostitutes I thought it was her he was painting. He was in a cold sweat, you know, and he made them look as ugly as he could and still they were never ugly enough."

"But you were ugly enough?" I ask.

A brief bout of coughing produces two red patches on his cheeks.

"Probably I was. He was very pleased with the picture."

The window on to the Esso station is still half-open. A pigeon is flapping its wings outside but avoids the opening and veers upwards, towards the high, chilly blue sky.

"Is there anything else you want to know?" he asks.

Oh yes, I think. There is always more. Always more and almost never enough.

"I've got a kind of appointment, you know," he says.

"Of course," I say, getting up. "Have you met the art critic who's writing a book about Aske?"

"Is she a bit sharp? She came here once asking for help with the book. Just a little. Aske had forgotten where the room we rented was."

"But you remembered?"

"Oh yes."

When the two of us stand upright in his little room we tower in it. No, he doesn't go to sea any more, he says. He does odd jobs now and then, and I have the impression that the spells between jobs are quite long.

"Do you ever meet him?" I ask. "Aske, that is."

He laughs then.

"It happens," he says. "You can hardly avoid bumping into each other in this town. Is it famous?" he says as I am putting my jacket on in the hall.

193

"Is what famous?"

"The picture of me?"

"I don't really know," I say. "It's rather an early picture, isn't it?"

"But it's expensive, isn't it?"

"Oh yes," I say. "It certainly is. I suppose too much so for my husband and I."

"Well, that's a shame," Skjalgson says. "If you like it, that is."

"You have certainly brought it to life for me," I say. "We'll just have to think about it first. The price."

And I can't help thinking on my way downstairs that his portrait may well be worth more than the social welfare I assume he will receive for the rest of his life, and almost irrespective of how it will be judged it will live longer than he will and his name may have stronger associations with his portrait than his own life.

An armada of ships has landed here in town. On my way back from the old sailor Rune Skjalgson I pass several of them. Their trim bows strive confidently towards the future, the hulls glitter and are flawlessly elegant, a gentle curve here, a daring line there. Long after the decline of Norway as a seafaring nation these vessels of glass and precious stones have inched their way in among the capital's hideous concrete blocks and cast anchor.

They make the town more attractive, as wealth does. Now, in the dusk the town's financial and government buildings are almost painfully beautiful as they reflect the golden beams of the dying sun off the fjord and absorb the deep blue and the turquoise of the sky. Precisely why so many of them insist on having such maritime associations is not easy to say. Perhaps it is the memory of the source of all our wealth – oil – that does it, or perhaps a gentle reminder that they can escape, lift anchor and set course for another tax climate if the harbour does not agree with them.

Glass towers in London. Brothels in Amsterdam. There are so many different kinds of escape and mine, battered and modest though it is, is merely to Vindern.

24

I PUT ON FAR too many lights in the large rooms in Charlotte
Andersensveien. I trawl the ground floor, turning on all the lights
I can find, only to make the dusk outside adhere itself, pitch black, to
the window panes, producing total darkness where before there were
only heartwarming dark blue tones. And now it is the right time to
draw the curtains. Mother's multi-coloured billows of curtain will
erase any memory of night if I give them the chance.

But now I can't see if there is anyone standing outside.

I had forgotten how defenceless a house with a garden can feel
when you have lived for such a long time with neighbours above,
beneath and beside you. How defenceless and lonely. There is a large
cellar here. An attic over the first floor. In addition, a floor that creaks
and trees with branches the wind can brush against the wall of the
house.

And a body that aches. There is a deep bath to sink this sore body
into, and I can keep my childish fear of the dark at bay with several
techniques I can remember from some solitary teenage summers I
spent here.

I leave the doors between the rooms wide open. I turn the TV on
low. I put the CD player up a bit louder. I won't hear if anyone
breaks in now. But you can't have everything.

Mother and Karsten's bath has become, as the town's architecture,
rather maritime after the last makeover. Yachts on the hand towels
and brass fittings in the oddest of places. There are yachts by
Jomfruland too, I know. Ida is already lying under a child's version
of them. Benny, when he goes to bed, will probably be under a duvet
cover decorated with anchors and manly ropes.

They don't have a bath like this, though, even if there is a gentle
ripple around the smooth rocks near them. Not only that, Mother's

wonderfully deep bath is surrounded by cheap and nasty bottles from which you can make huge amounts of foam. And it is more than long enough to stretch battered thighs in, too.

I have Karsten's cordless with me in the bath and I know that it is well past bedtime. I have talked to Ida twice already and I have to a) show confidence in other childminders, and b) ensure that I don't ring at precisely the moment the bedtime rituals are taking place. Unfortunately there is not a gentle ripple around the rocks on Jomfruland, there are massive breakers this autumn and it is a DISASTER.

Benny forgot to pack the mouse. I nurture a faint hope that she will sleep anyway since it is her father who is in charge on Jomfruland. Not so. Karsten and *Gran* insist on sleeping with Ida and have always done so. It is not so straightforward taking the place of a mouse.

But he has a splendid suggestion for solving the problem. I listen to him; I have to.

"Isn't that a little over the top?" I ask, calmer than I can believe.

"It's Gran's idea," Benny says.

"Whose did you say?"

"Your mother's."

"She thinks, in all seriousness, that you should drive to Kragerø to wait for the train where some kind conductor will give you the cuddly toy that I will have given to him? This evening?"

"Mmm."

"Have you had dinner?"

"Only Ida. The rest of us have just been for the most part, you know, *looking*."

"You haven't even had the sacred alcoholic drink?"

"I'm not daft," Benny replies. "Of course they've had a drink."

"But not you?"

"No. We've been cleaning teeth and all that."

"Quick," I say. "Knock back a couple of glasses of wine, then none of you can drive."

It doesn't help, it turns out, half an hour later when I ring Benny again to check on his alcohol intake. Karsten has promised that the mouse will be in place when she wakes up, and you shouldn't lie to children, he has been told. Whether you have had the sacred drink or not.

★ ★ ★

They don't know that I am not staying in Markveien and it is not because of photographers that I am keeping away from the gateway there. That is the way I want it. I am an adult and I can look carefully before I go in. First to the right. Then left and right again. Necessary rituals for survival.

The new death's head grins at me from the wall beside the door in Markveien. It has dripped. Thick greasy runs of paint form snail trails down the wall; they are shiny and would likely come off on my fingers if I touched them. From an anatomical point of view the head is no masterpiece, and it can hardly have taken a minute to smear it on, but that doesn't prevent it from being effective. On the contrary, the coarse base, the rough brushstrokes, the white stripes under it all help to emphasise its primitive character. Hundreds of years of experience of painting have demonstrated, if nothing else, that fear is at the heart of most primitive expression. The practitioner's and the recipient's.

Exposed to this Message, I sit in the car paralysed.

Oh, it helps that Markveien is deserted apart from the parked cars. They are dark empty shells abandoned by their missing owners or dead monster molluscs, empty shells under the swaying lights of street lamps swinging on such fragile wires between house fronts. The dark helps. The emptiness helps. My loneliness helps.

On the other hand it is obviously a greeting from Anlaug. Insistent, primitive. But not particularly dangerous. A whale in court shoes, Igi, is not the same as men wearing balaclavas.

On the pavement I do as Ida does: first I look left, then right and that is when I catch sight of it.

It is parked higher up the street and it may not be the same one, but it still looks like the oversized, misbegotten deformity called the *Dream Machine* that Anlaug was driving this morning. A giant of a machine, always painted in dark colours, with windows that you can't see through, and probably room for ten beer-swilling pigs. The dreams you find in this mobile fortress are not the kind you would want to know anything about. It is like an ambulatory rape factory and I hate it whenever I see it, even if it only contains a whale with court shoes and paint brush.

I stride angrily towards it.

Before I reach it two things happen at almost the same time. A couple turn into Markveien from Bergverksgata, and the *Dream Machine* comes to life. It sounds like an explosion in the empty street. The long flat section of rear lights bare their red teeth at me and the large ton-heavy metal body swings out into the street and guns hard and fast up towards Øvre Foss and the crossroads in Sannergata.

The couple turn round and watch it go.

"Halfwit," the young man says.

It might not have been her. It didn't have to be her just because the couple came and then the car sped off.

However, I keep my distance from them and I have them in the corner of my eye as I unlock the door. They didn't even look at the death's head. Anlaug isn't the only person in this town who paints on walls.

The mouse is, as expected, stuffed between the bed head and the mattress in Ida's bed. There is the smell of child's sleep and it gives me a kind of heady assurance. Or maybe it is the fact that I managed to go in through my own gateway.

I have the mouse in front of me on the desk as I look up Sjur Aske's address in Maridalen. I am going to take a peek at Aske's "Home". Perhaps even ask his brother a couple of questions about Martin Andersen's real role in the fall of TroJa or about what happened so many years ago in what is still his "Home". And if it doesn't feel safe I won't even have to get out of the car, will I?

Out through the passage door. Look around. First left. Then right.

No-one there. But it is like that with newly painted surfaces, it is difficult not to touch them. The death's head doesn't come off. Extremely quick drying paint, in the chilly autumn air. Or else Anlaug, if it was her *Dream Machine*, must have been *waiting* outside the gateway for some time.

I still have enough confidence, perhaps from being in the car, after going to Oslo station and delivering the mouse to a conductor with smiling eyes, children of his own and experience of DISASTERS. A mouse. And a whale in court shoes. The world outside the car door does not seem so menacing after all.

On top of that there is something very reassuring about driving in the dark. Reassuring and irresistible. I have left the town far behind me and passed the detached houses by Brekke on my way between the dense rows of spruces along by Lake Maridal when I feel it. The night whispers, the distinctive darkness that envelops lone motorists and gives them a feeling of control.

All night, this darkness says, wheels will whisper on the tarmac, all night you will be able to travel without feeling fear. Without ever weakening, just keep going, glide between these endless jagged shadows, without anything to hold you up, you can see the night through, right to the very end, until you know everything it contains. Don't stop, it whispers, don't let anything stop you now you are enclosed by night. Stay here.

It is tempting, the type of temptation drivers of *Dream Machines* of all kinds fall for.

Sjur Aske's smallholding is supposed to be somewhere near the sloping fields on the other side of the ruined church. I pull in to a lay-by to find the piece of paper with his house number and the Norwegian Automobile Association road atlas. The engine purrs along between the spruces and I am just reaching out to turn on the internal light when two powerful car headlights blaze out of the dark behind me. Headlights on full beam, dazzlingly bright full beam, operated by a driver with no intention of dipping them, and I turn my face away so as not to be dazzled. The car overtakes at a recklessly high speed for these narrow roads.

When I look up I recognise the car. I think I do at any rate. It is the back of a slim, gold Jaguar and there are not many people apart from Bella driving around in one like it.

She is driving faster than me, so I just follow her two red rear lights from some way behind. To the right of me a glimpse of water and then it is gone. A solitary smallholding in long fields. Bella's car disappears in front of me into the sharp bend at the end of the water.

It reappears under the blue light of a street lamp. It has slowed down and as the car turns into the gravel drive I can see it clearly for the first time. Not the driver though, but it is indeed a sleek, shark-like Jaguar and it is a gold colour.

It still maintains quite a high speed up the gravel drive, but it would be unlike Bella to let a bit of gravel stand between her and her goal.

I go past the gravel drive and continue up a little hill where the trees are dense enough to hide the car. Bella is an acquaintance. Even a sort of friend, although I know less about her then she knows about the law regarding shares. On the other hand she is probably closer to Aske than anyone. Benny said she helped him with everything from tax returns to minor dope offences. She had, of course, with or without any knowledge of the laws regarding shares, made great use of Martin Andersen before he died.

And as far as I know she does not make it a habit to cultivate relations with *workers*. Or, for that matter, smallholders.

It is interesting enough to leave the car for, interesting enough for me to cross the road on the dark stretch midway between two lampposts, to follow the narrow track between the clump of trees and the field, across towards this house situated in the middle of nowhere.

I move with silent footsteps under cover of night. And it is true to say that no-one hides in the dark, unless you have been following them that is.

There is a low building to the left of the house, too small to be a modern barn, bigger than a normal outhouse. It may have been a cowshed with enough room for a couple of animals. *The cat*, I remember, although there is nothing about this farm that reminds me of Aske's painting. The farmhouse is bigger, there is no steep hill behind it and in Aske's picture there is no outhouse. But there is something called artistic licence and right now as I approach the building under the shelter of dark this too is a little frightening.

There is a smell of damp earth and rotting grass here, and something sharp or bitter, perhaps the herbs. Between the two buildings there is a compact blackish area full of bushes and if I am going to spy on her, this sort of friend of mine, I will have to get in close.

In other words, behind the tangled shrubs. Hidden from the light in the ground floor of the farmhouse and, I hope, hidden from the bare bulb lighting the entrance.

There are two cars in the yard, pale and greenish in the gleam cast by the outside light. One is Bella's gold shark, the other is Sjur Aske's old Golf, which seems better suited to the shabby surroundings than hers.

The three-metre high doors of the farm building are within the range of the light from the farmhouse; the whole building is dark and gloomy especially for someone like me who can't stop thinking about *the cat*.

Their voices reach me first and I am looking in the direction of the farmhouse as they come down the steps. The shrubs obscure one of them for the moment, but the owner of the sports car wanders out into the yard, head raised characteristically high, and it is not a cat but a dog that I should be frightened of. Bella has Rita with her.

I don't know anything about wind directions, nor what effect youthful hash smoking has on a dog's sense of smell, but as far as humiliating experiences go, there are worse things than being *gnawed* at by Rita while hiding in the bushes.

I get away with it. Bella bundles Rita into her gold shark without the creature even sniffing in my direction.

"In there?" Bella asks, indicating the farm building with one raised, tiger-striped arm. "Do you keep your treasures in there? How *interesting*."

Bella in fighting spirits, I can hear. Bella also a little bit ruffled. The man following her is dressed in threadbare jeans and a thick sailor's sweater. His hands are thrust deep into his trouser pockets as he walks behind her, his long legs in rubber boots. It is Sjur Aske, whom Bella last saw when he was demonstrating against her exhibition, as far as I know, but obviously I don't know very much.

Sjur Aske tugs open the heavy doors; Bella makes no attempt to help him. While he does this she lights one of her menthol cigarettes and stands trembling in her thin clothes, tapping with the pointed, capped toe of her boot on the gravel. Her behaviour seems arrogant but is probably nothing more than a cover to disguise the fact that she is freezing.

"You can borrow one of my jackets," Sjur Aske says.

"Thanks anyway," Bella says in her West Side voice.

He disappears into the dark, rummages around for a moment and switches on a powerful torch. It casts a diagonal, yellow and white shaft of light from his hand down to the ground.

"My God," Bella says. "Are you expecting me to look at them with *that*?"

"Er," he says, "I think it'll give enough light, at least for a first impression. But we can take them inside if you would rather.

"Thank you very much," Bella says, following him. "I think we'll just get it over with."

The light flickers over the floor, but they obscure it, their bodies cast strange disparate patterns in the powerful spotlight and then they disappear from view, over to the left of the room; the broken streams of light flash in and out of my field of vision, none of them strong enough or still enough for me to gain any kind of impression of the room.

They continue to talk inside, not much, brief muffled phrases delivered in a monotone, mixed in with other sounds, clattering sounds and something being dragged over the floor. Then the light steadies for a while and there is silence. I hear the rustling of leaves around me and perceive the sounds my consciousness had filtered out. Afterwards a little tapping noise, possibly the toe of Bella's boot on the floor.

And there is no doubt about the brisk impatient sound of her heels on her way out. Sjur Aske's spotlight follows her. He still shines the light on the floor. Quite considerate of him. Bella's slim tiger legs roam towards the doorway in a flood of light.

Then he turns the torch off and hangs it up in its place. It takes me a few seconds to register them as anything but undelineated shadows. However, I can hear clearly what she says.

"You've made your point," she says. "But it is still first and foremost your problem, isn't it? In principle it is not something *I* need to bother about."

"I don't think you mean that," Sjur Aske says calmly, pushing the heavy door back.

"She was your mother," Bella says. "Not mine."

"That's not the point. It's not relevant."

"Isn't it? So *heartless* somehow. And here was I thinking it was your brother who was the prodigal son."

"He's got nothing to do with this." Sjur Aske's voice is a touch more strained.

"Are you sure about that?" Bella asks. "And here was I thinking *he* was the one you . . ."

"And you can cut out that uppety tone of voice with me," Sjur Aske breaks in. "You've seen it now. Perhaps you should sleep on it. Perhaps you should take advice from somebody who understands more about these things and then we can come back to the matter."

"Let's get one thing straight," Bella says. "And that is when I want to *take advice* from somebody who *understands more* about these things then I talk loudly and clearly to myself. And *actually* it's worked well up till now. Jesus! But you can be damn sure that we will come *back* to this matter, you needn't worry about that."

It is a grand exit, even observed from a bushy cover, and the tigerish roar of her engine as she hurtles down the gravel drive takes nothing away from it.

When can you be certain that someone is asleep? When all the lights in a house are off? When an attic window is left ajar? When there are no other sounds anywhere except for the whipping of the wind in dry grass, this rustling of the leaves close by or far away, if *far* is the corner of the house and if the rustling is caused by the wind or some small animal?

When your body is stiff from the cold, that's when you know. Then you don't know; you are not at all sure that anyone is asleep, but soon you begin not to care. I can always run, you think. If he can't sleep I can always run like the wind on these stiff limbs, down the gravel drive, over the fields. I've got a car, for heaven's sake.

The sickly green light over the porch doesn't help. As far as possible I'll have to avoid it. The moon, on the other hand, I can't avoid. In my foolish towny way I tend to admire the fact that it can light up a landscape, as long as you are far enough away from traffic and streets and the enormous glass expanses of commercial buildings.

Now I don't admire it, I curse it mildly, although mostly I am trying to stretch my short memory right back into the cerebral cortex where there may be traces of various abilities that cats have, which fantasising evolutionists think my body can remember because my ancestors could. They could move noiselessly in the shadows wherever there was shadow, put a foot down so carefully that twigs didn't snap and leaves didn't rustle.

That is not the way it happens for me. There is a crashing and banging, my breathing is like a dying whale's, my heartbeat like drumrolls, I snap twigs, I trip over clumps of grass, I am a treasure trove for any modern composer searching for authentic acoustic material as I sneak around, and the piece could be entitled "Hysteria" or perhaps "Fear".

I cast shadows too – flickering, fluttering and frozen – when I stand still, and it is just my breathing and my heart echoing around me. The shadow reveals a head, shoulders, upper body bent over. But no golden light appears in the house, no shouts reach my ears.

By the double doors to the farm building I am not a shadow, I stand there in full view, pale green and visible from the windows in the farmhouse, though not from the one that is ajar. From the moment Sjur Aske opened this door it has developed a chainsaw-like creaking sound. Perhaps it is a kind of alarm, I think, a special kind of farm alarm he activated without my noticing it, a creak alarm, long, drawn out and remorseless, that he can't help but hear whether he is in REM sleep or deep in Alpha or Beta or Omega sleep or whatever the *bloody* sleep is called.

But a shot doesn't ring out from a smallholder's rifle. I stand in complete darkness on the inside of the locked doors and here I can smell dust, white spirit and dried grass. No exhaust fumes, no petrol. This, I know, is crunch time, zero hour, the defining moment and I haven't given it a thought. I fumble around. I stagger sideways alongside the door to my right, let my hands grope and fumble, and scrabble around the wall, over the diagonal supports, over the tiles, and inevitably I knock it over. An explosion of sound on the floor, worlds meet, two tons of torch smash against a surface that must be made of iron. That is what it sounds like, and as I get down on all fours and crawl across the floor I am sure it must have been destroyed in the fall.

I must be covered in dust when I find it, grimy and lifeless. I switch it on. Lightning and flashes, explosions of light and laser beams, long V-shaped segments of space cut out in front of my eyes, and as the bearer of the light I make an attempt to shine it on to the floor. I don't suppose his hands can have been shaking like mine.

Relax, he can't *kill* you, I think. Of all the idiotic statements my brain could have slipped into my consciousness this deserves first prize since it has absolutely to be followed by a question. What do *you* know about that? How do you know that isn't precisely what he can do?

Somewhere inside me a little girl begins to whine. Stupid and childish. There are things she doesn't want to think about, questions she doesn't want to hear. The little girl notes that there doesn't seem to be anything sinister in here. Okay, she says to herself, great. That was what you wanted to know, wasn't it? Can we go now?

There is very little in here at all. A pile of wood along the back wall, some shelves made of coarse, unplaned wood with pots of paint and tools. A rusty barrel. Wooden crates of the kind that used to hold bottles of milk or beer a long, long time ago. A chopping block and a saw trestle.

No old sheep pen, no nasty rope ends by the wall. Although I would have got rid of them if I had even as much as suspected what they were used for.

Bella and Sjur Aske had disappeared from view to the left of the double doors. There are two old bookcases there, the kind with backs made of solid wood; they are heavy and inelegant and will have been replaced by something more practical from BBB or IKEA inside the house.

There is also a horrible, heavy coffee table from the Fifties that second-hand dealers have nightmares about; it is low and grey brown with four lumpen lion's paws for feet. A newspaper has been spread over the table's surface and on top there are three small cardboard boxes. This is where it comes from, this smell, something like white spirit but much more seductive. If I ever thought of becoming a sniffer this would be my choice. Terpentine. The little tang of resin, the full-bodied, entrancing fumes of pine and vegetable oil. Only pure petrol would smell more narcotic.

Small boxes contain tubes of paint, lots of them, rolled up and hard as rock, with faded labels and the sticky yellow remains of linseed oil between the paint stains. "Neapolitan yellow", one reads. "Titanic white." "Parisian blue." "Noir d'ivoire."

There is something moving and rather surprising about Sjur Aske keeping his brother's stuff from his early days as an artist.

The two bookcases stand back to back, a good half a metre apart, with something between them. Canvases, stretched out, most of them quite small, about 80 by 60 centimetres, but a few are much bigger. I pull them out and have a look at them in the light from the torch, one after the other.

The young boy with his shirt open at the neck sitting by a window. A meadow in summer, the tones muted in the evening light. Two old people by a roaring fire. A woman with a plunging neckline and a flushed face. Several dramatic mountainous landscapes.

They have all been finished with great care and in great detail in a kind of impressionistic style and there is not so much as a suggestion of artistic interest.

Work done in his youth, I think. Early, formal, private study of a young man who wants to get on in the world but doesn't yet know how to go about it. That is what I think until I look more closely at the signature on one of the landscapes. It is beautiful looped writing, formed with all the care of the skilled amateur.

"Merete Aske", it says. "1958." The same signature is on all the canvases, the only variation being the odd "M. Aske" and an "M.A." on the smallest ones.

This is the woman with the fumbling hands. With the repulsive punishments, with the hairbrush, the belt and the wild insane laughter. The woman who lay for days in a dark room only to appear half-naked and singing when he came home from school. This is the woman responsible for *the cat*.

And also such neat, detailed but stiff landscapes. With these patient, concentrated brushstrokes of pigment and oil. So he inherited something from her, I think, something other than hatred and fear.

But what does Bella care about that? What can Bella have seen here that was relevant to her and that she could get so angry about?

25

NATURALLY ENOUGH IDA did not show much interest when she saw the mouse. It is the morning now and I can hear from Benny that Karsten is a little hurt. He had probably expected wild celebrations after his rescue operation, undertaken after consuming alcohol.

"How hurt?" I ask, "a stroll over the rocks-hurt or woodchopping-hurt?"

"Stroll," Benny says.

"Then it's not so serious. It is when he does the woodchopping that you can expect something boring about *manners*."

The sun is chilly over by the rocks, he says, and there is ice forming on the puddles, which he and Ida go out to smash. No fantastic breakers. No LIONS either.

But Ida has had a series of morning experiences that have to be reported back. They concern silly children's things, all of them, *Gran* and *book* and the all-absorbing plans for her and Karsten to go *fishing*. I suddenly miss her desperately at the kitchen table in Charlotte Andersensveien and since this does not interest her very much I tell her father instead.

"You're very welcome to come down here," he says.

"I know. How's it going with Mother?"

"Brilliant. She and I are going to make bouillabaisse."

Provençal style, I know, just like the tiles by the stove.

"Did you know that Bella knew Sjur Aske?" I ask.

"No. Does she?"

"I saw them together yesterday," I say. "Quite by chance."

"Uhuh," he says. "Action still not silly, then?"

"Right."

But Benny is not so silly, either. He thinks, just like me, that

Bella plus Sjur Aske is strange. Maybe, I suggest, it wasn't just Martin Andersen who betrayed Otto Troels-Jacobsen when TroJa was hijacked?

"Maybe," Benny says. "But all that stuff about the demonstrations against Roll and so on – was that just a kind of game?"

Rent-a-Demo, I think.

"Well, they didn't seem to be on *friendly* terms, Sjur and Bella."

"And is this what's keeping you busy?"

"I'm going to visit the sister of someone called PAN today," I say. "Who went missing."

"Strange pastimes you have."

Says he, who dresses up in clothes that could never be mine. Maybe my mother's.

The spruces are much too high for me to see their tops and the black heavy branches form jagged arrows where they droop down from the trunk. Ten years after Aske painted his spruce trees in the *PAN* picture they might have looked like these. Underneath the heavily bent branches the dying wood closest to the ground attests to the life higher up. These trees die from the bottom up and in lines, all the same height. The twigs from the trees intertwine and then they shoot vertically into the sky because the light can't reach them from above through the dense growth.

I pass Hønefoss and the unending Lake Sperille through several kilometres of dense forest before reaching Nes in the Ådal valley. Somewhere around here Per Anders Nilsen was murdered many, many years earlier.

The mystery that exists in the long parallel sightlines between the trees is not one of variation, but of unity and conformity. All there is to be found alongside one row of spruces is another row, a dry impassable interweaving of twigs, dead at the same height, a hundred metres above the road. There are no fairy-tale adventures here, no winding paths, just more of the same – a measured and predictable if slow death.

It is not possible to go for a walk in forests like these, they are meant for driving through, meant for the slow purr of engines, numbing like the heat in the car, like the small skilled movements of hand, foot and gears. I repeat my movements, the forest repeats itself outside. Uniformity without meaning, one tree is like another, one life is like another, one death like another.

The houses are the only puzzles, the way they appear and disappear. Why here? Why not somewhere else? Why at this bend and why not at the next one? When I am driving through forests like these I always think that I am closer than ever to the minds of those who choose their victims at random and not through personal knowledge. This tree or that one? This person or that one?

The spruces have grown since Per Anders Nilsen went missing and now let even less sunlight in to the forest floor. However, when a field opens up and the river comes into view it hits me, then it is blinding and breathtaking.

The house lies slightly outside the centre of Bagn, directly beneath the sheer cliff the power station clings to. It has been painted white recently and has a long balcony with a heavy fretwork-patterned railing on the first floor. Full curtains with valance and ties in contrasting colours border the windows; a wealth of autumn flowers in pots and flower beds give the garden colour. Under an apple tree there is a small bird bath with two children in stone huddled under an umbrella. They look a little bored. "Amundsen" it says inside a garland of wild flowers on the post box.

There may still be traces of him inside, a shelf he put up on the cellar wall or sticker marks on the inside of a cupboard door which have proved difficult to remove. No-one disappears altogether.

The painter of wild flowers on post boxes opens the door after I ring. I assume it is her at any rate, since she is wearing a blue apron decorated with wild flowers. Edel Amundsen is a slight woman, probably ten centimetres shorter than me with the sort of straight back that comes with a certain defiance. A brother who went missing and a mother who hanged herself, that is enough to be defiant about. It is also admirable that she can bear such misfortune with a straight back.

"I rang you yesterday," I say.

"Uhuh, the psychologist."

Undisguised contempt in her voice.

"Did she send you," she asks. "The woman from . . . what is it called?"

"Loaf?"

"She said she was coming back, so I thought maybe . . ."

"You are talking about Ingeborg Dahl," I ask. "Aren't you?"

"That must be her name," Edel Amundsen says. "It's rather difficult to think of her as anyone but Helena's mother."

Can it be that this woman has not heard about her death?

"I may have been a bit brusque yesterday," she says. "Please come in."

She stands ramrod-straight and scrutinises me while I take my shoes off in the hall. Everyone has to, she says. "No-one can come in with outdoor shoes on." I turn down the offer of slippers.

In the sitting room Edel Amundsen sits at the furthest end of her old-fashioned sofa, her knees primly together as women of our generation only do when wearing a short skirt. Perhaps I should have accepted the offer of slippers after all. The floor is cold here and the temperature of the room can't be above 18°. She follows my gaze to the pine floor.

"Pine-fresh, liquid green soap," she says. "Not varnish. We have put up new panels too, with environmentally friendly paint. It is extraordinary how much poison people are willing to put up with in their own houses."

Still this straight back, this face that seems scrubbed clean with defiance. Now I recognise her odd smell too – it is the tar soap she washes her hair with, also toxin-free, I suppose. I would have expected there to have been more home crafts inside the house, but then I have my own preconceptions and I am a townie. The sitting room is pretty sober, frugal, rather randomly furnished. I imagine there to be things left by her deceased mother and an easy chair that may belong to a man called Amundsen.

She may have made the cloths and cushions herself, decorated as they are with wild flowers. There is nothing to suggest the existence of a teenage boy.

"She didn't dare come herself then," she says.

"Ingeborg Dahl?" I ask.

She nods.

"In fact, she hasn't *sent* me," I begin.

"It's not that I don't understand her," she interrupts. "I was perhaps . . . a little rough with her. But I was also sick of her

Christmas greetings and her reports. The gooey sentimentality that just covers over . . . You know. Money. Becoming a member and supporting. Newsletters. News about what? Other *victims and kin*?"

"I don't quite understand," I say, and once more put off telling her that Ingeborg Dahl is dead. It is underhand, of course, because I have twigged what is missing in this room and what keeps Edel Amundsen thinking she was still alive. There isn't a TV.

"That woman killed my mother," Edel Amundsen says flatly. "I still think that though I had no right to tell her. It was cruel of me and I regret it."

"Did Ingeborg Dahl have regular contact with your mother?" I ask.

"She did. She was very keen, too. For a while I think it may have done my mother some good. There was someone to talk to and someone who was interested enough to listen to her. But then she started putting ideas into her head. There's nothing very reassuring about her theories, is there?"

"What sort of theories were they?"

She is not listening to me now.

"I'm not sure," she says, putting her hands on her lap, "that someone in your profession can do very much about something like this. The woman came here and left my mother with the most horrendous traumas. All the same I can't say I have much respect for the profession you belong to."

"Why not?"

"You don't fulfil people's real needs, she says firmly. "Their religious and spiritual needs."

"No," I say. "You're right about that. We very seldom satisfy religious needs. These theories of Ingeborg Dahl's, what were they about?"

"Don't you know about them? She thought that both her daughter and my brother were victims of . . . what do you call it? . . . a mass murderer."

"A serial killer," I say, thinking about the absent TV set. How many people are there who haven't taken that distinction on board? What good does knowing it do us? Anyway, it doesn't interest her.

"While what my mother should have understood was that PAN went his own way," Edel Amundsen says. "That he made his choice. It was cruel, but it was his own choice."

Perhaps. It may be true. Although even this possibility would have created images that, if they were not horrific, were *cruel* at the very least. That is a word that Edel Amundsen likes since she has used it twice already.

"And you think it was these images that caused your mother to take her life?"

"Yes."

The light through the window falls on half of her face. It looks pasty and lifeless.

"Why do you think he went away?"

"It was his way," she says. "He had to do it. No-one has the right to deny anyone the chance to follow their own calling. He got on his scooter and *left*, and that's all there is to it."

"Was there any direct reason for him to go?" I ask.

"Oh, yes indeed," she says, "if one is interested in banalities. Our stepfather had just moved out and PAN was a lot closer to him than I was. On top of that the divorce was pretty harrowing. We thought for a while that he would head for his stepfather's. Even my mother was sure that he would go there. And it wasn't the first time he had stayed away. But none of this is important. The important thing is the choice."

I am interested in banalities. I think they are important. But they don't necessarily have the power of firm convictions.

"But other people have also thought that he didn't just go his own way, haven't they?" I ask. "Not just Ingeborg Dahl."

"You mean the police and the newspapers? Yes, they've been here now and then, most often the papers first. They didn't do my mother any good, either. But it is possible to stand back from them. It works."

This comes in a patronising tone, one finely mixed with bitterness. The patronising is for me, the young townie girl lapping up journalistic nonsense. The bitterness is all hers.

"You don't watch TV?" I ask.

"Nor do I read newspapers."

"You don't have material needs?"

"No."

But she has a radio, she says. She listens to the station that plays only classical music. She has it on when she's massaging her clients. A conviction, a semi-therapeutic business, a house that is slowly ridding itself of its poisons. There are many choices, some of them cruel.

"You don't know if PAN left to meet someone?"

"No," she says. "He didn't know many people outside this area. Apart from our stepfather, of course."

Her face is in shadow now, but her clear eyes follow me.

"Do you know someone called Aske?" I continue. "The artist?"

"No," she says. "I don't know him." Then she draws herself up. "But she asked me about him too," she adds.

"Did she?"

She takes a breath and looks out of the window for a few seconds, perhaps at the two stone children who are getting so bored.

"That's why you're here," she says, more to herself than to me. "Of course. I've had a bad conscience about it, you know. Because I lied to her. But I had almost forgotten about it when she asked. Not that that is an excuse."

She turns towards me again and gives me a vague sort of smile.

"It's probably more correct to say that I protected myself against an unpleasant memory. And you shouldn't do that."

You should of course. But not against all memories and not all the time.

The woman who likes the word cruelty has made a choice and it is, as she would have said, her own. And mine, since I am here. I presume she wouldn't agree with me about the latter, but it makes no difference. I make deals, a somewhat squalid business, and if she can clear her conscience with my visit, then perhaps we are quits. That is fine. There are all kinds of reckonings flying around everywhere, around me too.

"Is he very famous?" she asks.

"I think we could say that. About as famous as an artist can be in this country."

"Not in those days, he wasn't," she says. "And what's more . . . Yes, I'll come to that. As I said, the relationship between my mother and our stepfather was somewhat stormy and it had an effect on both PAN and me, but in different ways. I am two years older than him and I was, um, a little slow as a teenager. And I got much more involved in their conflicts. PAN just used to take off on his scooter."

Although she speaks quietly she has a control over her words that suggests they are part of am internal conversation that she has conducted before. Like a rehearsed text.

"I was very angry with them both, but more with my mother," she continues. "And so I was searching for a way to punish them. One of the girls I knew talked about this place, about his hut. I'm sure most of it was teenage bravado, but that was where it was all supposed to be happening. Booze and sex and so on. He painted her naked, she said, or almost naked. And paid for it."

I am glad that she looks away at this moment. Not because my face might betray shock at a little nude painting, but because of his hut. Aske's hut, she means. Somewhere around here, in the forest where PAN disappeared.

I have to think hard about something other than this information so that my face doesn't give away my interest. About painting nudes, for example.

Heady enough, I say to myself, risqué and wild and rebellious enough for giggling teenagers and awakening urges. Aske had a hut here. Aske had a hut here.

"So I went there late one night when they were squabbling. Into the forest and asked him if he wanted to paint me. I had probably drunk quite a bit. There was nothing very innocent about it, you know. *I* went to him, *I* took off my clothes. And I could see very well that he was much drunker than me and looked dreadful."

Young girls and enormous, muscular stallions. Forests and water and pitch black voids between the trees. *Now I'm coming to take you.*

"I was afraid, of course," she continues. "There was nothing elegant about it, the filthy hut and undressing while he stood looking at me and laughing. And he touched me. His hands were quite cold, I remember. Not much else happened. He drew. And drank. I also drank a little, not a lot. He talked a fair bit and got me to pose in a variety of ways. And then I got sick of it and asked if this was the best he could come up with, standing and drawing."

She looks down at her hands. The light from the window only reaches her neck, bent right over.

"Then he went out. Had to have a pee first, he said. And while he was away I looked at his drawings. It was just a mess, just a mass of confused lines, not me at all. Then I took off."

"And this was at the same time that PAN went missing?" I ask

"Some weeks before. I tried to forget it. I've never talked about it to anyone."

"And . . . nothing else happened?" I ask.

"No," she says firmly.

"Are you quite sure? You looked at the drawings and took off? Through the same door as he left by?

"He was standing out there," she says. "And he grabbed me. I was frightened and angry and then I said that his drawings were awful. Then he laughed even more. 'You're no artist,' I shouted. Or something like that. 'You're dead right about that,' he said. And then I ran."

"Did he follow you?"

"Only down the steps. But that isn't the point, the point is that it was true. It wasn't the Aske Ingeborg Dahl went on about. It was his brother."

"How do you know?" I ask very quietly.

"He told me. And the drawings. They were appalling."

I have had my part of the deal. She signals this by standing up and leading me into the hallway.

"Would you recognise him?" I ask.

"I don't think so. It was dark and I was quite drunk. And it's a long time ago."

I pull out a copy of *Home*. "Is that the hut?" I ask.

"It could be. But it's a bad painting."

"As bad as the sketches of you?"

"I don't know. They were just scribbles."

"If I send you some photographs," I say, "could you see if you recognise the man from the hut?"

"I've just told you I wouldn't know!"

"Could you at least have a look at them?"

Negotiations. Sub-clauses in small print. I get my deal and rough directions to the hut. I don't know if I have more poison on me after

I leave her. In the car I begin to piece things together. An apparent identification of an unpleasant drunken man in a hut at night. An assessment of artistic merit by a woman who adores wild-flower decorations.

It isn't much. But it is something. Modest ambitions. Either Aske or his brother were in the hut at the time PAN went missing. It isn't only girls who experience the strange fascination of forests and water and the pitch black void between the trees.

26

THE ROOF WITH the sunken ridge and the moss-covered tiles lies low over the single floor of the house. Behind the windows the pale brown curtains are drawn, one of them hangs crookedly and has a tear in it. It must be months, maybe years, since the grass by the rotting picket fence was cut.

Scattered over the small farm thin birch trees have taken root; on the west side of the house they form a bare thicket.

But the little glass porch is the same, although a couple of the window panes are broken and have been replaced with cardboard, now damp-stained. The sloping hill to the east of the house is the same, the curved, half-overgrown gravel drive up to the house too. There are no blazing red flames in the sky here, but it seems more likely that this is the model for Aske's *Home* than the smallholding in Maridalen.

I walk up the weed-filled gravel drive towards the house, past the rusting barrel under the downpipe, along the end wall where one window with its dusty curtain is in the dark. There is an empty Coca-Cola bottle leaning against the window frame.

A couple of dark planks lie rotting in the yard, some old paint pots are piled up under the eaves. It seems a waste of time but I bang on the glass pane in the door anyway. After waiting for less time then I normally would have if I thought someone was in I shield the fading light out with my hand and press my forehead against the glass. A closed door. A light bulb under a cotton lampshade faded by age; to my right thick, dark clothes on a row of hooks in the corner. It is too dark to see them properly.

The door is locked.

Someone is looking at me. Not from inside the house. From the dense growth of trees behind me. This is stupid and childish, I know.

A lonely woman in the forest, a child at night, primal reflexes in spinal cords and fear of reptiles in unfamiliar surroundings. So I turn round slowly and stare. There is no-one there. No frightening figure in the trees. Although the shadows there are deep enough, black enough, little by little the staring helps me to realise that I am frightened.

Because I don't see very much. Branches trembling in the wind. Shadows moving fractionally. A bare tree trunk stretching up into the sky. But I manage to walk slowly. I don't run. I stop at the corner of the house and notice that the barrel has corroded with rust and leaks. How long, I think, would it take a birch shoot, undisturbed, to grow up to my waist?

Two years? Five? – I have no idea, the child in the forest inside me says – and I don't give a shit. Then I walk faster, past the collapsed picket fence and into the bend where the path is almost swallowed up by the dense rows of trees.

He is standing under the spruce trees and it is just his face that gives him away; it casts a milky white, a soft dark light from beneath the slanting branches. Of course I give a start, twitch stupidly, like a woman, like a solitary person.

"Sorry," he says. "I didn't mean to frighten you. It's just so seldom that anyone walks around here."

What is he wearing? Something dark and stained, camouflage colours it looks like, the type *men* walking alone in the forest wear.

"I was up by the hut over there," I say. "Aske's hut."

It is supposed to sound brash and confident, but it doesn't.

"Aske's hut?" he asks.

"I don't know what it's called. Isn't it his?"

"That crumbling hole? I don't think it's called anything."

He moves. Takes a few steps towards the path. I can see him better then. He has a beard and he is wearing a battered cap. Must be a gun on his back.

"Is it your car, then, down the road?" he asks.

"Yes," I say, taking my mobile phone out of my pocket. Just so that he knows, as it were.

"I usually take the path across here on my way home," he says. "But I seldom meet anyone."

"No-one uses the hut, do they?" I ask.

"I don't really know. Now and then it seems as if someone has been there. Tracks in the grass. But they don't look after it very well, do they? Perhaps it is just kids who drop by once in a while and . . . you know, have parties."

"The door's locked," I say.

"It's probably the owners, then, who go there occasionally. It's got nothing to do with me."

I eat a sad-looking plaice at a roadside inn in Nes and, well, down on Jomfruland they are preparing a *fabulous* bouillabaisse. And soon it will be time for the drink. Ida maintains that she caught one of the fish HERSELF.

"Come on down," Benny says.

"Not this evening," I say.

Five hours' driving in one day is more than enough, but otherwise it is a nice idea. Tomorrow, I think, I am going to drop in on competent Chief Inspector Kielland and tell her that at least one of the men who was present at TroJa when Martin Andersen died was also busy sketching with clammy hands in the forest where PAN disappeared.

And then I can visit the fantastic breakers on Jomfruland.

It is getting dark as I cruise past Lake Sperille and the last rays of sun make golden stripes over the surface of the water. It is dark before I reach the tollgate at Sollihøgda.

There are branches outside the windows in Charlotte Andersensveien too, black and jagged. They remind me so much of the trees in the picture entitled *PAN* that I draw Mother's billowing curtains. Don't look. On with the CD player. Hear no evil. Only what is in the room, well-lit and very open.

While I am singing a children's song about a troll mother into Karsten's cordless phone I feel really foolish, but I do forget the branches. The mouse is in its place under the yacht duvet in Jomfruland with its mistress. She doesn't *need* a bedtime song, but it is *fantastic* to have it. Necessary rituals.

While watering the plants, which is what I am here for after all, I plan my little report for the competent chief inspector.

The oldest first: Otto Troels-Jacobsen had every reason to feel let down, not just by his daughter but by Martin Andersen who with his love for dangerous sports served Roll by procuring the support of the *Frogner Fannies*.

Furthermore, Troels-Jacobsen was supported by a Sjur Aske who was not only sneaking around Grønlandsleiret on the evening Ingeborg Dahl disappeared but was also familiar with Villa Troels, where she was found dead. Sjur Aske's loyalty is perhaps open to question. Apart from that he has something going with Bella and he likes to pay people to beat others up. He may have his own reasons for disapproving of Ingeborg Dahl's interest in his brother's – and thus his own – background.

Both brothers were not only present at the TroJa exhibition, one of them was drawing lousy sketches in a hut close to the place where PAN went missing. Aske has, of course, painted both the pictures called *PAN* and an *Hommage à Helena*. And out of the blue he cancelled the biography in which his terrible childhood was described. Not only that, Ingeborg Dahl, before she was strangled, was convinced that Aske had killed her daughter. She may well have told more people than me.

It is not finished, it is not cut and dried, but it is something. Enough at least, I think, settling into one of Karsten's chairs, to create reasonable doubt about whether Javed is guilty. That is *something*. Modest ambitions.

If it weren't for his original confession. And the video.

The video, it turns out on my way up to the bathroom, Edevart Riel's shy girlfriend can help me with.

I am not sure it is her because the woman's voice on the mobile phone is anything but shy. This is not Lill, the shaven-headed computer nerd of Riel's flat, this is her alter ego. She is a *dominatrix*, I remember, *Fräulein Todt* or something like that, and Fräulein Todt has also got a deal with me. Did I remember that?

Yes indeed. *Call me*, I said to what used to be Lill, call me if you find the video or any trace of it. This she *is* now doing.

Fräulein Todt has come a long way from down.boys or care for male juvenile depressives or whatever the address down.boys was intended to impart and we are talking *live*, she says. We are talking outside of cyberspace, beyond space nomads, out of the virtual body, we are talking flesh and blood, here and now, take it or leave it, good old-fashioned *real life, real time*.

"You mean," I say, "you mean . . . a person?"

"Yes sir," she says. "Right on."

"You're incredible," I say.

"Aren't I?"

"And it's okay to meet this person?"

"If you have the right connections," Fräulein Todt says.

"Have we?"

"More or less."

"And that means?"

"That I've got them," she says, a note of triumph in her voice.

"Ahh. So the question is whether I've got you?"

"Spot on."

"And the answer is?"

"I expect that can be arranged."

I am not sure what Fräulein Todt understands by me *having* her once something or other has been arranged, but then again you shouldn't always get hung up on details.

"The deal was," I say anyway, "that I would take it to the police."

"You don't have any other interest in the video, do you?" she asks.

No. No, I don't. Even if it were the unequivocal proof of my client Javed's guilt?

27

HIGH AND LOW. Night and day. There is a curious irony in the near-deserted night-time streets of Kvadraturen. During the day art is exhibited and sold here in sober, expensive rooms; at night the streets are given over to prostitutes and their clients. Buying and selling of another kind, a *body art* that is far removed from intellectual theory. High and low. The art that in its attempts to be free or rebellious and thus allies itself with low life and down and outs has never been able to avoid being elevated: irrespective of how rebellious or sordid the pictures are, they end up on plain white walls in such spartan surroundings as these. Anything but vulgar.

The owner of a valuable product does not need to make a big fuss about it. Nowadays the fashion for painting prostitutes has long since passed and there are other things in life that are low and *outrageous*. Nevertheless, the prostitutes captured in art have come out of it better than those painted with cosmetics. And, compared with working these streets at night, there is nothing very dangerous on display *inside* the exhibition rooms at all.

Aske painted prostitutes, I remember, as I drive slowly through Kvadraturen, painted prostitutes in an almost embarrassingly romantic way, in an *attic* by the port in Amsterdam, for goodness' sake. It is also a long time ago, and if he is dangerous it can't be because of the pictures or the prostitutes.

I cruise, as punters do, not in search of a suitable woman, but on the lookout for the entrance to something called *Down Under*. It doesn't signpost its activities, there are no neon signs or brass nameplates. To be precise, I am looking for shy Lill in her less than shy role as *dominatrix*, who is supposed to be standing outside the venue. How stupid, I think, how stupid that I don't know what this Fräulein Todt of hers looks like, so that I am forced to scrutinise the prostitutes like all the other drivers here.

Most of the punters arrive like this, by car. There are very few men strolling along the streets. I pass one coming out of Skippergata, wearing a dark outdoor jacket with his shoulders hunched, and I recognise him. Rune Skjalgson, the seaman who shared the attic and the booze with Aske in Amsterdam. Some people, it seems, are never done with prostitutes and dark, almost deserted streets. He looks frozen.

High and low. *Down Under*, I discover, is not in a cellar but in a loft. Fräulein Todt waves to me from a gateway in a quiet side street on the other side of Bankplass, waits while I park the car and then accompanies me into a backyard and up into a large goods lift.

"It's not without its dangers," Fräulein Todt says as we step out of the lift and into a large attic room painted black. It is difficult to imagine that anything could be without danger, if you take her clothing as an example. And I do. I look at it from the side, from a distance, with all the Oslo West upbringing I might still have in me. Whoops, a black man. Don't look at him. Oh no, a drunk. Shame on you, don't stare. Since those days I have done a lot of staring. It doesn't exactly build up your self-esteem if your psychologist can't even bear to look at you when you grin.

Faced with Fräulein Todt's collage of fantasies I fall back into my pre-professional shyness, the kind that camouflages itself as worldly wisdom. Boobs falling out of bras? Nothing human is strange to me. Chains attached to the nipples? My dear, I've been around, you know. A little whip in the belt? Well, that is . . . an interesting detail.

It is down to ignorance, of course, and for a second I regret not asking Benny to give me a lightning course in leather fetishes before I came here because I don't know if Fräulein Todt represents the average SM-er or if she is a veritable Christmas tree decorated with the Liquorice Allsorts of sexual fantasy. Thigh boots look great, but spurs? Is that normal?

There are supposed to be people who get their kicks from waterproofs or nappies. Apparently the Fräulein doesn't do these, but she includes most things. A military effect – is that little medal actually pinned to her breast or dare I hope that it is a joke? Fishnet tights that go way over her hips, a spiked dog collar, a PVC bodice with plunging neckline, the one with the holes for the breasts.

Fräulein Todt studies me without the slightest embarrassment as we queue for the cloakroom, and I am grateful that she doesn't use full hoods. I think I would find it a little difficult to talk to someone who had to unzip their mouth first.

"I suppose you could say that at least you made an effort," she says dryly.

I am wearing a short leather jacket, a tight top and narrow trousers.

"It's black anyway," I say. "If nothing else. The last time I wore leather trousers was in the Eighties, I think, and they weren't even tight-fitting."

"That's what I mean," she says. "An effort, not a successful effort, but one nonetheless."

"Thanks," I say. "Just as a matter of interest, where do you place yourself? As far as your outfit goes, I mean?"

"On a scale from one to ten?"

"For example."

"See for yourself," she suggests.

And that is what I do while I wait at the bar. It is rather dark here, as it has to be, and the music consists of the digital whipping beat, as it has to do. On the dance floor there is the bright sweep of bluish white light; otherwise the lighting is just as spare as it needs to be for the essential semi-covert eyeballing.

These are just tourists like me. In addition there are several wearing rather more sophisticated clothing, a fishnet top, for example, with a black bra underneath.

"Weekend SM-ers," Todt informs me. Fräulein Todt, I deduce, is full-time.

The professionals are pierced with great care, as you'd expect. The long-limbed guy in full fishnet outfit without briefs can be numbered among them. The heavily leather-clad men are in the majority and in the crowd it is not easy to separate the sheep from the goats, the professionals from the amateurs. When it comes down to it, naked men's torsos are commonplace, whether they have chains between their nipples and navel or not, so I conclude, leaving aside the accentuation of the G-string, that it is the number of tattoos that is the decisive factor.

A fully tattooed chest with neat loops tapering like an arrow towards the abdomen is fairly professional I assume, just as tattoo-covered arms must also be. The tattooed band around an upper arm doesn't count at all since before long the Crown Prince of Norway will be the only person of his generation without one.

There are several more bare boobs, besides Fräulein Todt's, but not that many, and she is almost the only person with spurs. All in all, she towers above the masses.

"Eight," I shout into her ear. "And ten if you only count girls." For this she vouchsafes me a contented snort.

A skinny girl with small eyes pushes her way between us in an attempt to get to the bar. She can't be much more than twenty and her face is a chaotic mix of pimples and small silver balls. They seem almost to have been thrown at her face and to be fighting for space – an inflamed spot here, a silver ball there. Since she also has freckles and pale skin her face looks like a lavish cream cake scattered with hundreds and thousands.

"What about real life, real time?" I yell at Fräulein Todt.

"I haven't seen him yet," she bellows, leaning her freshly shaven head across to the young woman between us.

"Have you seen Simon this evening?" she asks Hundreds and Thousands.

"No," she says with no interest. "But I've seen the video. It was pretty tame. I mean, apart from the fact that he *died*, and you never know if that is true. There was only the bit of apathetic stroking of his chest and who gets off on that?"

"Where did you see it?" I ask.

Hundreds and Thousands looks at me. Her eyes are two *blue* dots.

"Three shots," she says.

I look at her uncomprehendingly before I remember her generation's chronic shortage of money.

"Three shots," Fräulein Todt repeats to the bartender and is immediately served out of turn. On my way across the floor to Hundreds and Thousands' table it becomes clear to me that I have the consummate guide for the evening. Fräulein Todt moves heavily and not so elegantly among the masses, but she has an indisputable physical authority that is undiminished by either her plump tightly corsetted stomach or her naked chain-festooned, uplifted breasts.

As I sneak along in Fräulein Todt's wake I find myself behind a kind of queen who greets a respectful public with solemnity and warmth. People make room for her, people kiss her on the cheek with pleasure or rather timidly. Fräulein Todt takes it all with great calm. She dominates them as a dominatrix should, quite naturally.

Two of the shots were intended for the Hundreds and Thousands' girlfriends with the bodged head shaves and disappear immediately. Fräulein Todt sighs, waves a spiked arm and gets a sarong-clad minion to fetch more.

"Did you see the video at Simon's?" I ask Hundred and Thousands.

"Yes," she says, grabbing a pouch of tobacco from one of her girlfriends. "But he is so out of it, it's just good he got rid of it. He feels persecuted and stressed and restless. I mean, what pleasure is there in owning something if you become paranoid and stupid about it? Eh?"

"How did he get rid of it?"

Hundreds and Thousands looks at me as if she has just discovered that I am brain damaged.

"He sold it obviously."

"So it's about money?" I say.

In her mind's eye Hundreds and Thousands observes the CJD consuming my brain.

"What else could it be about? Not sex anyway. It's dull, didn't I say that? A *tea service* is more exciting than that."

"And now, I say, absorbing this interesting view of faïence and porcelain, "now Simon hasn't got it any more?"

"No," she says. "But he is gaga anyway. He has got it into his head that he should have given it to the police for some reason and now he thinks they're waiting for him around every corner. Too much acid and nothing to bring him down, don't you think?"

Apart from discussing Saturday night's TV I don't know anything as deadly as in-depth conversation about different kinds of drugs, legal or otherwise, so I get her on to another track.

"If Simon hasn't got it any longer," I say, "then who has?"

Hundreds and Thousands smiles sardonically at this. It can't be her, I think, and with some relief watch the sarong-clad young man coming with enough shots to keep all of them going. I don't mind getting this little fart a bit merry now that she has got here all by herself and I have no other unpleasant plans for her beyond sexual rejection should it come to that.

"Thank you very much," I say to the sarong man and hand him the money. "That was kind of you."

"Please, think nothing of it," he says with a warm shake of my hand warmly. "Kjell," he adds. "Or Thea rather. The process isn't quite finished yet, you know, and I think it's great to be open about it."

"Quite right" I say.

"Only two operations left."

"That's great. Good luck."

Kjell or Thea gives a big smile and leaves.

Hundreds and Thousands' two blue dots for eyes are focused on something beyond me.

"How much is it going for?" I ask. "The video?"

"To buy or just to watch?" Hundreds and Thousands asks vacantly. "I got to see it for free but some people paid. There's always some idiot waiting to be fleeced. Anyway it was probably an accident at work, too much E and not enough . . ."

The unfortunate mixture of cheap chemicals is, to my relief, drowned under a raucous noise from the dance floor.

"To buy," I shout. "Maybe."

"You can ask Simon, can't you?" Hundreds and Thousands says, still staring over my shoulders. "But I don't think he got a very good price. He's standing over there."

Fräulein Todt has also spotted our Simon and nods, frowning, in the direction of a group of men in front of a column by the dance floor.

"Which of them is Simon?" I ask, thinking that if she says that he is the one in the black leather there won't be any drinks for her.

None of the four men is wearing anything but black leather.

"He's the one with the G-string," she says. I have a closer look at them.

"Come on. They've all got G-strings," I say.

"Well, the fattest one. The one waving his arms about."

Fräulein Todt negotiates on my behalf. I don't know what specialised interests she furnishes me with, sexual or otherwise, but after a while she graciously waves her spikey arm, the queen's arm, the one that would be holding the sceptre if she weren't so pleased with her little whip. I am granted an audience with the queen and her knight Simon.

Simon proffers a clammy hand. He has a distinctive, gangling body with long thin legs under an upper body that seems disproportionate, not because it is broad but because it is so long. He looks a little as if he has been put together in the same way that children do group drawings of bodies: one child draws the head and folds the paper so that their neighbour can't see, then the next one draws the torso and the third the legs. Simon looks as if he has got half a torso too much.

Fräulein Todt, as a specialist in specialised requests, introduces me and mine. Simon's face and his three-day head stubble are shiny with sweat; his cheeks – the same three-day salt and pepper – flushed with agitation. He stammers a little. He runs his hand over his scalp. It is not certain that his and my specialised requests are going to coincide.

"The crucial thing," he says, "was that the press didn't get hold of it."

"Why's that?" I ask.

"Well, you know what it's like. They're circling overhead like vultures at the moment, right."

He shifts his weight from one foot to the other, then stands easy.

"This is what they *love*, you know that, don't you? To portray us as nutters who hack each other into small pieces for the sake of an orgasm. So when this nosy parker came wandering around I thought it best to nab it as quickly as possible."

"Before the press got hold of it?"

"Yes. The clues, they were out there on the net. It was just a question of time before they found out. But in this area I have a little more, a little more, a little more . . . shall we say *background information* than the mutts in Akersgata. So I beat them to it."

That may well be a slightly embroided version of the truth he presents me with, at least as far as his motives go. But then dazzling white motives are a rarity and the opposite is not necessarily pitch black, maybe just a little smudged.

Simon shuffles his feet. Simon sweats and rubs his head. Fräulein Todt passes him a pint glass of water and he drinks it as if he has just come out of the desert. Two thin lines of liquid run from the corners of his mouth down to his chin and the top of his neck when he puts the glass down.

"Where did you find it?" I ask.

"If it's a name you're after you can't have it, he says, wiping the remaining drops of water on his face.

"I'm not after a name," I say.

"There were quite a few people at the exhibition," he says. "You know that."

"That's right. It was fairly chaotic."

"Let's just say that one of them, one of the hundreds of people there, took it."

"That's obvious. But why?"

"How should I know? A souvenir perhaps."

"Or to make some cash out of it?"

"Or for more personal reasons?"

"That would mean you got it cheap, wouldn't it? It's a bit odd. Whoever it was, the person concerned must have realised very quickly that the video was important. And since I was there I also know that you had to concentrate quite hard to tell the two different programmes on the screen apart and on top of that to locate the master console."

Simon leans towards me with his damp, red face.

"Okay, okay," he says. "One of the people working up there was closest to it. We both know that."

"The police know that too," I say. "And the press."

"All right, all right. That is the problem, isn't it?"

"And the other problem is that you didn't pay that much for it?"

He gives a little nod.

"So you are not sure that the person who sold it to you will keep their mouth shut?"

Simon rubs his forehead in panic.

"That's not the point," he says. "The point is that . . . it'll turn up again. And I know that it's almost as if all people will have to do is stand in some cinema queue and they'll get to see it. It's crazy."

"You mean that there's some kind of risk?"

"Of course there's a *risk*. There are small boys here who have seen it and what has it taught them? What?"

He has thought about this. He has prepared his defence. It is not bad rhetoric, mainly because it is true to some extent.

"They don't know what to make of something like that," he says. "The young ones. They're full of stuff about all sorts of fancy sexual techniques they've got from the net, sexual thrills, but they don't have enough experience. There are some things that require knowledge, aren't there? Things you shouldn't do without having that knowledge."

229

He is sweating a lot. He has tears in his eyes. I believe him. I believe he would really like to protect these young boys and girls from fatal errors of judgement. But he is throwing dust in my eyes. It doesn't smart much, and it won't make me shed any tears.

"So why did you sell the video? You could have given it to the police," I say in a cold, prim voice, with all his sweaty conscience on my shoulders. "If you were so worried about what the press would do with it."

I regret this the moment I say it because I know what he will say.

"But that would have been the same," he says and he is relieved, in the way the accused are, when he gets a question that he is able to answer. "Don't you read newspapers? The video would have been in police custody for a day at most before, surprise, surprise, some TV station got a copy of it."

"You could have burnt it," I reprove, "buried it in the garden or hidden it in the loft. If you wanted to prevent young people from seeing it and getting into bad habits."

It is dirty. It is always dirty probing weak points, whether they are rhetorical or emotional. This is both and that is not so unusual. He folds in the middle. That is to say, he doesn't, but a convulsion runs through the elongated upper body of his. I can see it begging for mercy as he bends over, fumbling around for the empty glass of water. Fräulein Todt beckons for more.

"That's great," I say. "I don't give a shit how much you sold it for, but I need to know who you sold it to."

He holds on tight to the shelf where the glasses are kept.

"Not everything is about money," he says. Simon is taking deep breaths and I think about all the things that have nothing to do with money. Knowledge. Favours. And it is not that we lack words for such things, our little bargaining culture has loads of them. Mutual interests, they call it. Deals for mutual benefit. Confidential information, they call it, trust and understanding between parties. Of course he is right. It is this and not money *that makes the world go round.*

Simon makes it simple.

"This person," he says, "knows a number of things about me that . . ."

"That you would very much like him to keep to himself?" I suggest.

"Yes."

"In return for this he got the video."

"Yes. I assumed . . . I mean, I know who he is and that he has . . . his own specialised interests, so . . ."

"So you assumed he wanted it for his own purposes."

He nods.

"He has obviously broken your trust," I say, nodding towards Hundreds and Thousands and her girlfriend. "So there's no reason for you to be so loyal, is there?"

He needs another litre of water.

"I thought he would be here this evening," Simon says, after downing his bucket of water. "He's usually here. I thought . . . You know I have put some money by and . . . Do you think if we go together – you can talk . . . I mean if we both . . . And I've got this money. How about it?"

"Possible," I say. "We can try."

I know that this is more hypocritical than my little leather jacket and black clothes. In my present position I am a trader too, and since we haven't signed any papers our mutual understanding, our mutual trust, isn't binding.

He leads the way to the exit and the lift. Queen Todt, three steps in front of him, accompanies us with the solemn responsibility of her office through the leather and fishnet, the PVC and fishnet, the latex and fishnet and the relentless digital swish, swish, SWISH of the sound system.

We are pursued into the lift shaft by the sounds from Down Under above us. When the doors close behind us and we are outside in the yard, however, it is utterly still.

But not for long. First the searchlights; they are in the passageway and tear out two parallel cones of light in the backyard. Then the sound of heavy, determined steps and something that sounds like *beating*. The men step into the light, casting great looming shadows and it is not difficult to see where the beating sound is coming from. It is their baseball bats swinging into their open palms in a regular rhythm. Smack. Silence as their bats are raised again. Another smack.

I stand pinned against the wall and watch them coming. Strong. Rolling pitch. Smiling fiercely. Not one of them wearing a balaclava. They are in no hurry.

There is a rational thing to do when you have got something that looks like the Pakistani mafia making a beeline for you and that is to make a run for it. Simon and I share the same healthy instincts, and as we are in an enclosed backyard we head inside again, in and up to the security of friendly types with whips. Simon presses frantically on the lift button, but Fräulein Todt pulls his hand away.

She has already dialled a number on her mobile, and now she is mumbling into it with her back to the attackers. I think I hear her say "come".

I huddle against the wall, run with my head down and my arms over my head, as terrified as these guys want me to be. I can hear how amused they are. Simon has just been dragged over the tarmac by two of them when the lift doors open and release a horde of *clubbers*.

Not just any old clubbers. The sarongs and fishnets are fine for indoors. The figures that tumble from the lift are just as full as those of the baseball guys; these arms have pumped just as much iron, their thighs are just as muscular, they just don't wear training kit for a night on the town. The rougher element of the leathers has descended from Down Under.

Baseball bats smack heavily into open palms. Forged steel spikes glitter along the arms and knuckles of the men in leathers. Thud of bat into hand. Wheee goes a cat-o'-nine-tails.

Oh God, I think. For Christ's sake, spare us. Here comes the Pakistani-gay war.

And it does. It starts unconspicuously enough, with bodies swaying and an air of expectancy, then come the provocative, snarled shouts and mutual insults. We are on our way down into the backyard. Down with *dicksuckers* and *dagos*. Spat out, like gobs of filth. All the things that are usually swallowed can be expelled through clenched jaws, between teeth shining behind the smiles because what is to come will be much worse.

I don't want to be part of some clash between healthclubs. I don't want to know which version of machismo can pump more iron. I am not interested in the indignities that give you bigger biceps. I don't give a shit if *dagos* absorb more oxygen into the blood than *dicksuckers*. Whether or not leather trousers are better receptacles for male hormones than fancy training pants is a matter of complete indifference to me.

Javed's brother gives me a big sneering grin. If it was him who gave me a going over in my own backyard, he is about to avenge his brother's lost honour on people worse than therapists: homos.

All I want to to do is put my hands in front of my eyes and shut it out. But nothing in the adult world is so easy, even if the Pakistani-homo war is not directed at little girls of whatever sex or origin. Fräulein Todt cannot be considered a little girl; she has already formed an alliance with a black-leathered testosterone bomb against a giant from Oslo and Islamabad. I am pinned against a wall and if I could have whimpered like a genuine tranny I would have.

But there are enough noises without me contributing. Dull, repulsive, soft noises. High-pitched and piercing. Movements too – the raised bat, the dirty kick in the balls, the swinging fist that never stops, that rains down with such power and with such a shower of sparks reflected in the knuckledusters.

There is a hysterical, heaving mass of people in front of the lift doors, a tangled mesh of limbs, of men fighting for honour and identity of different kinds.

But, in front of the searchlights at the entrance to the yard there is no-one. Simon crawls over the tarmac towards me, without honour, him too. I nod towards the passageway.

"Are you crazy?" he whispers. "There is a car there. Blocking the way."

"Would you rather stay *here*?" I ask.

He is reluctant, but he is drawn by something that he is almost defenceless against, a woman with authority. In reality, a woman on all fours and bloody scared, but he has been kicked in the stomach and can't tell the difference.

"Come on," I say, pulling him along with me. The leather trousers and the fancy training pants have other things on their minds.

We are in the passage now, in the dazzling searchlight, and, right, it comes from a car blocking the entrance with its doors open. It is impossible to squeeze along the walls. On the other hand the man behind the wheel can't get at us, ironically, because he is prevented from doing so by the open doors.

"Run," I say to Simon. "Jump, for Christ's sake."

It isn't elegant. Simon lands on the bonnet and crawls up the windscreen and on to the car roof without the driver being able to

do any more than get out of his seat. He manages to get hold of me, however. He holds on to one of my legs as I slip around on his car roof, and then I kick myself free.

It wasn't so difficult. After tumbling off the end of the car, landing awkwardly and hurting myself, I turn round to find out why. He slams the doors on the left-hand side so that he can follow me. I run, of course, but I can *see* him, too.

It was easy to kick him away because he is an elderly man. He is wearing one of those freshly pressed, white pyjama-like outfits that I have always wanted for myself, and I imagine he must be Javed's father. The driver, if that is all he does, for those regaining their lost honour.

It is not difficult for Simon or me to escape from him.

We slow down when we hear the sound of sirens. Not because it makes us feel secure, but because we don't want the patrol car to stop us. We stroll casually past the police hand in hand; perhaps Simon doesn't look the type who likes women, but who can be *sure* any more?

Leaning against the thick stone wall of the Museum for Contemporary Art, he sinks down, gasping for breath.

"Why the fuck did you drag me along?" he asks.

"We've got a deal," I say.

A deal. We are members of the trading class, slightly breathless traders, but still fully paid-up members.

28

SIMON NEEDS A few cigarettes and a lot of talking to before I start up the child-friendly, non-smoking car.

"It's ages," he says, "since anyone came along and beat us up. The neo-Nazis used to like doing it some years back."

New times, new customs, I think to myself.

"These guys," I say, "weren't after gays in general. They had a special reason."

"Uhuh," he says. "And that is?"

"It's a bit difficult to explain," I say.

"As if it makes any difference that they think they've got a reason," Simon says.

He is right about that. He talks to calm himself down as I stare out on to the empty square between Gamle Logen and the gateway into the military area by Akershus.

Then I move position in my seat and groan a little.

"What's up?" he asks.

"Old sports injury," I say. "Must have opened it."

It is not so long since I was visited perhaps by Javed's brother in my own backyard and I can still feel it.

Simon is ready to keep his part of the deal.

The man with his own specialised interests has a little Internet business in a backyard in Sinsen. Free Space it is called with all the exaggerated optimism that colours language use in this area. Since he lives in his office, presumably it doesn't give him that much freedom or space. But the sign is inviting, set next to the door bells and beside other equally brash names, all flashing their apparent potential at us.

Is SignInDSign a little graphics enterprise or does it also conceal a one-man company with sofabed? Is Up Trading really on its way up or are they just dreaming? I fall for the all-pervasive tristesse of Hansen Competence.

Simon rings. He keeps his finger on the button for a long time but nothing happens.

"Well," he mumbles. "Waste of a trip. I suppose we couldn't expect anything else."

"Keep going," I say. "There's a light in one of the windows up there. Perhaps he's sleeping."

Simon looks up. "I haven't a clue whether that's his place," he says. "I'm sorry. I've only been here once before and . . . that was in rather special circumstances."

"You didn't much care where you were," I say, and at that moment the door lock buzzes for an instant. I am not fast enough. Simon isn't fast enough either although we both grab the door handle. Too late. The door is locked, as before.

Simon presses the button. I pull the handle. We had our one-second chance and it won't come again.

"It's pointless," Simon says. "He's up there. He pressed the release button. Why the hell won't he do it again?"

Perhaps he can't, I think, perhaps he wants to, but he can't. I put my finger on all the buttons in turn, I play them like an accordion. I press Hansen Competence with some urgency and then the doorbell beside the sign lights up.

"Yes?" asks Hansen or Competence.

"Security," I explain with authority, "Competence department. We're here because of a break-in on the floor above."

"Oh," Hansen or Competence says. "I haven't heard any break-in."

"No, but they have on the floor above."

Then Simon and I sprint up three flights of concrete stairs, which resound to the hammering of our feet.

Hansen Competence is standing in his office doorway and looks at us in bewilderment.

"One more floor," Simon pants, "at least I think so." Hansen or Competence nods.

They have broad red steel doors in this building. Simon hammers on the one with Free Space in thin plastic stuck on at face height.

Are there sounds coming from in there? Between the pounding of

Simon's fists and the echo it creates down through the concrete tube we are standing in it is not easy to decide. Hansen Competence stays on the landing below. With a small paper cup in one hand he stares wide-eyed as the Security Competence Department hammers away at the door.

"It's Simon," Simon roars. "I don't want to hurt you, for Christ's sake. Surely you know that? SIMON!"

Hansen Competence is sipping his coffee. Each to his own competence.

There's a thud from inside the door. It isn't an echo. The sound comes from inside.

"Simon, do you hear?" Simon shouts again as if his name were some sort of calming mantra. Perhaps it works.

Scratching noises. Something that may be a groan. The door slides open, only a few centimetres, and an eye stares up at us from close to floor level.

"There's no danger," Simon whispers. "It's just me and a friend."

He sticks his foot smartly into the crack of the door, however. Simon has been to see frightened people before.

"He's in there," says a squeak from the floor. "Oh, my God. Go away! Off with you!"

Simon crouches down and pushes the door open a little further. All I can see inside is the man's shoulders scrunched up as if in convulsions.

"You're not from Security," asserts Hansen Competence drily behind me. "You know that porn guy, don't you?"

"No," I say. "We aren't from Security. We're from the O–v–e–r–d–o–s–e U–n–i–t," I mouth.

"Uhuh," Hansen says, taking a gulp of coffee.

"We may well need some coffee too," I say. Interested, Hansen moves back. Simon opens the door to its fullest extent and makes room for me.

"This is Igi," he says to the human bundle between us. "She's okay."

He is very thin and grey-haired, not through ageing, and if what he is so afraid of has managed to kill the roots of his hair it must have been a very lengthy and scary process. He has probably dyed his hair because it matches his hideously expensive nylon trousers, which crackle as he presses himself against the door frame.

His fear, on the other hand, is obviously genuine and also quite contagious. He is staring hysterically at the closed door at the end of the short corridor, and I have to use all my strength to get his hands away from his face. He has already succeeded in making deep, inflamed gashes across his cheeks and a terrible reddening mark on his bulging carotid artery.

"Go away," he screams again. "Clear off."

The pupils in his distended eyes are tiny and he is in a cold sweat. But he is a long way off being in a coma, so we don't need the Overdose Unit quite yet. I stand up and walk two paces towards the closed door. He could do with a blanket. He is not wearing shoes and has only a tight vest over the top of his body. It may be fear or paranoia that is making him tremble so much, but the cold doesn't make it any better.

Then he screams again.

"No! Aren't you listening to what I'm saying? He's in there! Don't you understand? You mustn't go in there!"

When he stops thrashing around and calms down a little in Simon's arms, we pull him carefully out on to the landing. Hansen Competence hands me a paper cup, holding it at arm's length, as if I had rabies. But oh . . . his quick eyes follow us with interest.

"You can get on with your job now," I say. "Thank you very much."

"We support Children in Need," Hansen says. "That's also a kind of Red Cross in a way, isn't it?

"Yes," I say. "Excellent."

The sobbing bundle goes by the name of Paul. He is talking a little now, but it is incoherent and confused.

"He grabbed me here," he says, pointing to his neck. "Do you understand? Has he gone now?"

"Yes," Simon says, and as I walk the few steps to the dark door I hope that he is right, that *he* has never been there and therefore cannot be there now, either. I hold my breath for a moment before I push open the door. Fear, even if Ecstasy induced, is a contagious thing.

A small blue-flamed fire flickers in the room, otherwise it is in complete darkness. My extended shadow falls across the writing desk and the flickering TV screen. From the light of the doorway I can see the shape of a chair knocked on to the floor and part of a low coffee table where a plastic Coca-Cola bottle has spilt its contents over the table and the floor underneath.

There is a scratching noise in the dark, over where something is vaguely gleaming, it could be a window with drawn, semi-transparent curtains.

"Nooo," Paul howls panic-stricken from the landing behind me. His howl resounds all the way down the stairwell. "You mustn't go in there!"

I stand still as his scream fades away. I listen to the dark, my gaze fixed on the window, a boring regulation square, which slowly takes shape. Are the curtains moving a tiny little bit? Perhaps I haven't quite got used to the dark yet, perhaps it is a cat, or maybe a dog. My hands grope forward, first along to the left, then along to the right of the door. A switch. Click-click with my eager fingers. Click-click-click. But no light.

So he doesn't like ceiling lights, I think to myself, but he has got a table lamp. Bold steps across the floor, some groping around the illuminated screen. Behind me, out on the landing, Paul is sobbing. Perhaps it is not my fingers that make the tiny dry click somewhere ahead of me.

"FUCK OF THE CENTURY" appears on the screen. That is a little modest, I think. Why not of the millennium? I am only that flippant because my fingers find a friendly round switch, press it and the light comes on. The light comes on and a hell of a racket ensues over by the curtains.

"That's HIM," Paul roars from out on the landing. In the meagre light from the lamp the curtains flap, billow and bulge. I retreat, not at all flippant now, to the door and draw breath with difficulty. Something has been going on in here. It is more like an office than a living space, and it is not only the chair and the Coke bottle that have been knocked over. A black bookcase has poured its contents of files of all kinds over the floor; the sofa cushions have been violently thrust to the side as if someone has run or crawled over them. There is a pizza box lying open with its sticky slices clinging to the coffee table.

The remains of a fight. Or of lonely, frenzied paranoia.

If whatever is behind the curtains had wanted to attack me it would have done so already. Unless, I think as I cross the floor, staring at the curtains, it wants me to come closer.

As I stretch out my hand to touch the material it flies right up into my face. The curtain is over my head, something jabs me in the chest, scratches my hand, pecks at my eyes.

Two fingers pull tentatively at the curtain material. Mine. I lift one section of the curtain away from the window.

It is a pigeon. It blinks at me with its black jewel eyes and its feathers ruffle up in panic. The window is half-open to the night rain outside. This terrified bird could quite easily have sent our Paul, high on amphetamines, into horrendous hysteria on its own. With my arm well above the pigeon I push the window wide open. It is not just that I don't want to frighten it; I loathe pigeons in the same way that I loathe seagulls. It is an irrational reaction; it is much smaller than a cat, for example, and a lot less likely to attack humans.

It must be the uncleanliness, I assume, and I transfer all my remaining mental energy towards it. *Go away*, or as Paul says, *Clear off*. Uncleanliness according to anthropologists: a fallacy. You belong in the sky, I tell the bird, and unless you go you are going to make my whole body itch.

I clench my hand behind the curtain ready to push the paralysed bird out into its element when I suddenly see it. About a metre below the window there is the roof of a workshop or a storeroom. Nothing unusual about that, except for the cracked tiles under the window.

The pigeon flaps as my hand touches it and then recovers clumsily in the air, recognises its own territory and flies out over the roof, over the cracked tiles along the ridge.

Of course it could have been like that for long time. But the damp footprints that the rain is washing away look quite fresh.

Paul stares at the screen. I have put the sofa cushions more or less back into position, shoved the pieces of pizza back in the box and put it by the door, like a lazy cleaner, lifted the chair up and mopped up the worst of the spilt Coke.

"He was *there*," Paul whispers, pointing a trembling finger at the screen. Nobody works for very long in any part of the health service without getting sick to death of drugs. Paul is up and down and above all poisoned, not on a sweet, friendly E-wave but somewhere out on the perimeter perhaps, although he is not very forthcoming about what he has taken.

There refers to a chatline for those with particular penchants. Paul may have been trying to sell the video there, but he steadfastly refuses to talk about it.

"It's got nothing to do with it," he says. I ransack his room anyway and that just makes him laugh a little contemptuously.

Even when I click through the files on his PC he just chuckles.

"Bye, bye baby," he hums. "She's keen, isn't she?"

It isn't there. Not in his miserable video collection – hardcore, erection-fixated *stud*-porn – and not in his computer files, either. There are just business letters and some ejaculatory story or other. Some photographs. A flickering stream of Asiatic mens' bodies. No purple-faced murder.

I click back to where Paul was, the chatline that promises to arrange the fuck of the century.

"Wasn't he after the video then?" Simon, who has rustled up some coffee and a blanket, asks. He settles his large body on the sofa next to the shivering Paul. These two were supposed to have nurtured *particular penchants* I remember. Right now it looks as if it must have been stamps or maybe cuddly toys.

"Ye-es," Paul mumbles. "Maybe."

"So you were talking about it then," Simon offers. "On the chatline?"

"He asked if I had seen it."

"And you said yes?"

"I suppose I did."

"And afterwards you went into personal details, did you?" Simon asks. "Exchanged addresses?"

Paul curls up under his blanket. "Well," he mumbles.

"What! You gave your address on an open chatline?" Simon says.

"Mmm. I was *high*, wasn't I."

Simon looks at me in despair. This isn't net etiquette and on top of that it is bloody stupid.

"But that means . . .," Simon starts off.

"Yes, of course," Paul says. "I know, I know. Is there any pizza left?"

I pass him the box and he devours the cold pizza as if it were milk for a calf. Simon watches disapprovingly. I am very pleased. If he can eat, he can manage.

"But that means that you don't know who it was who came here," Simon says. "It could have been anyone out there listening in."

"Exciting," Paul says apologetically between bites.

"For fuck's sake," Simon says.

"How do those things out there work, what do you call them? You know, 'The Stallion' or 'Fuckmaster' or whatever?" I ask.

Paul almost chokes on his pizza laughing. "Well, they work on pledges, things you get a kick out of."

"And did you pledge anything?"

"Just the usual things," Paul says a little evasively.

"I don't give a shit what you do," I say. "It's the *words* I'm interested in. Your expressions. What did you call him?"

"The Beast," Paul says.

"In Norwegian or English? Did you say things like 'Hi Beast'?"

"The Beast," Paul says.

I turn towards the screen. "And you?"

"White Trash," Paul says.

"White Trash to the Beast," I read out aloud while typing. "What happened to you? I didn't finish. Did you?"

I am a little shocked by my pornographic imagination, but I have my back to them and I can blush unseen.

"What are you up to?" Simon asks.

"I am not really sure," I say. "But it might take a while now."

Not so long.

"RETURN OF THE BEAST" appears on the screen. "I'll be back, my lad. You can be very, very sure of that."

Paul gasps.

"Can we meet somewhere else," I type. "What about your place?"

"I'LL FIND YOU," the Beast writes. "WHENEVER AND WHEREVER."

"Where are you now?" I ask.

No answer.

"White Trash seeks the Beast," I write. "I want you."

No answer.

"White Trash has found the film," I write. "Would you like to see it with me?"

No answer.

"He has gone home, sweetheart," flickers on to the screen. "But there are others here, just as frisky. Me for example. I like . . ."

"We're going," I say and turn round. "Can Paul stay with you for a few days?"

"Ye-es," Simon mumbles. "Well, he can't stay here, can he?" Paul is lying with his arms across his chest.

"Fine," I say. "Then let's go."

I watch Paul getting his things together with meticulous care, like a schoolboy. A small rucksack, underpants, vests and the modern young man's bulging toilet bag. And the mobile phone, which I very quickly checked over and which Paul is not so doped up that he can't find. With muscular grace, he bends over and takes it from the back of the linen-covered sofa.

It is resting comfortably in his hand when I take it from him. Paul is a trusting person. So long as there is a masculine teddy bear close by he feels secure, even on his way down.

"What are you doing?" he asks sulkily.

"Ringing the speaking clock," I say, pressing the repeat button. The number Paul dialled last lights up in green on the digital display and I let it ring even though I'm quite certain that I recognise it.

Hi, the voice on the tape says, *you have got through to Aske's workshop. I'm not here at present. Please leave a message after the dialling tone.*

This is also what our machines do for us: they tell the whole world when our rooms are unoccupied and can be desecrated without fear of interruption.

"One more thing," I say after turning off the phone without leaving a message. "Simon here is not going to give you a bed until you have shown us where you delivered the video."

Simon looks at me with incomprehension. Paul shrugs his shoulders.

"It's a deal, boys," I say. "That's all."

I am not going to Aske's workshop on my own.

29

"**Y**OU HAVE TO make sure you have a bolt hole in life," Aske said, and if this is his, he chose it with great cunning.

Car Country in Ensjø is not somewhere you would connect with a place where art is produced. It is also an unsavoury part of town, even during the day, and now it is night-time, the rain is steady and there is no wind. The car workshops and showrooms surround us in the dark, heavy chains hang across the entrances, and somewhere behind the high fences guard dogs are loose in the parking areas. The confusing number of sheds, backstreets and workshops half falling to pieces make it difficult for you to find your orientation. Paul gets us lost several times.

"I've only been here once," he pouts. "I don't like coming here."

Who does except for chrome and plastic freaks?

"Find the way, babe," I mumble.

The really big companies have big signs, several metres long, above their shopfronts in glass or brightly coloured base sheet metal, but most of these signs are unlit now. There are no potential customers around outside opening hours. There is no point in illuminating something no-one wants to see. Even the showrooms are in the dark; the large shiny assets inside are protected by advanced alarms and are only visited overnight by the nightwatchmen and their dogs.

There must be thousands of cars here. The new ones are inside the high fences with the free-roaming dogs and the fixed-contract guards with their thermos flasks and flashlights. Second-hand cars are perhaps not so carefully guarded, at least not the ones behind the algae-stained walls in the passage that Paul finally decides is the one we are looking for.

There is no *Dream Machine* parked between the five-storey office and warehouse building and the low, rather delapidated, three storey building on the other side. "Knut's Quality Used Cars" it says in irregular Letrasign letters on a damp-stained veneered board above the locked door we park beside without a thought.

We walk down the narrow passageway between a tall, rotting fence and a blacked-out brick building on whose tin roof the rain plays metallic percussion. There is a smell of fungus here, like in the forest and out of place; the stink of piss, however, is more in keeping if less pleasant. Paul slinks along fifty metres behind us with his narrow shoulders hunched up, mumbling something, a low stream of curses against the night and the rain and the dope.

His over-sized trainers make squelching noises for every youthful, sluggish step he takes. It sounds soft and sad and vulnerable against the regular drumming on the roof. Do your shoelaces up, I want to say to him. Put more clothes on when you go out in the rain. Simon puts a hand on my shoulder.

"He's coming," he whispers. "Take it easy."

When the crash and the wretched animal's scratching noises root me to the tarmac, his fist closes around my arm, rock hard, panicked and painful. Half a metre to the right of my face the boards in the rain-soaked fence bend inwards, pressed down by the weight of the animal launching itself at it. For a moment I am hypnotised by this, by the curling, greenish black panels in the fence and the power behind them, the same violent numbing power that burns in the dog's throat and makes its claws scratch chunks out of the wood-work. If blood has a sound, this is what it sounds like. It sounds like crushed bones and torn flesh, if they could snarl.

Simon drags me away from the fence before I am conscious that there is anything else other than these loathsome roars emanating from the jaws of the animal, that there are others screaming too, myself included and Simon too, but what we emit is nothing more than raw terrified growls. It is Paul who *howls*. Howls and runs.

"It's a *dog*, Simon shouts. As if that helped. As if it would make any impression on a hypersensitive, spaced out brain. As if the rain and the dark and the smell of piss were not enough to make a captive, slavering dog the world's best reason for running away, when all you wanted to do was run away anyway. Paul is back by the corner of the brick building before we even realise it.

245

Then we run too, Simon in his sewn-to-fit, soft leather platform boots and me in my pointed slippery-soled boots. Young Paul may be doped up and whimpering, but more than anything he is frightened and wearing trainers. On top of that he can see his chance to slip away from us. Simon gets to the corner before me, sprints over the square between the brick building and a pale yellow office block and disappears down an alleyway, the self-parodying sound of ridiculously high heels ringing out after him.

In the alleyway I slip on the damp tarmac and land on my bruised and grazed hip. I waste time cursing and crying with the pain and then lose sight of them. With difficulty, I limp between the walls and aim to beat a hasty retreat to the car.

In front of me there is an empty yard. Somewhere, a long way off, I can hear the sound of muffled footsteps and what sounds like a heavy door slamming. Afterwards it is quiet. The crazed dog bays one last staccato solo, then it too is quiet, and the rain, relentless and regular and all-enveloping, takes over. My breathing is rasping and raw, as you would expect. But there is no longer the sound of fleeing SM-ers.

There are three doors here, as in folktales. All three are plain grey, metal-covered and scratched. A feeble light bulb shines above one of them. I try that one first and it is locked. The next one opens into a multi-storey car park.

I have never been here before, I say to myself. It is not like the rooms I walked through to get to the Pain Machine. It isn't even a multi-storey car park, I tell myself; it is a kind of warehouse. That's what it was in the dream too, my unsupportive brain reminds me. I stand motionless in the doorway.

There is a ventilation system here, wheezing away, heavy and monotonous. A line of bare light bulbs hangs from the ceiling, a good metre in length, above the highest piles of boxes. Behind the boxes it is pitch black. In front of them is an oil-stained concrete floor and a wide doorway leading to the room where the cars are parked. There are only three of them. Everything here is grey and dark and dusty, and no-one is running. The ventilation system groans, throaty and hypnotic.

I haven't been here before, but I can't even take another step into this room. I don't see any other exits, rooms or backyards, beyond which trainers and platform boots pound the ground. It is not something I decide. My body does it for me.

My body backs out of the doorway, and I know it is because I can't turn my back on this room. And I know something else. I am not in the slightest bit interested in trying the third door. Behind it Simon and Paul may be embracing each other, eating sweets or exchanging pornographic experiences for all I care; my only aim now is to get to the car, or less ambitious, to get out of the backyard.

The third door is open. He is standing there in silhouette, lit up from behind by powerful white neon tubes. His arm is long and strong, and he is beside me before I can come out of the paralysis. The metal door echoes as it slams behind us.

Inside is the workshop.

I'm not here at present, his voice said on Paul's mobile phone. Now, however, he is, and so am I.

It looks like a laboratory. Or maybe, my unsupportive brain behind me says, some hygienic slaughterhouse. The strong light. The white tiles. The zinc benches. There is no sign of paint pots with dry brushes in them; the floor is, like the walls, neatly tiled and there are no interesting Pollock-style spatterings of paint over the floors. So it must be a long time since he has done any painting.

On the other hand there is a lot of electronic equipment here: screens and cameras, and cables nicely laid out and secured to their bases with strong black tape. I avoid looking at his collection of tools. It covers a long wall, shiny, sparkling and tidily hung up. The only things that are not black or white here are electrical. Most of them are green, as most joiner's machines are, but there is no sign of sawdust here. I don't pay much attention to them, either.

"Welcome to my workshop," says Aske, nasal-voiced, and that is when I realise that he is drunk. I don't treat drug abusers. I don't know much about them, except that they are unpredictable.

He is pale, of course, thin and unshaven.

"I've got two friends out there," I say. "They're waiting for me."

"Oh really? Shall we invite them in, do you think? The more the merrier, or what? Although actually, *actually*, I think it's enough with you."

He folds over like a wooden doll, bends his upper body over his stomach, and then he laughs or coughs, or both. There are rasping,

247

whistling, gurgling and wheezing noises coming from him. It is seldom any comfort to discover that the man you are alone with is drunk, although it does have its advantages.

His guard will drop, I think. No matter how much he concentrates on me he will go into himself sooner or later. It is just a matter of letting him get warmed up, letting him talk, as everyone wants to do all the time, talk about themselves and themselves and themselves until the whole world consists of this one never ending *me*.

"Don't you want to see it now that you've come all this way?" he asks.

He leans over the long workbench and pulls out a thin wad of large dark plastic sheets. They are rigid and they make a swishing sound as he puts them on the flat screen. I am not married to a photographer for nothing; I know very well what they are – large format photo negatives. When he switches on the light I can see x-rays of a human torso – the spine and the ribs stand out sharply. It is somebody's insides, possibly Aske's, possibly a body he has borrowed from an acquaintance or a stranger on its way to becoming art.

"There," he says, pointing to something under the ribs, something he calls *lumps*.

"Is it you?" I ask.

"Very interesting," he says. "Is it me? That? Could it be? What does the psychologist think? At any rate it should be possible to make something out of them. Don't you agree? Isn't it attractive, in a way?"

There is a click, short, sharp and definitive, as he turns off the screen light.

He leans against the zinc bench, supporting himself with a long bony arm against the base.

"But I disappoint you," he says. "What you want to see is something quite, quite different. Action, as it were. We've got that, too."

On his way towards the video machine he brushes his hand lovingly across the wall where the polished tools hang. Perhaps it is a sign for me, perhaps he is just supporting himself on the wall. Before he reaches his collection of electronic equipment he spins round, stares at me and laughs.

If that is also a sign, a tell-tale sign, I interpret it without difficulty. He is very agile, despite being drunk.

On the video screen is what Paul, Simon and I have seen, the yellow and green flickering pictures with shadows that are more burgundy red than black. The hand on the chest. The closed eyes and the parted lips. The belt tightened round the neck. The tattoo. The face that is no longer sallow, but deep red, swollen and limp.

One more time. The hand. The face. The belt. And once more. I have seen it. Seen it enough times for my intellectual curiosity and to remind me of my failures, seen it enough times for a cool competent chief inspector.

He presses the remote control and the picture fades. In his other hand I can see one of his many knives.

"You saw it too, didn't you?" he says.

Oh yes. The cut. The one little frame where the camera does not pan across the body but jumps. The microseconds that mark a break before it reaches the swollen face. A cut. Almost undetectable, but it is there without a doubt. In what is less than the blinking of an eye can be hidden oceans of time or at least minutes, perhaps hours.

"It wasn't your little friend, was it? I've forgotten his name."

"Javed."

"Does that satisfy you?"

"Not much," I say. "Not right now."

He doesn't hear that, I think.

"It wasn't Javed, you see," he says in that rusty voice of his. "Someone Else. You've read Jung, I assume? The Shadow. The Other Person."

"Yes," I say. "I know his theories."

"Do you know what I like best about what he wrote?"

"No."

"*Whatever is denied always returns*. It wasn't your young lad who did these things. It was someone else. Someone wiser and more frightening. And he has been denied."

"What things are you talking about? Your pictures or . . ."

"Or," he interrupts. "It's not so easy to make a distinction, is it? What have we done that we can call our own? Wonderful, acclaimed works that people are so enthusiastic about or all the things that torment us at night and appear when we are sick, tired and wretched? Did I do that, that too?"

He has a knife in his hand, and I am surrounded by them, hanging up on all sides, knives, axes and sledgehammers, innumerable tools whose functions I don't know, but if I let them remain in my consciousness my imagination will run away with me, concocting endless fiendish tortures. I block out the sight of them as well as I can and begin small intense breathing exercises, forcing myself to remember random fragments of artistic praise that came this skeletal creature's way.

On the wall behind him hangs something that looks like a pair of pliers with leads attached to both handles. What does he use that for? The question shoots through my brain. And these dreadful small spikes, these oversized nails, what does he do with those?

Block it out. Breathe in. Aske is talking about himself. That's good. That's right. This is the only home advantage I have.

"She cheated," he mumbles. "You know that? All this wonderful, worthy moralising of hers and then she just cheated. Perhaps you've got a theory about that too, about what you do when the person you love is a cheat?

He's talking about Mummy, I think. It is always Mummy or Daddy when it is a matter of really serious cheating. Aske stretches out one of his bony arms and takes one of the strong 20 centimetre nails down from the wall.

"They're great for getting the remnants of marrow out of bones," he says, "if it hasn't all been boiled away. Then it is used as glue. Same kind that the Nazis made, although this is just from animals, of course. But it is what I use to stick the various parts together. I prefer the glue to come from at least one of the animals. It seems more reasonable. Just a variant, a different composition of the body it was once. Like a mutation."

He draws breath with difficulty and wheezes.

"But it's all humbug anyway. Cheating."

A bony hand rasps against the bristly hair on his cheek.

"I thought I shouldn't cheat," he says. "But that was very naïve indeed. You can't do it. Have you noticed that? We cheat whether we want to or not. You think it's great, I suppose, but that's your job."

Mesmerise him, I tell myself. Let him mesmerise himself with his own chattering. Although I am aware that there are people who get off on this too. I know. Block it out. Breathe in.

250

Then he stares at me, and holds his gaze. He has dragged himself away from the electronic equipment now and is standing against the large glass vat by the wall. It is half a man's height and filled with a yellowish liquid. It reminds me of Edevart's aquarium.

"It's terrible to die," he says. "You cannot imagine how revolting it is. They smell the blood, they say, the animals coming to the slaughterhouse that I buy the bones from. And then they panic as if they know what's awaiting them. I've seen them. It's an absolutely horrendous sight."

I breathe out. Quite consciously; maybe it's futile. Block it out. Everything except the knife in his hand and my own breathing.

"There are better methods, of course. There is a huge slaughtering complex somewhere in Texas, a veritable factory of death, where they have made a labyrinthine system so that animals can't detect where they are going. There are breaks in the sightlines and shorter horizons, you see. The smell of blood has gone and so the animals go in all right and don't absorb undesirable quantities of adrenalin into their muscles and panic. Because they can't see. Do you know who designed this complex?"

"No," I say.

"She's autistic," he says. "Interesting, isn't it? Absolutely alien to most normal people's emotions. But it works. Better meat, less fuss. More glue, for all I know."

He gives a small laugh. And then the mental leap, the characteristic feature of inebriation and the anarchic, perhaps creative, brain.

"That's also a kind of cheating," he says.

Again the coughing turns into laughter. He lets go of the glass vat and stands bent double for a second before he gets up, stretches and forces his stiff neck backwards like one of his own cruelly formed superhuman figures. I guess it must be a song coming out between his lips, a regular, growled humming with fragments of a melody in it.

"*Goin' to meet my maker*," he hums, "*Goin' to meet my man*."

With his knife hand he holds on tight to the metal cabinet to his right. I consider butting him in the stomach, hitting him in the soft underbelly, with my knee ready to bring up into his crutch.

"Ow," he says, covering his stomach with his hand and the knife. Jung would have loved that, the wonderful synchronicity of it, my own thought and his exclamation. The rest of us can take this atmosphere of slaughterhouse and captivity to explain away the coincidence of associations. But it puts me into a cold sweat, and I believe he knows that. At that moment I believe he can smell it. Smell my terror, the adrenalin seeping into my muscles, my tissue and my glands.

It is theatrical too. The hand against the stomach and the graceful way he raises it. Theatrical and coquettish and for that reason viscerally menacing. Talk, I think. I can hear my own gabbler winding up for the big leap, but it is not mine I want to work. It is his big mouth I want to work now, the streams of essential messages, the personal information and the emotional convictions that he has.

I want it, I chant mentally, inwardly and with pornographic precision, *give it me. More, more, more.*

"No-one can accuse me of not being a craftsman," he says. "There isn't a machine in this room I don't master to perfection, not a join I can't make with greater accuracy than the best carpenters in town, not a bone I can't boil cleaner than any slaughterer. And *still* they call me a charlatan. As if it were me who cheated!"

He slides his ungainly body down one of the cabinet's shiny steel sides. *Goodness*, I think. *Isn't he leaving himself open, the way he's sitting?*

Then he raises one emaciated hand to his mouth. The long blade of the knife sparkles.

You can't imagine how revolting it is to die, he whispers.

No, I can't imagine, but I know I have the smell of it on me already, acrid, humiliating and obvious.

"I thought I would get away from it," he says, "from all her lies when I went to sea. You know. The sea as a kind of cleanser. Metaphorically speaking. Intense. Male domination. I believed that kind of thing."

His voice is high-pitched and piercing now. He is sweating more than I am.

"Well, you saw it," he mutters. With his other hand he rummages around in his smart shoulder bag and pulls out a half-bottle of brandy. I stare at it as he takes a long, deep swig. More, I wonder, would more be better or less?

"You saw the clip," he mumbles. "You know what the Shadow does. Whatever is denied returns. Haven't I made room for it here, with all the bones? It's here all the time and it's as if it were never enough. It's insatiable, just like her. Once she said that she was doing it for Dad's sake, so that we would have enough money. But that was a sham."

He straightens up now and stands over by the bench, unsupported, with the knife dangling from his right hand.

"He came to see us, you know, Otto with the polished dome. Red and sweaty. And of course Dad was too stupid to see it, but it only took a few days at the factory and I knew that the fool didn't have a job there. Sort of foreman. An empty-headed idiot in overalls. He swept the floor, if he was given responsibility for anything. Where did his wages come from?"

"The pictures," I whisper.

"*The fakes*," he says. "It was Otto's idea. He thought she was so good at painting. He said. A talent. And then he came every week, several times a week, and was with her in the barn. And I thought he was distinguished, do you understand? I thought he was so much more bloody refined than Dad. And so I began to paint too."

Is there a ventilation system here too, or is it the rain making these vague, intermittent sighing noises? *Look at him*, I think, *give it him*.

"That's the only thing you can't tolerate," he says. "Your parents' humiliation. It's much worse than your own. You wake up from your own humiliation sooner or later or you repress it. But theirs. His. Do you know that? You can kill, slash, stab and hit out because of it."

Now, I think, *while he is distracted and distant.*

But he isn't. Aske stands there, lanky, his back bent, the knife hanging from his hand. "It wasn't me," he whispers. "It was the Shadow. I just steal and steal, I do, just like her. I'm no better than her, I just earn more But I steal. I do too. I copy and cheat."

The laughter is cracked and frightening, but I don't listen to it, though I keep my gaze firmly fixed on this man going through a series of strange, sudden jerks. There is something further away from us, something distant, semi-audible thuds at irregular intervals. I'm not sure they exist, but my perceptions are excited now to the point of hysteria, so I hear them, every single dull, longed for thud beyond the walls, out of our range, I hear them and I hope they really exist.

Talk.

"*Your mother*," I whisper. "*Give it me.*"

"If she faked art," he says, "couldn't I do the same with life?"

There is something alive outside this room. The distant sounds, not the wind or rain, they exist there and have their own rhythm. Aske straightens his back and supports himself on the surface of the table. I keep my eyes fixed on the long shiny blade.

He raises his arm and the blade describes a wide semi-circle in the air before he drops it down on to the zinc surface. The knife clatters against the bench for a second and he seems to be very taken by the short crisp vibrating noise it makes.

"Bong," he says, coming towards me. "Are you quite sure that you don't want a drink?"

I have been too fixated with the knife, too fixated by it and by the broad friendly smile spreading over his face. I haven't kept my eye on the bottle he has in his other hand and when I see it, in that flash of a second before it hits me, it is too late. He has also heard footsteps, and as I sink into the darkness they resound everywhere round the room, or perhaps it is just in my brain.

30

I AM BLIND. I am blind and I have no voice, not even a mouth. Perhaps there is a body in this room, but it has nothing to do with me. It can't possibly be mine.

There is a pale oval shape. Shadowy, as if it were out of focus or drawn with carbon, then rubbed out. Hollows for eyes. Deep cavities beneath. A skull. A face.

And a voice, disembodied and swaying in this boundless darkness.

"Let's go home now," it says. It would sound quite calming if it weren't for something, a body somewhere, hurting so much.

Somewhere in the dark there is a little red ball. It is burning. I exist around it, at least parts of me do, although it is not possible to say whether they are connected or if they are moving around detached from each other in the all-pervasive darkness.

There is something over my mouth, an extra layer of skin, something tight holding it in place. Above the mouth, my blind eyes and the continuous pain. It is too great to be only in my head. Perhaps my head is open, so that there is no difference between the darkness inside and the darkness outside. They are the same waves of darkness moving around inside me and around me.

I mustn't move, I know. The sounds outside in the dark tell me I mustn't move. Don't they? Perhaps it is memories of sounds. Perhaps it is this continual high-pitched buzz in my ears. I can't take such decisions. I can't know such things.

From out of the darkness come what sound like screams, long drawn out whining noises from a human or an animal or a machine. *Wheee*, it whistles, *wheee, wheee*. There is a thudding noise. It is not my heart. And then terror takes hold of me, plunges me into the breathless darkness. You can't listen to screams like these. I would rather fall or die.

My tongue is stuck to my palate when I come to. The darkness is thick, suffocating. The pain wanders up and down my body, shooting its rays from different places in these fragments that are me. I have memories of what sounded like screams and of Aske's face, but the memories are mixed up with the dream of the Pain Machine and the buzzing of my blood in my ears. There were footsteps. Perhaps a door slamming. Maybe a long time ago.

Everything is still. Apart from the beating of my heart and my laboured breathing through my nose, there are no sounds. It feels as if I am buried in heavy black cotton. Is there anyone waiting out there?

Then, after waiting for a long time in the stillness and the dark, I break it. My body does it, not me. My body is stupid and distant and acts by itself, pain-ridden though it is. It wriggles and lurches against a door that gives way, a door opening into a shattering, dazzling whiteness.

I lie in a foetal position on the tiled floor, in front of the large metal cabinet out of which I crashed. My eyes are streaming and needles of pain stab at me through the soft openings they form.

I don't see it. I can't see it. It is a product of my cotton-wool brain, of the torn fragments of dark dreams slumbering inside me. It has nothing to do with being confronted with dazzling white, crystal clear neon light, with these eyes of mine that can't stand light, that are streaming and smarting and making what is crystal clear blessedly indistinct. Although it calls me to action, my body condemns me to staying in a tight little ball, condemns me to crawling along the floor, to burying my face and eyes in my lap, protected by my hands that are powerless to do anything.

In this way I can look at it, after crawling over into a corner, through splayed fingers, peeping like a frightened child through latticed fingers and only then in panic-stricken glimpses. The glass vat is blurred, because my eyes are streaming so much, but it is not just my eyes streaming, my mouth is running with bile, as my fingers grope, claw-like, ecstatic, to liberate me from the extra layer of skin, the tape. I see and I don't see, I see and I refuse to see.

The liquid in the vat is pink now and there are threads of deeper red running through it, thin streams winding round the body inside. It is standing at an angle in the water, held down by the weight resting at the bottom of the glass vat, attached to an umbilical cord of a rope around its waist. The rope is taut, as if the body was struggling to reach the surface. As if it wanted to draw breath, as if it had a mouth to breathe with. And not just this dreadful severed section pressing against the glass lid.

I have seen hundreds of them before, the same mistreated bodies of dwarfs in all the art collections in the world. However, they are a sallow colour while this is an indistinct reddish colour, and they have a marbled surface, polished into a wonderful smooth finish, like skin. No-one polished this body. It was not necessary since no artifice or expertise could make the surface more skin-like than it already is. It has just been hacked or cut or sawn off, in many of the places where the red threads are seeping out.

It is a torso. A section of a body, a compact essence, the nucleus of a body without superfluous moving parts, without legs, without arms, without a head. Inside me it is like the whine of a thousand blades as the thin jets of blood rise in the vat and are dissolved as they mixed with the liquid. At some point, soon perhaps, the colour will be the same all the way around the body and it will be hidden behind an even film of pink, as if the glass had been painted that colour.

It is a man's body. Pale and hairy. Not Simon, I think. Paul? The bile runs from my mouth again, thick and in spasms.

But I can't search here, can't scrabble around on the floor to see if I can find any more parts that look like they belong to what is in the vat. I can only scrabble one way, clumsily, with my mouth and my eyes streaming. I crawl like a small whimpering animal towards the door. Towards the grey metal door leading to the corridor and to the storehouse that resembles the room where the Pain Machine belonged.

I raise myself into a standing position with the aid of the zinc bench and stand bent over it as I try to wipe my streaming eyes, my drooling mouth. There is a narrow rust-red stripe running down the gutter in the bench and I retch again. Nothing can make my gaze follow the brownish red trail to the blade of the saw.

I hold my arms above my head like a child as I stagger towards the door. Behind me in the glass vessel there is just one body, not two as in the Pain Machine. The other one, the twin body belonging to it like a shadow, is not attached, still free from the machine, like mine. Somewhere outside this room.

But not in the corridor. Not in the small damp yard, which is midnight blue, still and ice cold, and deep, jagged angles shimmer in front of my eyes. Of course I am running. It is just that I don't realise it. And that must be why my legs, detached and freed from my consciousness, strike out despite the odious baying from the dog. My legs avoid the treacherous angled corners, avoid the icy shadows, they lead me and find the open sky, the car, damp from the rain and shiny in the morning mist.

Behind it is there is a slim gold-coloured sub-aquatic presence, a golden shark's body in metal with a leopard by its side.

"My God", Bella says, "Igi, have you wet yourself?"

It is possible. It is even likely, but I can't tell her that. I can't tell her anything at all. I am pointing, I suppose, and I am shaking, too.

"And I was the one who thought that Aske had gone crazy," Bella says. "Does that mean that you've *seen* it? The masterpiece, I mean."

I stare at her. I stare and gasp like a sick fish. The *masterpiece*, I think to myself, and I have to lean on the car roof. On the other side of its golden body the amphibian opens a slender fin and a man's body wriggles its way out through the car door. Sjur Aske gives me a disapproving look across the golden surface of the roof. He is unshaven and one shirt collar is sticking out over the lapels of his jacket.

"This isn't exactly *a private viewing*," Bella says, "and the timing is original, one has to say, but we haven't *slept* for a second. We were having champagne and . . ."

"Bella, what are you talking about?" I gasp. Sjur Aske grunts.

"His e-mail, I guess. Isn't that why you are here? 'The masterpiece is finished,' he wrote, the pompous sod. 'Come and see it.' Flitted on to the screen at about five, *darling*, and had it not been for some fantastic picture devoid of any artistic merit whatsoever on the net that I had been thinking of showing kid brother here I wouldn't have checked the mail until well into the day."

"Well I'm buggered," Sjur Aske growls. "The lady's going to faint."

"*Let's go home now,*" I drawl and I don't know what happens next. I think I throw up over Bella's golden car and wake up again in the arms of the man who once doodled sketches of Per Anders Nilsen's sister.

" 'The last masterpiece,' " he murmurs. "That's what he wrote. *The last.*"

"Let's go home now," I drawl.

"Are you sure that was what he said?"

No, of course I am not. I am not sure of anything. I have dried threads of what was saliva round my jaw, I am incoherent and I have got nasty stains all down the front of my jacket. It's not my fault that my hair is all matted, but it feels like it. I am playing the rôle of the client and it makes my whole body itch.

Chief Inspector Kielland, on the other hand, looks cool and empathetic from where she is sitting in the morning sun in her office. The freshly pressed skirt is clean like her face, her voice is clear like her eyes, her hair has a glossy sheen like her shoes. I know this is what we offer all the clients at our smart centres of competence. This lofty, remote friendliness is what meets drunks, wife beaters and timid mice that dare not go on the bus on their own. It is not surprising they hate us.

"You were out at this SM place. Along with . . . friends?"

A vague kind of non-empathetic smile there, perhaps, or is it just me hearing the echo of my own studied, confident interviewing voice? *And what is it that frightens you about catching the bus, Gerd? Can you tell me a bit more about that?"*

Gerd can say something, if not in an articulate way. Gerd the Client confesses, slowly and disconnectedly, and notices every hint of disapproval or surprise in the voice of the cool woman sitting opposite. Gerd the Client puts her case with the greatest relief into the apparently much more competent hands that are metaphorically and also literally stretched out towards her.

"That's fine," my interviewer says. "Now you don't need to think about this any more."

I hope I have never said anything quite as stupid, and even though I know that it is being the underdog that makes me take this opportunity to strengthen my lost sense of self with such enthusiasm, I do it anyway. You wally, I think, and I am pathetic.

But it is not until she proclaims, in a voice as clear as a bell, her customary privilege as an interviewer – *Okay I think that's enough for the moment* – that I recognise her tiny novice therapist's error. Chief Inspector Kielland is angry. Not furious, but angry enough for me to see it in the slight toss of her head that makes her hair shine even more as she accompanies me to the door, angry enough for me to feel the pressure when she puts her hand on my arm.

"It looks as if you were right," she says, "you and Ingeborg Dahl. Apparently this guy's not content just with painting revolting pictures."

It is an empty victory of course, embarrassing and shocking. Perhaps I am mean-spirited enough to accept it nevertheless. The self-contempt envelops me, I can feel it, as it always does after humiliations of all kinds.

I want to go to Jomfruland, to the fantastic breakers and to be cured by a child's hands. I want solace and convalescence, to walk along the therapeutic rocks and beaches, I want to develop my mother's skills and to grieve and to go through the processes of recovering from shock and not to give a damn about the difference between *life* and *works of art*, between pictures and the person who painted them, lives and the person who took them. When did anything ever make sense, apart from on occasional dark nights, apart from on occasional moments with a child's hands close beside you?

The glass sky is over the town again, it reflects it, the gutters in the street and the house fronts. The reflection has a cold chill, as intelligent things do, it reflects what has been thought through and what is not chance, or at least it seems like it when it is morning and autumn and even the shadows are as transparent as water. As it does especially when you are filthy and cannot act in a rational way, but have to take your newly bought clothes with you and take your morning wash in the public baths because you can't, can't, can't do it either in your own home or in your family home. *Let's not go home now.*

We don't go home now because there is something about life and works of art, the authentic puss-dripping work of Satan that prevents us. Perhaps he is running around out there as a cobalt-blue, rain-freshened shadow, perhaps he is sitting hunched up by a rotting fence waiting for something to make him snarl like a dog. Maybe. That is the cool, competent chief inspector's problem and there is no reason to believe she will have any more difficulty tackling this than she has in distinguishing between *café au lait* and *caffè latte*.

As for me I will have to cleanse myself of my filth, first with water and then with anchor-bestrewn loving care from the family. My thigh throbs. This isn't a sore muscle strained, through fear, although I have enough of them, it is the advanced version of a baby monitor. I have had Ida chattering away a few times on the mobile phone already and assume that she has found some shells that Benny thinks she should tell her renegade of a mother about.

It isn't Ida. I am sitting secure in the sacred family car at the lights down from Bislet Bad, and the mobile shows a number that I don't recognise. It is the Beast's sign, I think. It is him. He is the one running and waiting, the one who knows who I am and can reach me. I have got central locking and have already activated it. And I am so good at talking to the furious, the demented and the needy.

"I thought you would want to know," Edel Amundsen says in my ear. "We were talking about the cabin, weren't we?"

"Yes," I say numbly.

"I don't think it's important, but the conversation we had made me think more about these things, PAN's leaving and so on."

God almighty, I think. How do I stand all this long-winded circumlocution? Routines are like bodies, they enable us to remember things that consciousness has forgotten.

"I'm a little busy just now," I therefore say, just like a therapist and in accordance with the formula.

"Really? It was my impression that you were interested. I only wanted to say that I went there to relive my memories, as it were, and confront my own degradation, I suppose you could say."

Shoot her, I am thinking, as the lights turn green in Hegdehaugs-veien. For God's sake, let this poison-free person suffocate in salmonella or in old asbestos dust. There are no parking places free in Josefines Gate I can see. I may have to walk several hundred metres without any form of protection. Haven't I got enough problems without being lumbered with Edel Amundsen's private exorcising of her devils?

"It was quite an experience, I can tell you," drones Edel Amundsen.

You were *drunk*, drunk and young and silly, I think. *Quite an experience*. More like hell, I think. Try to find a free parking spot in a predator-free zone around Bislet Bad and then let's talk about *quite an experience*. And then I remember PAN. Who is perhaps not just a picture and a boy who disappeared on his scooter among the spruce trees.

"Someone's living there," his sister says. "In the cabin."

Him, I think. Among the spruce trees in the cobalt-blue shadows and the raging nights. *Bones*, I think, and shreds of flesh and tissue and dark red muscles. I drive round the roundabout in Bislet for a second time.

"A massive woman," Edel Amundsen says. "Extremely aggressive. She literally chased me out of the courtyard and screamed at me. It was very unpleasant."

"When was this?" I ask.

"Just now," Edel Amundsen answers.

"Was she alone?" I ask without knowing quite why.

"It seemed like it. But I don't know. She had an enormous car parked down the road. One of those, you know, not a van, and it's got dark windows."

The *Dream Machine*.

Søren Dahl does not know where Anlaug is, but he has got her mobile phone number actually. There is only the business-like voice of Norway, Kristin Johnson, telling me that she is the answering service for Telenor. I leave a message, still not quite knowing why. Afterwards I call Bella who may still be with Sjur Aske. It would be fantastic, fabulous, wonderful, if Aske's brother or Bella herself could tell me, yes, Aske did once let a cabin, as it happens, to a whale in court shoes, and has never since, especially now, would never dream of going there again.

Bella has a migraine and police in front of the house. For myself I manage to sneak away as Aske doesn't know for certain where my stepfather's cabin is and therefore won't be able to find me there.

"They are gorgeous, dear," she says, but I'm not in the mood. A waste of some really dishy uniforms, Igi. It's really too bad, but what can a girl *do*? Not much, not right now.

Perhaps only when she is genuinely shaken does Bella manage to be tasteless.

"Do you know where Sjur is?" I ask.

"Of course it has got nothing to do with you, but he is here in fact. You can't talk to him right now because he's got Rita with him in the shower."

"Were you together all night?" I ask.

Then she laughs, a husky, sad Bella laugh. "I'm sticking with them, Igi," she says, "all night long."

"Ask him," I say, "if Aske uses a cabin out by Bagn."

"But I know that," Bella says. "He inherited that when Sjur got the family home."

"Does he usually rent it out?" I ask politely.

"Can't imagine that," Bella says. "Isn't it just junk? He never goes there, I know. Do you think he's *there*?"

Anlaug's mother is just as huge as Anlaug herself, but she can only whisper. She doesn't trumpet around like her daughter. She is standing, sweaty and clammy, in the doorway, in the suburb of Holmlia. It is apparent she is scared of authority, even such a miserable version of it as me. I take advantage of this.

Psychologist, I say. For her own good, I say. Hasn't been home for a while and doesn't answer phone messages, I say. A social welfare office here and a broken appointment there are enough, more than enough, for this large dough-like woman to let me into Anlaug's most sacred, most private room. Girl's room. If big brother doesn't see you, the big sisters from all types of therapy soon will.

Here there is a poster of a horse and a surprisingly well-equipped make-up table, but I am not here to probe anyone's soul expressed in form or space, not even Anlaug's. I am going for hard facts and thus the cardboard boxes from Loaf. The archive has a simple numbering system, even if I don't remember the numbers exactly. Was it 457 and upwards or 754? There can't be that many combinations and parts. *Victims and kin.* This, in principle, infinitely inclusive self-description covers just a limited number of people when they are required to pay subscriptions for it.

I find my opening, the gap we therapists all look for so keenly, the revealing absence. The gap is *the cat* that I can remember from Aske's biography and from the sheets fluttering on to the tarmac outside Søren Dahl's door in Grønlandsleiret. On the pages before and after the missing page is the rest of the unfinished part-medical and diagnostic life history of a Loaf member who didn't paint pictures of flames or make sculptures of bones because of an old, festering, deep sore.

Sjur Aske is right that his brother did not have a monstrous childhood, but it is not fiction for that reason. It is simply someone else's childhood, it is a theft not unlike the fakes she painted, the woman who signed the pictures M. Aske.

Disability Pension, it says in the box in the archives for occupation, *occasional work in a photographic shop*. The little series of courses of treatment within the system have been neatly noted down, as well as three convictions for violence. Someone, Ingeborg Dahl presumably, has entered an e-mail address by hand under the telephone number and street name.

It is still Kristin Johnson answering my calls.

She isn't on Jomfruland, however. Ida answers and I am happy about that. I have much more training in hiding all kinds of things from her than from Benny. There are quite a few things that *have to* be hidden from four-year-olds, and it is easily done while they chat away, as Ida does now about the tiny baby fish living in the rock pools and they are strange and deeply absorbing.

She thinks I am silly not to leave right away, but not that silly. However, she won't be a messenger for me. The nearest adult is Karsten and he isn't much more sensitive than a four-year-old, so he takes the message that I won't be coming just *yet* with great composure. Although he thinks I am silly too.

But now we are not going to Jomfruland. Now we are going *Home* at last.

31

As dusk falls I hear Kristin Johnson's telephone answer voice again, as I have heard it several times on the way here. Close into my ear where I am standing between the jagged spruce trees, deep into the shadows, which are not a clear cobalt blue, but black and dark and cold. It is only later I hear the short breathless convulsions I interpret as laughter.

Before I reach the trees Chief Inspector Kielland has already set her machinery in motion, so I am not alone in the forest.

There are shadows moving between the trees. Men in dark clothes looking for sightlines and paths to advance through the undergrowth. There are things that crackle here, communications, orientation and professional concentration on a fixed point. The fixed point is the cabin Aske christened *Home*, the fixed point is the life that includes *the cat* and a boy called PAN and a girl by a tall, sky-framed block of flats. The central point of rotation could hardly be less stable.

The cabin with the sunken roof lies shrouded in the darkness, its doors are as closed and inaccessible to us as the secrets enclosed in this life. Sure enough the *Dream Machine* is parked down the road, but we should not jump to any conclusions. The point at which we are gathering could just as easily be unoccupied. The person with the memories of *the cat*, PAN and Helena could have have sought refuge among the trees, or may already be a long, long way away. What we are looking for is a wounded animal and they tend to slink away. Ideas about what has been left behind in the cabin, if this is the case, are held in the chief inspector's neat night profile, or seen in the fevered whispering of the team, in the way my hand is clenched around the telephone.

If Anlaug is inside she knows that we have taken up positions in the forest, because the chief inspector tells her using the megaphone.

Her thin girl's voice sounds strained and a bit ridiculous in the darkness of the trees, distorted by primitive technology. *Shouting in the forest.* There is no response. The silence that follows is broken only by the distant crackle of communication and a low wind stirring in the treetops that point towards the first stars of the night.

It isn't Kristin Johnson who answers my next call.

"CLEAR OFF," roars a woman's voice into my ear.

"Anlaug, it's Igi," I say.

"Fancy that. I have actually TWIGGED that. This has got NOTHING to do with YOU."

"Are you alone in there?" I repeat.

"That's got SHIT to do with you," she says.

"Yes, it has."

"You have no RIGHT to HARASS me like this," booms Anlaug.

She is being childish, of course, and she is clearly, and with every justification, very frightened. "There are masses of WEAPONS in here," she says, "no shortage of them." When I ask her to come out, there is a long silence.

"I CAN'T," she says. "It's not MY decision."

No, I think. It's the Shadow's decision. What decides is the memory of the scooter and the block of flats and two young men on a bed. Not you.

The monotonous tone that tells me she has rung off is at first depressing and then persistent, lonely and frightening. *Bringg,* it rings out under the spruces, *bringg, bringg,* under the newborn stars.

It is the chief inspector who sets the deadline; it is finely judged, with time for a breather and decisions, but not enough time for anything to happen, anything crazy, defiant or monstrous, if Anlaug is not on her own there, or is not the only one to have a good reason to be frightened in the forest. That is how someone with a megaphone and a thin metallic voice standing among the evening trees thinks: the amount of time allowed must not be enough for someone to die.

But how long does it take to die, to kill another human? A few seconds, or years and years and years? Even under the stars and the spruce trees time can compress itself into a dot or stretch out as if to cover a hemisphere. The minutes that pass in silence after the megaphone's first authoritative demands last a lifetime. Helena's. PAN's. Anlaug's. *The cat's.*

Inside the silence the shadowy figures shift positions. Follow sightlines, occupy strategic parts of the undergrowth, take up more favourable positions logistically, sheltering behind tree trunks, raise and lower their visors and the infra-red night vision cross-hairs of their sights.

I talk on the phone about this. Entrust Kristin Johnson with the negotiating cards that are being laid out on the terrain and in the night, keep her informed with a mediator's neutrality about every-thing there is in the small print and the significant sub-clauses. "Look," I say in my friendly mediator's voice. "We have nothing to conceal. We just want a deal."

Isn't it cold in there? Isn't the night lonely and frightening? Isn't it wearing after a while to be so alone with the immense pressure that surroundings of all kinds create, not just trees and stars? I talk about methods, plans and systems and planning ahead, and I know it sounds as if we on the outside have no fears, that we can find our way around in the world, among its tangled branches and shadowy ravines. Only my knuckles give me away, bluish-white and tight as they are on this fist that is mine, squeezing the stupid little telephone.

There will be lights for her on her way across the field, I say. They are only there for her bearings, so that she will know where she is walking. They won't blind her. There will be men there, I say, but not until she has reached the edge of the forest. No-one will rush her.

I can say that because I have told her about the shadows and the men among the trees and about their firepower.

And then we strike a deal. When she comes out she is a sluggish, swaying shadow by the corner of the house. She waits, as we agreed, while the lights are put on. Ahead of her a path of lights is switched on in the slippery grass bowed down with moisture. It follows her large body, even more huge as a moving, struggling silhouette.

She spits at me when she gets close to us. A woollen blanket is put around her and she is accompanied into the trees by those who know their way in the dark. Down to the road where the *Dream Machine* sits.

And then we have to save a life. The life that is still inside, behind the walls, surrounded by the weapons that belong to the shadow-men and those of his own. With our intrusive, dense presence we have to try to keep him alive, nourish him via a cordless umbilical connection, maintain a balance in this way, because we are monkeys of the kind that see, hear and speak.

Now he has given up Anlaug, he has surrendered one of the weapons that prevent the shadow-men from going in. But only one of them. And we can't know, since he hasn't spoken yet, at whom he intends to direct them, the shadows inside or the shadows outside the house.

So we don't move. Because we want to save a life.

There is nothing smart about it. It isn't in the least bit satisfying. It is just a concealed throbbing pulse and the neutral maternal tone that is essential in the dark of the night. Not comfort. Just self-control and the wonderful quality we call being able to plan ahead. Systems, methods, plans: here we are. We can play it this way if you want.

You can think about it. Everything will be fine. *Nothing here is as dangerous as you think.* Apart from you, of course. Apart from memories of the scooter and the tall block of flats swaying in the sky and the two men on a bed, of course.

It is best if he doesn't think about this and that is why I speak the way I do. He mustn't think about it, we can't stop thinking about it.

I know he has been to sea and shared an attic and a prostitute with the man who was to become Aske. In addition, he must have, in some way or other at various points in time, shared something else with Aske, enough of his memories of what he did with PAN and Helena for Aske to paint pictures of them. How did he go about this? Did he present them as mere fantasies, his stories, in such a way that they were enough to fire Aske's imagination, but they didn't need to be taken too seriously?

There is a portrait of him that doesn't look like him at all or perhaps it does, deformed beyond anything human as it is. It is worth more than everything he has ever owned, certainly worth more than the scaled up state machinery surrounding him now, but not worth more, we have to believe, than the life he is threatening to give up.

With suicides, the day to come is the trick. Not the hope that it will be any better, but it is the almost business-like postponement of a decision. If things are dreadful the day after you can do it then. Or the next day.

But he knows more or less what tomorrow morning will bring. A cell. Interrogation. People round you, getting closer.

The only thing I can offer Rune Skjalgson is sleep. But then this is one of the real luxuries of our existence. A long sleep. Deep. Almost the same as death.

He mustn't think about that. We can't let him.

I remember that in Amsterdam Aske learnt to paint *ugly* pictures. At that time Rune Skjalgson hadn't killed anyone, but he had a history that would enable him to do so.

A history that was *ugly* enough for Aske to be able to punish his cheat of a mother by pretending that it was his own and her own history. Such a strange thing to do, such an uncaring thing to do. As if you could play with life. As if one thing were just as valid as the next, or just as usable.

Copies and originals. Pictures and the person who paints them. Lives and the person who takes them.

Sooner or later he will fire one of his weapons off in there in a moment of explosive fury. It will come to an end too, followed by silence, as with all explosions. In the silence we will stand under the trees and be as dispassionate as they are. He may be dead now, I think, and there may be someone who will miss him. Anlaug, who spits at me and hates me for having denied her a child to play with, may miss him even when she finds out what he did. *Victims and kin.*

I am not made of wood and so my girlish voice trembles when I whisper his name into the phone, into the stillness here outside and the stillness over there inside. Whispering in the forest. Not getting a response.

Systems. Methods. The shadows stir, press forward, as surroundings do when they are more than just stars and trees. They move into the silence, the men who understand sightlines and blind spots, they huddle together under dark windows, lean back flat and dark against the corners of houses, they move in a crouching run through the wet, sticky grass.

Then he tells us there is no point in using tear gas. He has a gas mask for that.

He must be tempted, too, by the knowledge that people are listening. Who can't burst in and *take* him, but who have to listen to him.

He talks about the cabin that Aske let him use because he owed him that much.

"We came here once," he says. "A few weeks before Aske went on his travels."

I think: PAN, a scooter among the trees, doodles on a sketchpad, drawn not by any brother of Aske's but by Skjalgson. He doesn't mention Helena and as I am here to save a life I don't press him.

But he talks about her mother. "She listened to me too."

Ingeborg Dahl and this organisation that suited him in every way. *Victims and kin*. It must have been so tempting to approach her since she was so interested in what only he knew was his *work*. And he was a very worthy Victim. She can't have been in any doubt about that as she painstakingly entered his childhood into her archive.

"She grieved," he says, "as mothers should."

So he was watching Ingeborg Dahl mourn Helena's death. Imagining this is more than you can bear, under jagged branches or anywhere. Maybe, I think, at some point he found it useful to keep an eye on her, this mother who made such connections between pictures and the person who painted them.

"But she kept going on," he says. "She rang me and went on and on. That idiot Anlaug had blabbed that I knew Aske and so the lady wanted to talk to me about these theories of hers and about him and the pictures. I didn't like that very much, did I? What she had worked out in that little brain of hers about what the pictures meant and who had painted them. Stupid of her."

That is the evening she died, I imagine, the evening I visited her and also got to hear her *theories* about Aske.

He reminds me about the weapons he has inside. "Yes," I say. "I am aware of them, all the time."

"They wanted to write a book," he whispers. "About Aske. Who knows what they would put in it? It could be anything. And when I went up to TroJa before his exhibition he had no *use* for me while all sorts of idiots were going round with tools they had no idea how to use. They were doing other things as well, if you watched."

In the ruins of a factory. On a bed. Doing other things that must have been strange to watch from the shadows for someone who already knew what it was like to strangle another person. Martin Andersen's *petit mort*: Javed. The big death: Skjalgson. The cut on the video, between a hand and a face. Between death as titillating fiction and as reality. The cut required no more than Skjalgson's brief experience at the photographic shop. What followed the cut required the whole of his story. And Martin Andersen's life.

Then it wasn't just Aske exhibiting pictures any longer. That is how simple it must have been, slipping the video between the ones that were going to be shown there. So simple. And so exciting.

Then he whimpers. He doesn't cry. I know there will be a time when it will be considered significant that this man cries, if he ever does. A time for notes, commentaries and analyses. Perhaps this is what we are keeping him alive for, the hope that he will cry one day, although under the spruce trees we don't know what we will do with his tears. We don't even give them a thought.

We let him whimper.

He is on his way back to his childhood now and he isn't coherent. But as long as he is talking he won't shoot.

Was it the book, I wonder, and the idea of what it might contain that triggered it all, or Aske's rejection and a random opportunity to take out his fury on someone? In the same way that his earlier fits of fury had also found an arbitrary outlet in PAN and Helena. Boy on a scooter, girl by a block of flats.

Ingeborg Dahl's death was not chance, she was a danger. And perhaps Aske, too, when he had seen the video and *knew*. Rune Skjalgson in Kvadraturen, not looking for a prostitute, but for the video.

Rune Skjalgson, not in the cabin, but in his childhood. Long before daybreak he gives in. He is absolutely freezing, he says. He doesn't want to be here any longer.

He was sitting against the wall, they say later, motionless, staring vacantly. They say his head wasn't there either, but a long, long way away. And he needed help to get up.

He takes me into his confidence a little when I go follow them in this room that smells of decay and booze and the sweat that comes from fear.

"He wanted it," he whispers. "Do you understand? He wanted to have his *self-portrait* before he died."

There is nothing more obscene than words.

"He wanted it," he repeats, in a way that I will never forget, in a way that makes him try to believe it himself.

271

Oh yes, I think. And Helena probably wanted something, too, before she died. They always want something, boys on scooters on the roads, making love in their beds. There is always something they want. Something they crave before they die. But it is never you.

He sits under his woollen blanket, freezing still, on the back seat of the car. There are blue lights here, engines starting, the chief inspector talking into her phone. We have saved a life, and now we are going home.

32

IDA IS SITTING quietly by the edge of the water in Paradisbukta. There is wet sand there, seaweed, shells and polished driftwood, all kinds of crap that you can stick your fingers into in interesting ways. This is a serious research project for the moment. Fat little fingers probe a variety of fascinating depressions and holes and textures. She is building. Trying things out, tentatively she takes a little taste, for the moment. Perhaps she knows that she will be stopped if she goes too far. She won't cover herself altogether in sand, she won't eat very much seaweed. A little, but not much, definitely not everything. She has tried and probably learnt from her experiences.

A little is also interesting. From where she is sitting she is not tempted by everything anyway. Everything means the entire rock, the high, glass blue sky, the silken fjord, the seagulls floating in the strange, soft reflections of the sun. I will stop you, I think, if you try to devour it, all of it, and you will still try. You will try for a long, long time to come.

A little is interesting, but it is not enough. A little creates all those painful dreams about more. Ida will also have them, sitting at the distance from us that trusting parents have to allow their children. Sniffing the world. Avoiding boring conversations with adults, but knowing that if she shouts we will come.

"My God," Bella says. "You can't imagine how crazy it is."

"Yes," Benny says. "Yes we can. There is a queue from here to the moon. Busloads from Askim, pensioners from Molde, librarians from Lillehammer."

"They're crazy," Bella says, curving her hands round a menthol cigarette. "I mean we can't print enough of those *fucking* posters of yours, even though there's nothing on them except for a few depressing *bones*."

"Frightened to death," Benny says. "I would call the bones frightened to death. Well-photographed bones scared out of their wits. The print is all right, too."

They are talking about *Impossible Body VIII*, the one with the screaming cranium in the stomach that is now stylishly advertising the TroJa Cultural Centre on black glossy paper in dramatic broad daylight.

"But the interest," Bella says. "It's desperate. And we're not talking newspapers here. I *avoid* newspapers now even if they are there the whole time. I've got ten *mad* arts students on my back and a dreadful *Ph.D. student*, do you understand? I mean, all in the course of a few weeks?"

"It's not going to go away fast so you had better get used to it," my husband says. "How are you getting on with your new friend?"

"Little Sjur? Well, he's very good with the old ladies although they aren't so much of a problem any more. I mean, for Christ's sake, there is no reason to be touchy when everything is going well. That's what they think as well."

"Are you talking about the Frogner Fannies?" I ask.

"Igi, there are children present," Bella says, sounding innocent. "They *adore* the Centre, just like the trade and industry correspondents. From a financial point of view, and between you, me and the bedpost, the most brilliant thing that poor Aske ever did was to get murdered."

The Frogner Fannies have acquired a new status since a fair wind blowing from the Stock Exchange and excellent attendance figures have made them even more disposed to being friendly towards Roll and Bella. It may also have helped a little that the head of the family, Otto Troels-Jacobsen, was touchingly reconciled with his daughter. It is conceivable that a nifty report by Bella about the contents of Sjur Aske's barn may have helped towards just that. Checking for potential fakes in TroJa's famous collection would not have done either father or daughter any good.

"And what about the fakes your father sold a long time ago?" I ask.

But this is, if possible, even more vulgar than the *Frogner Fannies*.

"Get postmodern," Bella says. "*No-one*, neither museums nor private collectors, is interested in finding out whether they own fakes. Something like that would just create chaos and price wars and destroy the market. And on top of that, dear, what is wrong with *copies*? The Romans were just as enthusiastic about copies as they were about the originals."

Far away, out on the oily, smooth water, the seagulls appear decorative. It is when they come closer that I don't like them. It is then that I realise that my own discomfort is passed on through a small, tense fear for Ida, for her eyes and for her head. But the seagulls remain in the air currents high above her. And she is building. Something with shells and driftwood that looks like someone's home. In a couple of days or weeks a wave will cover it, I know, but I won't tell her about that.

Somewhere, a few miles away, in Grønland police station, Rune Skjalgson confesses and atrocities stream out of the holes in his soul. Some of them come to me via the cool professional secrecy of Chief Inspector Kielland, some other ghastly *titbits* plop right out into the tabloids without any *known* source. His calm voice, the chief inspector says, chants as if at Mass to his listeners, churns out the monstrosities of his childhood as he lovingly thrills to the story of Aske's theft of his soul and history and a harrowed face.

Once in a while the true confessions slip out in coded packages, haikus telling of his own deeds rather than others'. There are some fleeting moments when he observed two men on a bed in the ruin behind the TroJa factory buildings, there is a scooter between the trees and a girl playing by a block of flats. There is the *Dream Machine* rolling through night-time forests and along rainy streets making him feel uncommonly invulnerable.

His defending counsel will have to dwell on *the cat*, his mother and the parts of Aske's biography that belonged to no-one but Skjalgson. The chief inspector and her machinery will have to exert themselves to decipher the codes and still they will never solve what is called the mystery, the reports of suffering, his and that of others. Copies and originals.

"Do you think he knew?" Bella asks. "Do you think *the poor man* knew that he was the Beast all the time?"

The poor man is Aske. He the Beast is Skjalgson.

"No," I say. "But perhaps he already feared it when Martin Andersen was found. He was so relieved that Javed had confessed and . . . then he visited us after Ingeborg Dahl was dead. He must have been close to admitting it to himself. Why else should he withdraw the biography? And he was searching for the video, just like Skjalgson, wasn't he? I don't think he let himself believe it until he had seen the video. Seen the cut."

"Took his time, if you want my opinion," Benny says. "But then he had done well out of not believing Skjalgson's stories were true earlier. What were they then, some kind of exciting fantasy? Something he could *use*?"

"Aske wasn't exactly a fan of traditional justice, as you know. Perhaps he was sorry for the guy. Just think of the *dreadful* childhood. Aske *took care of* him, let him use his cabin and so on."

"That was just cunning," Benny says. "Come on, Bella. Aske could have told the police about Skjalgson's weird fantasies instead of painting pictures of them."

"But he saved my life," I say. "When he shoved me into the cabinet."

"*And* knocked you down," Benny says.

"But Benny, *darling*," Bella says. "What could he have done when the bloody *Beast* was at the door? Give the poor man some *credit*?"

"Credit," Benny snorts. "He was happy enough to present his mother as a monster just because she wasn't a noble artist, but a lousy *imitator*."

Ida is building away, full of confidence and with no fear of the seagulls or waves.

"Roll is showing some interest in Zen Buddhism," Bella says out of the blue, "and is supposed to have visited a monk. There is something about a model he is sleeping with who is religious and has bulimia. The monster," she mumbles, stubbing out her cigarette in a shell Ida has given her for safekeeping.

"Do you mean the model?" I ask.

"God, no. I'm talking about the *Beast*. Just imagine, I saw him up there in the chaos before the exhibition. He was going on about that book. Aske asked him to leave, I remember. I thought he was just the usual pushy nutter."

Whatever is denied always returns, I think. Like the Shadow, I suppose, the dark companion. One day when the chief inspector and the state machinery have deciphered Skjalgson's code we will have to find out what brought him to TroJa. If it was fear of the book or a slow burning rage towards the man who *had* found a use for

Skjalgson's life. Or was it the force of numbers? Twelve plus twelve is twenty-four, Ingeborg Dahl said, ennumerating the age of her daughter when she died and Martin Andersen's age and the years between them. Twelve plus twelve is twenty-four and also perfectly rounded, and vital perhaps for that reason.

"He came here to find someone to *kill*," Bella says. "He had *planned* it."

"Come on," Benny says. "Aske provoked him."

One day when the codes have been deciphered the chief inspector will know just how Skjalgson met Javed and Martin and turned Martin Andersen's little death into the big one.

Javed spends his days at the department without any contact with his family and he is slowly beginning to believe what he remembers, that Martin Andersen was exhausted but alive when he left him. It was Martin who wanted it recorded, he says, and I suppose that is true. As it is unquestionably true that he left the video cassette in the machine when he went.

"Skjalgson took it," I say. "Afterwards. Then he went into the exhibition. And then he put it among the other videos to be played."

"Bloody hell," Bella says. "That wouldn't have been much of a problem. Everything was in a mess up there. If I had wanted to I could have dismantled one of Aske's *heaps of bones* without anyone noticing."

Ida shows interest in a group of impressive eight-year-olds, experienced and skilled in the ways of the world as they are. She stares at them with uninhibited admiration as someone who has things to learn has to do. First stare, then ape. Make bits of others' lives their own.

Benny and Bella continue their consultation therapy.

"And when Aske withdrew the biography," Benny says "do you think that was because he was *sorry* for Skjalgson?"

This is a sore point. Bella wants a new biography – the old one will even do – so long as it comes on to the market *fast*.

"He was *frightened*," she says. "Frightened of what the nutter would do if he read it. He had gone mad just because Aske put on a lavish exhibition."

"Absolute rubbish," Benny says. "He was frightened that others would start thinking like Ingeborg Dahl, that either it was him who had killed the two young people or he *knew* who had done it."

277

"The *Beast*," Bella says, "was *after* Aske. First he destroyed the exhibition and then the opening at Villa Troels. God knows when the Villa can be used for *anything at all*."

"That was a great bit of advertising," Benny says. "Fancy new Aske event. And so Skjalgson probably acquired a taste for exhibiting too. He could display his *works* and frighten the living shit out of Aske at the same time."

They continue like this for a while. Squabbling as a therapy while the chief inspector deciphers Skjalgson's codes, slowly, bit by bit. At one time or another Skjalgson must have listened to something told in trust that was significant enough for him to be able to talk about himself again or at least give very strong hints. The confidence came from Aske and must have been an intense experience for Skjalgson. The results of the confidence were pictures, enough for Aske, enough maybe for Skjalgson for a while. But not in the long term. Either the intimacy ended there or he needed something more than pictures.

It is not certain that what he is getting now will be any more satisfying for him. It is not certain that it is possible or desirable to satisfy him.

Ida comes back from the eight-year-olds, with new information to report to me. I lose the thread of Bella and Benny's consultation therapy. When I pick it up again they are back on the current boom-time for TroJa.

"Well, we get these fifteen-year-olds," Bella says, speculating on where his *body* is. "They have read about it in the paper and can't understand why it isn't on display."

Benny shudders.

"And that is a bugger," Bella says. "I mean I loved the man, but you can't help getting *a little* interested now that the question has been asked."

"What do you mean?"

Bella stands up and she is a leopard by the water, camouflaged, a survivor. Ida is studying the inside of a mussel shell. It is blue and white and strange. Benny's eyes are resting on her; his long eyelashes with mascara on them, just like hers. They have been playing with make-up. I know that these are the first steps for Bente on her way *out*.

"It was disgusting of course. I mean, you were there, Igi, so you know about his body. And that was a – what would you call it? A *unique experience*. A happening. A police matter."

What was in the shell, Ida perhaps remembers a tall, thin man telling her, is now out in the water, moving around naked and clean and free.

"The head," Bella says. "The best possible self-portrait, isn't it? You can't *imagine* what offers I have had for his head. And it is around somewhere, isn't it?"